Praise for *Southern Exposures*

"Ann Jeffries definitely has a skill for storytelling. There is vitality and high drama in Southern Exposures. The author did an excellent job with honing in and focusing on the three main, important characters of which the drama surrounds. I fell in love with the Alexanders. Job well done!"
—Jessica Tilles, Author/Editor

"Loved the way [Ann Jeffries] described the activities...I felt as though I was there witnessing everything [that she was] describing. [She] immediately got my attention with the colorful... attention to details. The book is very warm. The characters have to face challenges and each does it in a different way. Loved the focus on loving family— members of the family loving each other and believing in each other."
—Brenda Irons LeCesne, Esq.

"There are a lot of promising plots within the story. I thoroughly enjoyed... this [novel]. I think [Ann Jeffries'] ability [to] create emotion is a true talent. [She] did a great job creating suspense. The [characters'] stories seemed most authentic and enter- taining. Language and dialogue [o]verall... is a strong area for [Ann]."
—Karen R. Thomas, President, Creative Minds Book Group

Praise for *An Unguarded Moment*

"Ann Jeffries does an excellent job of weaving her characters' stories together and keeping the reader captivated."
—Nancy Engle, Author of *Murder at Mount Joy*

"An engrossing and sensuous love story that immediately grabs your attention and keeps you involved till the last page."
—Abraham Leib, Esq.

"This was a book I couldn't get enough of. I read at night to fall asleep and this had the opposite effect on me. I didn't want to put it down. Just a little more... Very well written with enough spice to keep things interesting. Never a dull moment!"
—Terri, an avid reader

"My overall view is that this is a good, intelligent read! It's the kind of story you never want to end."
—Janice Sims, Author of *This Winter Night*

"I really admire Ann's smooth writing style and the appealing premise of this project."
—Mavis Allen, Associate Senior Editor, Silhouette Books

Praise for *Touch Me In The Morning*

"I could not put my iPad down once I started reading. Loved the characters and story line which kept me guessing what was going to happen next."
—Pauline, an avid reader

"Ms. Jeffries has given us a love story about two adults who, having experienced some of life's darker moments, fall deeply and passionately in love. Her characters are real life and enable the reader to eagerly ride along with them on their adventure."
—Abraham Leib, Esq.

"I loved this novel; many times finding myself lost in their lives. The author did a fantastic job with character and plot development, and an unpredictable storyline."
—Jessica Tilles, Author of *Loving Simone*

An

UNGUARDED MOMENT

Family Reunion—In The Wisdom of the Ancestors Series

Ann Jeffries

Copyright © 2013 by Ann Jeffries
annjeffries@newviewliterature.com

Printed and Bound in the United States of America

Published and Distributed By
New View Literature
820 67th Avenue N, #7603
Myrtle Beach, South Carolina 29572
www.newviewliterature.com

Cover and Interior Design By
TWA Solutions
www.twasolutions.com

ISBN: 978-0-9915003-3-8

Library of Congress Control Number: 2014907677

First printing May 2014

This is a work of fiction. Names, characters, business, places, events and incidents are either the products of the author's imagination or used in a fictitious manner. Any resemblance to actual persons, living or dead, or actual events is purely coincidental.

For inquires, contact the publisher.

I bow in humble gratitude to:

The Creator

The Ancestors

Authors Evelyn Palfrey and Janice Sims
(My taliswomen)

Editor Chandra Sparks Taylor

Literary Agent Richard Curtis

Attorneys Abraham Leib and Stephen Ross

Khari and Yasemin Washington Brown
(You know why? Because you rock!)

Friends and mentors Brenda Irons LeCesne and
Rosezella Canty Letsome, Esqs.
(When I grow up, I want to be just like you)

and

a deep-knee bend to the truly amazing men I have known

"If loving you is wrong, I don't want to do right."

Otis Redding

"Me and Mrs. Jones, we've got a thing going on."

Billy Paul

Prologue

JaiHonnah fitfully tossed and turned in her sleep. In her dreams the hawk's eyes glowed meanly. Her fear increased exponentially. The ground beneath her feet shook, cracked like an earthquake before a gulf began to grow, widen, separating her from the man before her. The divide drew him away from her beyond her reach. She called to him, reached out toward him. He remained immobile, silent. Stone-like in his demeanor. *Didn't he see what was happening to them? Couldn't he feel the earth move, shudder, breaking apart? Breaking them apart.* She screamed his name over and over. She had to get him back into her arms, warn him of the danger. The hawk's curly talons dug into his flesh. She screamed his name again, imploring him to reach out to her, to take her hands into his, but still no response came from him. He remained immobile. The chasm continued to widen. She became frantic, fighting to breach the gulf, screaming for him to be careful of the hawk. Then something clamped around her, holding her still and pulling on her. Engulfing her in warmth, safety, pleasure.

Tugging her from her nightmare, he whispered, *"Let yourself go, baby. Relax. I'm here with you. No one but us, Jai. No one in the universe, but you and me."*

Wake up, JaiHonnah.

JaiHonnah pulled her eyes open as the man embraced her, enfolded her in his tenderness, and laved her from her neck to her ear. She held him tightly and cried.

Chapter 1

What the hell . . .?

JaiHonnah Reise Chapman woke with a start and looked around wildly, confused when the bright interior lights of the transatlantic jumbo jet flickered on and the lead flight attendant's voice pealed through the fuselage. She was pitifully grateful, again, that the nightmare had ended. She hadn't had much rest in the last week while planning for her return to the United States. Still a little disoriented, she batted and then briskly rubbed her eyes. *Had she been dreaming or had the attendant said something about being on the ground at Dulles International Airport in thirty minutes?* JaiHonnah looked at her watch through still bleary eyes, but it was still set to the time in Italy. Then she remembered. *The dream.* Her brow beetled. *It was so real each and every time. But, who was the man? Who had held her?* Her palms covered her face, blocking out the light. Momentarily closing her eyes in concentration, she tried to see his face, remember his name, his smell, his taste, his physique, something, *anything.* Try as she might, nothing came to her, no vision, no smell or taste. Only the drone of the aircraft engines and the sounds of the slowly waking cabin passengers surrounded her.

Snatching her hands away from her face in frustration and opening her eyes, she spotted an attendant who was distributing warm, damp, peppermint-scented hand towels to the weary travelers in the first-class cabin. "What time is it?"

"It's six A.M. Eastern Time," the attendant replied as she handed a towel to JaiHonnah and the man seated next to her before quickly moving on to serve the people across the aisle.

"Thank you," JaiHonnah said, stifling a yawn. She placed the warm towel to her face and inhaled. Then something dawned on her; her brow bunched. Removing the towel, she turned to her seatmate. "Did the flight attendant say that it would be another thirty minutes before we land?"

"*Si, Bella,*" the man, who looked to be an Antonio Bandaris clone or of Spanish descent, answered. "We are late, no?"

"We are very late, yes," JaiHonnah answered with some concern as she once again held the towel to her face. She sensed that the man was still watching her, but she did not turn to confirm her suspicion. Instead, she stood, excused herself and went to the rest room.

Her seatmate was certainly handsome and charming, as on-camera personalities with major television networks located in Madrid, Spain, tended to be. She enjoyed talking with him about his career in European broadcasting until his conversation became more of an inquisition into her personal life, and she noticed him surreptitiously slipping his wedding band from his finger. Sure that he recognized her, he tried to make conversation from the moment they boarded the aircraft in Milan, Italy. JaiHonnah was skillful in diverting his questions away from her—for a while at least. She didn't want to be rude, but as with most men with whom she came in contact, especially reporters, it wasn't her views on world issues that stirred their interest.

She hoped that her new life and career would let people look beyond the façade, she thought, looking critically at her face and sighing into the mirror She longed for the day when men didn't want to paw her on sight and women didn't hate her instantly for something that she had absolutely no control over. Silently she hoped that her new boss would find her worthy of employment because of her brains, not her body. Inwardly, she sighed again. She wouldn't be able to convince her potential employer of anything if she didn't get to the meeting on time. She left the rest room and returned to her seat.

The flight was supposed to arrive at five-thirty. That arrival time would have allowed her to be prompt for her interview. Now she realized that she would be really late. She frowned. Maybe she was wrong about the time for the meeting. She reached into her briefcase and pulled out her iPhone to check the text message that she received from one of her college friends, Vivian Alexander Jackson.

> *Jai—*
>
> *Everything is all set. Meeting with J. Roderick Baylor at seven A.M. on Friday, September 3, confirmed at his office. Address: 1255 Water Street, South West, Washington, D.C. Phone: 202-555-3414. Sorry I can't meet you at the airport, but I'll see you when I get back from Chicago. The keys to the condo are at the Watergate Complex front desk. Good luck!*
>
> *Love ya,*
> *Viv*

Well, she wasn't wrong about the time for her appointment, JaiHonnah thought and sighed. She put the iPhone back into her briefcase and leaned back into the seat, looking below at the dimly lit, checkerboard landscape of the Northern Virginia countryside. She regretted not taking an earlier flight out of Milan or she could have ordered one of her father's jets to bring her to the states at any time. If she had she would have had plenty of time to prepare for her interview. Instead she ended up on this red-eye. As it was, she barely had time to change Euro into American currency before her flight departed. Just getting through customs was going to be at least thirty minutes. *Who held a job interview at seven in the morning anyway?* she silently questioned. Being late was certainly not the first impression that she wanted to make with a potential employer. This scenario was not looking good. Not good at all.

She really *wanted* this job, not that she *needed* it actually. She was, in fact, a very wealthy woman. She really didn't have to work for a living. However, she had never traded on her wealth, her beauty or her family name. No, she needed this job because it was in her character to work—and work hard. She had something to prove to herself; that despite her appearance, family connection or wealth, she had a craft and self-reliance. She recognized that not too many companies were willing to take a chance on a new architect, even one with a lot of initials, including a Ph.D. after her name, and certainly not on a woman of mixed heritage without any real practical experience. Those who were willing weren't looking for her architectural or engineering skill and ability, she knew. Too often, they were more interested in her connection to her family's empire. She was determined to make a name for herself, to build a career despite her illustrious family background.

No matter what it took, J. Roderick Baylor, president of Baylor Construction Company, was going to hire her -- whether he knew it or not. Not for what she could do for him in her father's boardroom, and certainly not for what he might think that she could do for him in the bedroom. No, what she was offering Baylor Construction was her years of training, creativity and determination to do excellent work, to make her mark on the world's landscape. She already wasted too much of her life and, with the big three-zero staring her in the face, it was time to get busy. One failed marriage wasn't going to stop her and neither was her father, Jake Hawkins.

It was Big Jake who talked her into marrying Calvin B. Chapman III in the first place and wasting nearly two years of her life. Back then she was too young and too inexperienced to fight her father on his level. It was just another merger he and the Chapmans wanted anyway. Well, Big Jake got Chapman Forest Industries, bought Calvin and his father out for far less than its actual worth, and her divorce was thrown in for good measure. Her older brothers, Jacob, Jr. and Adam, were both heading major divisions of BlackHawk Industries under Big Jake's careful tutelage. Her father was after her to take over and run the part of his empire that acquired Chapman Forest Products.

At their father's instigation, her brothers both visited her in Italy on a couple of occasions to convince her to take a position in the family business, but being under her daddy's thumb was not for her. Nope, this time Big Jake wasn't going to interfere in her life. During her teen years he had groomed her as someone's hood ornament, and she hated every minute of it. Entering the Miss San Antonio Beauty Contest wasn't her idea either. Maybe, if she had lost the contest, things would have been different. Even before she won the Miss Texas Beauty Pageant and was first runner-up in the Miss America Pageant, she had about had it with Jake Hawkins pushing her around.

It was demeaning to be paraded around barely clothed in front of thousands of people who had a "body by Fischer, brain by Mattel" view of her, just like the man seated next to her now on the aircraft. The propositions she received were often lewd, obscene, indecent or vulgar. She hadn't tolerated that kind of behavior in her private life and she wouldn't in her professional life. She easily rejected offers to model for some of the top fashion designers, screen-test for movie roles and commercials from advertising agencies. Rather, she had opted for continuing her education toward making a respectable career for herself as an architect and civil engineer.

Living and studying abroad for the last four years since the divorce gave her the type of independence and self-reliance she needed. She did miss her family; her father and brothers, and especially her grandmother, Kiavi Ramose Littlefeather. JaiHonnah vowed that she would make time to visit her grandmother on the Navajo reservation in Shiprock, New Mexico. They also had business to discuss concerning her RAMOSE blind-trust account. JaiHonnah had not exercised her options in her portfolio since before she married Calvin. She gave her grandmother power-of-attorney to handle her financial affairs and to vote her proxy with her shares in her father's empire any way Kiavi Littlefeather saw fit. Her grandmother was a skillful businesswoman and JaiHonnah trusted her implicitly.

"Ladies and gentlemen, the pilot has turned on the fasten seat belt sign. Please put your trays and seats in the upright position in preparation for landing."

The announcement dragged JaiHonnah from her reverie. She was now ready to put thoughts of her old frivolous life behind her. This was the first day of the rest of her new, professional life, and she was determined to take control of it and to live it to her advantage. As she felt the landing gear lock into place and saw the flaps lowering, a new excitement tickled her spine. *Look out, J. Roderick Baylor, here I come!* The plane slowed and felt as if it had nearly stopped in midair, but the ground was coming up fast beneath them as the jumbo craft lost altitude. The wheels of the plane touched down and briefly bounced up again before heading smoothly down the runway. The pilot put on the brakes and the engines roared loudly.

As the plane taxied to the gate, the pilot said, "Welcome to the nation's capitol. The ground temperature is seventy-five degrees. Sorry for the delay, but thank you for flying the friendly skies of United Airlines. Hope to see you again on another United Airlines flight."

Not likely anytime soon, JaiHonnah mused as she hustled in preparation for deplaning. Before the plane came to a full stop, passengers leaped to their feet, aisles flooded and overhead compartments flew open. After eight hours in the air, she was going to be late for her first real job interview, and all United said was *"sorry about the delay!"*

JaiHonnah was the first person off the aircraft. *There were advantages to flying first class,* she thought as she grabbed a luggage carrier and positioned herself at the head of the carousel, impatiently waiting for her luggage and looking at her watch. As the carousel started to move she saw her luggage come out first. *Huh, maybe United isn't that bad after all.* She grabbed the two oversized bags, laid her exhibit case and briefcase on top and sprinted to a customs officer.

"Welcome home, Ms. Chapman. Seems you've been away a long time," the tall, darkly handsome officer said with all thirty-two showing, as he reviewed her passport flipping through the document to find an empty page.

"Thanks, but that's Mrs. Chapman, and I have nothing to declare," she said, clearly anxious to be on her way.

The smile closed in on the thirty-two. "I'll have to check your luggage anyway."

JaiHonnah huffed. "Look, I'm late already, couldn't we dispense with the—."

"Open up, *Mrs. Chapman.*" The man glared with a raised eyebrow.

This is not good, she thought. She wondered whether she put that expensive bottle of French perfume in her luggage or whether she packed it in one of her trunks, which were to be shipped later. Struggling to lift each piece of luggage, she glared at the man. As the customs officer examined each item in her luggage she caught the scent of the *Oui* perfume and so did he. His large hand wrapped around the exquisitely designed bottle. Fortunately, it was a half-full bottle. No tariffs. She smiled.

"Are we finished?" she anxiously queried with a big, Texas-size smile.

"Have a very good day, *Mrs. Chapman.*" He grinned, all thirty-two again present and accounted for.

JaiHonnah whizzed through the airport, dodging others as if she were on an escape mission. Fortunately, taxicabs were plentiful and she was third in line. The oppressive heat and humidity began to sap her energy while she waited. Finally, she hopped into the gray Washington Flyer taxi while the driver loaded her luggage and they were off. As soon as the driver was underway she leaned forward.

"There's an extra fifty in it for you if you get me to 1255 Water Street, South West, in thirty minutes or less."

"Lady, this is Washington, D.C.," he said in a raspy, but amused voice. "You couldn't get Congress to move for fifty billion, but I'll do the best I can. It should be pretty clear sailing on the Dulles Access Road, but government gridlock is going to get us once we're inside the Capitol Beltway," he said, laughing. "You must not be from around here."

"No, I've been out of the country for several years."

"Well, welcome back stateside. You here on business or pleasure?"

"Both. I have a job interview this morning and I'm visiting a college friend."

"Thinking of moving back to the states, are you?"

"Yes, sir, I think I am."

"Where you from, lady?"

"Originally, Hawkinstown, Texas. It's outside of San Antonio."

"Never heard of Hawkinstown, but I heard of San Antonio."

"I'm not surprised. It only has a population of one," she deadpanned.

The cabby laughed and they chatted all the way into Washington, D.C., as she constantly urged him to hurry. Traffic was horrendous as they came across the Theodore Roosevelt Bridge and hit a backup so slow that it resembled a parking lot. She was ready to get out and walk to make better time, but then she didn't know exactly where she was going. Washington streets were very confusing, but she was determined to learn all about the city that Benjamin Banneker designed and that she intended to call her home. She looked at her watch again. Time was passing too quickly.

A group of tourists passed slowly at an intersection on their way to the Lincoln Memorial. The Viêt Nam Veterans Memorial was already jammed and tour buses blocked the intersection leading to the Washington Monument. Finally the traffic signal changed, and they were able to crawl another block east on Constitution Avenue. JaiHonnah made a mental note to visit the Museum of Natural History as they passed the historic building with its gothic architecture. The city was pregnant with such solid monuments of architectural wonders. Directly ahead of her was the United States Capitol with its gleaming white dome and both houses of Congress ensconced in white-pillared replicas of historical European architecture.

JaiHonnah glanced again at her watch, nervously biting her lower lip. She would have time to see it all after she locked down this position. She checked her makeup again and brushed her hair into a French twist, piling the rest into a ball on the top of her head. Thank goodness for bobby pins. Maybe it was time for a new look, she ruminated while checking her appearance in her compact mirror. She could get her hair cut shorter instead of the nearly yard-long, heavy strands inherited from her Navajo and Spanish ancestry, which flowed over her shoulders and midway down her back. Long hair was fine for beauty pageants and even while studying in Europe, but that was then, the past. This was now, the future.

As they sat stymied in another long traffic light beside the colorful new Native American Museum, her grandmother came to mind. When she was a little girl, JaiHonnah remembered sitting for long, lazy afternoons brushing her grandmother's hair while her grandmother spun such wonderful Navajo princess stories. Her grandmother's hair was so long, silky, and thick that she could sit on it. Kiavi Littlefeather was now a world renowned author of children's fiction.

JaiHonnah's mother had worn her hair long, too, until the day she died more than fifteen years ago. JaiHonnah still missed Skai Hawkins so much, but so did everyone. Her mother, a registered nurse, was beautiful inside and out, her skin so clear, fresh and supple. Her beautiful, flawless complexion from her mestizaje heritage and her soft-spoken Navajo and Mexican accent even brought Big Jake to his knees.

Her father first saw her when he opened his eyes in the hospital. She was standing by his bed sponging his body after his injury at an oil rig. He was only eighteen at the time and she was twenty three, but he was in love at first sight. They were married and expecting their first child, Jacob Junior, eight months later. Eighteen months after that, their second child, a girl they named LaiLoni Skai, was kidnapped from the birthing clinic and never found. Next, her brother, Adam, was born and then JaiHonnah, the baby of the Hawkins family.

JaiHonnah knew that Jake missed Skai most of all though. She was his heart and soul. Such a pair they were with his big, six-foot-five, two-hundred-forty pounds, her mother's five-foot-five frame, and her body, which weighed one hundred twenty pounds soaking wet. God, how Skai used to laugh at her children's antics, JaiHonnah mused, smiling. Skai always had a Navajo or Mexican parable to fit each situation that JaiHonnah and her brothers got themselves into. Skai may have been small in stature, but she was a skyscraper in her family's eyes.

When the cabby laid on his horn, JaiHonnah snapped back to the present. "Are we there yet?" she nervously queried, checking her watch for the umpteenth time.

"Yeah, lady, just a few more blocks. Just across Maine Avenue and we will be there."

JaiHonnah again sat back in the taxicab, trying as best she could to be patient and control her anxiety. She wondered what this Baylor was like. Vivian hadn't told her much about him; only that he owned a young company that was climbing quickly up the business ladder. Even if it was a relatively new company, perhaps the owner was one of those bosses who would be reluctant to hire a woman as his sole architect or someone who only knew one part of the business—the money end—and only focused on that. Mentally, she went over her accomplishments: her undergraduate training at Spelman, her master's from Texas A&M University and now her double doctorates in architecture and structural engineering from Arcadia Laboratories, Politecnico di Milano. She had studied with some of the world's leading architects, those on the cutting edge of design. Of course she could talk about the awards and commendations she received, but even those accomplishments bored her to tears. No, she decided, her portfolio would speak louder than anything she could verbalize about her academic background. She had selected her best, prize-winning works in a cross section of all of the architectural treatments she created or designed. Perhaps Mr. Baylor wouldn't appreciate those studies in African architecture that she chose to include. Maybe she should have picked more pieces with the gothic approach. After all, this was Washington, D.C., and the home of European architectural clones.

She wished that she knew more about J. Roderick Baylor, but she didn't even have time to Google him. Perhaps, then she'd know how best to approach the interview.

"We're here, lady," the cabby said. "It's only 7:50. We made pretty good time considering the traffic and all."

"Oh?" JaiHonnah said, snapping the door open. "Not if I've already lost the job, we didn't."

The cabby chuckled. "Lady, as beautiful as you are, nobody in his right mind would turn you down for anything, including a job."

She gave him a smile. "From your lips, sir, to Mr. Baylor's ears."

The four-story red brick building in a warehouse district looked deserted until a convoy of trucks with a **BCC** insignia pealed out from the parking lot adjacent to the building. A small gold plaque at the door read: Baylor Construction Company. When no one answered the door JaiHonnah turned, stepped off the curb and hailed the passing vehicles. Finally one of them stopped. She stepped up to the passenger door as the driver rolled down the window.

"I'm looking for Mr. Baylor, a Mr. J. Roderick Baylor," she said to a disgruntled driver.

"Oh, you mean JRock. He's gone, lady. He was here until about seven-fifteen. Pissed off though 'cause he was waiting to have a meeting, but the bastard didn't show. Now there's gonna be hell to pay. JRock he don't like to be late doing nothin', and he was spittin' nails when he left."

JaiHonnah sighed. "Oh, no."

"You one'na JRock's women?" the driver asked, grinning at her. "You certainly are pretty enough."

"His woman?" she indignantly flashed. "No, I'm the person who he was waiting for!"

The drive ruefully shook his head. "Lady, if I was you, I'd leave Dodge City now on the first thing smokin'. JRock, he don't..."

"I know, I know," she interrupted hastily, impatient. "Do you know where I can find him?"

The man scratched his head, apparently in thought. "Lady, I know where he was goin', but..."

"Please, this is very important," she begged. "Could you take me to him?"

The man looked at his watch and then at her contemplatively. "Ah-ite, lady. Get in. I'll take you to where he was heading, but ain't no telling whether he's gonna be there now and if he is, he's gonna kick my butt for not being on the job he sent me on."

JaiHonnah sucked up her grit and quickly paid the cabby who put her luggage in the back of the truck. She climbed into the dusty cab with the Baylor employee. She was very nervous now, looking at her watch, wringing her hands, and worrying her bottom lip.

"Tough man, huh?" she asked the driver as they rode through the traffic-clogged city.

"Lady, steel is softer than him," the driver lamented, shaking his head thoughtfully. "Hope you got a hard hat."

"No, just a hard head," she mumbled, summoning her courage.

Finally they arrived at the job site at Pennsylvania Avenue and 21st Street, North West. A fourteen-story building that took up the entire city block was growing up out of the ground. A big sign at the site read: BAYLOR CONSTRUCTION. DOTHAN ELECTRICAL. AVERY PLUMBING. Cement trucks were lined up around the site with their motors running and barrows rolling. Men in hard hats were everywhere on every floor of the open-frame, concrete structure. A huge crane swung its long arm over the edifice and lifted tons of wet cement up the skeletal structure while a convoy of backhoes churned up a blizzard of dust and dirt as they backfilled around the base of the structure.

"C'mon, lady, let's see if he's still here," the driver tentatively grumbled.

JaiHonnah didn't have to be invited, but when she exited the truck cab a dry dust cloud coated her from head to foot. She cupped her hands over her face, coughing and looking around for anyone who might be the tough-as-nails Baylor.

"Hey! JRock!" the man escorting her yelled and then, with fingers between his teeth, whistled loudly.

Other men at the work site stopped and turned in their direction. They began whistling, too, but not for Baylor, she noticed. The dry, dusty wind was lifting her above-the-knee linen skirt and tugging at her criss-crossed blouse as she fought through the blizzard. The catcalls were for her, but she was too anxious to find her potential new employer to care what was going on around her.

"JRock! Hey, JRock!" her escort called again. "Over here!"

JaiHonnah covered her eyes against the blowing dust and tried to see who was approaching.

Out of the storm of noise, dirt, dust and lewd comments, JaiHonnah saw a mountain of a man bearing down on them. Suddenly the earth seemed to shift, tremble from under her feet and the sun was born. Moving toward her was the brawniest man ever created. The white hardhat on his head didn't mask much, including the scowl on his all-too-handsome face. The dust parted for him like Moses opening the Red Sea. All six feet, eight inches, two-hundred-thirty pounds of molten masculinity was bearing down on her with a vengeance. Sharp, piercing, black eyes like those of a hunter seeking his game surrounded by thick lashes and eyebrows furrowed to the bridge of his flaring nostrils, neatly trimmed mustache, and full, luscious mouth. JaiHonnah saw muscle mania from the neck down under a Million Man March T-shirt that must have been painted on by one of the master artists. A black Adonis with a narrow waist, a pronounced six pack and long, sculptured thighs under the low-riding jeans, Baylor's tall, powerful torso moved relatively swiftly in the ruthlessly laced brogans on his feet. He was intimidating with his imposing size and, as he cast his eyes around at the melee, the noisy catcalls immediately ceased. JaiHonnah involuntarily caught her breath.

"Murray, what the hell are you doing here?" he bellowed. "You were supposed to be over at McKinley High School thirty minutes ago!"

"Boss, this lady is looking for you. Said she—."

"Move it, Murray!" the mountain rumbled with malice.

"Sure thing, JRock. Color me gone!" Murray said. "I'll put your luggage in his truck, lady," the driver whispered to JaiHonnah before he scurried away.

Then Baylor swung his laser-beam gaze to her. JaiHonnah had forgotten to breathe. She felt like she had been moving at the speed of light and suddenly hit the proverbial brick wall, J. Roderick Baylor. She choked as his eyes seized her.

"Well?" he asked none too politely.

"*You're* J. Roderick Baylor?" she asked in disbelief.

His brow furrowed, lips thinned to a straight line, and his fists punched his hips. "Is that a trick question?" he clipped sarcastically.

"Uh-uh, I've come about the job. I mean, I'm sorry I was late, but, you see, my flight got in—."

"Job? What job? I already filled the secretarial positions. Didn't your agency tell you? Damn! You called me all the way down here... Look, lady, this is no place for a woman . . ." he rapidly spat, clearly frustrated.

"Secretary? No, I'm not a secretary, Mr. Baylor. I've come about the—."

"You're the baby-sitter then, Mrs. Betterman? Oh, okay. I've read your qualifications, but somehow I thought that you'd be older. Never mind. I can deal with... Look, my girls are still away, but your credentials and references are acceptable, so I'll try you out on a temporary basis. I want you to start in two weeks when they return—."

"Baby-sitter?" she interrupted, her confusion began to clear like the dust. "I'm no baby-sitter!" Her ire rose, then settled when JaiHonnah reminded herself that she wanted this job. "I'm, uh, uh..."

"Speak up, woman! I don't have all day. Who the hell are you?"

"I'm your new architect and civil engineer," she said confidently, squaring her shoulders, and extending her hand. "I'm J. Reise Chapman."

The look on his face was priceless; sold for about two cents with expectations for five cents change JaiHonnah thought, but she noticed his fists tighten on his hips.

"Damn! I'm going to kill Vivian!" He scowled, turning his back to her in apparent frustration and issuing a string of imaginative expletives.

JaiHonnah was left with her outstretched hand hanging in midair as Baylor communicated with the heaven above. She had enough of his arrogant, chauvinistic tantrum though. She could feel the hair standing up on the back of her neck, her temper peaking. She didn't have to take this kind of behavior from this Neanderthal. He acted just as arrogantly as Big Jake, and JaiHonnah wasn't having it. Job or no job.

She grabbed a thick arm muscle in a failed attempt to turn him around. He lifted his eyes from her hand and looked over his shoulder at her. Her voice rose in direct proportion to her ire. "Look, Mr. Baylor, I've had years of training, and I'm qualified to do the job. If you think you can do better with that paltry little sum you're offering, go ahead and try it, but you'll be missing out on the best architect and civil engineer in the western world!"

"Oh, really?" he said then snorted derisively. He turned toward her, his arms akimbo.

"And another thing..." she continued.

Roderick's eyes flashed over the sensuous curves of the lady architect and engineer as she read him the riot act for his behavior. *She has spunk,* he'd give her that. She'd need it in this male-dominated business. What could Vivian have been thinking by recommending this woman to him with her distracting beauty? Her tall, leggy, statuesque form was clearly aerobicized into a soft, tight package and stood out ahead of any woman he had ever seen. Even his former wife hadn't sent sensuous shock waves through him like this golden-bronze beauty. Although covered with dust, she was still an exotically voluptuous woman; far too beautiful for a job in a construction industry that was predominately male dominated. That thought annoyed him. Thick, raven hair was piled on top of her head with baby-fine wisps caressing her perfect oval-shaped face and high cheekbones. He was hard-pressed not to gaze at her pearl-white teeth and expressive mouth as she talked. She had wide, round whiskey-brown eyes which sparkled against a golden-bronze complexion that had to have been manufactured. No one's skin could look that smooth, that clear, that clean, but she was wearing very little makeup, he noticed.

Her full bosom rose and fell, cutting his breath. No hourglass could possibly be more perfectly shaped, and the legs attached to that shape would make Beyonce envious. The hands were delicate and expressive, captivating him with their grace even as she wangled a finger in front of his face. Ordinarily, he resented the way men at construction sites behaved when attractive women passed by, and his men knew he wouldn't tolerate it, but this time, they were right. She was spectacular. Then he noticed that she was wearing wedding rings. That brought him up short. No matter how attracted to her he was, she would be safe from him and any one of the men who worked for him. She was a married woman and that suited him just fine.

He didn't need to interview her or review her credentials. He implicitly trusted Vivian's judgment.

"When can you start?" Roderick asked, shifting his weight.

JaiHonnah stopped her tirade in mid-syllable. He had caught her off guard with that question. She was just getting ready to shift into second gear.

"Immediately." she quipped, quickly regaining a professional demeanor.

Confident, he thought, as he stifled the grin that inched toward his lips. "I'll give you a try, but only because Vivian seems to have a lot of confidence in you and your ability. She's my lawyer and I trust her judgment. However, I expect you to be on time for appointments."

"And you won't be disappointed," she said, bravely, her chin defiantly upraised.

"We'll see," he said, smirking, and then excused himself to step a few feet away to answer his phone. Turning his back to her, Roderick pulled a cell phone out of his pocket and thumbed it on. Looking at her was entirely too distracting so he listened to his sister until he could get his hormones back in sync. "Kelley, by the way, J. Reise Chapman goes on the payroll as of today. Get her contract and insurance papers processed through administration. I'll bring her in when I come...Yes, she's a woman. I'm going over to the D.C. Office of Licenses and Inspections to check on some of the other job sites and then I'll be in...No, nothing's wrong. Any other calls?...What did she want? Never mind. I'll check with you when I come in. I'm out."

He ended his call and turned back toward her with a scowl, JaiHonnah noticed. She figured that this time his foul mood had nothing to do with her and, for that, she was supremely grateful.

"All right, let's go. I've got things to do today, and you might as well tag along," he growled, taking her elbow and leading her to his truck.

JaiHonnah didn't know that *'tag along'* meant an all-day affair, being carted around like so much extra baggage with less sensitivity than porters treat airline luggage. Roderick went about his business as if she weren't even there. He drove his big, black, extended-cab pickup to and from at least eleven of his construction sites never stopping once to eat a real meal. Her tan, linen business suit and French silk blouse were ruined and her Italian shoes were a mess. She was dirty, tired and starving by six o'clock that evening when he finally parked in his office building garage on Water Street.

"You'll have to come into the office with me now and sign some papers before you leave, Mrs. Chapman. Just some routine forms for our employee records, benefits package, and your employment contract. Vivian's law firm also does the company's accounting and taxes. She's hell to deal with if I don't keep everything intact for the IRS and the insurance carrier."

"Oh," was all that JaiHonnah could manage as she peeled her tired, aching body out of the truck cab. Although the day was intriguing and she learned a great deal about some of Baylor Construction's ongoing projects, her shoes were killing her feet. The September moist heat matted her underclothes to her body. Her legs ached from trying to keep up with Roderick Baylor's long, quick strides around and through each job site. Her hair looked like it could have been the prototype for Medusa. All she wanted was solid food, a bath and a bed before the jet lag completely shut her down. Thank goodness it was Friday. She would have the weekend to decipher all of the notes that she took and to prep for her first day in the office on Monday.

They entered a spacious and nicely decorated reception area on the ground floor of his office building. An attractive woman, casually dressed, sat on the edge of a desk talking on the telephone. She motioned silence as they entered.

"No, Monique, I don't know what time Roderick will be in. He's been on the road all day, but I'll be sure to tell him that you called again... Yes, kiss the girls for me..." She held the telephone away from her ear and they could all hear the venom and the loud bang as Monique slammed down the receiver.

"Hey, JRock," the woman said softly. Then she turned to greet her brother's companion.

"J. Reise Chapman, this is Kelley Baylor, my sister and my best friend." He said and smiled. "Kelley is also the Vice President of Baylor Construction, Chief of Staff of the Baylor corporate structure, and she keeps me on a short chain."

"Hello, Kelley," JaiHonnah said wearily with a half-hearted smile, extending her hand. "You can call me Jai or JaiHonnah. I'm pleased to meet you."

"JaiHonnah, welcome aboard. You certainly are a surprise," she said, chuckling. "When Vivian recommended you, we thought that J. Reise Chapman was a man. It will be nice to have another professional woman in the office. You're tall too. You wouldn't happen to play a little round ball, would you? We have a company team—."

JaiHonnah interrupted, smiled, and held up both hands. "If you mean basketball, it's not my game."

"With your height, I'm surprised you don't play," Kelley said.

"Everyone makes the same mistake because I'm tall, but I do play handball, racquetball, tennis, and a decent game of golf when I'm awake." She smiled wryly indicating her fatigue. She turned her attention to Roderick. "Mr. Baylor, you said something about papers?"

"Uh, yes, Kelley, did you…"

Kelley pulled a folder from the desk behind her and handed it to JaiHonnah. "Yes, right here. Why don't you have a seat and look over these papers? I've indicated where you should sign." When JaiHonnah moved away to take a seat at an empty desk, Kelley turned back to her brother and guided him away for a little privacy.

"What is it this time?" he asked solemnly.

"You're not going to like this, but…"

"If that was Monique on the telephone, I already know I'm not going to like it. Don't candy coat it, Kelley. What's the problem?"

"JRock, don't get angry, but Monique is putting the girls on a flight back to D.C. tomorrow morning and—."

"What the hell—?"

"C'mon, JRock," she said, sighing. "You know how Monique can be. She wasn't cut out for motherhood. She says that Shelly and Shelby are driving her crazy, and it's not convenient for them to be with her right now. She has a screen test for a feature-length film or something in two or three weeks and she says that her nerves are shot."

"Damn. They're only four years old. She's the adult. They haven't seen her for a year. Can't she cope for a month?"

"We're talking about Monique, JRock, not Mother Teresa. Don't let it get to you. The girls want to come home. They said they missed their daddy."

Roderick's shoulders slumped, and he raked a hand over his close-cut hair. "God knows that I miss them, too. I can't wait for them to get home."

"I knew you'd be happy about that part of it at least..."

Roderick looked at her suspiciously. "What's the other part that I'm *not* going to be happy about?" he asked cautiously.

Kelley sucked in her breath and said in a rush, "Monique is coming with them."

Roderick rolled his head away from her in disgust. "Damn," he said softly.

"There's more, JRock," Kelley said quietly. "Not about Monique. BlackHawk has been nosing around our operation."

Roderick's head snapped toward Kelley. "BlackHawk?"

"Yes. I smell trouble big time," Kelley asserted.

"I expected as much, but not this soon," he said thoughtfully.

"You've been doing too well to go unnoticed by the conglomerates. That last article in the *Wall Street Journal* about you taking Baylor Construction public under the new parent company, Baylor Design and Development, has a lot of people sitting up and taking notice, uh, and now this," she said hesitantly showing Roderick a new issue of *Black Enterprise* with his picture on the cover. "Apparently you've shot up the charts of the top 100 Black-owned and operated businesses. The publisher called to congratulate you. He was the one who told me about BlackHawk International. He said that he had lunch with the old man who owns BlackHawk. He also said that it was BlackHawk's CEO who brought up your name specifically. Your friend Nick Collins, the one who owns NICO Communications, called too. He wants to feature you in an interview on his cable television and radio networks. Nick also confirmed that BlackHawk might be positioning itself to acquire your company in a hostile takeover attempt when you take it public. He suggested that you reconsider your decision."

"I've considered all of the possible ramifications. I'm not going to change my business plan because BlackHawk is flapping its wings."

"Honey, they might be circling overhead waiting for you to announce the new Baylor Design and Developers, then dive in and scoop up the restructured company."

"Predatory birds, like BlackHawk, don't attack until the prey is dead. The carcass is still moving." He grinned and kissed his sister on the forehead.

She ruefully shook her head and smiled. Then she eyed JaiHonnah over Roderick's shoulder. "Uh, JRock, I think we're being rude to JaiHonnah."

Roderick had almost forgotten that J. Reise Chapman was in the room during his tirade. Monique always had a deleterious effect on him. She particularly drew his evil side out when it came to their girls. His argument with Monique the previous evening had him out of sorts all day. She knew exactly what buttons to push, and she pushed them with precision, and often. It was always about their daughters. The twin girls were his heart and soul. He never wanted to let them go to visit their mother in the first place, but unfortunately Monique, with her egocentric way, was their mother and his girls had a right to know her and to love her. God knows there was so little love in Monique to begin with. How he could have let himself love and marry a woman like her, he would never understand, but he would never let it happen again. Women with marriage on their minds were out of his life for good! It was him and his girls. That's all he needed or wanted.

"You're right, Kelley, I have been rude."

They moved back toward JaiHonnah.

"After you co-sign the papers, you've got to put a move on it, JRock. You're due at the Congressional Black Caucus dinner at eight o'clock. Cocktails start at seven."

"Yeah, yeah, I know. What time will Vivian be here?"

"Oh, I forgot to tell you. Vivian was called out of town. One of her client's cases is going before the federal appellate court in Chicago."

"I don't like going to these grip-and-grin things!" he fussed then glanced hopefully at his sister. "Why don't you go instead of me, Kelley?"

"Oh no, little brother." She held up both hands and shook her head in protest. "I've got other plans for tonight and they don't include being your substitute or your date...again." Then, with a twinkle in her eye and a sly grin on her lips, Kelley said. "Why don't you take JaiHonnah with you? It certainly would be an opportune way for her to quickly get into the mix."

JaiHonnah was penning her signature to the last of six documents when she heard Kelley mention her name. Startled, she looked up at them, her eyes wide.

"Me?" she squeaked. "Oh, no, I, uh, caught the redeye in from Milan. I need a bath and some food and a bed. I couldn't possibly go to a..." She noticed that her protests seemed to be falling on deaf ears as she looked from Kelley into Roderick's engaging eyes.

Roderick acquiesced. "You're right. You've had a long day and so have I. I'll have to pass this one up. Give me a few minutes to freshen up, and I'll give you a ride home. Where are you staying?" Roderick asked. He didn't like the disappointment that he felt. Was he actually hoping that he could spend more time with her?

"JRock, you've got to go to this gala," Kelley insisted. "Remember you're making an important presentation? You're on the dais representing the United Black Contractors and Construction Industry. You can't just not go. Besides, it means more exposure for Baylor Construction and Baylor Developers."

"If I show up without a date, I'll never get out of there. C'mon, change your plans, Kelley," Roderick entreated.

"No way! I haven't had a real date in a month of Sundays, and I don't intend to spend the evening protecting you from the female sharks," she said, laughing. "Besides, everyone knows that I'm your sister. I wouldn't be any protection at all. If JaiHonnah won't be your date tonight, Michael Jordan, Dr. J, or David Robinson might consider it. They called earlier to make sure that you were coming tonight. You can hang out with your boyz the way you used to."

JaiHonnah tried not to listen to the conversation, but Roderick seemed to really need moral support. *Well, what the hell*, she thought. Being a hood ornament, just one more time might not be that distasteful. Besides, she had always been a sucker for a hard-luck story. Moreover, it wouldn't be a *real* date, she rationalized. Business associates, even if they were employer and employee, attended business functions simultaneously, didn't they? Well, so what if Roderick just happened to be the most handsome boss ever created? So what if he was wearing a wedding band? She was wearing wedding rings too. Sitting next to him at a purely business function for purely platonic reasons was no admission that she was being forced to slip back into a frivolous social life that she detested. She sucked in her resolve. She could do this for a few hours.

"Okay, okay, I'll go," JaiHonnah relented, "but I have to have a bath, wash my hair and—."

"I'll get your luggage and be right back," Roderick said, striding out of the door.

"But where am I supposed to get ready?" JaiHonnah asked to Roderick's retreating back.

"Upstairs," Kelley said. "JRock lives on the third and fourth floors of this building. He converted it into a 4000 sq. ft. condo. It's convenient for him to live and work in the same place. It also means that his daughters have access to him all day. It makes for a very convenient arrangement for all concerned." Then she shifted gears. "Thanks, JaiHonnah. I hope that you understand that you're not expected to do this type of double duty as a part of your regular responsibilities, but this really does help the company. Let me assure you that JRock is a gentleman to a fault. He's a master when it comes to playing basketball or handling this company, but social affairs make him edgy. He hates the pettiness and posturing that goes on, but in Washington, fifty percent of the business gets done at these affairs."

A number of questions buzzed in Jai's mind. Basketball? Did Roderick Baylor play basketball and run a construction company? Daughters? If he had daughters, where was the mother of his children or a wife? She had no time to ask those questions and wondered whether she really wanted to know the answers.

"Yes, I know, and another fifty percent gets done on the golf course," JaiHonnah lamented. "What's the attire?"

"Sharp and shiny," Kelley said gaily. "After all, we are talking about the premier Black social event of the year. Black Caucus week started last weekend. The President of the United States opened the confab. It's been going strong all week. Everyone who is anyone in Black society nationwide will be at the closing gala ceremony tonight, including representatives of every sorority, fraternity and social organization; business leaders, church leaders and the press and news media. It is rumored that maybe the President and First Lady will attend tonight, too. A popular Black Republican is the keynote speaker tonight. It should be interesting considering that the speaker will be addressing a group that has, in the past, sworn allegiance to the Democratic flag."

"Yeah, I'll bet." JaiHonnah sighed. "I'd forgotten what living in the states entailed."

Roderick returned with her luggage and escorted her into the elevator. When they exited on the third floor, she marveled at the beautifully converted warehouse. The natural red-brick walls and partitions were lacquered and showed a deep grooved texture. Two large, red leather lounge chairs sat before a fireplace with a fluffy rug at their feet on wide-planked, gleaming Brazilian cherry hardwood floors. Sparsely decorated with large, hand-painted oils in vibrant colors by Black artists she recognized, large green plants, and rich brown micro fiber upholstered furniture, it was decidedly a man's abode. Large, wide windows offered a panoramic view of the Washington skyline. No frills, with a combination of efficient office/living space. A giant flat-screen, digital, high-definition television surrounded by high-end, surround-sound, studio-quality stereo equipment was the only entertainment in the room. She noticed the open-concept kitchen with pots and pans hanging from hooks in the huge ceiling beams, a large center-post prep area. The dining area contained a round, butcher-block table with two chairs and two booster chairs. All in all the space was huge, yet very comfortable and homey looking.

"This way," Roderick said as he led her through a large playroom and then into a bedroom of particularly beautiful yet functional furniture. Definitely a room for his daughters with all the frills. It was gaily decorated in peach and cream colors with big stuffed animals everywhere. A bathroom with a corner shower stall and an old-fashioned, claw-foot tub sat amid cream porcelain fixtures low enough to the floor that his girls could reach them with ease. A reading area in an alcove housed books, video equipment and a desk with a computer. It was the kind of room every little girl dreamed about, JaiHonnah mused while eyeing the double beds with canopies. She could bury herself in the deep pillows that adorned them.

"Is this alright?" Roderick asked.

She smiled, looking around in awe. "It's wonderful."

"Good. I'll leave you now. My room is through those double doors," he said, motioning with a nod, although he didn't know why he told her that. It wasn't as if she would need to seek him out. "I'll be ready in thirty minutes, and I'll meet you back downstairs in the reception area." With a lively step, he left the room.

JaiHonnah watched him go and wondered where Roderick got all his energy. She had followed him around all day. He seemed as fresh and energetic as the Energizer bunny. He just kept going and going... She shook her head. "Oh, well," she said aloud, "once more into the breach." She headed for the shower.

Roderick was pleased that JaiHonnah agreed to accompany him, he decided as he stepped into his wide open, glass block shower stall. Under ordinary circumstances he'd rather do anything than have to go to one of these affairs, but if he was going to get the new company, Baylor Design and Developers, off the ground, this was part of the wind that would lift its sails.

His image as a former professional basketball player could get him in the door, but initially people rarely took him seriously as a businessman. Especially not one who grew up on the wrong side of the Anacostia River on Bad Ass Place. Hell's Kitchen, Cabrini Green, Bedford Stuyvesant, East L.A., all of them combined were not as tough as his old neighborhood. For every dilapidated, rundown project house there was a sad story of untimely death, despair or degradation. He carried the memory of the desolation in his heart no matter where he was. Too many of the young brothers he grew up with just weren't around anymore. He could have just as easily been among the missing in action in that urban war zone. Only a strong woman, his mother, Sarah Baylor, stood between him and life on the streets after his father, John Baylor, died of prostate cancer. Sarah lived long enough to see all of her five children finish college before she succumbed to a stroke brought on by high blood pressure. Roderick was the youngest of three boys and two girls. He was nearly nineteen years old when his father died, but he still remembered him.

John Thomas Baylor served his turn in Viêtnam when it was still considered a minor skirmish. When he returned, he worked two jobs— one fulltime during the day at the Post Office on East Capitol Street, near their home, and the other part time as a night watchman at Washington Gas and Electric on Benning Road. Roderick still remembered his father talking about giving back to the community. No matter how bad the neighborhood got, John Baylor refused to be moved. He said that if he could survive the Viêt Nam jungle, nothing in his neighborhood could scare him away. He worked with Rap Incorporated when Marion Barry, who later became the mayor of the city, headed that organization back in the sixties. His father had been there during the 1966 March on Washington, and helped to organize the Postal Workers Union as did his mother who also worked at the Post Office until her death. They were gone now, but Roderick's dream for Baylor Plaza Park in his old neighborhood in honor of his parents was one step closer now with J. Reise Chapman on board. She, and the presentation he would make at the gala, would help to bring that dream to life and the neighborhood around it would again live.

JaiHonnah, he contemplated as he lingered in the shower distractedly lathering himself. Her name rumbled through his thoughts like the thunderstorm that he could see brewing through the large glass skylight above his head. In the distance, the continuous faint flashes of lightning spectacularly creased the darkness. Her scent was like a hot summer breeze. She took the air from his lungs and made him sweat. "JaiHonnah," he whispered, almost as a prayer as he lathered the soap over his face. Then he tried to shake off the thought of her, burying his face in the hot, pulsating spray. What could he possibly be thinking? She was an employee, just like any one of the others he had on staff. She was wearing wedding rings for crissake! However, even if she weren't, Monique was living proof of the prophecy, once burned, twice shy. JaiHonnah...correction, Mrs. JaiHonnah Reise Chapman was off limits. Out of his reach. Out of bounds. He looked down at his growing phallus. "You hear that, buddy?"

JaiHonnah lotioned the fragrant cream over her now rejuvenated torso before she slipped into her black French nylons with a patterned rose at the ankle and lace at the top. She let her mind wander as she continued dressing in the little girls' bedroom. She had a room much like this when she was growing up, she reflected as she looked around. It seemed so long ago, but the good memories of her own childhood were still fresh.

Now, however, she thought as she slipped into the black, form-fitting Vera Wang original with plunging décolleté both back and front, she was no one's little girl anymore. Now it was the latest in haute couture Parisian fashion for her. Her outfit didn't allow for a bra. Thank goodness everything on her hadn't gone South, yet, but now that she had a job she was going to have to take full advantage of the Watergate's exercise facilities to keep her body toned and to keep up with the demanding pace of her new duties. Thanks to J. Roderick Baylor, her life was beginning.

"JRock," she whispered with a small smile edging the corner of her mouth. That's what everyone called him. It should be Rock of Gibraltar, she mused. That's what he seemed to be she recalled as her mind wandered over the events of the day. He had apparently been some kind of basketball icon. She hadn't followed sports much when she lived in the states and rarely paid attention to sports in Europe except soccer. So his celebrity was lost on her. She watched him as he deftly handled his business. He was impressive. Women in the D.C. government's Licenses and Inspections Office openly swooned when she and Roderick came in to arrange for and schedule inspections of his job sites. He seemed impervious to the flirtatious glances. JaiHonnah was certain that one woman kept him longer than necessary at the scheduling desk as she batted her mascara-caked eyelashes at him and moved her tongue over her lips while twisting her hawk-claw faux nails between a string of faux pearls. *Ugh!* How disgusting, JaiHonnah shuddered as she smoothed her dress into place, but, she recalled the Rock of Gibraltar never took his eyes off his list of inspection dates and standards.

Other men and women flocked to him for an autograph or to induce him to have dinner or drinks with them. He was courteous and kind to people who approached him and his engaging smile never dimmed no matter how often he was intercepted. She liked his openness and generous nature.

"Enough already, Jai," she muttered, chastising herself aloud when her nipples plumped. *Her new life did not include getting it on with her boss! If it did, her career could begin and end with one fell swoop. Plus, he's married, and you're obligated to play the part of a married woman.* Yet the thought of him still sent strange sensations coursing through her body. "Be still my heart."

In Italy playing the role of a married woman hadn't kept the wolves away as successfully as she had hoped, but here in the states, a woman wearing wedding rings used to mean something. She hoped that it still did, even though her former husband had proven her wrong on that score many times. A chastity belt wouldn't stop Calvin Chapman, though, she reflected. Rather, it just made the hunt and conquest that much more exciting for him. He was a charmer alright. Not as tall, masculine or as ruggedly handsome as the Rock of Gibraltar by any stretch of the imagination. Calvin was more of a pretty boy with European charm, and the women fed his ego. Just once she would have liked for him to just say no to any of the women who openly pursued him right in front of her face. Her self-esteem took a beating, but she was still ticking. She pulled herself up by her own Manolas after her divorce and now, again thanks to the Rock of Gibraltar, she was stepping a little livelier. She checked herself in a full-length mirror. Her appearance was chic, sophisticated, yet she had the air of a professional businesswoman. She liked the look. Better yet, she liked who she would become: an employed, independent woman. "Well world, ready or not, here I come!"

Roderick was leaning against the high reception desk chatting with Kelley. It was a good thing that he had something to hold on to when JaiHonnah Reise Chapman walked off the elevator. She was breathtaking. *Breathe, man. Breathe.* His heart, his loins, his blood accelerated.

"Sorry I took so...long...uh, but I couldn't get...uh, my hair dryer to ..." *God, he's gorgeous!* She sighed inwardly -- "uh, work in the socket, I mean plug, I mean, uh ..." *Shut up, Jai. You're making a fool out of yourself. But he's so fine! Adonis, eat your heart out. Please don't smile. Oh, God, forgive me.* He smiled and the lightning struck. *I don't know about the Rock of Gibraltar, but the Walls of Jericho must be crumbling.*

"Uh, no, you're not late. These things rarely start on time anyway," Roderick said, smiling around a large lump in his throat. *That's right, breathe slowly, but God Almighty, why me? You had to send an angel to tempt me? Alright, I'll go to High Mass and confession for what I'm thinking. Satisfied? I'll repent, but let me sin tonight! At least let me lust in my heart!*

"JaiHonnah, you look like new money!" Kelley exclaimed.

"Thanks, Kelley. I hope that my attire is alright. I haven't been keeping up with the fashion in the states. Most of my things are being shipped, so I had very little to choose from."

"You just set a new standard," Roderick said, swallowing with difficulty.

JaiHonnah didn't know or understand why Roderick's appreciative gaze warmed her and pleased her in intimate places while at the same time excited her beyond belief.

"Uh, little brother, close your mouth, you're drooling," Kelley whispered for her brother's ears only. "G'Night, you two," she sang louder as she left the office.

Roderick and JaiHonnah stood gazing at each other, barely aware of Kelley's departure. The air was full of electricity, but it wasn't coming from the storm raging outside.

Roderick cleared his throat. "Uh, should we go?"

"That's what we're all dressed up to do, isn't it?" JaiHonnah smiled up at him. "What would we do instead?"

Please don't ask me that question at this particular moment, he thought. Lusting in his heart would only be the beginning of one sacrilegious, decadent, and heat-filled night.

"Of course, I meant to say that we should be going," *to bed, together, now,* he mentally added.

Roderick led JaiHonnah to the garage. He opened the door of his custom black Mercedes Benz for her, helped her in and then got in on the other side. He could barely breathe as she crossed her long, silky legs at the knee and the split on her left thigh rode up. Her intoxicating, fresh scent filled the space as his nostrils flared, savoring the aroma. The garage door crawled up, and they drove out into the torrential rainfall, but another storm was brewing inside them.

One Gentleman cologne was doing everything but cooling JaiHonnah's senses, she thought. When Roderick rested one large, strong hand with long fingers on the floor-mounted stick shift, she nearly lost it. Recalling the old adage about the size of a man's hands in proportion to other more intimate parts of a man's unique anatomy had her shifting subtly in her seat. Or was it the size of his feet? Which she noticed were long too. He stood at least six foot seven. She was sitting next to this God's Gift to Womankind and having erotic thoughts about them being together, naked. He had entirely too much charisma and animal magnetism to think about. *He's your boss,* she reminded herself. *He's married. Remember?* She inhaled and exhaled slowly. She cleared her head of thoughts of him and busied herself looking at the beautiful Washington skyline.

Things had certainly changed considerably along Pennsylvania Avenue, she noted. It had been a long time since she had been in Washington. Roderick pointed out some of the buildings that Baylor Construction had worked on. The company was the contractor for the interior of the new downtown convention center and the new baseball stadium. Tonight would go a long way toward making many other major projects happen. All of the city council members and the mayor would be there.

* * *

The gala was no small-town affair JaiHonnah and Roderick both noticed as they fell in line behind a row of limousines waiting to drive under the portico to unload their passengers. There were top executives from some of the most prestigious and influential companies in the country in attendance. A valet opened JaiHonnah's car door and helped her to the curb while a second valet whisked the car away. Roderick put her floor-length matching coat around her shoulders and offered her his arm as they entered the wide marble foyer that led to the Atrium Ballroom.

The mayor, his wife and their entourage formed a receiving line as the official hosts of the gala, greeting the guests as they arrived. Huge ice sculptures placed strategically around the anteroom, adorned in bright, late summer foliage and greenery, glistened and melted in tiny spotlights. An army of young waitstaff moved skillfully among the throngs of people offering trays of hot and cold hors d'oeuvres. Other waiters carried champagne glasses precariously perched on trays. A jazz combo played up-tempo selections on the open mezzanine level overlooking the rapidly burgeoning crowd.

Women clad in beautiful and expensive evening regalia glided around the expansive salon, accompanied by male companions who looked quite dashing and prosperous in their couture tuxedos and black or white ties. None looked more elegant than Roderick Baylor and JaiHonnah Chapman as they entered the reception area outside the ballroom. Heads turned as they advanced through the crowd. They were met every step of the way by people who approached and greeted them warmly. Photographers seemed to capture them with each word that they uttered. Both Roderick and JaiHonnah were impervious to the flash of cameras.

Roderick furtively glanced at JaiHonnah as he talked with members of the South African delegation and she spoke in fluid French with a noted Afro-French sculptor. He prayed that she would not look more lovely and stunning than any other woman in the room. His prayers were not answered. Her dress lay softly on every perfect curve of her hourglass figure. A matching black, sequined, choker graced her long, slender neck and the diamond-stud earrings sparkled brilliantly in the ambient lighting. Her shimmering, black-tinted nylons accentuated her long, shapely legs, and her shoes had a diamond-studded strap at the ankle and one across her perfectly pedicured toes. The bodice of the dress defied the laws of gravity with its ability to remain in place, cupping her full breasts, Roderick thought. Her thick, heavy black hair was mounted gracefully atop her head in an old-fashion Georgian style reminiscent of the 18th century with wisps of hair dangling around her lovely face and onto her neck and bare back. She was an absolute vision, he thought, but he wasn't the only one who noticed her. She garnered appreciative stares from popular actors and other entertainment moguls. She certainly was no stranger to so many who hugged her warmly and laughed with her over what he assumed was some shared memory.

JaiHonnah couldn't stifle the smile that brightened her face when she noticed Roderick's glances. His black Perry Ellis tuxedo with shawl lapels and white shirt with a band collar and onyx studs did justice to his tall, sleek frame. A Gucci watch, gold nugget ring and Lorenzo Banfi shoes completed the ensemble, and she wasn't the only one who noticed. Women flocked to him in droves.

"Your date this evening, I've seen him before somewhere," Geneva Simpson, a former Ms. Louisiana, now owner of Geneva Cosmetics International, said casting her eyes shamelessly over Roderick's torso as she sipped champagne.

"Not satisfied with sleeping with my husband anymore, Geneva?" JaiHonnah quipped with a smug smile.

Geneva slowly turned her soft, green-eyed gaze and sly grin toward JaiHonnah and took a lazy sip of her drink. She was a stunning beauty of Cajun heritage. "But, Jai, darling," she said, grinning, "you know that was only for sport. Calvin is great for a few rolls in the hay, but I didn't want to buy the farm. You are entirely too sensitive about your husband. No one takes marriage as seriously as you do. I should think that by now you would have put all of that fidelity and monogamy silliness behind you. I certainly have, along with your husband."

"I have, too, but, of course, you always did favor my leftovers."

A perfect eyebrow arched. "Well, well. The sleeper has awakened," Geneva said, and then breathed salaciously. "Living on the continent has put a little steel in your britches, has it?" She again leveled her sultry eyes on Roderick. "It will be a real challenge this time ferreting that long, tall sip of chocolate soda away from you."

"*Laissez les bon temps rouler,* Geneva. He doesn't belong to me, but as you said, I've learned a few things over the years. I'm no southern belle anymore and as far as your affair with my husband is concerned – *Et trois.*"

"Mrs. Chapman," Roderick gently interrupted, "I believe we should take our places on the dais." Then taking JaiHonnah's arm and turning to Geneva, he said. "If you'll pardon us, please—."

"Roderick Baylor," Geneva recalled. "You played some type of sports, didn't you?"

"Yes, many years ago, but—."

"Mr. Baylor, this is Geneva Simpson, CEO of Geneva Cosmetics in—."

Geneva interrupted JaiHonnah's introduction and moved well within Roderick's private space. "You're Monique Baylor's husband, aren't you? I haven't seen her here tonight," Geneva said, looking around the room casually, sipping her champagne lazily, and eyeing him suggestively. "She's here, isn't she? I hear that she's doing some movie or something in Hollywood. She usually doesn't miss one of these soirees, but she doesn't seem to be with you tonight."

"What was your first clue?" he asked, abating his anger at the mention of Monique's name, but not waiting for Geneva's response as he guided JaiHonnah swiftly away. "Friend of yours?" he asked as they wound through the crowd.

"Just someone I used to know," she answered, dodging one guest after another.

"And your husband's, too, apparently," he mumbled to himself.

JaiHonnah stopped in her tracks. She hadn't realized that Roderick had overheard her conversation with Geneva. This was a real breach of her privacy, she thought as she narrowed her eyes, knitted her brow, and glared up at him.

Roderick hadn't realized that he'd spoken his thoughts loud enough for her to hear him, but the look on JaiHonnah's face said otherwise. "I'm sorry. That just slipped out. I overheard parts of your conversation."

"My private life is—," she started.

"None of my business," he finished for her. "You're right. I won't let that happen—."

"JRock," Lionel Porter, President of Porter, Dare and Silver Construction in Atlanta, interrupted, extending his hand and broadening his already too large smile to encompass JaiHonnah. "It's good to see you, and who is this lovely lady?" He stroked JaiHonnah with his eyes.

"Good evening, Lionel. This is Mrs. J. Reise Chapman," Roderick said through a set jaw. "She's recently joined our staff. Mrs. Chapman, this is—."

"Mr. Porter needs no introduction, Mr. Baylor," JaiHonnah said, smoothly, extending her hand. "I'm very familiar with the work your company did in designing some of the Atlanta Olympic village. In fact, I submitted some of my concepts to your company."

Porter gave JaiHonnah another long perusal as he clasped her hand warmly in both of his. "I recall them vividly," he said, leaning too close. "Look, I'm going to be in town for a week or two going over some details with members of the Olympic Committee about refurbishing the structures and chatting about the next Olympic site. Perhaps we could arrange to sit down over dinner and discuss your designs."

JaiHonnah sensed the tightening in Roderick's demeanor. Obviously, Baylor and Porter were competitors, but there was uneasiness between the two men she also noticed that seemed to go beyond business, but couldn't quite discern what.

"Well, only with Mr. Baylor's approval, of course. I design exclusively for Baylor Construction now."

"Loyalty. I like that in a person," Lionel said, still gazing at her. Without breaking eye contact with JaiHonnah, he said to Roderick. "You're fortunate to have such a talented associate on board, JRock, and so beautiful too."

Roderick sensed what Lionel was up to. He had a great deal of recent, painful history with the man. Loyalty, ha! The man didn't know the meaning of the word, nor integrity or honor.

"Mrs. Chapman's time is very limited, Lionel. She has more than enough to keep her busy with Baylor Construction projects."

"Well, I see," Lionel said with a raised eyebrow and sly grin poised around his thin lips. "But I should mention that unlike your company, our firm is in a position to offer partnership options to talented architects—after serving an appropriate apprenticeship period and a relatively nominal buy-in, of course."

JaiHonnah's interest increased, but her sense of Roderick's discomfort with Porter caused her to hold back any further query about the partnership potential.

"I'm at the Mayflower. Why don't we—," Porter began, directing his statement to JaiHonnah to the exclusion of Roderick.

"Excuse us, Lionel, but we have to be seated," Roderick said abruptly, gently placing his hand at JaiHonnah's back and continuing their journey to the ballroom door.

Once inside, they were greeted by gala organizers who led them to the multi-tiered dais and seated them. For several minutes they were alone on their long row of opulently decorated tables that sat above the floor of the ballroom. Neither spoke as they reviewed the leather-bound program that had been given to them when they were seated.

Focusing on the program was difficult for Roderick. Emotions that he could not identify or understand streaked through his mind. Even though Lionel was openly making a play for his new architect, Roderick sensed that he had been too overbearing intervening in Lionel's discussion with JaiHonnah. Of course she had a right to speak with anyone she chose, even Lionel Porter. Roderick had felt justified in his actions at that moment, but now a cooler head prevailed. However, the thought of someone making a better offer to JaiHonnah Chapman for her services annoyed him. Companies raided other companies for talented employees all the time. It was a cost of doing business. That's what many of these gatherings were about—an opportunity to network and move on or up in one's chosen career field. If JaiHonnah's work was half as competent as Vivian had boasted, in time J. Reise Chapman would certainly be looking for greater and more rewarding career opportunities. Although he recognized that he could not stop her from leaving his company, for some reason unclear at the moment, he wanted to try. Markedly, however, he knew that his feelings had less to do with his need for her professional skill, and more to do with some innate desire to protect her from something.

The nerve of this man to raise any issue related to her private life, JaiHonnah fumed silently sitting next to Roderick. His comment had no place in a strictly business relationship. And the way he ramroded over her potential opportunity for greater career advancement, a partnership with a world class firm, no less, was shameful. His incredibly selfish and chauvinistic behavior was infuriating and demeaning. Certainly she was capable of speaking for herself. She was, after all, an independent woman, wasn't she? Although the idea of a partnership was intriguing, she could have and would have declined the opportunity. After all, she had just signed a one-year contract with Baylor Construction. Now, because of Roderick's high-handed behavior, she felt bound and determined to pursue it. She would contact Lionel Parker at her earliest opportunity.

The dais began to quickly fill around them. They rose from their seats frequently to meet and greet others seated above and below them. Later, the orchestra began to play, the doors to the ballroom were opened and the other guests flowed in, finding their seats at the reserved tables throughout the room. Once seated, the lights dimmed, a spotlight shone on the Chairman of the U S Senate's Banking and Financial Services Oversight and Investigations Committee, with a superstar actress at his side, opened the evening's festivities. Reverend Justice from the largest congregation in Chicago and who happened to be the grandfather of one of her close friends, Constantina "Tina" Justice, gave the prayer. Once the prayer ended, wait staff surged over the room and the seven-course meal commenced amid murmurs and whispers in the crowd. Roderick and JaiHonnah still had not spoken to each other as they dined on pheasant under glass. JaiHonnah did chat with a congressman from Maryland, while Roderick talked with a noted black female publisher on his left.

When the endless speeches and presentations began, JaiHonnah, now very weary, listened half-heartedly. J. Roderick Baylor was briefly introduced as he rose from the table and strode to the podium amid appreciative applause in recognition of his years as a professional athlete. He thanked the audience and set about his task without delay.

When Roderick finished his remarks the audience was spellbound by his words. Roderick's voice was confident, clear and stalwart, muting the audience for moments after he finished. Then, as if it all finally sunk in, thunderous applause broke out. People leaped to their feet. Clamorous roars went up with great fervor. Even the dais, the wait staff and the orchestra rose in enthusiastic adulation. Roderick seemed unaffected by it all as cameras flashed in his face and the adulation heaped on him. He had only spoken for ten minutes just as the others before him had, but what he put into his presentation packed more of a wallop than a youthful Muhammad Ali punch.

JaiHonnah was still standing and applauding with others as Roderick retook his seat beside her. Her eyes sparkling, speechless, adoration flared in the pit of her stomach. What a waste tonight would have been, she thought, if she had gone to bed and missed this blueprint for the future. She glanced around at the boisterous crowd still standing and applauding enthusiastically. Clearly Roderick had struck a chord in his audience and in her. How selfless he is, she contemplated as the din quieted. Despite her best efforts, JaiHonnah found it impossible to concentrate on the official keynote address. She had already heard the unofficial version from J. Roderick Baylor. She could not stop thinking about him. She wanted desperately to touch him in ways that were inappropriate between an employer and employee. He had managed to thoroughly impress her in less than twenty-four hours.

That morning he was working shoulder to shoulder with his men; something that, as the head of a large company, he really didn't have to do. By noon he was troubleshooting at multiple job sites; another task that was usually performed by lower level staff. This evening he was the businessman extraordinaire and the consummate orator; truly a man for all seasons.

Under ordinary circumstances, Roderick shied from adulation. He had nodded his head to the crowd hoping the din would be quelled, but while it continued unabated, he had felt twenty feet tall when he looked into JaiHonnah's eyes. Her smile lifted him, warmed him. Spontaneously, his heart pounded hard against his chest.

Soon after the dinner and speeches concluded, the entertainment and dancing began. This was the time that Roderick would usually make his excuses and head for the exit, but not this time. Tonight he wanted to dance. Fortunately a down-tempo piece played as he pried himself away from another group who had monopolized his time. He spotted JaiHonnah across the ballroom talking with a famous young golf pro and an entertainment mogul and headed in her direction.

"Mrs. Chapman, may I have this dance?" he asked, extending his hand to her.

Wordlessly she left the group, took his hand, and accompanied him to the dance floor. When he took her into his arms, her nipples hardened and stood on end against the soft outline of her dress. Too much caffeine, jet lag and too little rest, she assured herself as Roderick moved against her needful body. Then when he pulled her closer and rested his cheek against her brow, her eyes closed and she was lost in the magic of the moment.

Roderick felt he could not conceal his emotions with the soft scent of her hair playing havoc with his senses. Her statuesque form fit so perfectly in his arms, against his body. Her velvet-soft hand in his palm and the rhythm of the famous male vocalist caused a warm, peaceful sensation to filter up his spine. He relaxed, his breathing became quiet and his nature began to rise effortlessly. His eyes began to close, blocking out everything around him except her. When he stifled a moan, something snapped him back to reality. *What did he think that he was doing?* This was not the prelude to an evening that would end with JaiHonnah Chapman in his bed. This woman was married and an employee, damn it!

"Uh, I think we ought to be going," he said, his voice husky and low. He cleared his throat. "It's late and you must be tired."

"Yes, uh, yes, I am very tired," she said, struggling to regain her composure.

"I'll get your wrap and have the valet bring the car," he said stiffly.

"That will be fine, Mr. Baylor," she answered, clearing her throat and stiffening her stance. "I'll just get my purse and meet you in the lobby."

Roderick strode away from her as she watched him disappear across the crowded dance floor.

"I'll finish what he started," an all-too-familiar voice said behind her.

She felt the hand on her arm. The hair stood up on the back of her neck. She didn't have to turn around to know who it was.

"No, thank you," she huffed as she began to thread her way through the dancers.

"Jai," the voice said still behind her and again clutching at her arm, stopping her in her tracks. "You don't really want me to make a scene, now do you?" the voice harshly whispered.

The man pulled her back against his body, and she tensed, gritting her teeth.

"Take your hands off me," she answered through clenched teeth.

"No," he whispered, still holding her against his body. "Not until you dance with me."

JaiHonnah let out a long, labored breath then turned to look into Calvin Chapman's light, brownish-green eyes and sun-tanned complexion. When he leaned forward to kiss her, she turned her face away and made her way to the dais to retrieve her purse with Calvin following in her wake.

"What do you want, Calvin?" she asked, checking her purse to avoid looking at him.

He eyed her suggestively. "Is that anyway to treat your husband?" he asked, grinning.

She looked at him and whispered, "You're *not* my husband."

"Oh, then you're not still calling yourself Mrs. Chapman and wearing the rings I gave you on our wedding day?" he asked, taking her left hand in his and holding it up displaying the rings. "Maybe I'm mistaken." He kissed her fingers.

She eased her hand away. "It's jewelry, Calvin. What's your point?"

"A man ought to be able to dance with his wife..."

Her chuckle was derisive. "What, tired of doing the horizontal mambo with someone else's wife? As I recall, that's always been your forte."

"Our contract only stipulated that we would not disclose our divorce publicly or privately. A man needs a little variety..."

"This gala is like Baskin and Robbins for you. They have thirty-one flavors of your favorite women here tonight, including one of your favorite flavors, Geneva Simpson. *Bon appétit,*" she said as she turned away as coolly as she could. Calvin put his hand on her arm to delay her again. When her chilly gaze went from his hand to his eyes, she registered the surprise in his face. He hadn't expected her to stand up to him. For tense moments they glared at each other.

"I think that we need to talk, Jai."

"Calvin, I don't give a damn what you think."

Roderick watched the quietly animated exchange between JaiHonnah and a man whom he did not recognize. The experience seemed to be causing her stress, he realized as he threw her coat over his arm and closed the distance toward her.

With eyes lowered and moving at a rapid pace, JaiHonnah didn't see the Rock of Gibraltar before her until she smashed into his chest.

"Are you alright?" he asked, leering at the man following her and locking his jaw.

"Yes, yes, I'm fine. Please, can we leave now?" she asked with annoyance.

The man stopped his pursuit as Roderick enveloped JaiHonnah in her coat. Roderick and the man momentarily glared at each other and then the man melted into the crowd. Roderick put his arm around JaiHonnah's shoulders and led her to where his car waited. The valet seated her and Roderick generously tipped the valet before he got in behind the wheel. He noticed JaiHonnah's silence as she looked out of the passenger side window.

JaiHonnah's temples were pounding. She closed her eyes against the pain and leaned her head back against the soft, glove-leather seat. She was weary and her nerves were shot. Seeing Calvin was totally unexpected, but she had survived the encounter. It pleased her that she could look at him without the least twinge of feeling except disgust.

"I'm sure that you're going to bite my head off for this, but what was that all about back there?"

"It doesn't deserve discussion."

Case closed, he thought as he drove down Connecticut Avenue. A flagman stopped them while a road crew cleared a large tree limb from the street. Waiting patiently for the road to clear, he turned on the XM Radio to the soothing voice of Anita Baker. Whatever was going on, JaiHonnah clearly was not willing to discuss it with him, and he already apologized for interfering in her private life once tonight. He wasn't going to let that misstep happen again. Not now, not ever, but he still felt drawn to her defense against whatever or whomever was bothering her. She seemed strong and resilient, yet she had a quality that made him want to protect her, to take her in his arms and comfort her. While they danced it had taken every fiber of his being to keep from lowering his mouth to her earlobe, her neck, and her bare shoulders and rewarding his tongue with her taste. He glanced at the time, 1:45 A.M.

The flagman finally waved him through and a short time later he backed into his garage. Opening her car door, he noticed that her eyes were closed and her breathing was slow and light.

"Mrs. Chapman?" he said just above a whisper, stooping down by her side. She did not answer. "JaiHonnah?" he said again, but still no answer. "Some exciting date I am," he mused.

Roderick smiled to himself and lifted the sleeping lady in his arms. He quietly kicked the car door closed. She shifted her head against his cheek, still sound asleep. The elevator opened and as it rose he gazed at her exotically angelic face. Wisps of baby-fine hair outlined her hairline. Perfectly matched and shaped eyebrows over long lustrous lashes feathered her closed eyes. A small, barely visible mole was to the left of her sumptuous mouth. He tried to take his gaze away from her beautiful and perfect countenance, but had no real inclination to do so.

The elevator doors opened, and he carried her into his daughters' bedroom. He quickly realized the short double beds would not comfortably hold JaiHonnah. He pushed open the double doors and moved from his private sitting room into his bedroom. His oversized sleigh bed was the only option. Slowly he lowered her into his bed, and then removed her shoes and coat. He unsnapped the choker around her neck and stopped. No bra. This was a real dilemma. He took a clean shirt from his closet and threaded her into it before removing her dress. God, if she were his he wouldn't want another man gazing at her, let alone undressing her. He pulled the shirt down around her and slowly peeled her dress from her body. She shifted and the shirt rode up over her hips revealing a strawberry-shaped birthmark high on her thigh below V-shaped French lace thong. "Give me strength," he whispered as he continued to undress her. Covering her against the air-conditioned chill with a sheet and comforter, he hung up her clothes, and left the room.

Roderick lay awake in his den on a sofa bed recalling the events of the day and especially those involving his new employee. She was certainly magnificent, a beauty beyond belief, but he was confused. Vivian Alexander Jackson, an enigma in and of herself, must have recommended JaiHonnah to him for some reason other than friendship. What confused him was what that reason entailed. He could rarely figure Vivian out, and he was too exhausted to try it tonight. He trusted her and admitted to himself that because of that trust he hadn't reviewed JaiHonnah's résumé.

His focus then turned to JaiHonnah. She was certainly no stranger to this level of elite society. He had expected her to be talented in her field, but he found it awe-inspiring that she was multilingual and adept at the social graces. However, on a personal level, how could she have a casual conversation with Geneva Simpson, a woman who apparently had an affair with JaiHonnah's husband? Well, hell, hadn't he conversed with Lionel Porter, a man who had an affair with Monique?

Moreover, who was the man from whom she was escaping at the gala? Less than twenty-four hours had elapsed since he first met JaiHonnah Reise Chapman and already his interest in her had grown beyond a purely professional relationship. She was keeping him awake thinking about her and wondering about the mysteries that lay behind her beautiful eyes. She moved like a gazelle, gracefully and fluidly. All that day his every thought had been about her; dangerous thoughts that his body was hard pressed to conceal and her sensual scent controlled him. That was why he kept on the move. For the first time in a very long while he felt vulnerable to a woman.

Chapter 2

JaiHonnah rolled to her side and stretched her body full length, yawning lazily and taking a deep breath. That had been a beautiful and erotic dream that she had. She enjoyed the feeling of being lovingly carried and disrobed. Even now her body warmed at the thought. Strangely, the man in her dream resembled J. Roderick Baylor. *He's probably been in a number of women's dreams,* she thought as she struggled to wake herself. She inhaled Million, then Burberry Touch cologne and her eyes shuttered open. She didn't move, but her eyes skittered around the unfamiliar room.

Where the hell am I? When she began to focus, she realized she was in a massive sleigh bed—alone—and it didn't appear that anyone else had slept there but her. Clearly tracing the events of the previous night, she recalled having a pounding tension headache and closing her eyes just for a moment. Some moment, she recalled. It was broad daylight outside. She sat up and looked at the long-sleeved shirt covering her body and spotted her dress hanging on the back of the double doors, her nylons draped over it. *Oh hell,* she thought. *What have I done?* She quickly got up and noticed her robe and slippers lying at the foot of the bed. Grabbing them, she slipped them on. A noise at the back of the building caught her attention. Cautiously she walked toward the French doors, which opened onto a large upper deck. As she walked out onto the deck to the railing, she covered her eyes against the bright September sun. At a distance she noticed Roderick Baylor at the top controls testing the engines of a one hundred, twenty-foot cruiser docked beside a private ramp in the Eastern Power Boat Marina. Although his back was toward her, she noticed that he was wearing a baseball cap turned backward with Miami Heat stenciled across the brim. When he turned to head for the lower deck, her eyes laved from his sleeveless Georgia Tech muscle shirt and cutoff jeans down to his deck shoes. "Magnificent," unexpectedly escaped her lips.

Roderick had risen early on Saturday morning to check his messages and determine what time his daughters would be coming home. They would be arriving at Dulles International Airport on a 2:00 P.M. on a nonstop flight from Los Angeles. Since he hadn't met with his new housekeeper and baby-sitter yet, he made a list of all of the things he knew his girls liked. He would stop at a grocery store in Virginia on his way to the airport to make sure that fresh fruit was in plentiful supply. His daughters, Shelby and Shelly, were fresh-fruit fanatics just like him. He always had to make extra servings of frappe for breakfast because his daughters could drink as much as he could.

Then he set about the task of preparing *The Mighty Magic Heat* for probably the last of the late summer voyages down the Potomac River. The girls loved to go out on the boat with him, especially the longer cruises down to his summer place just beyond Virginia Beach. This was the middle of the hurricane season and the high heat sometimes created severe thunderstorms like the one the night before. The boat had been littered with debris, but he was nearly finished with the cleanup. How he had so much energy after spending a nearly sleepless morning thinking about the beautiful and alluring woman in his bed amazed even him. He couldn't remember a time when undressing a woman had been so torturous and the feel of her soft-as-velvet skin had his senses in overdrive. He had to shake it off though. She was his employee *and* a married woman. A double no-no, he had to remember.

As he checked the engines, he noticed a figure standing on the deck off his bedroom. He cut the engines, grabbed a towel to clean his hands, and climbed down the ladder on the side of the boat to the dock. As he walked up into his well-landscaped backyard around the swimming pool and lawn furniture, he couldn't help the smile that grew around his lips. Married or not, she was something to behold with her hair loose and cascading around her.

"Good morning, Mrs. Chapman," he called up to her, turning his cap around to block the sun.

"Good morning," she said, smiling back. "You're up awfully early."

"I usually don't sleep this late in the day."

"Late?" She frowned. "What time is it?"

"Eleven-fifteen," he said, checking his watch.

"Eleven!" she gasped. "I didn't realize..."

"Uh, don't worry about it. It's not a work day at Baylor Construction, and apparently you needed the rest. There's coffee, orange juice and fresh bagels in the kitchen. You're the only one in the building, so you shouldn't be disturbed. Take your time; I've got to leave shortly. I'll help you with your luggage and take you to your place when I return. In the meantime, make yourself at home."

"Thank you, Mr. Baylor. Sorry to impose on your hospitality."

"Not a problem, Mrs. Chapman," he said, smiling.

As he started to turn to leave, JaiHonnah called to him. "Uh, Mr. Baylor?"

"Yes, Mrs. Chapman?"

"Uh, under the circumstances," she said with a raised eyebrow, holding up his shirt, "don't you think that we could dispense with the formalities?"

He chuckled, turned the cap backward again and grinned broadly, but knowingly. "Yes, ma'am, I believe that we could," he said as he turned to walk back toward his boat, "JaiHonnah."

A lopsided grin crept along her mouth, and she shook her head slowly. *Dangerous.* She inhaled the thought with a slight shiver. There ought to be a law against a man being that handsome and that sexy and that masculine and very intelligent too.

After breakfast, JaiHonnah took a long, leisurely soak in Roderick's oversized Jacuzzi. While the jets invigorated her body, she savored the manly aromas of shaving creams and aftershave lotions permeating the air. She closed her eyes, inhaling deeply, her thoughts turning to the man who wore those scents. God, he was such a dichotomy: sports icon, businessman, orator, blue-collar worker and apparently, a responsible parent.

JaiHonnah took him at his word to make herself at home and looked through photo albums that contained pictures of his family. In addition to Kelley, he had two older brothers and another sister. The individual portraits indicated that all of his siblings were married except for Kelley. He also had a bevy of nieces and nephews. There were pictures galore of his girls, but she found none that included his wife. *How odd*, she though.

With such a charismatic personality, where the hell was his wife that he needed a date? She wasn't about to seek that information from Geneva Simpson. What was more intriguing was that business with Lionel Porter. *Nope*, she thought. *No way am I going to start thinking about him in any way other than as my employer, the boss.* Work, her fledgling career, that's all she needed to focus on. However, the thought of his earth-shattering smile threatened to obliterate her stance. His natural charisma seemed impossible to resist. His blatant sexual prowess made her question her long-held abstinence from physical relationships.

In the midst of her ministrations, JaiHonnah heard someone frantically ringing the front doorbell, snapping her out of her thoughts of Roderick. He told her that she was the only one in the building. She eased out of the Jacuzzi dripping wet and grabbed Roderick's terrycloth robe hanging on the back of the bathroom door. Quickly she went down the open, interior steps to the first floor as the ringing, and then banging, intensified. When she opened the door, an almond-colored, porcelain-doll beauty with flowing golden brown hair breezed by.

"Who are you, and where is my husband?" she demanded, eyeing JaiHonnah.

Something about this woman annoyed JaiHonnah immediately. She rarely took an instant dislike to anyone, but this woman deserved that singular honor.

"Your name is . . . ?" JaiHonnah asked, arms akimbo and brow knitted.

"I'm *Mrs.* Baylor! Monique Baylor! Roderick is my husband."

"Uh-huh, well, *Mrs.* Baylor, Mr. Baylor left a while ago. I do not know where he went or when he'll return, but I'm sure that you're welcomed to wait for him." Geez, she had just been wondering about Roderick's wife, and there she was as if she had conjured her up. *Well, be careful what you think about…and all that.*

"And just who do you think *you* are?" Monique asked, rolling her neck.

"How many guesses do I get?" JaiHonnah asked flippantly.

Monique huffed. "I'll bet you're that hussy who was with my husband at the gala! I heard all about you from Geneva Simpson last night! Well, let me tell you a thing or two, Miss Whoever-the-hell-you-think-you-are, Roderick Baylor is *my* man and he loves *me*! So you can just pack up your stuff and get the hell out of our lives."

Now she knew she didn't like this woman, but she was in no position to argue with the boss' wife. It was bad enough to be found soaking wet in a married man's bathrobe, albeit innocent. She wondered for a fleeting moment why, if she was Mrs. Baylor, she didn't have a key to the place? Nevertheless, the hair stood on the back of JaiHonnah's neck. This woman wasn't going to push her around no matter who she was.

"I'd worry more about Geneva Simpson, if I were you, Mrs. Baylor, but unless you sign my paychecks, I'll be here until Mr. Baylor returns—as requested. Make yourself comfortable, it may be a while," she said, turning and walking up the steps.

"Just a minute, you!" Monique stormed. "I'm not finished with you!"

"Yes, you are!" Roderick said coldly, standing in the door, carrying two little girls.

JaiHonnah turned at the sharp reproach and spied the two, beautiful, little, identical, chubby-cheeked cherubs in Roderick's arms clinging to his neck.

"Who's the pretty lady, Daddy?" one asked.

"Yeah, Daddy, who is she?" the other chimed in.

Roderick's jaws were already tight after finding that Monique had taken his daughters and left the airport before he arrived. Finding them sitting in the limousine alone with the driver when he drove home didn't improve his disposition. Overhearing a portion of Monique's tirade nearly sent him over the edge, but he didn't want to fight with her, especially not in front of his girls.

"Wait here, Monique!" he ordered sharply as he climbed the stairs behind JaiHonnah.

As they reached the residential level, JaiHonnah turned to face him. "I'm sorry, Mr. Baylor, if I've caused a problem for you. I wasn't sure that your wife was who she claimed to be. I didn't intend to let the situation get out of hand like that."

"No apology necessary," he said, his anger melting with JaiHonnah's smile. He eyed his bathrobe engulfing her. Damn, it never looked that good on him!

"Daddy," one of the little girls whined.

"Oh, yes, baby, this pretty lady is Mrs. JaiHonnah Reise Chapman. She's an architect and engineer who's going to be working for our company. JaiHonnah, these little golden nuggets are my daughters, Shelby and Shelly Baylor." He smiled at both of his daughters.

JaiHonnah smiled at the two little girls and shook each one's hand. "It's nice to meet you both."

"Is she your girlfriend, too, Daddy?" Shelly asked innocently. "Mommy said—."

Roderick interrupted. "Uh, no, sweetheart, you and your sister are my special lady friends," he said making his daughters giggle.

Roderick was annoyed that Monique might involve their daughters in her usual scathing attacks on his character.

"Ja-Ja-JaiHon," Shelby struggled with the pronunciation.

"Ja—Hon—*nah*," JaiHonnah said phonetically.

"What kind of name is that?" Shelly asked innocently.

"Native American," JaiHonnah said, smiling. "Navajo to be specific."

"You're an Indian? Like in the movies? Like Pocahontas?" Shelby questioned with mounting, youthful surprise and wide-eyed wonder.

"Pocahontas is an Indian Princess who is real pretty too," Shelly added.

JaiHonnah laughed. "No, I'm no princess."

"I want to hear all about it," Shelby said.

"Well, if Mrs. Chapman has a few minutes to spare and doesn't mind, I need to talk with your mother."

"You're not going to yell at each other, are you, Daddy?" Shelly asked with a furrowed brow.

Roderick felt a flush of embarrassment and saw the same discomfiture on JaiHonnah's face. He smiled at Shelly and kissed her pert little nose. "We're going to have a conversation, baby, that's all." Then to JaiHonnah, he said as he lowered the girls to their feet. "Uh, may I impose on you . . .?"

"Say no more." She nodded knowingly. "I'll keep your 'little golden nuggets' occupied with some stories that my grandmother, Kiavi Littlefeather, used to tell me when I was their age," she said, taking the girls by the hand and leading them into their playroom.

Roderick wanted to stay and hear the stories, too, but he had Monique with which to deal.

When he returned to the office reception area the chauffeur was placing the last of his daughters' luggage in the foyer, and Monique was crisscrossing the tile floor in a huff. He knew what was coming, but he had to hold his temper and remember that she could hurt him. She had the ability to hurt him badly.

As soon as the chauffeur left, Monique confronted him. "I don't like it, and I won't have it!" she flared as Roderick came down the last step.

"Neither will I!" he said coldly.

Monique stopped pacing and put her hands on her hips. "How dare you parade that hussy around in front of my friends! And I resent—."

"Get out, Monique!" he growled, cutting her off.

"What do you mean 'get out'?" she flared.

"What word didn't you understand?"

Monique took a deep breath. "I have more of a right to be here than that...!"

"Watch it, Monique!"

"And just what are you going to do about it?" she yelled.

Roderick went to the telephone and dialed 911 on speakerphone.

"D.C. Police Department," came the voice over the intercom. "What is the nature of your emergency?"

"This is Roderick Baylor. I have an intruder at 1255 Water Street, South—."

Monique disconnected the call. "If I go, my girls go!" she hissed.

They glared at each other until the telephone rang and Roderick assured the police officer that all was well. Roderick blew a hard breath and looked away in frustration. In that statement lay the danger. He shoved his fists into his pockets, mentally counting backwards. "What do you want, Monique?"

"I want that woman out of my house and away from my girls...now!"

"This is not *your* house! It's *my* office and *my* home! You will not dictate to me who I have as a guest in *my* home!"

Monique gathered herself and like a chameleon changed her approach.

"How can you be so cruel as to bring another woman between us, baby?" she asked sadly.

"What in hell are you talking about? Between us? Do you have a short-term memory-loss problem or something? There is no 'us.' There hasn't been for four years. We are divorced, remember?"

"A minor technicality," she said airily, with a dismissive flip of her hand.

"Monique, why did you bring the girls back early?"

She moved closer to him and rubbed her hands from his chest down to his abdomen. "Couldn't it be that I missed you?" She slipped one hand down his thigh.

"No, it couldn't. Why are you here?"

She stroked Roderick's granite-like jaw and started to place a kiss on his mouth.

He turned his face away, took both of her hands and stopped her from stroking him. He took a step back.

"We need to talk, Roderick."

"About what?"

"Well," she hedged, "I have an opportunity to star in a film, and I know that you know people in the film industry."

"And?"

"I want you to use your influence to get me in to see the director and maybe if you offer to invest in the film I'd have a better chance of landing the role that I want to play."

"Is that all you want? You brought Shelly and Shelby home early just to ask me to make some contacts for you in Hollywood?"

She eased up to him again, snaked her arms around his neck and nibbled on his chin. "That's not all I want."

JaiHonnah came down the steps just as Monique started to kiss Roderick. She felt a flush rising to her face and turned abruptly to ascend the stairway. Roderick noticed her, backed away from Monique, and cleared his throat.

"Uh, Mrs. Chapman, is there a problem with the girls?" he asked, moving to the bottom of the steps. He looked up at her. She had dressed in a pair of brown slacks with a high waist like matadors wear that accentuated her long legs. The matching jacket had black piping and Spanish designs along the edges, short sleeves with a contrasting black shawl draped over her left shoulder. Her heels looked like those worn by flamenco dancers. Her posture was straight, aristocratic. Her makeup was minimal, but expertly applied and not overdone. Her hair was knotted in a ruthlessly tight bun at the back of her neck. She looked like a Spanish aristocrat.

JaiHonnah didn't turn around. Why a man being intimate with his wife should rattle her so was a mystery. She sucked in a deep breath, dug out a weak smile, and finally turned around. "No, no problem," she said. "The girls fell asleep and I thought that this would be a good time for me to leave. I didn't mean to interrupt."

Roderick flushed. He really didn't want her to go so soon. He felt something earlier when she stood on the deck holding his shirt by one slender finger and impishly smiling at him. When Monique said his name, it grated on his nerves, but when JaiHonnah called him Roderick for the first time while she smiled at him and his daughters, his heart did flip-flops in his chest. He couldn't understand his reaction, but he liked it nevertheless.

"I'll take you—," he started.

"That's not necessary. I can take a taxi. I'm only going to Vivian's condo at the Watergate Complex."

"I said I'll take you. I'll get your luggage and we can leave whenever you're ready." Then turning to Monique, who was wearing a very smug smile, he said. "We'll finish this when I get back."

"I can't wait," she said, breathing sensuously. "Don't be too long, darling."

When Roderick and JaiHonnah arrived at the Watergate Complex, Roderick insisted on taking her luggage to the condo and putting it in the master bedroom. He looked around the very spacious area and then turned to JaiHonnah.

"I'm glad that Vivian is finally letting someone use this place. It's a shame to keep it closed up."

"It's a beautiful condo and a very special place for her. It's where she and Derrick lived before he died. They were very much in love and very happy here."

"Yes, I know. Derrick and I were very good friends. He was one of the greatest basketball players ever and an even better pediatrician. He was my daughters' doctor when they were born. He loved children as much as I do." He sighed. "I'm sure you know the story."

"Yes, I do. Although I haven't lived in the states for many years, Vivian and I are still very close. She and I met in our freshman year at Spelman. Later we were roommates. I remember when Derrick and Vivian married and adopted their first health-challenged child, Linda. I think that Vivian has adopted more children with medical problems since Derrick died. Their natural son, Derrick Jr., must be, what, three years old now?"

"Four and a half, going on thirty," Roderick chuckled, then he looked away. "Uh, JaiHonnah, I seem to be apologizing to you a lot for my behavior, and I hope that that hasn't changed your mind about working for Baylor Construction. We do have a good team in place, and I'm going to hire quite a few new people. We're a growing company with a very good future..."

Holding up her hand to ward off his apology, she smiled at Roderick. "I'm looking forward to working for Baylor Construction, Roderick. I'm not sorry that I badgered you into hiring me."

"Badgered? Oh, you mean how you read me yesterday at the Donovan site?" he asked, grinning. "Well, I deserved it. I, uh, I mean, I had a really bad week, until last night. I never said thank you for going to the gala with me. It was your moral support that got me through the entire evening."

"You certainly didn't need me," she said, chuckling. "You were magnificent."

Roderick nearly blushed. "Uh, thanks. I'd like to find a way to repay you for your kindness to my girls too. Maybe we could ..." his cell phone rang in his pocket. "Yes," he answered, his tone very annoyed. His face contorted. "Look, Monique! I told you that—!" he noticed the smile slip from JaiHonnah's face as she walked away to give him privacy. "Tell the girls that I'm on my way," he said before he closed the phone.

He walked toward JaiHonnah as she stood in the kitchen, buried his hands in his pockets, sucked in a deep breath, and lowered his gaze to her eyes.

"I have to go now, but I'd like—."

"What time should I report on Monday?" she interrupted, stiffening and looking away from his intoxicating eyes.

"Monday? Oh, yes, nine o'clock is fine. I'll go over the projects that we have in place now and the ones that I'll be bidding on, but I'd like for you to have dinner with my family."

JaiHonnah extended her hand. "Thank you, but no. I'll see you on

Monday at nine sharp," she said in a very dispassionate and professional tone. "Please enjoy the rest of your weekend."

Roderick took her outstretched hand and shook it. It was so soft and warm, but she withdrew her hand quickly. "Well, then, uh, you have a good weekend, too."

"Thank you," she said, moving swiftly toward the front door.

Roderick reluctantly followed. He paused at the door. His eyes roamed over her beautiful, dewy face, and her raven-black hair. Her fresh, clean scent caused his body to react and his nostrils flared. "Uh, about what happened...I mean with Monique..."

"Have a good weekend, boss. I'll see you on Monday," she said, again turning away from his face so close to hers that she could hardly breathe.

"Uh, yes, Monday," he said somewhat frustrated.

Then he was gone, but the heat still lingered long after he left.

* * *

"No! No way, Monique! You're not staying here!" Roderick raged.

"Then the girls and I will go to a hotel," she huffed.

"He's at the Mayflower!" Roderick said with a hard stare. "And you're not taking my daughters anywhere near that bastard!"

"Who's at the Mayflower?"

"Lionel the Lover. Lionel Porter, the 'love of your life,'" he said, snorting facetiously. "Isn't that what you called him when you walked out on me and our daughters? Isn't he who you told me made you want to sing in the morning? The one who put the stars in your eyes when he took you to bed? *My* bed?"

Monique nervously looked away as they sat at the dining room table. She rose to clear the dishes and strode into the kitchen area.

"You know, Roderick, you're an even better cook now than when we were living together. I wonder what else has improved over time," she said with a little lift in her voice, dismissing his comment as if it hadn't been spoken. "I noticed that you're still wearing the wedding band that

I gave you. You know," she said, coming back to the table and slipping her arms around his neck and nibbling at his ear, "it's been a long time since we, uh—."

"And we're not going to either, Monique," he said coldly, removing her arms from around his neck.

Monique moved swiftly before he could rise and sat on his lap, straddling him. She smoothed his face before snuggling close.

Roderick had no reaction. He had suspected it before, but now he knew she wanted something more than she already stated and whatever it was, it was big.

"Daddy! Mommy!" the twins laughed and giggled as they charged into the room.

Roderick lifted Monique from his lap in one fluid motion, stood and reached for his girls, swinging them up into his arms. His arms were full and so was his heart. He snuggled them close, nuzzling them both at the neck as they laughed and giggled.

He smiled broadly. "My little cherubs ready for bed yet?"

"Tell us a story, Daddy," Shelly implored.

"Yes, Daddy, tell us the story about Skai the *real* Indian princess," Shelby demanded.

"Skai? Honey, I don't know that story."

"Pocahontas told it to us today while you and Mommy were talking. Didn't she tell you the story, too, Daddy?" Shelly asked with a quizzical expression.

"Pocahontas?" Roderick asked, confused.

"Yes, Daddy, JaiHonnah," Shelby corrected. "I said it right, didn't I, Daddy?"

"Oh." He smiled. His daughters were such a delight. "Yes, baby, you said it right, but Mrs. Chapman didn't tell that story to me."

"But that's what we want to hear, Daddy," Shelby whined.

"We'll find the book tomorrow and..."

"It's not in a book, Daddy," Shelly corrected. "It's a secret story and only Indian princes and princesses can hear the story. That's why we want you to tell us."

"Yes, Daddy, because JaiHonnah said that the prince's name is JRock Walks With Tight Fists and that we were his princesses, me, Shelby Moonglow, and Shelly Sunbeam."

Roderick chuckled. "Walks With Tight Fists, huh?" he asked quizzically.

"Yes, but the princesses learn the secret of how to open his fists and then . . ." Shelly's little voice lifted along with her shoulders, "we don't know what happened. We fell asleep. We want to know the secret of how to open JRock's fists."

Roderick roared a laugh he felt from deep within his core. He had not had anything to tickle his funny bone since before his daughters left for California to visit their mother. It felt so good to have the joy back that his daughters brought into his life. It was also great to have something good to laugh about.

"I want to know the secret, too, my little cherubs. We'll have to ask Princess JaiHonnah to tell us the rest of the story, okay?"

"Call her now, Daddy," Shelly entreated.

"Yes, Daddy, call her. I know she'll come. She's a nice princess," Shelby pleaded.

"Please, Daddy, please," Shelly pleaded.

Roderick actually considered making the call, but he didn't know the telephone number. Of course, he could just look in her employment file. He was sure that it was still on Kelley's desk downstairs.

"Enough! It's past your bedtime! Really, Roderick, you placate and appease these girls' every whim! You're too indulgent!"

Roderick had nearly forgotten that Monique was even in the room. Her voice and sharp reproach grated on him. "I did it for their mother, why not for them?" he shot back, forgetting momentarily that he was holding his daughters.

Monique fell silent.

Then he smiled and hugged his girls. "Your mother is right. It is past your bedtime. I bought some new storybooks for you. We'll read one of those tonight and then we'll hear the rest of Mrs. Chapman's story another time."

"Aww," the girls whined.

"But, I do have a surprise for you two."

"What is it, Daddy?" Shelby asked.

"How about a trip on *The Mighty Magic Heat* soon, if the weather is still good?"

The girls were elated. He read two stories to them, kissed them both good night at least a dozen times and tucked them into their beds. He returned to the living room smiling to himself with his fists dug deep into his pockets. "JRock Walks With Tight Fists." He laughed quietly to himself and shook his head. He unclenched his fists in his pockets.

Roderick worked well past midnight on his cruiser that night getting it ready for the next opportunity to take an extended trip with his girls. He showered on the cruiser and stretched out across the king-size bed in the master cabin. Turning out the light above him, he laced his fingers behind his head, and lay bare with the hot, late summer breeze off the river flowing over his body, drying the moisture left by the refreshing shower.

The Eastern Power Boat Marina was alive with the usual Saturday night parties and music wafted in from many directions. The boat rocked gently against the dock. He flipped on the FM radio and tuned to Howard University's jazz station, WHUR. The mellow horn of Paul Taylor's *"I Want Your Love"* filled the air. He closed his eyes and was flowing with the music until he heard someone climb aboard the craft. The bright moonlight caught Monique as she stood poised in the doorway of the master cabin wearing a very revealing black négligée. In her hands was a magnum of chilled champagne and two fluted glasses.

Monique's eyes lasciviously roamed over Roderick's nude body, enhanced by the dappled moonlight. Her perfect breasts heaved beneath the barely veiled bodice of the négligée.

"I see you were expecting me." She grinned, dropping her eyes to his phallus.

"What is it that you want, Monique?" he asked coldly, covering himself with a sheet.

"Another chance."

"Another chance to do what?"

"To be your wife. To love you and make love to you the way that only I know how." She moved closer to him, putting one knee on the bed and holding out the champagne bottle to him. "You haven't been able to love anyone since I left, and you know it. That's why you're still wearing your wedding band. You know you want me." She leaned over him, removing the cover and kissing his chest, letting her hair feather his abdomen. "Why don't you just let it happen? Stop fighting yourself and me because you're still angry with Lionel. He was never half the man you are and by the look of you now, he never will be." Her tongue slid down his abdomen. "I can make you feel again. Touch me, darling. I want you so badly."

Roderick unlaced his hands from behind his head and began applauding slowly, but firmly. "Another award-winning performance by Ms. Monique Miller," he said facetiously. "Now, if you're through with the Camille act, what is it that you want from me?"

Roderick witnessed the return of the chameleon.

"That was cruel, Roderick!" she scoffed.

"You have five seconds."

"But, darling . . ."

"Four seconds."

"Honey," she whined.

"Three seconds."

"Alright!" she blared. "I need money!"

"How much this time?"

"Five hundred thousand."

He didn't bat an eye. "I'll speak with Vivian on Monday. In the meantime pack up your bags, tell the girls whether you'll see them for Thanksgiving or Christmas, kiss them good-bye and leave by noon."

"Vivian Jackson shouldn't have anything to do with this! It's strictly between you and me!"

"Do you want the money or not, Monique?" he asked more calmly than he thought he could.

She drew back the magnum of champagne as if to use it as a weapon.

Roderick was on his feet in a flash, towering over her.

"And don't pull this stunt with me again or I'll instruct Vivian to take you back into court to rescind the million dollars a year in alimony that I'm already paying you," his tone low and threatening.

Monique backed away from him, her face contorted in anger. "You want that witch! Well, she'll never love you like I did, Roderick!"

"Thank God for that! Now good night and good-bye, Monique!"

Monique huffed, but left the cruiser. Roderick didn't have to ask to whom Monique was referring. He lay back across the bed as Phyllis Hyman's dulcet tones soothed him with, *"Somewhere in My Lifetime."*

"JaiHonnah," he whispered as he drifted into sleep.

Chapter 3

JaiHonnah tossed and turned fitfully in bed and tried to reach for the blaring telephone. Finally she captured it and dragged it to her face buried under the pillows.

"Yes," she garbled.

"JaiHawk!" a voice blared over the receiver without formality.

"Daddy, hi, how are you?" she asked, rolling over heavily. She'd recognize that Southern Texas drawl anywhere.

"I'm fine, baby," he said, chuckling. "Rough night?"

"Just jetlagged I think. I didn't sleep well."

"Apparently not, by the looks of things. What's with you and this boy J. Roderick Baylor?"

"Nothing, Daddy, he's just my..." something dawned on her. "Daddy, how did you know where to find me and why did you ask me about Mr. Baylor?"

Jake laughed. "Now I've got your attention, huh?"

"Daddy!" she warned.

Jake laughed louder. "No mystery. Syndicated Society Column carried full-page coverage of the Black Caucus Gala. You're almost as beautiful as your mother."

JaiHonnah sat up in bed. "Don't try to sweet-talk me, Jake Hawkins! You own and publish the newspaper. Answer my questions."

Jake laughed again. "Ah, dahlin', you're getting too quick for your old man."

"Don't give me that *ole man* stuff either. You won't be fifty two until next year. Now what are you up to?"

"Nothin', dahlin'," he said and laughed. "You're too suspicious. Always have been."

"With good and sufficient reason I hasten to remind you, now talk."

"Well, I did see your lawyer in Chicago on Friday. She blew in like a Texas tornado trying to separate me from some plans I've got in the works. I asked her when she last saw you, and she gives me this cryptic grin like a chessie cat. That little lady don't know who she's fooling with, I'll tell you. I figured that, if you were in D.C., she knew where you were staying and seeing that this boy, J. Baylor, is a client of hers, too, I had someone get in touch with him for me. See, I told you it was all innocent."

"Yeah, like Enron was a bookkeeping error," she quipped.

Jake laughed loudly. "Now you ain't sleeping with this Baylor boy are you, JaiHawk?"

"And just who spent the night in your bed, Daddy?" she quipped.

"Draw it mild, baby girl. Draw it mild," he said and laughed.

"Don't start with me, Jake Hawkins, and stay out of my business. If I catch you or any of your BlackHawk flunkies nosing around, there's going to be hell to pay!"

"That's my girl! I love it when you get your dander up! But you gotta catch me first, and you know that takes an early bird. It's nearly noon back East and you ain't even out of the sack yet." He roared. "Why don't you pack up your duds and bobbles and come on home? I'll send the little Lear up to get ya."

"Uh-uh, I'm not coming home yet. I'm going to see Grandma, and maybe I'll stop in to see you and my brothers, but don't you start making any plans."

"Aw, c'mon home, JaiHawk," he whined. "Been a long time since you made me a mess of fried green tomatoes, corn puddin' and spoon bread. Can't nobody cook like you and yo' mama."

"I'll see you when I'm ready, Daddy, but if you do anything to interfere..."

Jake roared with laughter. "Bye, JaiHawk. I love you."

"I love you, too, Daddy." She hung up. "Trouble's brewing! I can feel it!" JaiHonnah lay back in the bed and tried to figure out what her father was up to. How did he know that Vivian was Roderick's attorney? she wondered. She knew that her father had her under surveillance out of his fear that someone would attempt to kidnap her as they had her older sister, LaiLoni, just days after her sister was born. Jake never found her. Skai had believed that their daughter was still alive somewhere so Jake had continued to search for his daughter even after Skai's death. Jake had not been wealthy when her sister was abducted and couldn't retain private investigators to search for her, but with each of his other children, Jacob Junior, Adam and her, Jake kept an investigative team busy twenty-four seven. Because the investigators were unobtrusive, she and her brothers grudgingly tolerated Jake's paranoia. He, after all, had lost a daughter, but she'd have to be on her toes and get some track shoes while she was at it. Jake Hawkins didn't just drop Roderick's name on her for no reason. Her father was up to something. He built BlackHawk International with his bare hands, and he had the Midas touch. Scary, she thought. BlackHawk consumed companies as if they were popcorn, and Jake had a voracious appetite.

The doorbell rang simultaneously with Vivian Jackson's entry into the condo.

"Soup's on!" JaiHonnah heard Vivian yell.

"Vivian Alexander Jackson, what are you up to?" she asked, laughing and pulling herself out of the bed and going into the kitchen.

They hugged each other tightly and warmly. Vivian's eyes always smiled and lit up a room. She was tall, too, and thin. More athletic and certainly more energetic. She wore her hair cut very short, which accented her round face, broad nose and full lips. She bore a striking resemblance to Jada Pinkett-Smith in her younger years.

"Good to see you, sister woman," Vivian said, smiling.

"You, too. It's been a long time since you were in Italy, Viv."

"It's been a long time since you were in the states, kiddo."

"That why you railroaded me into coming home? Just because I haven't been here in a while?"

"That and some other reasons," she said, smiling cryptically.

"Viv, you wouldn't by any chance be in cahoots with Big Jake or representing BlackHawk, now would you?" she asked, one eyebrow arced.

"Called you, did he?" Vivian asked and then grinned slyly.

"Yeah, how'd you know?" JaiHonnah asked, knitting her brow and folding her arms. "I just hung up from talking with him."

"Hung some bait out there to see whether Big Jake would bite," she said, reaching for plates in the kitchen cabinet. "He took it hook, line and sinker," she said and grinned. "My client is the Sierra Club. Big Jake wants to do some clear cutting in the National Parks for BlackHawk's pulp and paper division; the company that used to belong to your former husband and his father, Chapman Forest Products. Big Jake is using the lobby group, the Forestry Industry Consortium, to spearhead his operation, but everyone knows that Jake Hawkins pulls the strings and the consortium dances like puppets to his tune. So, I slapped a restraining order on the consortium, and the appellate court heard oral arguments on Friday. Took the court two hours to uphold the restraining order. Big Jake is fit to be tied," she said and grinned as she took the plates to the kitchen bar and started opening the food containers that she brought.

"You go, girl!" JaiHonnah said, laughing. "Serves him right!"

"Your daddy didn't come down with yesterday's rain, Jai. I just tilted him a bit. He didn't get to where he is without knowing how to dodge a few pitfalls. I've got my work cut out for me."

"Daddy loves you, Vivian, because you can be as tough as he is. He'll think twice before he comes back at you."

"Yeah, but it's the third thought that I've got to be careful of," she said and laughed. "Now, tell me why I couldn't reach you here Friday night, sister woman."

"You called?"

"Of course, I called. I wanted to make sure you got in alright. Alejandro, the desk clerk, said that you never showed up. You had me a bit worried. Where were you?"

"I went to the Black Caucus Gala," JaiHonnah said casually as she started serving herself from the food containers.

"Oh," Vivian said with a raised eyebrow. "With whom, may I ask?"

"My boss," she said, beaming.

"You got the job?" Vivian asked and smiled brightly.

"Yes!" she said enthusiastically, jerking her fist through the air.

Vivian opened the bottle of champagne that she brought and poured it into fluted glasses. She handed one to JaiHonnah and raised her glass for a toast.

"To JaiHonnah Reise Hawkins-Chapman, career woman soon-to-be entrepreneur," Vivian saluted, tapping her glass to JaiHonnah's.

They both took a sip and smiled at the delicious flavor.

"Vivian, I haven't even started working yet and you've already got me on the cover of *Forbes* as the Woman of the Year. You've got more confidence in me than Carter has little liver pills."

Vivian put down her glass and took JaiHonnah's hand in hers. She looked at JaiHonnah seriously, but with warmth. "Look, you academically over-qualified, friend of mine. My plan is to have you back in the land of the living, not the land of the walking wounded. You stayed in Italy so long because you didn't trust your own judgment when it came to making your life work for you. Calvin Chapman is legally a thing of the past. I understand your rational for letting people continue to believe that you're still his wife, but it's time to move on."

JaiHonnah leaned toward Vivian with a warm, but directed gaze, clasping her free hand on Vivian's.

"And you, Miss Fix-It, have you moved on? You're flying all over the known universe arguing major cases; running your own law firm. Keeping the President on the right track. Adopting and raising all those wonderful children. You are one of the wealthiest women in the world and twenty-nine years old. Who's making your toes curl?"

Vivian leaned back, removed her hands from JaiHonnah's and began serving herself from the take-out containers. "That's different, Jai. Derrick made all of those things possible for me. I'm still very much in love with him. I'd trade anything to have just one more moment with him."

JaiHonnah placed her hand on Vivian's shoulder, searching her eyes. Vivian finally looked at her. "Viv, everyone loved Derrick. He worshiped you like a goddess. He was a wonderful man, but he's been dead for a long time."

Vivian looked away from JaiHonnah. "I know that in my head, Jai, but not in my heart. I know that to be a fact every time I look into Derrick Junior's eyes. So often all that I can remember is that Derrick died holding Derrick Junior on April Fool's Day, the night that our son was born. The children that we adopted together barely remember how wonderful he was, but the other children, especially Derrick Junior, will never know what a fine man, talented doctor, and great father Derrick was, but I'm doing just fine. I've got my family and my friends."

JaiHonnah breathed out slowly. She could sense the pain and loss that Vivian still felt. She didn't want to belabor the point so she decided to change the subject.

"Speaking of friends, are you and Roderick, uh, special friends?"

Vivian cocked an eyebrow. "And just why would you want to know that Miss I-went-to-the-gala-with-my-boss?" Vivian asked, arms akimbo and a grin on her lips.

"No reason," JaiHonnah tossed flippantly tasting a forkful of food.

"Yeah, right!" Vivian said, chuckling.

"Well, are you?"

"For your information, contrary to what he may appear to be, J. Roderick Baylor is a very moral and principled man. He doesn't play the field. He and I are purely platonic friends first, we have a client/attorney relationship second and, finally, we have some investment interests together. That's all. He's a great guy and a wonderful father. I love him like a brother, but we're not into each other now, nor have we ever been. He and Derrick were very good friends. They played professional basketball together and against each other. That's how I met JRock, and he was a rock for me when Derrick died. Enough said?"

JaiHonnah just grinned.

"So where *did* you spend Friday night?" Vivian asked with a raised eyebrow.

"You're too good of a lawyer, Vivian Alexander Jackson, and rumor has it that you're being watched for a potential federal judgeship. It was the talk of the Black Caucus Gala."

"And maybe you should have studied the law instead of architecture and engineering considering how well you've dodged that same question. Out with it, Jai."

JaiHonnah blanched. A tingle that she didn't understand flitted through her. "Well, yes, I did spend the night at Roderick Baylor's condo, but it was totally innocent. He put me to bed because I passed out. Jet lag, fatigue, and too much gala, but he was a perfect gentleman...I think. Nothing happened."

Vivian laughed. "That goes without saying. JRock is nobody's one-night stand or flavor of the moment. I have a lot of respect for him. He's got high principles and standards."

"And a wife from hell," JaiHonnah added.

"Monique showed up, did she?"

"Yep, in the flesh," JaiHonnah said and then asked casually as she ate. "Sooooo, what's with them?"

Vivian seemed deep in thought.

"Viv, what's the story on Roderick and Monique?" she prodded.

"Oh, uh, can't discuss it. I'm his attorney also. You'll just have to get to know him on your own. Just as I won't discuss you with him or anyone else, I won't discuss him with you." She continued eating.

"I understand. It was just idle curiosity."

"Uh-huh," Vivian said and grinned knowingly.

"It was," JaiHonnah protested. "However, I have to admit that, from what I've seen so far, I can understand why you love and respect him."

"And trust him, my friend. Now, let's eat, and you can tell me all about your new job and let's see if I can convince you to stop letting Calvin continue to pull your strings by permitting everyone think that you're still Mrs. Chapman."

* * *

Roderick was sitting with his feet propped on his desk in his den going over reports when Monique entered the room.

"Roderick, I'm ready to leave. I'll be at the—."

He didn't look up at her, but held up one hand, silencing her. "I don't need that information, Monique. Call Vivian late on Monday or early on Tuesday. She's already back in town. By then, I should have talked with her."

"As close as you two are, you're probably sleeping with her too!" Monique flashed.

Roderick raised his eyes only. "Whatever, Monique. I expect you to call Shelly and Shelby at least twice a week and to arrange your time for them to visit with you when you're not preparing for some movie role. Otherwise, goodbye." His eyes went back to his reports.

Monique huffed and strode out of the room.

Roderick took a deep breath and exhaled, happy that Monique was finally out of his home. He continued to look over the reports. He was getting nowhere fast. Trouble was brewing like a shadow of a dark cloud moving over him. Laying the reports aside, he steepled his fingers. He'd have to find a way to underbid BlackHawk Construction. Although he had not met the man who headed the conglomerate, he respected the man's business acumen. They had gone head-to-head on more than a few occasions. They were running about even up, but there were ten new projects that Baylor Construction and BlackHawk were both after. Roderick knew that his proposals would have to be more cost effective than BlackHawk's and that the concepts would have to be more functional and appealing to the potential clients. He couldn't afford to lose to BlackHawk or any other competitor now. He hoped that JaiHonnah's creative, architectural visions would give him the edge that he needed. He made a mental note to thank Vivian for recommending her. The portfolio that JaiHonnah left for him was spectacular. The woman was, without question, extremely talented.

Roderick picked up and then put down the reports again, leaned back in his chair and again steepled his hands. *JaiHonnah,* he thought.

She certainly was something, he smiled to himself. She could handle herself very well with Monique and wasn't intimidated by her at all. Then there was the incredible impact that she had on his girls. They were still whining for him to call her before they left with Vivian and her children. *JRock Walks With Tight Fists,* he mused. Well, perhaps sometimes he was wound a little too tightly. Relaxation was an occasional experience, not a usual one. Other than spending time with his girls or his family members, there wasn't really anyone with whom he wanted to unwind. About that, Monique was right on target. Although he dated discretely, occasionally, he hadn't been able to love or trust another woman. Monique taught him some very valuable lessons. Never trust a woman you don't know and never love a woman you don't trust. Well he wouldn't have that problem again anyway. He wouldn't fall in love again. The bigger fool he was, the harder he fell. When the telephone rang, Roderick snapped out of his reflective state.

"Baylor," he answered.

"JRock, if it's alright with you, I want to keep the girls overnight."

"Vivian, you've already got a bunch of children. Shelly and Shelby can be little unguided missiles, you know."

"That's why I'm putting them all out."

"What?"

"They want to camp out in the backyard overnight in tents and sleeping bags. I just spent a gazillion dollars on camping equipment to make it happen, so you gotta let the girls stay, unless you're ready for a fight from them," she said, laughing. "Missiles are on the launch pad and are ready to fire."

"And I suppose I'm the target?"

"You got it," she said, chuckling.

"Okay, the ladies have this round. I'll pick them up tomorrow."

"Let me deliver them to you. I'll bet that they'll be up until the wee hours and sleep late. I'll also bet that you're sitting there all alone working. It's a beautiful Sunday. Why don't you find something fun to do while I have your girls? Maybe go to the movies or a concert. Go out to dinner with a friend."

"Naw, I've got to work on this BlackHawk problem and solve it before they pull a raid on my projects, my staff or on Baylor Construction. You and I have to talk early tomorrow about Monique and a few other things. How's your time?"

"How about a game of racquetball at six in the morning?"

"Sounds good. See you then, Vivian."

"If I survive the night," she said and laughed.

"Hang in there, kid."

They hung up.

True, committed friendship was hard to come by, but with Vivian Jackson there was no question that she was his friend first, last and always, Roderick thought as he leaned back in his chair. He loved her like a sister, and he ached for her loss of her husband and his good friend Derrick "DJ aka Dunk and Jam" Jackson. He understood the kind of love that Vivian and Derrick had for each other, even though he never experienced it himself with Monique. Looking at them together or apart he felt the glow, the heat and the passion, but Derrick wasn't the only one who was deeply in love and committed to Vivian and that person was still hurting too. Roderick picked up the telephone again and dialed.

"Dr. Charles Montgomery, please," he said when the switchboard answered.

A few moments lapsed and then. "Doctor Montgomery."

"Hey, brotherman, you wanna try to prove that white boys can jump?"

"I got your 'white boy,' JRock," Chuck said, laughing. "When and where?"

"See you over at Georgetown's McDonough Arena in thirty minutes. Maybe Coach Thompson can give you some pointers on how to play the game before I run this clinic on you. I saw him Friday night at the Black Caucus Gala. He told me your game was looking awful weak," Roderick said, laughing.

"You wish, bro. Bring folding money. I got my eye on your yacht too, so bring the deed," he said and laughed.

"Bet," Roderick said with a snort.

Roderick and Chuck had a few lively pick-up basketball games, which lasted several hours. Chuck's tall, thick frame towered over Roderick's. Chuck had dark brown eyes and hair that he wore long and tied in a short ponytail at the nape of his neck. Both tired and still talking trash to each other, they sat relaxing in the sauna.

"So where you been, JRock?" Chuck asked.

"Man, working. Trying to make the cheddar."

"Like you need the cheese," Chuck said and snorted.

"Gotta do something with the rest of my life after basketball. You know how that is. You and Derrick did the same thing, made a mint and then walked away from the game. Then you started whole new careers and became big-time doctors."

"Derrick was big time. Me, well, I just lived in his shadow. Miss the hell outta that man though."

"You two were like the Gayle Sayers and Brian Piccolo of the NBA, inseparable," Roderick said and laughed. "You and Derrick go way back."

"Yeah, he was twelve and I was nine when he taught me how to play round ball. I owe DJ a lot; hell, I owe him everything I have."

"He felt the same way. That's why he made you Derrick Junior's godfather instead of me," Roderick said and laughed. "He knew you'd end up paying big time as fast as DJ is growing."

"Yeah, but at least Vivian let's you see Derrick Junior grow up. She won't let me see him or any of the other children either. She still blames me for Derrick's death."

"She knows you weren't responsible for Derrick's death, Chuck. I had heard the rumors about his condition. Then one summer I happen to meet Derrick and Vivian while they were vacationing at his home in Bimini. I told him what I had heard and he told me that he didn't want Vivian to know about his heart condition. Said it made him feel like less of a man, and he didn't want her to worry about him all the time. He didn't want her to treat him with kid gloves."

"Yeah, but she blames me for not telling her about his condition. Vivian and I were friends, good friends, before I introduced her to

Derrick, and you know how Vivian is about friendships," he said. "She'd turn the world on its ear for a friend, and she feels that I betrayed that friendship. How can I argue with that, especially against the best lawyer in town? I'm between the proverbial rock and a hard place. Derrick was my best friend since forever, and he made me swear not to tell her, and I kept that promise."

"And you're still in love with her even now," Roderick said, "aren't you?"

Chuck groaned. "Like crazy," he said sorrowfully. "I fell for her the first time I saw her sitting in O'Hare Airport at 2:15 P.M. on December 29 nearly seven years ago. She was coming back from a family trip to San Francisco for the holidays. I did everything I could to get her to talk to me, but she wasn't having any of it. Initially, I thought that maybe she was prejudiced. You know, the racial thing, but thank the gods a blizzard hit D.C. and when we landed, she was stranded. I offered her a ride and she still wasn't giving me no chat. I finally convinced her and gave her a ride home. I was never so happy to see twenty inches of snow." He laughed. "It took a while, but I finally got to know her. She was still in law school. Then I made the mistake of introducing her to Derrick before I finally got up the nerve to ask her out on a date. Derrick didn't have my problem. He took one look at Vivian and, as they say, that's all he wrote."

"Your mistake was not telling Vivian how you felt about her in the beginning, before you introduced her to Derrick."

"You heard? I wasn't sure that she could love a white country boy from the Pocono Mountains of Pennsylvania. If I had it all to do over again, I'd tell her the truth, quick, fast and in a hurry."

"Derrick knew that you were in love with her, Chuck. He also knew that he wouldn't live long with his condition. He loved you and Vivian, and he knew that you'd be there for her after he was gone."

"Yeah, well, he never figured that making me swear to keep his condition a secret from Vivian would ultimately make her hate me this much. Don't follow in my footsteps, JRock. If you find someone who you can love, tell her. No camouflage."

"After Monique, I don't even want to think about it."

"Speaking of Monique, I saw her today at the Mayflower. I was over there having lunch when she came in with…"

"Lionel Porter," he said, finishing Chuck's thought.

"Yeah, him. You gotta get a divorce and move on, JRock. You're still a relatively young man, even though you can't ball worth shit," he said and chuckled. "So what are you doing with that once overactive libido of yours?"

Roderick made a gesture with his hand and Chuck laughed loudly.

"That action will stunt your growth and make you go blind, JRock."

"Is that your professional medical opinion, Dr. Montgomery?"

"Let's just say that I've raised the practice of self-gratification to an art form, so I'm speaking from personal experience."

"Well, I've moved on. The only reason Monique and I communicate is because of Shelly and Shelby, and that's fine with me."

"So what's with the wedding ring? You're still wearing it, I see."

"Protection," Roderick said and snorted. "When I was balling, women were giving it up outta both panty legs. That stuff gets old, ya know."

"Yeah, I know," Chuck agreed. "Been there, done that!"

"Don't get me wrong. I love being with a woman as much as the next red-blood, but I want someone to want me for me and not for what I do or what she thinks I can offer. Seems like every woman I run into is like Monique: wants the fast track, bright lights and big city. That's not me so I wear this ring to keep down the hassle. Plus, it keeps me and my family out of the press."

"Does it help?" Chuck asked.

"Humph, not much," he said, shaking his head. "For some women, it must be a sign of a challenge."

Later that day, Roderick paced his office feeling at loose ends, edgy. He worked as long and as hard as he could, played basketball as long and as hard as he could, but still his unspent energy and emotions were wreaking havoc on him. He even stopped by Vivian's home to help her children and his set up their camping gear. His daughters were having such a good time with Vivian's children that they barely noticed him. So he left with many kisses and hugs from the children and returned to his quiet home. Being alone was one thing, but being lonely was entirely different. There was too much daylight left to go to bed, and going to bed meant going alone. He didn't want to put himself through that ordeal.

JaiHonnah's intoxicating scent was still on his sheets and in his shirt, and it was driving him crazy. The simplest thing to do was to put the sheets and shirt in the laundry basket, but somehow he couldn't bring himself to do that. He had to do something though. JaiHonnah was on his mind since he met her for the first time on Friday. It was now Sunday afternoon. He was wearing a trench in the floor just thinking about her and visualizing how it would feel to kiss her—to make love with her. Not just have sex with her, but to really make love. *Make love?* Now where had that thought come from? He certainly wasn't a school-aged adolescent anymore. He had been with women, plenty of them. Enjoyed them too. Somehow he had shied away from forming lasting relationships. Sex was sex, no more, no less, but somehow that didn't compute when he thought about JaiHonnah. Not that he should be thinking of her in those terms at all. She already had a commitment to love, honor and cherish. Vows that she made to another man. He was no home wrecker.

He had to get out of the house, stop thinking about her or go mad.

Roderick cast off the ropes at the stem and the stern, climbed aboard *The Mighty Magic Heat* and started the engines. He slowly piloted the craft away from the dock out into the Anacostia River past the Washington Navy Yard and under the Frederick Douglass Bridge. It was a warm, sunny afternoon. Other boaters were also out enjoying the last vestiges of summer and waved as they drifted by him. As he rounded the fountain at the tip of Hains Point he started south into the Potomac

River with aircraft coming in overhead for landings at Washington's Reagan National Airport. Suddenly he reversed his direction. "Who am I trying to fool!" he chastised himself aloud as he swung the yacht around and headed north up the Potomac River. Once clear of the Arlington Memorial Bridge and the Theodore Roosevelt Bridge, the John F. Kennedy Center for the Performing Arts stood, its white marble glistening in the bright afternoon sun. Over the top of the Kennedy Center, there it was, the Watergate Condo Complex made famous during President Nixon's era in the White House. Roderick docked at the Harry T. Thompson Boat Center near the Rock Creek Parkway and sat looking up at the Watergate wondering what explanation he would be able to offer for just dropping by uninvited and unannounced. Nothing came to mind.

* * *

JaiHonnah had just put the last of her clothes into drawers and tucked her luggage away in the storage area. She made lists of things that she needed to get to make the condo feel like home and groceries she needed to buy. Her stomach growled while she belted out Whitney Houston's *"I'm Every Woman"* at the top of her lungs. Thank the ancestors she didn't have to sing for her supper, but she was having a good time all by herself.

After pulling her hair into one thick, loose plait with a barrette at the end, she tied a wide, thin leather headband with Navajo design around her head. The afternoon sun drew her attention to the French doors, and she couldn't resist going out onto the wrap-around terrace, inhaling deeply and looking at the beautiful boats crisscrossing the Potomac on this lazy, warm Sunday afternoon. As she headed back into the condo to the kitchen to make something to eat, the telephone rang.

"Yes," she answered.

"Mrs. Chapman, this is Alejandro at the front desk. You have a guest in reception."

"Oh, who is it?"

"A Ms. Baylor is here to see you."

"Oh, great, send Kelley up." She hung up the telephone and went into the kitchen to make mimosas and put on a couple of steaks. It certainly was nice of Kelley to stop by and pay a visit. JaiHonnah hoped that the woman would share a meal with her because she liked Kelley Baylor's personality. It was real relaxed and easy going as compared to her "little" brother, JRock, she mused. The man towered over Kelley, but she seemed to know how to hold him and his dichotomy-ridden personality in check. JaiHonnah hadn't had the same success with her own older brothers, Jacob, Jr. and Adam. JaiHonnah knew that she was going to enjoy getting to know Kelley and the rest of the Baylor family.

When the doorbell chimed, JaiHonnah opened the door with a big smile. Slowly it faded from her face.

"Mrs. Baylor, what can I do for you?" JaiHonnah asked, an eyebrow cocked.

"It's what I can do for you," Monique Baylor said. "May I come in?"

JaiHonnah stepped aside and Monique drifted in, her eyes scanning the exquisitely furnished and decorated condominium.

This was no social call, JaiHonnah surmised. Monique Baylor had a purpose, and the sooner she heard what was on Monique's mind, the sooner she could get back to enjoying the rest of her afternoon. Maybe she'd just give Kelley a call and invite her over. "I trust that this will not take long. I was making an early dinner," JaiHonnah said as she headed toward the kitchen.

"Don't play coy with me, JaiHonnah Chapman. You know why I'm here."

JaiHonnah stopped in her tracks and turned slowly to see Monique assume a very superior posture. Fingers of one hand impatiently drumming on her slim hip, she looked like a fashion model in a pose that screamed "Danger Zone." JaiHonnah knew that pose all too well. She had struck it often enough when competing for beauty pageants and portfolios. She no longer had to conform to anyone else's view of her and certainly not the Moniques of the world. Digging her hands into her pockets, she stood with her shoulders squared and met Monique's pointed glare.

"No, I don't know why you're here, but I'm sure that you're going to tell me very quickly, now aren't you?"

"I want you to stay away from my husband. He and I are just going through a difficult time now. We still love each other very much, and we're trying to find a way to make things work between us. When we made love last night—"

JaiHonnah held up one hand, interrupting Monique. "Look, Mrs. Baylor, I don't need to hear about or know about what goes on between you and your husband. It's none of my business, and I resent your attempts to bring me into your marriage. I'm sure that he explained that we have a purely business relationship, nothing more. I work for Baylor Construction. I accompanied him to the gala, but only as a colleague. My being in your home and wearing your husband's robe when you arrived was coincidental and totally innocent. Nothing—absolutely nothing—happened between us that night. Rest assured that nothing will happen between me and your husband."

"Well, perhaps I'm being premature, but Roderick has a long history of womanizing. I understand from Geneva Simpson that your husband is very wealthy, handsome, and virile and has cheated on you more than a few times. I'm sure that you can sympathize with my dilemma. It's just that I'm not going to be around very often, and my husband is a very handsome, wealthy and powerful man. Although I know that he loves me completely, and he has promised that he won't have other affairs, I wouldn't want anyone to get the impression that he's fair game. The children and I are the most important people in his life. That's why I'm willing to give him another chance, but some times he could miss me so much that he might...well, let his defenses drop and succumb to the charms of another woman again. As you've, no doubt, observed he is a very virile man. Of course, if he were to wander ever again, I don't know whether I could forgive him, and the children would suffer terribly under those circumstances. I'd be forced to leave him, and to take the children away from him for their welfare."

Somehow Monique's soliloquy on her relationship with Roderick didn't wash with JaiHonnah. She watched Monique casually stroll around the living room spinning this tale, but not once did Monique look her in the eyes. Monique's discourse was certainly at odds with what little Vivian had said about Roderick and, from what she, herself, had observed, Roderick was no womanizer. He didn't accept any of the overt propositions during their workday on Friday. Women had flocked to him at the gala before and after his speech, but he had looked very uncomfortable during each encounter. He seemed to be a faithful husband.

"Mrs. Baylor, if this is some type of veiled threat, save your breath. I can empathize with your dilemma, but I am a happily married woman," she lied. "I have no designs on your husband. As I have said before, Mr. Baylor and I have a professional, business relationship. He's my boss and I'm his employee. Nothing more, nothing less. I accompanied him Friday night because Kelley could not, and both Mr. Baylor and his sister thought that two people representing Baylor Construction would make a good impression.

"I'm happy that you and your husband are working on your marriage, particularly for the sake of your beautiful daughters. They are very special little girls who need both of their parents. I hope that it works out for all concerned, but as for me, I'm not in the mix."

"Then we have an understanding and we need not mention this little talk to Roderick?"

"There's nothing—."

There was a knock at the door, interrupting JaiHonnah. She excused herself, confused over why the guest had not been announced. When she opened the door, her heart nearly stopped.

"Uh, what are you doing here?"

"Hi, gorgeous, can't I come in?" Calvin Chapman asked, grinning.

"This is not a good time, maybe later or tomorrow."

Calvin grew more belligerent. "No, Jai. I won't wait in line for the Texas princess again!"

JaiHonnah didn't want to make a scene, particularly not in front of Monique Baylor. She had witnessed her ex-husband's outrageous behavior before. "Alright, Calvin, come in, but I'm not alone, so let me do all the talking, understand?"

"Well, of course, dahlin'," he said, mimicking a Texas drawl.

JaiHonnah led Calvin into the living room where Monique strolled around the room looking closely at the priceless artifacts and decor.

"Mrs. Monique Baylor, this is Calvin Chapman," she said to Monique. "Mrs. Baylor is married to J. Roderick Baylor, President of Baylor Construction."

Monique stepped forward and offered her hand. "You're JaiHonnah's husband?"

Calvin's expression changed immediately when his eyes settled on the porcelain beauty of Monique Baylor. "I am, yes." Calvin was obviously captivated by her, JaiHonnah realized as she listened to him chat Monique up. She had experienced this reaction in him with other women he met when they were still married. She hoped that, at least, this time he wouldn't totally embarrass her. Calvin was true to form though as he kissed Monique's hand and her almond-colored skin flushed. JaiHonnah excused herself to turn off her ruined steaks. She knew that, the moment her back was turned, Calvin would have Monique's vital statistics, name, address and telephone number in his iPhone as quick as the wink she noticed that he gave Monique. She seemed to be very receptive to Calvin's barely veiled interest, JaiHonnah thought. *This behavior from a woman who, only moments ago, was talking about rekindling her marriage with her own husband?* JaiHonnah sighed deeply and shook her head. She couldn't really fault Monique Baylor's attraction to Calvin. He was eye candy with a suave James Bond-like European demeanor. He had the face and physique that demanded attention and he used it to his advantage. It was all too much to think about. It was none of her business what Calvin, Monique or Roderick for that matter, did in their private lives. She just wanted to be left out of it to get on with her own life—whatever that was going to be.

Shortly after Calvin arrived, Monique prepared to leave. JaiHonnah walked with her to the door.

"Well, Mrs. Chapman, I'm sure that you and your husband have lots to talk about as do Roderick and I, so I'll be leaving. I hope that I can depend on your integrity and your discretion."

"Say no more, Mrs. Baylor, I do understand."

JaiHonnah closed the door and leaned against it. And she thought Big Jake was trouble. Monique Baylor was trouble personified.

JaiHonnah stood awaiting an explanation from Calvin for his spontaneous and unwelcome visit.

"Now that Mrs. Baylor is gone, why are you here, Calvin?"

"You, baby," he said. "I miss my wife. Let's order dinner."

"Not interested," she quipped. "How did you track me down, and why exactly?"

Calvin looked around the living room, casually touching the priceless figurines and viewing the artwork. "Oscar and Buffy DuPont. I was visiting them in their condo earlier. They're on the eighth floor and mentioned that you were living in this building too. Nice digs. Almost as nice as your villa in Italy. I'm sure that your loft in Paris is not quite this modern, but the only way I can see where you have been living is to visit you with your brother. You never seemed to be in the same country whenever we came for a visit."

"Now that you've taken the grand tour, Calvin, either tell me what this visit is about or get out."

Calvin turned to face her, squaring his shoulders. "Monique Baylor is the woman who's married to your boss."

"You mean you didn't have enough time to get all of the information you wanted from her?" she asked sarcastically. "My, my, Calvin, you must be slipping. Usually you would have had all of that information, plus the amount in her personal checking account rounded to the last dollar. Now what do you want?"

"I told you, Jai, I want you. I still love you and I want to try to put our marriage back on track. We were good together. I know you couldn't have forgotten already. I want you back in my life."

"Tell it to someone who gives a damn. Now stop lying and tell me what your real reason is for coming here."

"Baby, you know—."

JaiHonnah held up one hand. "Yes, Calvin, I do know. Now if you have nothing else to say..." She started moving toward the door.

"Your old man," he blurted. "He's got a big deal cooking, and my father and I want in on it. This deal could be worth billions."

"So, talk with Jake about it, not me. I'm not involved in my father's business."

"You own a part of BlackHawk Industries. You're on the board of directors. I'd say that you're very much a part of his business."

"Under advice of counsel, I put all of my holdings in BlackHawk in the RAMOS trust account, Calvin. I did that before we were married. You know that RAMOS is a blind trust. That information was a part of our prenuptial agreement. I also don't exercise any board responsibilities. I've given my proxy to my grandmother, to manage RAMOS in any way that she deems appropriate. Now, as I've said before, talk to Jake, not me."

"My father and I tried that, but we can't get anywhere with him. He's still pissed off about the divorce, but if you call him and tell him to let us in on this deal, he'd do it in a heartbeat."

"No way. I'm not getting between you and my father, so, if that's all—."

"Not even for old time's sake?" he asked, moving toward her grinning.

"Especially because of old time's sake. You and your father screwed up, Calvin. You thought that just because we were married, Jake would roll over and let you take advantage of him. Or because Jake didn't have the benefits of an education, like you did, and because he came up the hard way, you thought that you could take advantage of him. You married me thinking that you could twist him around your little finger through me. Well, you blew it, and Jake took your company away from you and your father. He didn't do anything behind your back. As I recall, he got up close and personal. What went on between you and my father had nothing to do with me, and I'm not getting into it now. Whatever Jake is up to is none of my business."

"He's looking for his successor. Rumor in the global financial market is that Jake wants to step down soon as CEO and chairman of the board of BlackHawk Holding. When he does, I want to be in a position to step into his shoes."

JaiHonnah narrowed her eyes and almost laughed in Calvin's face. "You must be delusional, Calvin. If my father is ready to step down, which I strongly doubt, the leadership of BlackHawk will probably go to Jacob Junior. My father has been grooming him and Adam for that position since Jacob crawled out of the cradle."

"Oh, Jacob's his father's son, alright. So is Adam, for that matter, but old Jake wants someone who's better than either of them to lead BlackHawk, and I believe that someone is me. With the right word from you, Jai, Jake wouldn't take such a hard line against me. He'd be more apt to pick me, if you told him that we were getting back together."

"Back together? You are delusional, Calvin," JaiHonnah said, waving off the thought.

"You look fantastic, Jai." Calvin breathed sensuously, pulling her toward him. "Remember our wedding night?"

"Why would I want to remember being raped?" she asked dispassionately, trying to free herself from his clutches.

"Hell, how was I supposed to know that you were a virgin? You'd been a princess of this or that for a long time. Thought someone would have seasoned that ripe cherry before I got to it."

"Once, is one thing, Calvin, but every time you touched me—."

"That's the way I like it. You remember, don't you? I'll bet you haven't had a man since me. That cherry is probably still as tight as I remember."

She pushed against his chest to free herself, but he held her tighter. When he bent to kiss her mouth, she turned her face away.

"God, woman, you've got the greatest tits, ass and legs I've ever seen," he said and laved her throat with his tongue. "You still taste like more."

"And you've had plenty more, Calvin. Now get the hell off me!" she said, struggling harder to free herself.

He reached for her breast, gripping the fabric of her blouse tightly as he pawed her. She wrestled free and the fabric ripped, exposing her breasts. Shock gripped her and without a thought, JaiHonnah let her fist fly across Calvin's face, drawing blood with her diamond rings.

Calvin gloated, tasting his own blood. "I see you remember," he said, grinning with some sort of madness that JaiHonnah couldn't identify in his eyes. "That's just how I like it. You want it rough, baby, I'm your man."

"Get out of here, now, or I'll call security!" she screamed at him.

"Uh-uh," he said, eyeing her exposed full bosom. "You're pretending to be my wife, now you're going to act like it."

Calvin grabbed JaiHonnah by her hair and wrestled her to the floor. "No! Please no! Calvin, please don't . . .!"

"You, bitch! You know this is how you always wanted it! Go ahead and fight me. I love it, but I'm going to have you any way I want you!"

"Not again!" she screamed, fighting him as fiercely as she could.

* * *

Roderick weighed all the pros and cons a thousand times in the space of the few hours that he sat on his boat looking at the Watergate Complex. The final analysis came up the same way, no matter how he looked at it. He didn't want to wait for Monday to see JaiHonnah again. He tried to think of a plausible explanation or excuse for coming to see her, but only the truth would do. He wanted to get to know her better, not just because she was his employee, but because he wanted to be her friend, and he wanted her to trust him. He questioned Vivian about her, but getting blood from a stone was easier than getting information out of

Vivian Alexander Jackson about a client. What he did glean from what little Vivian did say was that JaiHonnah would welcome his friendship.

He remembered her pained expression after she talked with Geneva Simpson at the gala. He heard enough of the conversation to know that JaiHonnah's husband was often unfaithful to her. The man must be out of his mind, Roderick thought. If he were married to a woman like JaiHonnah, nothing this side of heaven would make him want another woman. Nevertheless, he knew how it felt to be disrespected in a marriage. Monique was a master at that game. If this new acting career of hers failed, she could give drama lessons on how to lie convincingly. JaiHonnah, he believed, was a different type of woman and Vivian had confirmed that JaiHonnah was a warm, giving individual. He wanted her to know that if she needed a shoulder to cry on, his was available. And he wanted to know who that man at the gala was who had upset her.

Courage, brother, he thought to himself as he raised his hand to knock on her door, but, before he knocked the door flew opened and two people stood before him bearing their teeth at one another. Clearly there had been a fight, and it didn't take much thought to see what had happened. JaiHonnah looked distraught and trembled with fear or anger, tears flowing over her face. Her clothes were torn half to shreds, her hair tossed in every direction, and bruises were evident on her shoulders, arms and chest.

The man's torn shirt was stained and he was wiping blood from his mouth. Deep red angry scratches were on his face, neck and chest, and his slacks were open and unzipped.

"Get out!" JaiHonnah screamed, shaking with emotion, tears streaming down her face. "Don't you ever touch me again!"

"Don't play coy with me, Jai! You wanted me as much as I wanted you. You're going to do what I want when I want or..."

JaiHonnah suddenly saw fear in Calvin's eyes. When she turned to follow his gaze, a mountain moved past her and crashed down on Calvin so fast that her eyes only caught a glimpse before it was too late.

Roderick had let go of three successive blows to Calvin's face before she blinked. She caught her breath and grabbed Roderick. He unconsciously pushed her away.

"Roderick," she screamed, "please stop before you kill him! Roderick!" she sobbed more frantically, more tears streaming down her face. "Please, Roderick, no!"

Roderick finally heard JaiHonnah's cries as he straddled Calvin, beating him about the head and face. He looked toward her trembling torso in mid-swing and dropped Calvin like garbage. He went to JaiHonnah and engulfed her trembling body in his arms. Calvin, dazed, disheveled and badly bruised took that opportunity to flee the Wrath of Gibraltar.

JaiHonnah couldn't control her sobs. She felt the mighty mountain close in around her. Melting into him, her knees bucked. He lifted her and sat on the sofa with her in his lap, rocking her gently for some time, the adrenalin still coursing through his body.

"JaiHonnah," Roderick finally said, calming himself more for her sake than for his as he held her tightly against his chest.

Roderick's voice was low and soothing as he held her. Her lips were at his throat. Involuntarily her arms were around him holding on as she shuddered and her breasts heaved against his chest for what seemed like an eternity. Roderick lifted her chin.

"Look at me," he requested, gently.

JaiHonnah's shudders calmed as her tear-filled eyes opened and met Roderick's concerned gaze. He wiped her tears with his thumb, still holding her against his chest. Oddly, but still in shock, JaiHonnah heard Phyllis Hyman's "Under Your Spell" playing in the background as their gazes locked.

Damn! Roderick thought to himself holding her and looking deeply into her watery eyes. He knew it wasn't premeditated, but it was bound to happen. His mouth covered hers in the sweetest caress he had ever experienced. Every thought of apprehension vanished. Every bit of self-respect and self-control diminished. All he could feel was a sensation with the strength of an atomic blast as it whirled around them. His heart beat wildly in his chest. His body tensed, fighting his growing erection, which had shot up with rocket force. Heat spread throughout his body. He fought to exercise some sense of control. He had to understand who that man was and what he had done to her, but for the moment all he could manage to do was to kiss away her pain.

Nothing had ever made her body tingle like this. She didn't understand it. Couldn't catalog it. Couldn't draw it, but she could taste it. She could feel it and, frightening as it was, she could bask in it forever. She had built solid, invisible walls around herself, but in one precious touch of Roderick's mouth on hers the walls were no longer invisible, they were gone. Her pain diminished.

Someone above had to help him peel his mouth from her sweet nectar. He didn't have the strength to do it alone, but divine intervention was slow in coming. He had kissed her to comfort her, he told himself, and he believed it. It was madness. Finally, sanity arrived.

"I want to call the police," he said, quietly stroking her face. "Whoever that was should be arrested."

JaiHonnah's spell was broken. "Police?" she said, sobbing out a breath. "No, uh, no, that won't be necessary." She pulled away from Roderick, clutching the torn fabric over her breasts and attempting to smooth her disheveled hair. She took in a deep breath. "I'll be fine."

Anger and disbelief knotted his stomach. "Fine? JaiHonnah, it doesn't take a genius to see what he did to you! That's the same man that I saw you arguing with at the gala. Who was that bastard?"

"That was my, uh, that was my, uh . . ." She visibly trembled.

"JaiHonnah! Who is he?" Roderick demanded, holding her again.

"My husband," she said, sobbing.

"Jesus Christ Almighty, I'll kill him!" he bit out.

"No, Roderick. Please, just hold me. I'm fine." She buried her face in Roderick's chest, mangling his shirt in her fists.

"Yeah, right! That's why you're shaking from head to toe. I don't give a damn if he is your husband. That doesn't give him the right to abuse you. Please, let me call the police. At least, put it on record what he did to you. I'll be with you every step of the way. He'll never hurt you again. I promise you that. If I ever get my hands…"

JaiHonnah put trembling fingers to Roderick's lips, silencing the threat. She gathered her courage and looked into his scowl. "I'll be fine," she whispered with more calm than she had ever had against one of Calvin's attacks. She wasn't a little girl anymore. She could handle this, she told herself.

Roderick's blood was hissing through his veins, making them protrude through his skin. How could anyone touch this woman in any way other than lovingly? Her soft fingers against his lips cooled his temper slowly. She was being so brave and so foolish, he thought. He had to give whatever support that she needed, but in his heart he'd gladly kill that husband of hers with his bare hands. He took her soft fingers from his lips and kissed them.

"Alright, no police, but you should go to the hospital to be checked by a doctor. I have a friend, a very good friend who's a doctor at Georgetown Medical. I'll call him."

JaiHonnah shook her head. "No, no. I'll just wash my face and comb my hair. I need to change my clothes." Tears rimmed her eyes and began to overflow.

"JaiHonnah," Roderick's anguished face and voice thick with emotion implored her.

JaiHonnah spread her fingers on his chest holding him off. She rose from his lap and went into the master bathroom. The thought of Calvin touching her made her empty stomach erupt. She held her head over the commode until the sensations dissipated. Deep, cleansing breaths brought her back into control. She shed her clothes, throwing them into the trash, and stepped into the shower. She scrubbed her body, fighting back the tears with every stroke, melting against the shower wall and then sliding to the floor. The shuddered, painful sobs bursting her heart, her mind, her soul.

He's dead meat! Roderick vowed as he paced the living room floor for half an hour. His fists were balled at his sides. Why had he waited? Had he come earlier instead of sitting on his boat trying to justify why he wanted to see her, none of this would have happened to her. He would have been here for her. What kind of animal was her husband? Roderick grabbed the back of his neck, rubbing forcefully. His muscles tightened. His hands ached. He looked at his knuckles. They were bruised from connecting with Calvin's face, but nothing seemed broken or even sprained, he thought as he flexed his fingers.

Then he finally thought of the kiss that he shared with JaiHonnah, and he slowed his pace, breathing deeply. What a hell of a thing to do to a woman who had just been raped, he chastised himself. She was in pain, probably in shock, and all he could do was want to kiss her. He closed his eyes against his inner turmoil. What she needed was to go to the police and then to the hospital. Instead he had to add insult to injury and kissed her. True, it wasn't a kiss that would frighten her into thinking that he would hurt her. It was only meant to comfort her, calm her, protect her. Nothing, not anything justified his behavior. He wanted to go to her now, to apologize for taking unfair advantage of her, but he could hear the shower still running. He couldn't go to her now, invade her privacy and frighten her even more than he already had. No, he had to wait.

He thought of calling Kelley or Vivian, but decided against it. JaiHonnah was obviously a private person. The decision of what to do was hers, not his, to make. No, he would wait for her to decide and then he'd kill her husband.

He forgot about the pain in his hands, and his muscles began to relax.

No more tears, she told herself as she sucked up her remaining strength, but she ached. She would put this behind her, just as she had done before. Calvin would never control her again! This time she had fought him. Hard. There was little solace in that fact, but she had overcome her fear of her ex-husband.

When JaiHonnah finally emerged from the bedroom, she dug deep for a slight smile, still fighting back the urge to cry.

"Well, Mr. Tyson, besides your loss to Desiree, how did the rest of your day go?"

Roderick wanted to take her in his arms again and tell her that everything would be alright, but he could see that she was valiantly trying to hold herself together.

"Not bad for an old street fighter," he said. "But I don't open my door after nightfall anymore."

"Good idea." She exhaled a nervous, hesitant breath, not able to meet his gaze.

"JaiHonnah, about the—."

She put up one hand to silence what she thought was coming and then wrapped her arms around her waist, rubbing forcefully. "Let's not talk about it anymore. I appreciate your kindness, but my reputation has been damaged enough for one day. I don't want you to think that what happened here is the kind of thing that I do ordinarily. It was just an unguarded moment. I hope you'll forget everything that's happened and not let it hamper our working relationship."

Roderick put his hands on her arms and gently turned her around to face him. "Your reputation has not been tarnished or even come into question, JaiHonnah, but if I ever find that your husband has brutalized you again..." He let the lethal threat hang.

Her eyes never lifted to his as she studied the third button on his polo sport shirt. "He won't, but thank you for your concern. I appreciate that. We should put this behind us."

An index finger lifted her chin. "Would you permit me one more transgression?" he asked, trying to meet her eyes.

"What?" she asked, still unable to look him in the eyes.

"At least report this to Vivian," he said and lifted his hand to silence her when she would have interrupted. "She has a cooler head on her shoulders than I have on mine at the moment."

JaiHonnah sighed in thought then nodded in agreement. "I'll talk with her tomorrow. I'm too shaky, tired and hungry to be coherent tonight, and Vivian will grill me on every detail, I'm sure."

"Hungry? Good. I've worked up quite an appetite myself. Have dinner with me. We could go out somewhere."

She looked at her casual attire and his. "I don't think that I feel up to that or that they'll let us into any five-star restaurant wearing these clothes."

"Now what fool would tell Mike Tyson that he couldn't come into a restaurant without a tie?"

JaiHonnah shook her head and smiled slightly. The emotional pain of the afternoon still gripped her. What a wonderful friend Roderick would make, she thought. Vivian was right not to confide too much about him. JaiHonnah wanted to learn on her own. She couldn't understand though why a man such as this would want to rekindle a relationship with a woman like Monique. Based on the little she had observed, they were as different as night and day. Yet, the kiss... What about the kiss?

As if reading her mind he said, "Don't worry, Jai. I have something more relaxed in mind for dinner."

Chapter 4

Asmall, hard, black ball ricocheted against several walls, zinging back at high velocity before making the journey to another. Two, dripping wet, racquetball players— one male, one female—raced up and down the narrow court.

"That's enough," Vivian Alexander Jackson said, stopping the play mid-volley. "Okay, who peed in your cornflakes this morning?" she asked, grabbing a towel and wiping the sweat from her face.

Roderick bent over resting his hands on his knees, his chest pumping as he tried to catch his breath. Sweat dropped freely onto the hardwood floor.

Vivian tossed a towel to him and stood with her hands on her hips waiting for an explanation.

"You trying to kill me, counselor?" he asked between labored breaths. "You're beating the hell out of me, and you want to know who peed in *my* cornflakes? That's rich."

"The thought of killing you hadn't crossed my mind lately, but I'll consider it. JRock, you're playing like a man with a vendetta." She lifted the goggles from her eyes up to her sweatband. "Now let's have it."

Roderick stood slowly, still trying to catch his breath. He pulled off his goggles, wiped his face with the towel and ambled to the wall. Leaning his back against it, he slowly slid down to a sitting position, his hands bracing his knees.

"Have you heard from JaiHonnah today?"

Vivian eyed him suspiciously. "JRock, hadn't you noticed? It's 6:45 A.M. Most right-thinking people wouldn't call me at this time of the morning. So what's up with Jai that I need to know about this early?"

"I'll let her tell you, but I want your promise that you'll keep me in the loop on this."

"No deal. If Jai has something on her mind, you'll have to get any information from her, not from me."

"This is important to me."

"Obviously, if you're asking me to violate attorney/client privilege or my commitment to my friendship with Jai. That aside, you'll have to have her permission before I'll discuss anything with you about her.

"Is that what you wanted to talk with me about or does it have something to do with the former Mrs. Baylor?"

"You heard she was in town then?"

"Yes, the bugles blew, the thunder rolled and the lightning crashed. Suddenly she's here. I didn't have to wait for the drum roll." Hanging the towel around her neck, she studied Roderick. "So how much does she want this time?" she asked without expression.

Roderick lifted his eyes to hers. "Are you psychic or something?"

"How much, JRock?"

"Half a million."

Vivian didn't hold her tongue and the expletive wasn't deleted, Roderick noticed when he glanced up into her flashing eyes.

"Give her the money, Viv," he said evenly. "I want her out of my sight and out of my life."

"Done," Vivian said, too coolly for Roderick's comfort.

"What? No questions, counselor?"

"You're free, Black and over twenty-one. I'm not your priest or your conscience. I'm your lawyer. You don't have to confess your sins to me. You tell me you want something done, unless it's illegal, immoral or unethical, consider it done."

"Alright, counselor, you can take off the kid gloves and tell me what you're really thinking."

"I won't say what I'm thinking unless or until you tell me why, after we worked so hard to reach a much too generous, but nonetheless amicable, out-of-court divorce agreement, avoiding all the court battles and press coverage, you suddenly turn around and give Monique *carte blanche* access to your bank account. Are you still in love with her?"

"Hell no, Vivian! You know that. I wonder whether I ever really loved her or whether I just married her because I got her pregnant. Damn, we weren't even together a year."

"Then why are you giving her this money? What are you getting in return?"

"Hopefully, getting some peace."

"Is that all of it? You're not hiding some guilty little secret that's going to pop out nine months from now, are you?" she asked with a raised eyebrow.

Steel locked his jaw. "If it does, every lab in this area will be working overtime at my expense churning out DNA test results. I want to wring her neck, but I swear, I never laid a finger on her."

"Alright, I believe you. You've never lied to me, and I don't think that you would over something this important, but I want some guarantees from her that are legally binding and that include forfeiture of the money if she reneges."

"I just want some peace in my life, but she still has a right to see Shelly and Shelby."

Vivian thought carefully. "I don't want your girls to become pawns in some high-stakes chess game between you and Monique."

"They already are. Monique . . ." Roderick thought and realized he was trapped.

"Has threatened you with a battle royal over custody of the girls, hasn't she?" Vivian knowingly added.

Roderick looked away and exhaled in frustration. "Not directly, but she's vindictive enough that if I don't give her what she wants she'd take it out on me in court. I won't have my girls dragged through the muck and mire to serve Monique's whims. The divorce is not public so I don't want it to come up in a custody battle. As far as the public knows, Monique and I are still man and wife. She'll keep quiet if I pay her and help her with this movie she wants to make."

"Let's get real for a moment, JRock. After all, we are talking about Monique. If she thinks she can lead you around by the nose because you fear losing the girls, she won't stop at making a spectacle of your family or five hundred thousand dollars. That would only be the starting point. What and how much are you willing to give up to appease her?"

Cold eyes landed on Vivian. "I won't risk losing my daughters over money or have them hounded by the press and news media. You saw what happened to Michael Jordan when his wife divorced him. What happens when any high profile people divorce? Their lives get shredded in the press. I won't tolerate that happening to my family, Vivian. As long as money is all that Monique wants from me to keep quiet, she's welcome to it."

Vivian shook her head. "Alright, JRock, I'll handle it with Monique—and her attorney."

"Good, I don't want to be bothered by her again."

"Done. Now, can we finish this game?"

Roderick peeled himself away from the wall and looped his arm around Vivian's shoulders as they walked toward the door. "Naw, you've whipped me enough for one day. Let's have something to eat before we leave. I have something else to talk with you about, and you're not going to like it I'm sure."

Vivian only cocked an eyebrow at him as they left the racquetball court.

Roderick and Vivian sat at a small table in the Racquet Club bar having frappe.

"I saw Chuck Montgomery yesterday," Roderick said casually, but eyeing Vivian carefully. He noticed her body tense and her eyes flash and narrow. He kept his voice even and calm. "We played a few games over at Georgetown. He tells me that—."

Vivian held up one hand. "I don't want to know this," she hissed.

"Vivian, please, just hear me out. Both you and Chuck are my friends—long-time friends. You were friends even before you met Derrick. You and Chuck were once closer than you and I are now. He told me how you two met when he brought you home from the airport during a blizzard. You were still in law school at Georgetown then, he said. And later, after you two got to be close, how, when he thought that you were lost, hurt or in trouble on your way home for the holidays, he drove all night talking to the state highway patrol and the truckers over his CB radio and looked for you between here and South Carolina. He never gave up until he found you. When your house mate was attacked, Chuck personally took care of her for months. When your mother needed that biopsy on the lump in her breast, Chuck found the best team of doctors in the country and flew them to South Carolina to perform the procedure. And then, when your little brother was thinking about where to go to college, Chuck dropped everything to go with you two..."

"JRock, you're treading on thin ice," Vivian flashed.

"I know, honey, but your brothers and cousins asked me to look out for you, and I promised them that I would."

"Kenneth and Benny have their own lives to lead. I love them both, but they don't understand what I'm feeling, neither do my cousins, James and Donald. I know that everyone in my family and all of my friends think that Chuck Montgomery is the best thing since sliced white bread—no ethnic reference intended—and I can't and won't interfere in their or your relationship with him, but, as far as I'm concerned, Dr. Charles Patrick Montgomery is a closed case. Now, I understand that all of you men go skiing every season together on those male-bonding weekends of yours, and I'm cool with that, but I don't need to hear about Chuck Montgomery anymore. I get enough from my former house mates. Melissa, Gloria, Bill, Alan and David think that Chuck can do no wrong, but they're wrong!"

"Viv, Chuck was Derrick's best friend. They were closer than brothers. You know that. That's why Derrick made Chuck executor of his estate and godfather to Derrick Junior and the children that you adopted together. Derrick loved you more than life, and he knew that Chuck would always take care of you and be there for you and the children."

"And did he know that Chuck would betray my friendship?" she demanded. "Yes, you're right. At one time Chuck and I were inseparable, but he thought very little of that friendship. He had an obligation under the terms of that friendship to tell me that my husband—his best friend—was dying, and he didn't. He kept that from me, and Derrick and I had less than a year in our marriage. I will not forgive Chuck for that."

"That was Derrick's decision to keep that information from you, not Chuck's. Derrick knew he had hypertrophic cardiomyopathy. Plenty of athletes have had the disease and lived long and productive lives. It nearly killed Derrick to give up professional basketball when he did, but he never wanted to be treated like an invalid. He also didn't want you to worry. Only his parents and Chuck knew about his condition. What choice do you think Chuck had under the circumstances? Either he betrayed Derrick's friendship or yours."

"He made his decision and now he has to live with it just like I do."

"Losing Derrick was hard on everyone, especially Chuck. He worked on Derrick in the hospital for more than an hour trying to revive him after everyone in the emergency room knew that Derrick was gone. Chuck kept trying and finally the hospital emergency room staff had to restrain him, but he kept fighting to get Derrick back, not just for himself, but for you." He took a deep breath. "Vivian, you're no racist, and I've never known you to have a malicious bone in your body. You're one of the fairest, most even-tempered, and caring and loving women I know, but, for the life of me, I don't understand how you can be so unyielding where Chuck is concerned. I know that you don't resent the relationship that he and Derrick had." Vivian looked away, and Roderick put his fingers to her chin and turned her face back toward him. "You've held steadfast to this animosity toward Chuck for over four years, why?"

Vivian didn't answer him, but in her pained silence something dawned on him.

"You love him. You're in love with Chuck," he said as the realization gripped him. Vivian did not deny his theory.

She abruptly rose from her seat. "I've got work to do, JRock. I'll handle this thing with Monique and call you later. I'll arrange to bring the girls over to your place this afternoon. We also have to talk about BlackHawk. My investigators tell me that the company is on the prowl for fresh meat, and you're looking like dinner."

"Viv . . ."

She walked away, and Roderick slumped in his seat. His good friend was not just mourning the loss of her husband, she was castigating herself for being in love with Chuck Montgomery, her deceased husband's best friend.

Chapter 5

Roderick positioned himself in one of the first-floor conference rooms with a clear, unobstructed view through a glass wall to the office entrance and to the Anacostia River at the back of the property. Other employees had already arrived for work and were going about their routines. He frequently glanced at the clock. He had gone to and from the coffeepot in the reception area three times, walked up and down the steps to his second-floor office twice and thumbed through the magazines and newspapers in the reception area at least five times. The door to the office opened and Roderick caught his breath. When a client entered, he exhaled and glanced at his watch. As he looked up toward the office door again he glimpsed Kelley's quizzical grin. She left the reception area counter and came into the conference area where Roderick had finally lit.

"Okay, little brother, what's going on?"

"Uh, nothing, why do you ask?"

"Because you seem as nervous as a cat on a hot tin roof. I know that you and Vivian had a game earlier. You've been here all morning. Usually you're out checking our construction sites by seven. You certainly aren't dressed for job sites today. Nice duds," she said, smiling. "Adolfo?"

"Uh, I guess so, uh, I really don't know. It was just hanging in my closet..." He glanced toward the door and then his watch again. "Just thought I'd wear something different today."

"What time is JaiHonnah Reise Chapman coming in?" she asked.

Roderick caught his sister's knowing grin and looked away. "Uh, around nine, I believe. I really don't know. She's just another employee, Kelley," he affirmed.

"Uh-huh," she said knowingly.

"Well, she is," he said, a bit more forcefully, but his eyes kept darting to the entrance of the building and then to the clock.

"In that case I'll be here when she arrives and you can go on with your day."

"Uh, no, I have some things to do in the office today."

"Like the Sokol proposal?"

"Uh, yes, I reviewed it yesterday. The products seem to be of high quality at the right price. I want to have Lyle do a cost comparison with other electrical equipment suppliers before I sign off on the purchase." He glanced at the door and then the clock. "I also signed the Garner Building bid. I believe we're better than the other two competitors. Uh, Kosar Plumbing Supply went up on its inventory price sheet, so next month, I believe that we should . . ." the door opened, and his attention strayed until another client came in, then he glanced at the clock, then his watch. "...Uhm, where was I? Uh, oh yes, Kosar, uh, the door, uh, I mean..."

"She'll be here, little brother."

Roderick blushed. "Is it that obvious?"

"Not even a blind man would miss it." She gave him a sideways glance. "I like her, too, JRock. Apparently so do my nieces. I stopped by Vivian's yesterday, and JaiHonnah was all Shelly and Shelby talked about. Something about a real Indian princess."

"Yeah, and a prince called JRock Walks With Tight Fists," he mused.

"From the look of your fist, someone got a knuckle sandwich," she said, holding up his slightly swollen hand and looking at the cuts and bruises. "Care to tell me about it?"

"Uh, no. Uh, what time do you have?"

"The same time you do. Relax, JRock. JaiHonnah will . . ."

Kelley saw her brother's face light up before she turned to see who was coming through the office doors. He moved so swiftly toward the reception area that he had to put on brakes at a low-swinging gate. Kelley followed him, smiling broadly and shaking her head.

"Good morning," Roderick said around a large lump in his throat.

"Good morning," JaiHonnah said. "Uh, I decided to come in a little early to set up my office before I met with you at nine. I hope that's alright."

The sun rose for him when JaiHonnah smiled. Roderick couldn't tear his gaze away from her fresh, clean countenance and sparkling eyes. His eyes searched for that small mole beside her perfectly shaped mouth. It had fascinated him during dinner on his boat the evening before.

"Uh, sure, that's fine. Uh, let me help you with your things," he said, taking some of her belongings. "Your office is upstairs next to mine."

"Good morning, JaiHonnah," Kelley said in a sing-song fashion.

JaiHonnah grinned. "Good morning, Kelley."

"After you get settled in, come and find me. I'll introduce you to the rest of the staff." Many of whom were converging on Kelley with a barrage of questions about the beautiful, new employee.

Roderick led JaiHonnah up the open staircase to the second floor. She was pleased at the decor and arrangement of furniture in her office and noticed that her name was already stenciled on the glass. Green, healthy plants gave the room a warm, homey feeling. The rear wall was made up of French glass doors that opened onto a deck overlooking the beautifully landscaped backyard, swimming pool, and the Anacostia River beyond. There she noticed *The Mighty Magic Heat* where she spent an enchanting, leisurely evening having dinner with her boss after the horrifying afternoon ordeal.

JaiHonnah turned and bumped into Roderick's chest. She smiled up at him and cocked her head to one side. "You know, we're not going to make any progress today if you're constantly worried about how I'm doing," she said.

Roderick dug his fists into his pockets, lowered his head and raised his eyes to hers. "It shows, huh?"

"Yep. I told you last night that I would be fine, and I am."

"You also said that you would call..."

"Vivian at her office. I remember. Now you scoot," she said, taking his arm and leading him toward the door.

Roderick stopped. "Uh, are you sure that you don't need any..."

JaiHonnah narrowed her eyes and raised an eyebrow.

"Okay, okay, I'm going, but will you call me if you need anything?"

"I will, yes," she said. "I'll be in your office at nine."

JaiHonnah smiled to herself and shook her head after Roderick left. He was being so protective and solicitous. After they returned from dinner the previous night, they sat talking late into the evening about Washington politics and the impact that it had on their work. Roderick was a great deal more complex and intriguing than he seemed on the surface. He offered to stay the night in one of the spare bedrooms in the condo, and when she declined his offer, he called her twice after he left. Each time he asked the same questions about Watergate security and whether her doors were locked and bolted. She appreciated his interest in her welfare, but she really needed to feel confident about her ability to stand on her own two feet and weather the trials and tribulations of life the way that any other professional woman did. She had been someone else's responsibility for too long. Now she could take care of herself.

* * *

Vivian put down her pen and looked across her desk at JaiHonnah. Her thoughts were not evident on her face, so JaiHonnah ventured into uncharted waters aware that Vivian was watching her.

"Well, that's about it, Viv. I just thought, well, I mean, Roderick insisted that I discuss this with you. I'm fine though and there's no need for this to go any further. Besides, Buffy DuPont called this morning to tell me that she and Oscar had to call the house doctor for Calvin. He claimed that he had been mugged, but didn't know his attacker and didn't want to call the police. I'm sure that by now, Calvin has left the country and gone back to Europe. Buffy said that he didn't want to worry me and wouldn't stay in the states. He probably won't bother me anymore." When Vivian didn't say anything she started to rise from her seat. "Thanks for making the time..."

"Sit down, Ms. Chapman!" Vivian's voice came like a low rolling thunder across her desk.

JaiHonnah reseated herself and looked away from Vivian's piercing stare.

"Now listen to me, JaiHonnah. You are my client, and what you have disclosed to me clearly falls within the confines of protected information between us, but if I thought that it would do any good, I would drag you kicking and screaming to the police precinct to file charges against that bastard! I may still have someone do some legal research on the question of whether, as an officer of the court, it is my duty to report what may be a felony to the proper authorities!" With both hands planted on her desk Vivian rose and leaned across it toward JaiHonnah. "How *dare* you take this so lightly like you're reading it off the pages of the *Washington Post!* This is your *life* and your safety we're talking about, and I'll be *damned* if I'll let you bury yourself away again and act like nothing happened! Women have the right to say no and to have that decision respected. You've come too far and worked too hard to get to this place in your life, to let that bastard do this to you again and get away with it."

JaiHonnah rose to pace Vivian's office. "He didn't just 'get away with it,' Viv. I told you, Roderick nearly killed him. If I hadn't stopped him, he would have done just that. That's why I believe that Calvin won't try this again."

"Is JRock going to play bodyguard 24/7?"

JaiHonnah looked away. "No," she said quietly, "of course he's not."

"Then don't tell me that this couldn't happen again."

"Viv, I know that you're angry, and so am I, but please don't take any independent action. I want to be able to handle this on my own. I went through the abused spouse therapy sessions—group sessions and private counseling—for years while I was in Europe. I know that I didn't do anything wrong or anything to encourage Calvin to attack me. I understand that what he did was an act of violence, not of love. I'm angry and hurt, but I'm not afraid anymore. I'm not going to let him make me regress into a shell over his brutality. He has the problem, not me, and one day he'll pay dearly for what he's done."

Vivian relaxed and sat down. "Alright, Jai, I'll do as you ask, but..."

"I know. Roderick felt the same way. He doesn't agree with my position and he's being too protective, just like my father. Roderick's been stopping by my office to check on me like I'm going to fall apart any minute. I wish that he didn't think of me as some fragile piece of china that has to be handled with care. I want him to think of me as a competent and confident professional."

"That's a switch. Before you wouldn't want him to think of you at all," she said, offering JaiHonnah a slight smile.

JaiHonnah grinned and looked away from Vivian's inquiring expression. She wondered whether Vivian could see the blush that she felt rising in her face. That's how Roderick affected her. He made her want to smile and even laugh out loud. She recalled that she had done a lot of that during dinner on his yacht. She couldn't help it, though. He was nice to be with.

* * *

The week passed relatively well for Roderick. Summer was loosing its sticky grip and fall was being ushered in with balmy days and cool nights. The trees were doing their part with brilliant colors to catch the sunlight.

He was learning a new management technique—delegating. It was working very well. Now he could spend more time in the office rather than running all over the city checking each detail at every job site. He attended meetings as necessary. He convinced himself that it was his daughters whom he raced back to see every day, but he admitted to himself that if JaiHonnah was still in the office when he returned, he would have no complaints.

He enjoyed working closely with her, and she picked up quickly on the concepts that he wanted portrayed in the properties that he was developing and rehabilitating. She had an easy way about her; never seemed flustered during that first week although they had many crises with which to deal. She took them all in stride and worked very well with the rest of the staff. She even took on some of the responsibilities of clearing designs or design changes through the myriad of government offices that had to put their stamp of approval on every minute alteration. She seemed to be able to get everything completed effortlessly and in record time. By the end of the week, Roderick was very impressed with JaiHonnah on a number of levels, the least of which was her work.

One afternoon during her first week on the job, JaiHonnah took her lunch outside and sat on one of the picnic tables that surrounded the swimming pool. She enjoyed her first few days of work although they had been very hectic. She was shortly joined by three other employees: Bruce, head of accounting; Marilyn, scheduling manager; and Philip, a crew boss. Bruce, while not a classically handsome man, had a good sense of humor which made up for what he lacked in the looks department. He asked her out a couple of times, but she begged off saying that she was married. It wasn't that he was unattractive or boring. Rather, it was her decision not to become involved with anyone, especially not a coworker. Marilyn, a cocoa-brown, bottle-blond pixie, JaiHonnah learned, was a bit of a gossip. She knew everything that there was to know about everyone's business. Moreover, she flirted openly with both Bruce and Philip. Philip was going through a nasty divorce. Tall, and a bit soft around the middle, he still had a twinkle in his moss-green eyes. Although Bruce tried to get Philip back into the dating scene again, Philip was very reluctant.

"So what's happening this weekend?" Bruce asked, looking at JaiHonnah.

"I'm going to visit some of the museums and tour Washington," she said as she ate her turkey salad.

"Oh? Want a guide?" he asked. "I can be great company."

JaiHonnah smiled. "I'm sure that you can, but I've been here before. I already know my way around the city."

"Oh? So you've got someone else, is that it?" Bruce asked.

"Yes," JaiHonnah said, slowly, holding up her left hand and wiggling her ringed fingers. "I'm married, remember?"

"Humph, wish my wife would have said that a few times," Philip muttered, shaking his head before he bit into his hero sandwich.

"You need to come off that stuff, Phil. You were tippin' out on your ole lady long before you found out that she was tippin' out on you," Marilyn said.

Philip cocked an eyebrow in her direction. "It's a poor mouse that don't have but one hole."

"You expect that your wife is supposed to be faithful to you when you're not faithful to her?" JaiHonnah asked.

"Sure I do. Women don't have the same kinda needs that men do. I mean, it takes women forever to give up the body. A man gets the scent of a woman he wants and *wham,* it's a done deal!"

"Ha!" Marilyn scoffed. "And who do you think these dynamos are tippin' with?" she asked rhetorically. "With somebody else's ole lady, that's who. But then, all you men think alike. You can't help it though. Your brains are in your other head."

"Not me," Bruce crooned, taking JaiHonnah's hand. "I'm the faithful type." He raised her hand to his lips.

"So am I," JaiHonnah said smoothly, removing her hand from his before his lips could touch her. "And I intend to keep it that way." When she winked at Bruce everyone laughed.

"Humph, not the way JRock's been keeping tabs on you," Marilyn said with a sly smile. "He never spent this much time in the office before you came along. Seeing him in the office more, gets my vote. I love to see that man walk! All those muscles moving...and everything. And when he goes swimming in the backyard pool, I damn near orgasm on cue!"

"Yeah, you and every other woman in the office," Philip muttered testily. "I'm surprised that the building doesn't tilt to one side. I don't see what all you women see in him."

"Like I said," Marilyn offered, leaning in close to Philip, "your anatomy is different. You're thinking with the wrong head, right, Jai?" she said, winking.

JaiHonnah blinked, surprised at Marilyn's comment.

* * *

When Roderick pulled his pickup into the garage at his office, he noticed that all of the employees' cars were gone. He expected that since it was the end of the work week with the promise of probably the last beautiful Indian summer weekend ahead. He allowed his staff and crews to knock off early on Fridays during the hot summer months. Pulling three bags of groceries out of his truck, he headed to the boat to store them. As he returned to his office through the back door, he heard Kelley talking on the telephone.

"Yes, I did enjoy spending time with you, Henry, but we've been together several nights since we met... No, there's nothing wrong with that, but I do think that we should slow down a bit... No, there's no other man in my life... I can understand your position, but I hope that you can understand mine... Yes, we'll talk over the weekend. Thanks for calling."

Roderick stood leaning against the door smiling at his sister. She noticed him and rolled her eyes, shook her head and sighed deeply. He chuckled aloud when she hung up the telephone.

"That's what comes of being a beautiful woman in demand," he teased.

"Right!" she snorted. "Borrrring!" she huffed.

"So who's the guy?" he asked.

"His name is Henry Tillery, regional sales manager for Young, Gupta and Herring Plumbing Supply and Equipment."

"Never heard of them."

"Neither had I. The company is based in the Midwest somewhere."

"So why is he so borrrring?"

"He doesn't talk about anything but business. We went to the Kennedy Center, and all he talked about was work. We went to the movies and he talked about business all through the exciting and romantic parts. We went to the H2O restaurant to do some dancing and what did we do?"

"Let me guess. You talked about business?" Roderick answered, amused.

"You must have been there," she said, deadpan. "I can understand a man being interested in his career, but he was pumping me for information about construction deals. Says he wants to get the jump on his competitors. I had hopes that what he wanted to jump on was me," she said flatly. "I haven't had a gleam in my eyes in the morning in a very long time. I'd like to curl up with something other than a good romance novel at night."

"Kelley, you can be a little intimidating, you know," Roderick teased.

"Look, little brother, if a man finds me intimidating then he can just keep on keeping on. I want someone in my life who *I* find intimidating."

"Whoa, be careful what you ask for. Remember Lee, and Lyle and Norton? Real hard cases."

"Yes, but great lovers. At least I know what I want and I'm not afraid to ask for it, Mr. I Haven't Had A Date In Four Years."

He had no comeback for that, so he let it pass. "Have a good weekend, Kelley. See you sometime on Monday."

"Oh, JRock, are you leaving today?"

"Yes, why?"

"Well, Jai and I went to The Grill Fish for lunch today."

"And?"

"Office grapevine has it that she doesn't have any *real* plans for the weekend."

"So?"

"Just thought I'd mention it. See ya, little brother," she sang.

Roderick looked away with an embarrassed smile before climbing the steps to his office. He wasn't a bit surprised to see JaiHonnah still working with two little helpers spread out on the floor at her feet mimicking her every move. The girls spent a considerable amount of time in JaiHonnah's company, and they seemed to be enjoying one another immensely. JaiHonnah would simply put them to work on some *special* project. His girls enjoyed how JaiHonnah praised them for every little hieroglyphic they designed. Today was no different.

He stood watching them for a few moments. Something about the scene before him tugged at his heart. The three of them seemed so right together, almost intimate and nurturing. *God, she's beautiful,* he mused. She was not just beautiful outside, but inside too. She interacted with his daughters as if she had always known them, and they responded to her in the same way. She was the first one of the office staff they wanted to see in the morning and the last one at night. Come to think of it, that's how he felt too. JaiHonnah's radiant smile lit his mornings and fired his emotions. Her gentle caring warmed him, and he felt that his four-year, self-imposed immunity to women and relationships was waning—fast. He was beginning to think about things that he was unwilling to address: love, marriage, more children. He shook off the thought. JaiHonnah was his employee, nothing more. Besides, she was a married woman, and he had always respected the sanctity of marriage. That wasn't going to change, not even for the remote chance of sleeping with *Mrs.* Chapman.

"Alright, little cherubs," Roderick said, sticking his head into JaiHonnah's office. "You two finished redesigning yet?"

The girls and JaiHonnah looked up at him, and his heart missed a beat or two.

"Hi, Daddy!" Shelly and Shelby simultaneously screamed as they flew at him.

He collected his dose of his twins' healing kisses and hugs and delivered his own barrage of kisses and squeezes to their faces and little necks. Their love would be all he needed to sustain him for the rest of his life, he thought as he stood with them in his arms.

"Well, little cherubs, are you ready to go?"

"No, Daddy," Shelby whined. "Jai hasn't seen our pictures yet."

JaiHonnah smiled from deep in her core. Seeing Roderick with his girls always made her smile. He was so affectionate and loving with them, and the girls reciprocated. They talked about him constantly, she noticed, but very little about their mother. It came as no real surprise, and it seemed natural for little girls to love their father so much, but shouldn't they miss their mother too? she wondered. She had to stop thinking about Roderick and his family. He was, after all, a married man, and she respected the bonds of matrimony.

"Well, let me see how well you've done today." She took their little drawings and praised them highly, pinning their work to her cork board along with the girls' other "creativity." Roderick's office was also full of such notable pieces.

"Daddy, can Jai come with us on *The Mighty Magic Heat?*" Shelly asked innocently.

"Yes, Daddy, can she come, pleeezzze?" Shelby added.

Roderick was taken by surprise. "Certainly, she's welcomed to come along."

All eyes were on her as she squirmed under Roderick's directed stare and the twins looked down at her with their big, bright greenish-brown eyes.

"Please, Jai, will you come with us?" Shelly begged.

Shelby reached her arms out to JaiHonnah. When she took Shelby into her arms, Shelby put her arms around JaiHonnah's neck and snuggled close. "Please come, Jai," Shelby implored, hugging her tightly. "It's a lot of fun on the boat and my daddy's a good driver. He won't let the big boats hurt us."

Bewilderment caused her stomach to do a long, slow dive. How was she going to dodge this loving invitation? It was hard enough spending time with Roderick during the normal workday and trying to stifle her growing interest in him, but to spend a weekend on his boat in close proximity to him would be disastrous for her, she thought.

"Maybe another time," she said. "I've got a lot of work to do."

"That's against the rules," Roderick said. "At Baylor Construction, no one works the weekends or holidays except the boss, and even I'm taking this weekend off."

He wasn't going to let her off the hook easily or at all, if he could help it. It was hard enough thinking of her being all alone and unprotected in the evenings at her condo. Leaving her alone and unprotected while he was away was totally unacceptable. He would not be able to enjoy himself knowing that her husband might show up again and try to harm her. JaiHonnah's heart was too tolerant. A woman deeply in love would obviously forgive any transgression her man perpetrated. Obviously, she must be in love with her husband since she didn't want to press charges against him for his brutality. That was the only plausible explanation. Nevertheless, he didn't understand why she had told her husband never to touch her again. Roderick knew that, if he were her husband, the thought of never touching her again would have spelled something tantamount to a slow, agonizing death.

He had to stop that type of thinking. He was happy with his life the way it was, he tried to convince himself. He was surprised that the girls asked her to go with them, but he really didn't object. Shelly and Shelby rarely took to anyone as openly and freely as they did to JaiHonnah. For that matter, neither did he. Earlier in the week, he thought to ask JaiHonnah to go with them, but changed his mind because, outside of business meetings and conferences, she had barely noticed that he was around. And indeed he had been around—a lot.

"Look, your daddy is almost ready to go. You three go without me this time, have a wonderful trip, and tell me all about it when you get back," she said, smiling brightly.

The girls pouted and Roderick's demeanor stiffened.

"Jai, may I speak with you privately?"

JaiHonnah set the girls to work at another task and then joined Roderick in his office.

He leaned his butt against his desk, folded his arms across his chest and crossed his long legs at the ankles. "Jai, I can understand that my daughters can be more than a notion and then some. They've been following you around since you got here, so I can understand why you're reluctant to spend the weekend with them—."

"Oh, no, Roderick," she interrupted. "Shelly and Shelby are wonderful little girls, and I enjoy spending time with them."

"Then is it me that you don't want to spend time with? Have I said or done something to offend you? Do I make you uncomfortable?"

"No, of course not. It's none of those things. I just feel that we should keep our relationship on a professional level."

"It's about that kiss, isn't it?"

"Well…"

"What's wrong, Jai? Are you afraid of me? Are you afraid that you'll wake up and find me in your bed?"

"I've already ended up in your bed once, but you wouldn't do that to me. I know that."

"I don't go where I'm not invited and I don't accept what's not offered openly and honestly. You ended up in my bed alone, remember? I slept on the sofa bed in my den. So what's it going to take, Jai, to get you to agree to come with us?"

"Well, if more people were going…"

"How about eleven, twelve, or fourteen more people? Would that make you feel safer? Give me a number, Jai. Any number of people, and I'll make it so."

"Eleven? Who…?"

"Vivian, her children and my nieces and nephews are going to spend the weekend with us at my place near Virginia Beach. She took *The Vivian Lynn* out early this morning. She's probably halfway there by now."

"Oh," JaiHonnah said quietly, "I didn't know that. You didn't mention that Vivian was going too."

"I didn't think that the idea of spending a weekend with a bunch of children was a selling point. And by the way, it's not uncommon for me to take members of the staff and crews, both male and female, on boating trips during the season. I haven't ended up in any of my female employees' beds. Sexual abuse and harassment are crimes, and I don't practice either one."

She had hurt his feelings. She could see it in his eyes. She approached him and then heard someone clear his throat behind them, and they both turned.

"I second that position," Chuck Montgomery said. "But I'm about to lock my lips on some mighty sweet cheeks."

"Chuck Montgomery," JaiHonnah said, her smile brilliant. "Come here, City Cowboy, and give me some of that good loving of yours."

Chuck engulfed JaiHonnah in his massive arms, hugging her tightly.

They parted, still holding on to each other.

"Good to see you again, Sweet Cheeks," he said.

"You too, City Cowboy."

Roderick cleared his throat. "Uh, I didn't know that you two knew each other."

"Jai and I have a little history. She spent some time here with Vivian while...well, we got to know each other very well."

"We sure did, Dr. Montgomery," she said, hugging him again. "Chuck was still doing his residency at Georgetown Medical when we first met, and he was a real big country cowboy fanatic. Since I grew up on a ranch, he used to grill me about ranch life. I used to hang out with him, Vivian and her house mates whenever I was in town, and he used to take us to the country dance clubs. He taught me how to do the Down and Dirty," she said, laughing.

"The what?" Roderick asked, amused.

"It's a line dance, JRock. Something like the Electric Slide, but with a lot more action."

"Big as he is, Chuck usually can't walk and chew gum at the same time," Roderick joked.

"Yeah, we'll just see about that," Chuck said, good naturedly before turning to JaiHonnah. "So how come you didn't call me and let me know that you were in town, Sweet Cheeks?"

"I thought that Vivian would have told you that I was...oh, I'm sorry, Chuck, I forgot."

"Don't apologize, but how did you end up in this no-basketball-playing, overrated, knock-kneed, pigeon-toed hoodwinker's office talking about sexual harassment?" Chuck asked.

"Stop it, Chuck Montgomery," she said, grinning. "That's my boss you're talking about."

"Well now that's something to dance about, Sweet Cheeks. That means you'll be around for a long time."

"Yep, and we're going to make time to talk, you and me."

"You'll have your chance, JaiHonnah, if you stop holding up progress.

Chuck is going to Virginia Beach with me," Roderick added.

"It'll take me an hour and then I'll be ready to go," she said.

"I hoped that you'd say that," Roderick said, his voice lowered. He noticed that his heart was beating more rapidly looking into her beautiful eyes and at her tantalizing smile. "Now move it, mate," he joked. "The ship sails in one hour." She could take one year, but he knew that he wouldn't leave the dock without her on board.

JaiHonnah saluted and rushed away. She thought about how sudden and impetuous her actions were. What was it about J. Roderick Baylor that struck something deep within her? Why did she want to constantly be in his presence? She shook off her troubling thoughts. She wasn't going to analyze it to death because it felt too good. She was almost giddy.

Chapter 6

Roderick and Chuck cast off the ropes, pushed *The Mighty Magic Heat* away from the dock, and climbed aboard. Roderick took the controls and brought the sleek, white, cabin cruiser out into the tranquil Anacostia River. Chuck went to play a board game with Shelly and Shelby. JaiHonnah stood next to Roderick and watched as he skillfully navigated around other boats and marveled at the way he handled the big water craft.

"Want to run her?" Roderick asked, stepping back from the controls.

"May I?" JaiHonnah asked as she moved into position.

"Sure. Here, take the wheel."

"I want to warn you that I haven't done this in quite a while." She smiled, remembering her childhood and her father's yacht. At eight years old, Jake set her in the captain's chair after they cleared the port in Corpus Christi and helped her steer into the open waters of the Gulf of Mexico. The Hawkins family spent many vacations cruising the Southern coastal waters down to the Cayman Islands, just the five of them and a crew. When they lost her mother, the summer family outings stopped. It was both a poignant and painful memory.

Roderick positioned JaiHonnah in front of the wheel, then he stood behind her helping her steer until she got the hang of it. The fresh scent of her hair as well as her butt rubbing against him as the boat swayed in the ripples and wake was driving him crazy. His arms were around her holding the steering wheel, and his nature was rising. He had to relinquish the wheel for fear that she would feel his heat. She seemed to master the controls as he explained how to maneuver.

"Slow the pace until the other traffic passes," he said as she eased off the throttle and smoothly entered the Potomac River heading due south.

For a while Roderick just sat back watching JaiHonnah at the helm. He breathed deeply at the sight of the most luxuriant example of femininity he had ever experienced. Removing his sun shades, he pinched the bridge of his nose between his eyes. He had to stop looking at her or she'd soon notice the effect she had on him. He felt a familiar tingling growing up his spine. It always seemed to happen when he gazed at her for too long. He was drawn to her like a nail to a magnet, but she vexed him beyond reason.

Beyond their meetings and conferences she made herself scarce. She seemed to always be going somewhere when he was coming in. They glimpsed each other during the business days through the glass wall that separated their offices, but if he looked up at her, she would look away. She made friends with everyone on staff and on the work crews. She would have lunch with him in a group, but his offers to lunch with her alone were politely rejected. He wanted to be her friend, but couldn't understand why she was so reluctant to spend time with him.

Maybe he was emitting something else that made her feel uncomfortable in his presence. In a few painful seconds he realized that maybe she was afraid of men because of what her husband had done to her. His physical response to her was immediate from the moment he first saw her. He wasn't a master at masking his feelings. Maybe she picked up on his attraction and was afraid that he was like her husband, that he would brutalize her. The beating he gave her husband would only serve to solidify her fear of men, if, in fact, she feared them already.

Or maybe she was reluctant to be more open because she was married. He learned that JaiHonnah's husband was Calvin B. Chapman III, an international financier who had homes in Switzerland, Spain, Argentina, and Denver, Colorado. Now he could put a name to the face that he battered. He overheard Marilyn, the office gossip, talking to other employees about how handsome and wealthy Calvin Chapman was, amazed that he married a woman of African and Navajo descent. Not so surprising to Roderick, though he wondered why JaiHonnah, an intelligent, resourceful and competent woman would remain married to a man who obviously didn't honor or respect her. Even in the worst of times with Monique he never would have considered hurting her physically, though Monique seemed to favor rough sex.

Then it dawned on him. Monique. JaiHonnah must believe that he was a married man with a wife living in California while she worked on making a movie. Everyone, except his immediate family and Vivian, believed that they were still married and he couldn't confide the truth to JaiHonnah under the terms of his divorce decree; terms that he established to avoid public disclosure and for the protection of his daughters.

Then he thought back to that kiss. JaiHonnah hadn't fought him, rather she submitted, maybe out of fear or embarrassment or shock. He hadn't seen any of those emotions in her eyes afterward, but what did he know about how a woman would react after being attacked? He had no frame of reference. He would have to be more careful when with her, but how could he mask the tremors he felt when he looked at her? Issuing an expletive under his breath, he stood hiding his erection. He'd been too long without a woman.

"Did I do something wrong?" JaiHonnah asked, barely hearing the expletive that Roderick issued and noticing his abrupt move.

"Uh, no, you're doing fine. Stay on this course and watch the dials. This chart will guide you through and around the shoals. The helm is computerized and linked to the sonar equipment. I'm going to check on the girls and Chuck."

"You trust me to run this yacht without a co-captain?" she asked with a quizzical smile.

A wave of pleasure rushed through him and somersaulted in his abdomen as he gazed at her upturned face. Something long buried awakened in him. Something powerful, frightening.

"Well, if you run us aground, I'll take the towing cost out of your next paycheck," he managed to say without making a complete fool of himself.

"Aye, aye, sir," she said with a saucy salute.

"Carry on, mate."

Mate, he thought to himself. She was someone else's *mate*: Calvin B. Chapman III. One half of a marriage license. The thought of that gripped and wrenched his gut.

Exuberance and excitement peppered JaiHonnah's spirit as she stood alone at the helm of *The Mighty Magic Heat*. She wondered how Roderick came to give his craft that name. Her father's yacht had been christened *The Skai Hawk* in honor of her mother. Growing up on the desolate, barren Navajo reservation, her mother loved taking every opportunity to go to sea. Skai loved Jake even more for giving her beautiful fantasy cruises.

Vivian's yacht was called *The Vivian Lynn*. Derrick renamed his yacht after he and Vivian fell in love. Maybe that's what Monique created in Roderick, a mighty magic heat. She slumped back in her seat. Here she was with another woman's husband, piloting a yacht that he obviously loved, and named for the woman he loved. "Roderick," the name slipped from her lips in a smooth whisper. The sight of his finely chiseled body caused her to choke off her breath more than once since she met him.

That was only natural though. So many females on his staff and work crews expressed great appreciation when the hot summer heat caused Roderick's T-shirt to cling to him. They positively swooned when the September heat caused him to remove his shirt altogether. The days that he went swimming in his backyard pool wearing a pair of black swimming trunks, nothing else got done. One of the women, Bonetta, had to take a pill to calm herself. The women in the office talked about a half-dressed man in a soft drink television commercial and how the man in the ad couldn't carry Roderick's empty soda can to the trash. She hadn't seen the television ad, but she got the meaning nonetheless. Roderick was magnificent—and married, she reminded herself.

Pausing in her thoughts, she checked the heading and noted that she was right on course. Then her thoughts went back to Roderick. He was married alright. The elegance and beauty of his yacht with its deep pile carpeting, finely honed woodwork, gleaming fittings and tastefully decorated staterooms surrounded her in a feminine embrace. Definitely a woman's hand fashioned the craft's interior. Monique certainly had good taste in furnishings—and in men—JaiHonnah thought.

She could understand Monique's desire not to let a man like Roderick out of her sight for long, but her movie career must be mighty important to her. JaiHonnah respected independent women who wanted to fulfill their career goals and objectives while simultaneously raising a family. Monique obviously didn't totally trust her husband to steer clear of other women, but she had to trust him a great deal to leave him. Of course, he must have given Monique his full moral support. She had sensed that about Roderick. If he was in your corner, nothing on Earth could move him.

Her father had the same type of personality and presence. Jake Hawkins didn't suffer fools lightly either. If she and her brothers hadn't been around to stop him, Jake would not have rested until he saw Calvin and his father destitute for what Calvin did to her. She should never have let Jake see the bruises on her body, but, when she was wheeled into the San Antonio hospital, she was barely conscious. All she could remember on that fateful day, when her eyes finally opened, was a mountain looming over her with tears falling from its face. It was Jake's tears that had awakened her. Much like the mountain of a man she stopped from killing Calvin, both Roderick and Jake were immovable.

* * *

Roderick piloted the craft into the dock at Tangier Island. Night had fallen, and it was too dangerous to run with all the heavy commercial traffic on the Chesapeake Bay. They gassed up for a pre-dawn departure; had a long, leisurely dinner on the deck; and then battened down the hatches for the night. Roderick was restless though. He got out of his bed in the middle of the night, checked on his girls, and then went out on the deck. Resting on a chaise lounge, he looked out on the moonlit waters and steepled his fingers, deep in thought.

JaiHonnah was on his mind, and her image wouldn't let him rest. He needed time away from his bed, which was in the cabin across from hers. Was his unexplained interest in her just a bit of a diversion or was it deeper, his need to protect her? Clearly, her beauty was haunting him. He hadn't allowed himself to gaze at her during dinner. They had all focused on his twins and their infectious antics at the dinner table. However, he hadn't forgotten that JaiHonnah was there. Her soft fragrance mesmerized him as she and Chuck caught up on each others' life over the past years. It did not surprise him that she had traveled extensively in Europe, Asia and Africa. She spoke French, Spanish, German, Japanese and, of course, Italian fluently talking with his daughters as they tried to mimic simple words she taught them. He enjoyed hearing stories of her travels, but he knew all too well that he couldn't let himself get close to her. Letting himself be vulnerable would never happen again. If he did, he'd sink faster than the *Titanic* and just as deep.

No matter how hard she tried to turn off her brain, it didn't work. Roderick would seep into her thoughts through her twilight dreams. From the first time she saw him, something about him captivated her and, for the first time in her adult life, sexual desires were playing havoc with her psyche. Regardless of her resolve, she still felt a longing that she couldn't seem to get past. Maybe it was time to open herself up to men again as Vivian had urged. Certainly, Washington, D.C. was fertile ground for that. The city had some of the most handsome and eligible men in the country. It was, after all, a predominately male-oriented city, and eligible men were in and out of the offices of Baylor Construction all of the time.

Groaning, JaiHonnah gave up trying to sleep. The sexual tension was just too great. She put on a robe and silently tiptoed past the other cabins until she reached the deck. She looked up at the warm glow of the moonlight and accidentally bumped into a chair. Out of the corner of her eye she noticed someone move. In the moonlight she could see Roderick's features.

Roderick woke from a light sleep when he felt someone bump into his chair. Then he heard her melodic voice.

"Uh, Roderick, I'm sorry. I didn't see you."

"What's wrong? Are you alright?" he asked, quickly sitting up and swinging his bare feet to the deck.

"Yes, yes. I'm fine. Just a little restless. I couldn't sleep."

Roderick stood. "Here," he said, positioning another chaise lounger near his. "Why don't you sit a while? The salt air may make you rest better. I know it helps me."

JaiHonnah sat in the chair and Roderick reseated himself in his chair beside hers.

"You couldn't sleep?"

"I was making a very good effort at it."

She loved to hear him laugh. He didn't seem to do very much of it, but here, sitting in the moonlight on the Chesapeake Bay, his deep-throated chuckle was infectious and she joined in.

"I'm sorry. I should know better than to stumble around in the dark."

Her voice was so alluring he thought. It made his heart sing. "You're forgiven. It's a shame to miss out on these nights before winter sets in. I'm glad you woke me."

"It is beautiful out here. The water looks so peaceful and calm." She sucked in a deep breath, snuggling into the chair.

"Look," Roderick said, pointing up into the sky.

"A shooting star."

"You have to make a wish," he cajoled.

"I haven't a clue what to wish for."

Roderick noticed how the soft, moon glow caressed her long, shiny, black hair; creamy, flawless skin, and dark, topaz eyes,.

"What did you wish for?" she asked when she turn to look at him.

"Uh, me, well, nothing really. I guess I have almost everything I need or want."

It took Roderick only a few seconds to realize that it was a lie when the words fell from his lips. True, he had vast financial resources for which any man could hope. He was only twenty-two when he signed his first multimillion dollar contract and thirty-two when he left the NBA ranked number one in his position in the league. He wanted to do something else with his life, spend more time with his family and friends and have more children, but of course Monique's blatant infidelities had squashed that desire.

His nostrils caught a whiff of JaiHonnah's delicate scent, and his thoughts turned to her. His eyes wandered from the top of her head down her perfectly shaped body and legs to her toes, which stuck out from under her long, silky robe. She was stunning.

Even in the relatively dim moonlight Roderick stirred something inside her. His manly physique was perfectly sculptured, she noticed. In spite of herself and her own self-admonitions, her eyes feasted on him. It was dangerous for a man to be that virile, sensuous, and handsome. She had to look away or she might find herself openly swooning the way some of the other women in the office did when Roderick wasn't looking. She closed her eyes to his allure.

"Tell me more about living abroad," he urged, hoping that a stimulating conversation might take his mind off the want of her.

"It's a different world there," she began.

They talked for what seemed like hours, until the dawn caught them both asleep in their chairs on the deck.

* * *

As the sun grew higher in the bright morning sky, Roderick slowed his yacht waiting patiently while an aircraft carrier, a giant oil tanker and then a submarine moved into the oldest naval shipyard in the nation at Norfolk, Virginia. His twins were beside themselves with awe as they frantically waved at the vessels. Cargo ships under foreign flags and luxury liners also passed in parade order. Once all of the vessels cleared, Roderick crossed the Chesapeake Bay Bridge Tunnel, and then approached Cape Henry. As he rounded the cape, the expansive Virginia Beach shoreline and skyline loomed beside them. Hugging the shore around pleasure boat tours, he cruised down the coast to Sandbridge.

When Roderick slowed the yacht's engines they glided into docking position, JaiHonnah held the girls' hands lest they, in their excitement, tumble over the bow. Vivian's children and Roderick's nieces and nephews were already on the beach and racing toward the dock. Roderick momentarily reversed the engines and the large vessel floated into its slip.

Chuck, Roderick noticed, covered his eyes in disbelief when the sleek docked *Vivian Lynn* came into view.

"Man! How could I let you trick me into this?" Chuck bellowed. "Vivian is going to think that I put you up to this, and she's going to kill both of us!"

Roderick laughed. "She's too good of a lawyer. She won't kill us in front of witnesses. Besides, you said that you wanted to see the children sometime before you died, didn't you? Well, Chuck, old man, there they are."

Chuck's face lit up as he heard Vivian's children enthusiastically calling to him. He bolted toward them as Roderick docked. When the boat was moored, the children engulfed Chuck, and he reveled in their glee. Roderick looked up toward the middle deck of his house on the beach and saw Vivian's stiff stance with her arms folded across her chest.

"Uh-oh," JaiHonnah said, suddenly standing beside him. "Vivian looks like she's ready to commit homicide. Uh, did you tell her that Chuck was coming with you?"

"Nope, and I'm going to need protection when she goes for my throat," he said with merriment laced in his voice.

"Gee, and you left the Army, Navy, Air Force and Marines back in Washington," she said. "Well, I, for one, think that you did the right thing. Chuck loves and misses those kids terribly. Look at them. They obviously love and miss him very much too. Maybe this will help Vivian and Chuck heal the breach between them."

"Or have her hanging me up by my gonads," he said.

JaiHonnah laughed. "That's alright; I'll protect you—from the rear."

"Yeah, a lot of help that's going to be," he deadpaned.

"Sorry, fellah, this one is going to be tough."

"If all else fails, I'll remind her that she's Shelly and Shelby's godmother."

"She already has children, Roderick. Taking on two more wouldn't even raise her eyebrow," Jai said.

Roderick enjoyed having JaiHonnah beside him. She had a beautiful smile, captivating laugh, and a wonderful sense of humor. She turned her captain's baseball cap around backward on her head and then adjusted his in the same manner.

"Well, shall we brave the lioness in your lair?" she asked.

He glanced up at Vivian's unyielding glare. "Uh, maybe not. I'd better sleep on the boat tonight."

"Want some company?" she asked, looking up at Vivian.

It was an innocent remark he realized, offered as a joke, but he was dangerously close to saying yes, no matter how the remark was intended. He'd been too long without a woman, and JaiHonnah Reise Chapman was no ordinary woman—a more beautiful woman inside and out than he had ever known.

"If I didn't know better, I'd think you meant that," Roderick said with mock playfulness in his naturally deep baritone.

Something inside JaiHonnah clicked when she realized what she said and Roderick's response. She was afraid to look up into his face. His sunglasses covered his eyes completely, but she could not look at him. If she did, one look would confirm the dynamic that was clearly building between them.

"Well, onward, once more into the breach." She tried to laugh as she walked away from Roderick, but it came out sounding as shaky and nervous as she felt.

Roderick held back, watching JaiHonnah disembark and surround herself with the children. He'd promised himself that he wasn't going to do or say anything remotely personal to her and, less than twenty-four hours later, he had broken his own vow. He had ventured down that road, and he wasn't sure why, but he wasn't ready for that conversation to end. It was pointless to argue with himself now. He'd rather face the wrath of his attorney.

"Counselor," he said, hugging Vivian's stiff body and kissing her on the cheek.

Vivian didn't return his greeting.

"I have two words for you, JRock: *justifiable homicide*," she said, jabbing him in the chest with her index finger.

Roderick grinned at her and folded his arms across his chest. "Tell me that the children aren't happy to see their Uncle Chuck?"

Vivian glared at him. "That's beside the point, but I'll deal with you later," Vivian said, pushing Roderick away and embracing JaiHonnah.

Roderick noticed that Chuck got nothing but a quick icy glance from Vivian before she and JaiHonnah left the second-level great room in his beach house. Uh-huh, he thought as he watched the two women leave. Then he looked at Chuck who was wiping his sweaty brow.

"Am I bleeding anywhere that you notice?" Chuck asked.

"Check your pulse and see if your heart is still there," Roderick joked.

"*Whew!* That was a close one!" Chuck said, shaking his head thoughtfully.

"Give her time, Chuck. I hope she'll come around soon."

"Until she does, I'm keeping a very low profile."

"Chuck, you're seven feet tall. You weren't born with a low profile."

They both laughed and began to settle in.

"This is a fantastic place, Viv," JaiHonnah said as Vivian showed her around the large three-level, octagon-shaped beach house, with panoramic views of the sea and shore. Decks completely circled the upper two levels of the structure. The lower level contained a three-car garage, video center, a second complete kitchen and bar. Also on this level, the exercise room housed the latest equipment, a bath, sauna and game room that looked out on a stone patio that lead to the shoreline.

"Yes, it is. JRock and Derrick built identical homes. Derrick built his retreat on an island in Bimini. When I can't find time to go to Bimini, JRock lets me use his place to relax. He loves it here, but I'm more curious about that gleam I saw in your eyes, *Ms.* Jai."

"Sun is very bright here, that's all," JaiHonnah proffered as she tried to maintain her composure.

"Sun too bright in JRock's eyes too, I suppose," Vivian said with a sideways glance.

JaiHonnah put up both hands in mock defense. "Don't start, Viv. I hadn't planned to come on this cruise in the first place, but the girls really wanted me to come. Everything was going fine until I said something incredibly stupid to Roderick. We have a strictly . . ."

"Business relationship," Vivian said, finishing JaiHonnah's sentence, but watching JaiHonnah closely. "I know, I've heard the drill. Practice saying it about a hundred more times, maybe then I'll believe it."

"Vivian!" JaiHonnah flashed.

"JaiHonnah!" Vivian mimicked.

The two women glared at each other and then roared in laughter.

The day was filled with fun and frivolity. The children swam and played raucous games on the beach with JaiHonnah, Chuck and Roderick while Vivian perched in a deck chair supposedly reading a novel. JaiHonnah and Roderick later took the children for a long hike along the shore purposely leaving Vivian and Chuck alone together to prepare dinner.

Shelly and Shelby walked between Roderick and JaiHonnah holding their hands. The foursome chatted while the other children played as they walked slightly ahead of them. An elderly couple approaching them on the beach, beamed when they recognized Roderick.

"Could we please have your autograph and a picture, Mr. Baylor?" the elderly man asked while his wife dug into her straw beach bag. She handed paper and pen to Roderick then stood by his side while her husband snapped several pictures.

"It's nice of you to remember me," Roderick said. "What are your names?"

"McKinnon. Ils and Morganna McKinnon," the man said proudly.

"You were my favorite basketball player, young man," the elderly woman said as Roderick wrote a special note. "My husband and I still look at videotapes of some of your games. Pardon me, Mrs. Baylor," she said, smiling at JaiHonnah, "but your husband used to give me goose bumps." She squeezed herself. "I'll bet he's been a fine husband to you from the looks of these beautiful children of yours. You two make such a lovely couple."

"But I'm not—." JaiHonnah tried unsuccessfully to interrupt.

Ils steamrolled on. "Yes, young man, I was getting pretty jealous of how my wife used to act when she saw you playing basketball. I'm glad to see that you have a beautiful, young wife. Maybe now my Morgana will stop her daydreaming about you."

"Ah, stop your fooling, honey. You're making them blush. That's alright, Mr. Baylor, even with such a pretty wife you're still a young and very handsome man to me."

"Not as young as I used to be, ma'am," Roderick said, smiling.

"Well, son, you and your beautiful wife certainly look too young to have so many beautiful children, but young people in love these days can do anything together. When you and your wife have been together as long as my wife and I have, your children will be your crowning glory. We've been together for fifty years, and we have sixteen children and a mess of grands and great-grands. You two look so happy now, you couldn't miss being happy later in your life."

"Uh, thank you," Roderick said, handing the autographed sheet of paper back to the elderly man.

"Nice meeting you, Mrs. Baylor, Mr. Baylor." The couple waved as they walked away.

JaiHonnah and Roderick didn't speak or glance at each other as they walked farther down the beach. Then, almost simultaneously, they gave each other a sideways glance and broke into hilarious laughter, gripping their sides and doubling over. The children all gathered around them, confusion fixed on their faces.

"What's so funny?" one of Vivian's sons asked.

Roderick and JaiHonnah were still laughing too hard to answer. The children shrugged and went to play along the sandy shore.

Roderick and JaiHonnah saw the smoke billowing from the barbecue pit before they and the children reached the house. Chuck and Vivian cooked a huge feast.

"Where's Chuck?" Roderick asked.

"Basting on the grill," Vivian answered matter-of-factly.

Both JaiHonnah and Roderick actually turned and looked at the grill as if she might be serious.

"Viv, what did you do to him?" Roderick asked after assuring himself that the ribs on the grill weren't Chuck's.

"He had to leave. Some type of emergency. He took a cab to the airport in Norfolk. Said he'd call you next week—if you're not on a platter with an apple stuck in your mouth," she added with a raised eyebrow, waving a very big knife and barbecue fork in front of his face.

JaiHonnah laughed. "Whew, you had me going there for a minute, Viv, but I promised to protect Roderick. Chuck is a good person. I hope you two had an opportunity to talk."

Vivian's eyes slid toward JaiHonnah. "This grill is certainly big enough to hold two," she said with a devilish grin.

"She's completely innocent, Viv. It was all my fault. Jai and Chuck didn't know anything about what I was up to."

"And what time are you two leaving on Monday morning?" Vivian asked, sharpening the knife.

"Uh, early—very, very early," Roderick said, eyeing the knife.

"Good, but leave your family here. I may just use them for ransom," she quipped.

"But, Viv. . ." Vivian cut her eyes at Roderick. "Uh, done," he said, holding up both hands backing away in mock surrender. He went to help the children set up the tables on the beach for dinner.

Chapter 7

Early Monday morning Roderick backed his yacht out of the slip and waved good-bye to the children on the dock who enthusiastically blew kisses and waved. He turned the craft northward and in a few minutes, they were under way and out of sight.

"Alright, captain, she's all yours," Roderick said to JaiHonnah.

"Aye, aye, sir," JaiHonnah returned with a saucy salute before taking the wheel.

Roderick returned the gesture and then turned JaiHonnah's cap backward on her head to match his.

"You know, Roderick, I haven't had so much fun in years. Thank you for letting me come along. Your nieces and nephews are a real joy."

"You're welcome to come along anytime you like, Jai. I've enjoyed this trip more than most of the ones I've made lately. I'm sorry that Chuck had to leave. He and I don't get much time to just kick back and relax anymore. Shelly and Shelby and the rest of my family enjoy seeing him, Vivian's children and the big boats so I usually make this trip every weekend when the weather permits. This gives my brothers and sister some quality time with their spouses too. Sometimes I can convince Kelley to come along. I bring Vivian's children with me when she's out of town or tied up. I'm sorry that the boating season is nearly over."

"Vivian certainly has a fine family, and they're a joy to be around. I don't know how she does it. She's a very successful lawyer, a wonderful mother, an author and an orator, and with all of the organizations she's involved with, she still finds time for her friends."

"I know that I don't have to tell you that she's an exceptional and selfless woman. It's still very painful to think that Derrick died holding Derrick Junior on the day he was born, April 1 and didn't get to see his family growing up. Having the children that they adopted together helped Vivian get through his death. She still adopts children who are orphaned and have heath challenges. Seeing these children get the medical care that they so desperately need and welcome them into her family are what keeps her charged up. They make her very happy." Roderick asked his next question very carefully. "Have you considered having children?"

JaiHonnah exhaled deeply. "I wanted to years ago, but now, well . . ." she shrugged. "The time has passed very quickly. Perhaps, when I'm better established, I'll adopt...I mean, we'll adopt a child like Vivian has."

For a solitary second JaiHonnah had let down her guard and almost slipped up. Actually, she wanted children more than anything. Although she had experienced a trauma years ago, she could still hear the doctor's words ringing in her ears as she lay battered and bruised in the emergency room. *"I'm sorry, Mrs. Chapman, but we couldn't save your baby."* It was her gleeful announcement to Calvin that she was pregnant that precipitated their quarrel and subsequent fight that doomed their marriage. He insisted that the baby wasn't his and that she have an abortion. After that experience years ago, her hope of ever becoming a mother died.

Roderick's jaw tightened along with his fists when JaiHonnah mentioned that she and her husband would likely adopt a child together. The thought of her husband being anywhere in close proximity to her tore at Roderick's gut. However, she was, after all, a married woman who apparently still wanted a life with her husband. Roderick had to look away from her and wrestle for control of his emotions. He settled his mind on the thing that made him happiest.

"I don't know what I'd do without Shelly and Shelby. They're growing up so fast. It seems like only yesterday that I brought them home from the hospital. They've been twisting me around their little fingers ever since."

Roderick was being more transparent than he expected. He had to stop that, he thought. JaiHonnah didn't have to know that he suffered through, what he later realized, was a loveless marriage. Almost immediately after his girls were born, Monique walked out on him and their daughters, confirming that she never really loved him and stating that Shelly and Shelby weren't his. She claimed that the twins were really Lionel Porter's offspring. He never tested her on that question, and Lionel never laid claim to the twins. If he was not the twins biological father, then Monique had every right to take them away from him. As far as Roderick was concerned though, they *were* his daughters, and he loved his girls more than his next breath. Giving up the marriage was not difficult for him, but the threat of losing Shelly and Shelby still struck fear in his heart.

Vivian had skillfully handled the divorce negotiations, but he had not even told her that the twins might not be his. Even without that knowledge, Vivian was masterful in her approach to Monique and her lawyers and won him his freedom and total custody of the girls. Acknowledging that the twins would, at some point, need to know their mother, he insisted that Vivian include provisions in the custody settlement for visitation rights for Monique. Though she never committed herself to the girls, and rarely exercised her custodial option until recently, her request to have the children always came with a price tag. He had paid dearly for Shelly and Shelby to have time with their mother. This time the price was higher than usual. He was beginning to worry about her motives, but he didn't want to let on to Vivian, and certainly not to JaiHonnah, how worried he actually was.

Roderick's pained expressions gave JaiHonnah reason for concern. He seemed fine all weekend—playing with the children, reading stories to them at bedtime and having a relaxing evening with her and Vivian before they all turned in for the night. They slept in his handsome house by the ocean and got up early to make a huge breakfast, which was quickly gobbled up by the household. After breakfast he walked with his twins alone on the beach for nearly an hour. She saw them in the distance sitting on the sand dunes far up the beach deep in conversation. The twins were crawling over him, hugging him. He is a good father, she thought, warm, caring and very giving. What she didn't understand was what had changed his demeanor.

"I've wanted to have more children. A houseful like Vivian or like that couple we met the other day on the beach," he said spontaneously, not looking at JaiHonnah.

JaiHonnah felt something in his demeanor that she couldn't identify, but then she was no expert on J. Roderick Baylor. She wasn't an expert on what made any man tick. She spent her entire adult life reacting to whatever was thrown at her. Doing whatever came next. She never felt in complete control of anything, least of all her own emotions. Now she was beginning to feel something more than blatant lust for this Rock of Gibraltar and she wanted to share in his...*Stop it, Jai!* she chastised herself. *He's a married man who just told you that he wants more children with his wife! Get it through your head. He loves his wife, no matter what!*

Nearly half the distance home, Roderick began to see white caps forming on the choppy waters. Storm clouds were moving in low from the southeast and the wind picked up considerably. JaiHonnah was having difficulty holding course, so he took over the helm. Heavy weather warning signals were coming in over the marine radio frequencies advising boaters to rig their vessels and anchor for the night. Small-craft warnings were being signaled to each vessel on the Chesapeake Bay. A hurricane, although still well out to sea, was skirting the Atlantic Coast, bringing high winds, rough waters and heavy rain at its edges. Even larger ships were told to exercise caution. Roderick, along with other small craft owners, heeded the warnings.

Roderick marveled at how calmly and swiftly JaiHonnah acted as he shouted instructions to her over the loud thunder while he piloted the yacht into Point Lookout Sound and dropped anchor. Together they stowed the furniture and loose deck items as the sky blackened, torrential rain fell and a furious wind whipped. They were soaking wet, drenched to the bone, when they were finally able to batten down the hatches and race into the interior of the craft.

They were laughing as they shook the water from their faces, hair and arms. The craft tossed in the shifting and turbulent waves, wind and rain. JaiHonnah's breasts heaved up and down, molded by the wet T-shirt. Roderick's eyes caught the shape of her hardened nipples through her wet clothing. He looked away and pulled his T-shirt over his head, wrung it out and used it to wipe his face, chest and arms. Then he noticed blood as JaiHonnah shook the water from her hair, arms and hands.

"You're hurt," he said as he instinctively gabbed her fingers.

"Oh, I hadn't noticed," she said, looking at the small cut on her index finger.

It wasn't a bad cut, but Roderick stuck her finger under cold water. The sensation that sprung from her finger in the warmth of his hands sent shock waves through JaiHonnah. Looking at his finely sculptured bare chest, her core constricted, fighting off the heat of having him in such close proximity to her. He acted so quickly that she didn't know what he was doing until she felt his arms surrounding her while he held her hand under the water. She never felt the pain of the cut, but she certainly felt his taunt half clothed body rub against her as the boat rocked in the tumultuous waters. Her breath quickened involuntarily and became labored. The tips of her breast hardened more against her sopping-wet T-shirt as he continued to tend to her finger. She turned her head toward him and looked up at him over her shoulder. Her eyes went slowly up the ridged plane of his broad chest to meet his and lingered, mesmerized by the passion she saw there.

She realized that she was trembling, not from the chill of her wet clothes against her skin, but from her own desire. He secured a small bandage around the cut and then kissed it. Slowly, she turned in his loose embrace. He stood before her balancing himself and her against the rocking motion of the boat. Tentatively, she traced the outline of his mouth, slipping a finger in and out of his full lips. His hand went to her cheek, caressing it softly and moving the raindrops away with his thumb. Then his rain-moistened face was all that she could see blocking out everything around them, lowering to meet her upturned face and hungry mouth as it whispered his name. His lips brushed over hers and then softly engulfed her mouth in his. His suction on her bottom lip caused her breathing to quicken. He moaned deeply as she parted her lips, and he explored the warm inner chamber with his tongue. Her body moved against his, and her arms circled his neck, her fingers stroking his head and his back. She rose to her tiptoes and deepened the union as his powerful arms encircled her and pulled her even closer to his rock-hard body. Her swollen breasts ached to be held as she shuddered against the hard plane of his chest.

Dizzy with a raw desire that she had never felt before, she pulled against him and a needful whimper escaped her throat when she felt his engorged manhood pulsating against her abdomen. Her heart was beating a rapid tattoo against her chest with the feel of him in her arms. His moist scent stoked the fire that was beginning to rage within her. At that moment nothing else existed for her except him.

Roderick was lost in the ecstasy as one hand slid down JaiHonnah's back and cupped her butt, drawing her up even closer to him. Her hardened nipples teased his bare chest and caused him to groan his unbridled desire. He shivered with anticipation as his shaft strained against the wet fabric that separated them. He didn't have the presence of mind to question his motives; his need for her was too great to be quelled. JaiHonnah's lithe tongue took control of his senses and spun electrical shocks throughout his body. He deepened the kiss, his body straining with barely contained desire. His chest heaved in syncopated rhythm with his pounding heart and pulsating manhood. He was about to explode with a desire so deep, so thick that it rocked his entire body.

A loud crack of thunder punctuated their deep moans. Roderick tore his mouth from hers and peered down into her upturned face. He rested his forehead against hers and closed his eyes while he tried to get his senses under control.

"Stop me, Jai," he whispered, his deep voice thick with emotion. "Tell me no and I'll let go of you."

"Stop you?" she whispered breathlessly. "I can't stop myself unless you do it. Push me away from you, Roderick," she whispered, moving her lips against his throat, her hands kneading his neck and his back.

He tipped her chin up. "Look at me, please, and tell me that you don't want me to touch you. Tell me, Jai, and I'll stop. I won't force you to do anything. I'll walk away."

Her eyes raised slowly to his, searching his depths. "Do you want me to lie to you?" she asked, the anguish showing on her face. "Do you want me to tell you that I don't want to touch you in ways that I know I shouldn't? To touch you in ways that I have no right to touch you? To touch you in ways that I have never touched a man before?"

"I want no lies."

His head once again lowered and the passion was even stronger as he captured her mouth and groaned his deep pleasure.

JaiHonnah's body trembled as Roderick led her to the master cabin. Once inside he raised her rain-moistened face to his. Slowly he kissed each cheek, then her forehead, both eyes, her nose, then her mouth, sucking gently at her fleshy bottom lip and worrying the small mole. He did not touch her in any other way, gripping the railing above the bed instead to restrain himself from crushing her to him with unleashed wanton lust.

JaiHonnah's trembling fingers spanned the broad, thick, ribbed plane of his chest settling on his nipples first with her fingertips then with her lips; the touch, the feel, the scent of him driving her pass mere passion. A groan rumbled through his throat as JaiHonnah's soft fingers ignited him and slid down his stomach to his flat abdomen causing it to concave even more, throbbing with desire. Slowly he unzipped and then unfastened his cutoff jeans, and they fell from his firm muscular hips. He placed her trembling hand on his shaft. Her fingers met with surprise along the silky circumference of his black briefs. He was long and thick causing her to gasp. Her fingers, although long and slender, could neither span the distance from its base to its large, smooth rounded mushroom head nor reach around the circumference to touch her fingertips together. She nearly froze not knowing what to do. Her experience with a man was limited to her brief marriage to Calvin. Never had he been tender with her. Never had he brought her to this heightened state. Suddenly she wondered whether there was enough room in her body to take Roderick's impressive size into her.

Roderick felt her reluctance. He sensed that his size and length had shaken her. He guided her more to forewarn her of his girth and length as he placed his hand on hers and moved it along his shaft. He didn't want to frighten her or make her feel uncomfortable. If she pulled back from anxiety or in fear, he would not have continued, but once she became aware of him, she handled him gently—and almost too proficiently—as his groans deepened at her touch.

Roderick's body strained against the sweet ecstasy that she caused. His fingers contained no blood as he held a death grip on the bed railing above his head to balance himself against the rocking craft and JaiHonnah's attention to his sex. His jaw tightened until his teeth ached from the excruciating pressure as he breathed in short, quick pants. His abdomen concaved and convexed in rapid succession straining to hold on to his fleeting self-control while his silent cries for divine intervention were lost in the thunderous rage of the storm. Her lips on his chest were lethal. Her tongue on his abdomen, deadly. Her touch on his manhood, fatal. He could not resist her. It was not within his control. His already rock-hard muscle expanded even more as JaiHonnah's soft, warm hand surrounded it, exercising it slowly, and her tongue lathered the tip and down the pulsating vein to the base. His nostrils flared and his breath quickened with each tender stroke. He placed his hand on hers and stop the exquisite pain before he exploded. Roderick marshaled his emotion before he spoke, clearing the large lump in his throat. He raised her face to his and whispered against her lips.

"I don't want to frighten you. I won't hurt you, just tell me when to stop."

JaiHonnah's face showed her concern and confusion. "Did I do something wrong?" her voice quivered.

He caressed her worried face, smoothing away her concern and smiled slightly. "No." He breathed. "Too perfectly."

With both hands Roderick slowly lifted her wet T-shirt over her head and loosened her single plait releasing her hair that shimmered slick with rain and looked like pitch-black silk over her shoulders appreciating the beauty of her full breasts. His fingers gently unfasten the white, lacy, French front-clasped bra releasing the most exquisite pair of breasts imaginable. He slipped the garment from her shoulders and lowered himself to a sitting position on the bed to nibble at the light, cherry-chocolate circles centered with plump raisin tips. JaiHonnah shuddered and goose bumps peppered her skin. Her hands dug deep into Roderick's hard, fleshy, muscular arms and shoulders. Her head fell back as his tongue blazed a trail from her breasts down her flat stomach. He lingered at her navel while he loosened her shorts and slid them down her thighs. His tongue continued its blazing trail along the top edge of her thong, the satin barely covering its charge. Roderick's hot kisses through the fabric sent wild sensations spiraling throughout her body. Slowly he removed the eye-patch-like thong kissing gently where the fabric had been. He gripped her butt pulling her forward shifting her onto her back on the bed and serving himself from her hot, sweet nectar. The teasing she took from his mustache against her bare skin sent her quickly up, reeling. The flashes of lightning outside the cabin paled by comparison with the array of flashing lights behind her tightly closed eyes. A low, steady hum grew from deep within her core rising to her throat and finally exploded as the orgasm ripped through her like a rapier. Never before had she experienced this sensation, and the fear that she would never survive another such eruption gripped her. She wanted Roderick with an intensity that she had never felt for any man, including Calvin. Roderick didn't let her recover before he began to heighten her senses anew. This time he raised her thighs to his shoulders, giving himself unobstructed access to her hardened breasts and to her unprotected core. He feasted there until she released more succulent nectar, and he again sent her to the edge of oblivion and over the brink.

JaiHonnah's body was quaking out of control when Roderick retraced the trail he had blazed earlier up her body to her now rock-hard nipples to her neck, which he lavishly bathed to her chin, and then capturing her open mouth in his.

Roderick's excursion over JaiHonnah's velvet-soft body was long, but exquisitely pleasurable. He relished the taste of every inch of her, monitoring her reactions to assure that his need didn't overwhelm or frighten her. His last ounce of self-control nearly spent, he began the last part of the journey as he allowed her to open to him at her own pace. He had to see her eyes to know her needs.

"Look at me, please, Jai," he whispered. "I need for you to tell me if I become to much for you."

JaiHonnah's eyes floated open and sparkled like rare gems. Tears welled up in her eyes and flowed over the brim.

Roderick's body tensed at the sight of her tears. "I've hurt you," Roderick worried, as he began to back away.

"No," JaiHonnah whispered, holding him in place. "I've just never felt like this before or ever been so happy. My tears are for joy, not sorrow."

"Jai, please, are you telling me the truth? I couldn't bare it if I hurt you in any way," he pleaded. "I want you so badly that I may not be capable of holding back."

JaiHonnah pulled his head to hers, kissing his face gently in several places, then settling against his lips.

"Make love to me, Roderick. Please forgive me, but I don't want this feeling to end," she whispered breathlessly against his mouth as she licked his lips. He groaned from deep in his core, opened to her and their tongues danced together in an age-old rhythm.

Roderick began the slow gyration of his hips, inching his way toward the depth of JaiHonnah's core. Each inch through the narrow, wet, tight corridor tested his ability to stay lucid, but he had to monitor her reaction. She might not tell him if he was too large or too long for her, he feared. As her sheath closed in tightly around him, he placed his fingers at her wet sweet spot worrying it gently until her hips bowed up and moved in tandem with his. The arc in her back, the whimpers from her throat and her grip on his neck and shoulders told him that she was reaching another climax. Sweat pouring from his body and hers warned of an impending cataclysmic explosion. The sweet sounds of her liquid fire lifted his phallus as he moved back and forth inside her. He couldn't get close enough or deep enough without hurting her. She adjusted to his size and pace as they breathed each other in. They looked into each other's eyes until their visions began to gray. Unable to hold off his need any longer, his pelvic thrusts quickened his pace driving harder and deeper. They did not heed the warning as they voiced their climactic ecstasy and went over the edge into oblivion together.

Their bodies trembled for what felt like an eternity, cutting off all conscious thought and lapsing into a cacophony of unintelligible sounds. The thunder of their hearts drowned out the sounds outside the cabin. Nothing existed for them beyond that place.

Roderick nuzzled JaiHonnah's chin up to her ear as she kissed his neck and down to his muscular shoulder. His arms of granite wrapped around her, completely keeping her close to his heat and his heart.

"Are you okay?" he asked, squeezing her to him.

JaiHonnah took his face in her soft hands, smoothing away the worry.

"I feel like I have never felt before. I feel beautiful and wonderful and complete. I didn't know that it was humanly possible to feel this way, but I didn't want you to be disappointed. We can't do this again, can we?"

Roderick would have laughed if that lump hadn't grown in his throat. He was thinking the very same thing. He had never been so completely satisfied. No woman had cared so completely for his pleasure as well as for her own. Once into the uncharted, unfamiliar, but devastatingly wonderful and fulfilling JaiHonnah Reise Chapman would not be enough.

"Yes, Jai, we can do this again. Just give me a minute. I just want to hold you. You're pure magic, Jai," he said against her lips. "In your arms I can do or be anything you want me to—and then some. You've taken me places that I've never been before, but I want to go there again—now—with you," he said, his voice again laden with passion.

Never as a younger woman had she felt gentleness, tenderness or sensitivity with Calvin's crassness when he touched her, but Roderick pulled at the woman within her. He made her weak with need with every caress. She suckled his tongue, and her body took on a life of its own, rocking gently against his until her need for him began to spiral out of control and her hips pistoned against him. Her inner muscles clamped him in place and she felt him building within her. She worried that she could not please him, which motivated her to try harder. In her quest, however, that exquisite sensation that he had caused her to have, built again. Her breathing became positively erratic, hypnotized by his hardness against her and inside her. She heard him catch his breath as they molded their mouths together. She sighed needfully as her eyes drifted shut. His perspiration moistened her and heated her. How incredibly sexy he made her feel. She had a practiced walk and stance when in competition designed to be alluring and enchanting, but that experience never rivaled the energy she felt with him resting between her thighs. Her core was pulsating with intensity, and her emotions both surprised and shocked her. His mind-numbing kisses created an incredible fire once again as she stroked him.

"Roderick," she groaned as his large hand cupped her buttock.

"Are you alright?" he asked, lifting his head and looking into her eyes with concern.

She smiled at him and tasted his mouth. "I'm fine, better than I've ever been before," she whispered, "but I'm not using any form of birth control and we didn't use any form of protection."

"I know," he whispered, concern knitting his brow. "That was my responsibility, but I didn't expect this to happen. I wasn't prepared and I couldn't stop myself."

"Neither could I," she said on an exasperated breath. "I don't do this type of thing, ever. I want you to know that."

She didn't have to tell him that. He knew instinctively that she didn't practice to entice men into compromising positions. She certainly wasn't like Monique. In his mind, Monique couldn't hold a candle to JaiHonnah. With Monique it was like a wrestling match. She demanded he perform at her pace, which was quick, fast and in a hurry. She never let him love her his way, slow and easy, savoring the moments of intimacy. Monique took what she wanted from him and rarely gave anything in return. Too often after being with her he lay unfulfilled. She was like a jackhammer bouncing up and down on top of him until she climaxed and then hopped off him before he neared his peak. No pleasure, just performance was all she wanted from him. His efforts to romance her, after their hasty marriage, were rebuffed, leaving him to feel foolish and very much alone. He was patient with Monique while he watched his seed grow in her womb, but never felt any real warmth from her. With JaiHonnah, he felt alive and alone no more. The warmth that flowed from her to him bathed his soul and enlivened his spirit. He could go on making love to her forever, he thought.

"I don't do this type of thing either," he said, caressing her face and gently kissing her mouth.

JaiHonnah didn't have to be reassured. His tenderness and caring showed in his eyes and resounded in his loving touch. Calvin was her first and only lover, but he never touched her the way that Roderick did. She heard about and read about a climax, but until now she had never felt one. She felt like a virgin again being loved for the very first time. Indescribable sensations coursed through her body heightened by the feel of the Rock of Gibraltar against her and buried deep inside her. Nothing in her experience with Calvin ever reached this level of intimacy. She was now even angrier with Calvin. Not only for what he had put her through, but also for what he had denied her—complete satisfaction. A renewed hunger deep in her soul roared to life. Her pounding heart and tears worked in tandem.

Roderick felt JaiHonnah's body moving below him and saw tears rolling down her face. The sight completely captivated him. They were tears of joy she had told him and her feather-like kisses served to confirm her statement. He had satisfied her and she had thrilled and satisfied him to his core.

Slowly they began to move against each other. His body shuddered as she brought him to life still buried deep inside her. He could feel every sensation in her. He threaded his fingers through her damp hair and held her head in his palms. He lifted his upper torso off her, resting his weight on his elbows and let his pelvis do the work she wanted. He kissed her with his soul laid bare and open, delving into the warmth and velvet of her mouth.

JaiHonnah was breathless and still wanted more of him. Her body was hot, pulsating and gyrating against Roderick's. She locked her legs around his waist wanting him deeper inside of her. Calvin never made her feel any way but defiled. She stroked Roderick's back and then arched hers, serving up her body to him.

"My God!" Roderick groaned as he sucked in a ragged breath through gritted teeth. He buried his head between her breasts and raised himself almost to his knees, slowly and strongly entering and exiting her with a pleasure that defied description. Hot buttered syrup flowed between her legs. He arched his back and groaned a deep guttural sound. "JaiHonnah," he moaned. "Oh, JaiHonnah."

With one strong arm and her thighs wrapped around his back he lifted JaiHonnah without breaking contact.

When Roderick buried his face between her breasts again, the climaxes came in rapid succession. She lost count of them and nearly lost her mind. His mouth touched her in ways she never dreamed possible; the intimacy between them was overwhelming. She was shrieking inaudible words, but the storm drowned out the sound. Her heart pounded in her chest, and with every touch she knew her next breath would be her last.

Roderick was losing himself again in Jai. She tasted of sweet nectar and he delved deeper for more. She was driving him to the brink of insanity—a feeling he never had before captured and held him. His engorged muscle pulsated, twitching again as if he had not released thirty minutes before.

His name on her lips had never sounded so erotic. She quivered with his every touch and caress. He kissed every inch of her slowly and deliberately until he could no longer stand being outside of her. She rocked the foundation of his world when he again quickened his lazy thrust in her tight, wet portal. The rapture began and heightened with each inch-by-inch stroke. They were lifted up outside of themselves to a heightened state beyond reality.

Roderick slammed his eyes shut against the tears of his joy. JaiHonnah's tears met his. Kneeling on the bed with her wrapped securely around him, she made him feel things he didn't know existed, with every touch of her warm, soft hands over his wet body. She clung to him whispering her pleasure against his ear. He knew that if he never breathed again, in that moment in time, he had lived.

Like two lost souls they reached for a new beginning. They were thrust into a new life that would never be the same again. They became one new life force.

Chapter 8

Morning came, the storm ended, the lovers lay still clinging together on the damp sheets totally spent and sated from their night of ecstasy. Sleep crept in as they lay in the coolness of the mid-September morning, still reeling from the all-night rapture.

Roderick held JaiHonnah, her body half covering his. He pulled a cover up over them both. Her forehead rested against his growing beard. He listened to her soft, steady breathing and a smile bowed his mouth. Closing his eyes, he drifted into a sweet slumber.

"Ahoy, *The Mighty Magic Heat!*" A blaring horn crushed the silence.

Roderick and JaiHonnah were jolted from their dreams. Roderick bolted up and quickly slipped into his cutoff jeans. He opened the hatch, blocked the sun from his eyes with his hands and climbed onto the deck. JaiHonnah followed wrapping a robe around her. A U.S. Coast Guard cutter lay off his starboard bow.

"Are you Roderick Baylor?" a lieutenant blared.

"Yes, is there a problem?" Roderick yelled back.

"Urgent message to call your wife, sir," the lieutenant yelled back.

"Urgent?"

"Yes, sir. Said she's been trying to reach you all weekend. Frantic she was, sir."

"Thank you," Roderick said and waved. He immediately brushed past JaiHonnah to the telephone.

Roderick dialed Vivian at his beach house. When she answered, there was fear in his voice. "Vivian, the girls, are they alright? The rest of my family?"

"Yes, JRock, everyone is fine," she said with confusion evident in her voice. "Why? What, did you think that the storm was enough for us to evacuate?"

"I don't know." He exhaled slowly, rubbing his hand over his face in frustration. "Monique sent the Coast Guard looking for me with an urgent message. I thought—oh, I don't know what I thought," he said with a huff.

"Monique? Oh." Vivian breathed heavily. "Her lawyer probably got in touch with her about the money."

"You think that's what it's about?"

"Well, I don't know for sure, but, if it is, remind her that any negotiation over this issue has to come through me. My office knows where to find me."

Roderick exhaled deeply. "Thanks, Vivian. Kiss the girls for me."

"Sure thing, JRock. We'll be back tomorrow or the next day. The children are fine and having a wonderful time. You relax. I'll talk with you when we get back."

They hung up, and Roderick slumped in his chair rubbing his face in frustration.

JaiHonnah froze when she heard the lieutenant say that Monique was frantically trying to find Roderick. She glanced up at the lieutenant who had what she considered to be a smirk on his face when he spotted her next to Roderick wearing his robe. She knew what it must have looked like to the lieutenant: some tryst with another woman's husband. Caught on a clandestine rendezvous on the yacht of a high-profile man. The kind of thing that sold newspaper copy and fired the rumor mills of yellow journalism and tabloids. The type of exploits read about every day in the society columns. Little snide innuendo, dirty jokes, career-ending rumors of escapades and insinuations. The type of crushing coverage that would obliterate the beauty that passed between them. Her once high hopes for her re-entry into life would crash and burn, bringing this gentle and tender mountain of a man down with her. The thought fixed her to her spot when he rushed past her to call his wife. She could not listen to what he might have to say to Monique, the lies that he would have to tell to save his marriage. It would be too painful to hear him reaffirming his love for his wife. She knew and understood what it was like to be the wife of a man who had affairs during their marriage. She was disgusted with being placed in the role of the other woman. Particularly after she had told Monique that there would never be anything between her and Roderick except a strictly business relationship. She stayed in her place watching the grinning face of the lieutenant as the Coast Guard cutter pulled away.

What had gotten into her? Was she so starved for affection that she slept with the first man who touched her emotionally in years? For crissake, this man was her boss. Was she crazy? She had known him for barely three weeks. The things that they had done to each other and together in one night many married people had not done in a lifetime together. What must he think of her? Easy? An office pet? A little side stuff while his wife was away? How could she face him? Had she lost all self-respect? Burying her face in her hands, breathing in his scent, she shuddered at the thoughts, but, oh how he had loved her. She had been so happy, but this wasn't love, it was sex. How could she let herself get into this situation?

"Jai," Roderick whispered from behind her, engulfing her in his arms, a large, warm hand caressing her breast. He kissed her ear and she felt his heated phallus against her spine as his tongue slid down the back of her neck to her shoulder. "Why are you still out here on the deck?"

Momentarily she slumped against him trying to fight the magic that he was re-creating, but it had to stop. She had to walk away.

"I'd better get dressed," she said as she abruptly tore herself away from his warm, erotic embrace and re-entered the cabin. She felt Roderick's surprise at her haste. Moving swiftly to her stateroom, she closed the door and locked it behind her. She cupped one hand over her mouth, hugging herself around the waist with the other to stifle her whimpers. She could still smell him on her hands, her body.

"Jai, what's wrong?" Roderick pleaded, knocking at the door. He was confused and didn't understand what had happened. Less than thirty minutes had passed since they lay together completely naked and sated in their rapture.

"Nothing, I'm fine. I'm just going to take a shower and get dressed," she said, summoning her courage and will to get past this bleak point.

"Are you sure? You don't sound like yourself. Open the door, Jai, please."

"Roderick, please, I just need a few moments alone."

Roderick's hand slid down the door. A chill skidded up his spine. Something was terribly wrong on the other side of the door. He could have broken through it to get to her or opened it with his keys, but he didn't want to frighten her or bully her. Although a dense foreboding gathered around him, he had to wait for her to come to him.

"Alright, I'll make breakfast," he said through the closed door and then moved away.

JaiHonnah turned her face up to the spray and let the shower water wash away her tears, the musky scent of him and her together, but it could not wash away the memory. She had never known love like that. Never felt the ecstasy. Never visited the rapture. It was all too mind numbing. She could still feel his soft kisses on her mouth and everywhere on her body. His fullness had filled her and inspired her to coax him for more and more, which he delivered over and over and over all though the night and early morning. Suddenly she felt ashamed of her behavior.

After her shower, she dressed in a loose, oversized sweater; leggings; socks and ankle boots. She braided her hair in two plaits and pinned them together at the top of her head. Taking a deep breath, she opened the cabin door and gasped as she saw Roderick.

He was leaning back against the opposite wall looking at her with his dark, piercing eyes. His long legs were crossed at the ankle, his cutoff jeans hung low on his hips and his arms were crossed over his bare chest. The beauty of his body made her want to gasp again.

"I'm sorry," he said, looking at her down-caste eyes. "Whatever it is that I've said or done or not said or not done, I apologize. Now, can we go back to bed and get some sleep, please?"

"Shouldn't we be getting back? It is a workday, remember," she said fluidly, trying to pass by him.

Roderick stopped her with a gentle hand on her arm. "Yes, it is a work day and yes, we should get back to town, but neither of us has had much sleep in the last twenty-four hours. By now Kelley is in the office. She'll handle everything very well until I get back. Besides, I wouldn't be any good to anyone today. I want you back in my arms again and back in my bed," he said softly.

"Is that an order, *boss*?" she flashed.

The question took him by surprise. "An order? Of course not!" he said, narrowing his eyes and knitting his brow.

"Then, if it is a request, I'll pass."

"Jai, I don't understand. What's gotten into you?"

She turned her eyes to meet his gaze. "Marriage means something to me. For a moment I forgot that fact. I don't intend to compound my mistake or repeat it!"

"Mistake? You call what happened between us a mistake? It was anything but that for me, Jai. It was the first right thing that's happened for me since my daughters were born. I won't let you lessen the value of what we shared."

"What we shared has ended. Please, let go of me. If you're too tired to pilot this boat back, then I'll wake you when it's time to dock her," she said coolly, looking away from him.

"Jai, please . . ." he started, but he sensed that she would not be swayed. He let go of her. "I've made breakfast. You eat, I'll get us home, but this isn't over between us, Jai, and you can take that to the bank!" he said vehemently as he headed for the deck.

Roderick wanted to shout or do something to relieve the tension in his chest. Passion of two types—ire and desire—melded together wrenching his gut. Her distancing herself from him caused a shudder to shake him. For many of his thirty-six years he practiced control of his body and his emotions on the basketball court and in the boardroom. Now in the space of a few weeks, his practiced and finely-honed skill was illusive. He held his breath momentarily and let it out slowly. He turned the vessel's ignition and the engines roared into action.

It was nearly noon when Roderick guided *The Mighty Magic Heat* into his berth in his back yard. He was still bewildered over JaiHonnah's sudden change in demeanor. Before he could stop her to discuss what was going on, she disembarked and walked swiftly through the yard past other employees having lunch at tables by the pool. He glanced up and saw Monique standing on the bedroom-level deck in a stiff stance, arms akimbo glaring at him.

"Damn it." He groaned aloud in frustration.

Some of his employees tied off the boat as he climbed down the ladder.

"Good trip?" John Seals asked with a broad grin.

Roderick didn't answer. He tossed his oversized carryall over his left shoulder, dug his fists into his pockets, and walked past the employees without a word.

"Hold all my calls, Kelley," he snapped as he breezed past her in the office reception area and climbed the steps two at a time.

"JRock, Monique is . . ." Kelley started.

"I know! I'll handle it!" he grumbled still moving up the steps.

At the second level he stopped in front of JaiHonnah's office. The door was closed and so were the vertical blinds. He started to enter then remembered that Monique was upstairs. He wanted to see JaiHonnah badly, but decided to deal with Monique first. He took a deep breath and climbed the remaining steps to his residential level of the building. Monique was pacing the living room floor like a lioness stalking for prey.

"What was so important that you had to send the Coast Guard after me?" he snapped, not looking at her as he walked pass her and directly into his bedroom.

Monique followed. "You slept with her, didn't you?" she flashed, her voice laced with venom.

Roderick tossed his carryall onto the bed, turned and swiftly closed the distance between him and Monique. He towered over her and dug his hands into his pocket. "What do you want, Monique?"

Monique's face contorted in shock as she back peddled away from him until her back was against the wall, fear still evident in her eyes. "That bitch, I want you to call her off!"

"*Who?*" he railed.

"I mean Vivian Jackson, your lawyer. I want you to call her off."

"No! Now, is that all?" Monique did not answer. "Fine! Then get hell out and stay out!" he bellowed.

He held open his bedroom door for her to leave. She quickly exited and he slammed the door behind her. His temples pulsating, he headed for the shower.

JaiHonnah was too agitated to focus. She heard the shouting between Roderick and Monique above her head, but couldn't make out what was being said. Then a door slammed and everything grew quiet. Had they made up so quickly? Had Roderick lied and told Monique that nothing happened between them? Of course he would try to convince her. She was the mother of their daughters, and, JaiHonnah remembered, Monique had threatened to take Shelly and Shelby away from Roderick if he was unfaithful to her. Roderick loved his daughters and would do anything to keep them, including convincing Monique that nothing happened. She glimpsed Monique standing on the deck when they docked, but she had not made eye contact with her or the employees whose telling glances and grins assured her that they knew what had happened between her and her boss—their boss and Monique's husband. She felt the humiliation more gravely when she entered the office and all conversation seemed to cease. She glimpsed Kelley's warm smile, but did not stop to talk. Instead she went straight to her office, closed the door and drew the blinds. She turned on her computer and tried to focus on her work, but it was no use.

How could she be so stupid? she wondered. Was she so starved for affection that she'd broken the cardinal rules on never sleeping with the boss or another woman's husband? She felt bare and naked. Everyone in the company would know. She wanted to run away and hide like before, after her marriage ended. Maybe that was the answer. Maybe leaving the city would serve the same purpose. She wanted to go home to see her grandmother. She was always there for her before; her moral support system. JaiHonnah lifted the telephone receiver to call and noticed an electronic message flash across her computer screen. She replaced the receiver and opened the e-mail. It was from Lionel Porter asking her to call him at his hotel. She picked up the receiver again and placed the call.

"Well, Mrs. Chapman, I'm glad that I had this opportunity to talk with you. I would like to meet with you tonight, say eight o'clock at my hotel. The food here is very good. What do you say? Can you make it?"

"Could we perhaps do this tomorrow, Mr. Porter?"

"I'm sorry, but I'm leaving for Atlanta in the morning very early. I'm very excited about your work and, if it is at all possible, tonight would be better for me."

JaiHonnah agreed reluctantly and hung up the telephone. She was already running on raw fiber and very weary from her erotic, all-night experience with Roderick. She put her fingers to her lips. "Roderick," she whispered. The thought of him was too overpowering. Her heart beat wildly with the vision of him making love to her. She gathered her things and left the office.

Roderick turned over in his bed and looked at the clock on the nightstand. It was 5:45 in the afternoon. He had not intended to sleep that long, but he was tired, angry and, above all, confused. He closed his eyes recalling, with a growing need in him, the previous night and morning with JaiHonnah, how they had made love during the storm. Incredible love, he thought. He could see the excitement and feel the heat in her warm, responsive body. She couldn't just turn that feeling, that heat on and off like a light switch. It had to have meant something to her. Something more than just a roll in the sack. A one-night stand. That's how she was treating it, though, and what was the "boss" business all about? She wasn't the type of woman to sleep her way up the career ladder. She had talent, a real gift and a good eye for capturing what a property needed to bring it to life or to make it stand out. He rolled on to his stomach crossing his arms under his chin. What had he done to make her change so drastically? He thought back over every blissful moment. They had a wonderful time, he thought. An experience beyond belief. A defining moment in time. He was looking forward to her spending the rest of the day and night in his arms. What had spooked her? He had to have answers and he wasn't going to get them laying in bed—alone.

Later, Roderick descended the steps and went to JaiHonnah's office. He knocked and then entered. She was gone. He went down to reception and saw Kelley still working in one of the conference rooms.

"Hi, sleepyhead." She smiled as he walked in.

"When did Jai leave?" he asked, leaning forward on the back of one of the conference room chairs.

"Well, hello, Kelley, how was work today? Did I have any important calls?" she said teasingly. Roderick smiled slightly and she noticed. "That's better. Now do you want to start over or meetings?"

"Hi, Kelley, I love you, now, when did Jai leave?"

"You've certainly got a one-track mind today," she said and smiled devilishly. When Roderick didn't return her smile, she continued, "Early. I'm not sure of the exact time."

"Did she leave a message for me?"

"Nope, she barely said good-bye. Must have been some storm," she said and smiled with merriment in her voice.

Roderick glanced at her. "You are talking about the weather, aren't you?"

"Now what do you think?" she asked, giving him a fleeting look.

Roderick didn't answer her question. "I'll be in my office," he said, going toward the door.

"JRock," Kelley called to him. He turned with his hand still on the door. "I hope it works out—for both of you," she said soberly.

Roderick left without a word. He hoped so too.

Chapter 9

JaiHonnah entered the posh Mayflower Hotel on Connecticut Avenue. She appreciated the Concierge Desk in the lobby where a young man stood talking on the telephone. He quickly ended his conversation.

"Good evening, Ms. . .?" he said.

"Good evening. Mr. Lionel Porter's room?" she asked.

"Uh, your name?"

"Mrs. Chapman."

The man picked up the telephone and dialed. Shortly, he said, "Mr. Porter, Mrs. Chapman has arrived.... Yes, sir. Right away, sir..." he said as he hung up. "Mr. Porter is in Suite 415, Mrs. Chapman. You may go right up. He's expecting you."

"Please call Mr. Porter again and ask him to meet me in the Lobby Lounge," she said coolly. She turned on her heels and walked away.

JaiHonnah didn't have long to wait before Porter entered the lounge and came directly to her table. She rose when he approached and extended her hand.

"Mrs. Chapman," he said, taking her outstretched hand and raising it to his lips.

JaiHonnah quickly removed her hand. There was something about him that made her more than a little uncomfortable. His unctuous smile. His posturing. She was going to have none of that from him or anyone else.

"Good evening, Mr. Porter," she said in a professional tone.

"You know, Mrs. Chapman, I have a very expensive dinner waiting for us in my suite," he said, breathing sensuously.

"Thank you, but I've already had dinner, Mr. Porter, so shall we move on to the reason for this meeting?"

Porter appeared taken aback, the grin slipping from his lips. "Mrs. Chapman, may I call you JaiHonnah?"

"Mrs. Chapman will do just as well," she said dispassionately.

Porter reared back in his seat, obviously calculating his next move, JaiHonnah thought. She had seen his type before. She put on her this-is-only-about-business face and fixed an unyielding stare. Lionel Porter wasn't a particularly tall man, but thin and wiry. His rakish countenance was too pretty to be considered handsome, but it was clear that he thought himself irresistible. This time she was not going to be struck by a handsome face and a masculine physique. She appreciated the fact that Porter paled by comparison to Roderick in every dimension. *Roderick.* She had to stop thinking about him and comparing every man she saw to him. Washington had a wealth of handsome men, but of those she met since her return to the states, none made the grade as compared to Roderick Baylor. She had to put what happened between them behind her. Porter apparently settled on his next move, she thought, as he leaned forward on the table.

"Chapman? Uh, are you, by any chance, married to the international financier, Calvin Chapman, formerly the owner of Chapman Forest Products?"

The question caught her off guard, but she recovered quickly. Obviously, Porter had done some investigation of her background. Probably Googled her. Maybe he even knew her father since an arm of her father's conglomerate was also in construction. "Mr. Porter, when we met at the gala, you said that you had seen my work. That was not accurate, was it?"

The complete slippage of the grin on his face confirmed her suspicions. He cleared his throat. "Well, actually, no, I hadn't, but I had your submissions sent by overnight mail the very next day. I've studied them very closely. How did you know?"

She dodged his question, just as she had done before, by asking one of her own. "Now that you've had an opportunity to study my work, what are your views?"

"Mrs. Chapman, you do go to the heart of a matter."

"Your time is very valuable, Mr. Porter, and so is mine. So, about your views..."

Porter finally launched into a serious discussion.

* * *

Roderick turned off his computer and sat back in his chair. He glanced at the clock. It was eight-fifteen. He had last called JaiHonnah at eight and gotten no answer, just the voice mail instructing the caller to leave a message. Hell, he had left half-a-dozen messages already! She hadn't returned any of his calls. Enough was enough! Roderick rose from his chair, slammed off the light and headed for his garage. He peeled rubber as he headed for the Watergate Complex. Only the alternating red and blue flashing klieg lights in his rearview mirror and a siren slowed his progress. He pulled to the curb, turned off the engine and reached for his license and registration.

A few minutes later, the police officer handed the ticket to him for speeding and running a red light and then asked. "Mr. Baylor, would you mind giving me your autograph? I mean, it's not for me, it's for my boy. He's thirteen and you're one of his role models."

Roderick slumped in his seat. "What's your boy's name?" he asked as he reached for a note pad.

"Chad, Chadwick Hochstein Jr.," the officer said proudly.

"He's a very lucky boy to have a role model like you for a father," Roderick said as he scribbled a long note telling the boy exactly that.

The officer looked at the note and smiled broadly. "Thank you, Mr. Baylor, and please, drive carefully and responsibly. We don't have that many high-profile figures in this town that young kids can appreciate. We need to keep the ones who do deserve high praise alive and well."

"Thanks, I'll remember that," Roderick said as the officer left. He looked at the officer's name on the ticket, picked up his iPhone, and flipped to his voice recorder app. "Note: Two front-row, center court tickets for Chadwick Hochstein Senior and Junior to the Wizards' opening season home game." He turned off the phone and started the engine.

When he arrived at the Watergate Complex he saw a former senator and his wife leaving the building. They nodded briefly in recognition. The desk clerk, for the price of an autograph, confirmed that JaiHonnah was not at home and remembered seeing her go out earlier in the evening. Roderick looked at his watch and decided to await her return. He was determined to talk with her before the day ended. Twenty-four hours earlier they were locked together in a blissful union. He didn't want that to be the last time they were together, regardless of her marital status. They would just have to work that out together. Chapman didn't deserve a woman like JaiHonnah. Why she hadn't divorced that bastard was a mystery, but one Roderick was going to solve.

* * *

JaiHonnah rose from the chair in the lounge and extended her hand to Porter. This time he shook it without fanfare.

"You'll be hearing from us, Mrs. Chapman. I'm sure that once you've seen our operation and the potential that it offers you, you won't be hesitant to accept our proposal. The City of Atlanta has become as vibrant as any city in the world. Making a move there will not work to your disadvantage. I know that we can offer you what you're looking for, and the question of salary is no question at all."

"Thank you, Mr. Porter, I'm completely familiar with Atlanta. As my résumé indicates, I did my undergraduate work at Spelman, but as I've also indicated, I'm not in a position to accept any offer at this moment. I will come to Atlanta at my first opportunity for a visit and interview with your partners. That's the best that I can agree to at this time. Thank you for making the time to see me, but it's getting late, so I'll say good night."

"I'll be looking forward to that day. Good night, Mrs. Chapman. It's been a pleasure talking with you." He smiled, taking her hand in both of his.

JaiHonnah left the hotel and hopped into a waiting taxicab. "The Watergate, please," she said to the driver. Then she settled back in the seat to ponder Porter's generous offer. It wasn't the money that interested her, it was the opportunity for a partnership in a very prestigious corporation—and, more important, a way to break her attraction to one J. Roderick Baylor. Out of sight, out of mind, she thought.

Hell, who was she kidding? He had rocked her world and turned it upside down. Maybe that's what other women had meant by the term *penis power*. Roderick had it, alright—and then some! God, she lamented, how did I get myself into this fix? A month earlier J. Roderick Baylor was just a name on a text message. She expected that he was some old, balding, fat cat. Not the Black Adonis she saw parting the noise, dust and dirt with his presence. Not the eloquent orator who held her and thousands of others spellbound amid an evening filled with dynamic speeches. Not the tender, loving man she witnessed with his daughters. Not the man whose brute force landed on Calvin with agility and speed. And certainly not the man who took her to his bed with such care, warmth and tenderness that her heart still skipped a beat just thinking about what they shared. JaiHonnah exhaled slowly. She had to make a move. It was inevitable.

Other notables came in and out of the Watergate lobby as Roderick sat in the bar waiting for JaiHonnah to return. He chatted briefly with some, and signed autographs for others while he waited. However, he kept his eyes on his watch too. It was nearly ten-thirty. Where could she be so late? he wondered. Finally, a taxicab pulled up and he saw her get out. It pleased him that she was alone and looked more beautiful than he remembered. Her blinding beauty more exotic than before. His body hummed a needful refrain when she entered the lobby.

"Good evening, Mrs. Chapman," the desk clerk said stopping her as JaiHonnah started to pass the desk. "A package arrived for you while you were out," the man said, handing a long, white oblong box of flowers to her.

"Thank you." She took the box.

"Oh, and there's a gentleman waiting to see you. He's over there in the lounge." The man nodded toward the lobby bar.

JaiHonnah turned and nearly gasped. It gave her heart another jolt when her eyes locked with Roderick's. *Damn, why does he have to be so handsome?* His eyes were washing over her like a tidal wave and she felt that tingling sensation growing in her core. He stood with his strong legs slightly apart and his hands in his pockets. He didn't need that crewneck, cable-knit, navy-blue, bulky sweater pushed up at the sleeves to remind her that there was a massive, hard-as-rock chest and abdomen beneath it. Nor could his designer slacks hide how much he appreciated the sight of her. The memory of his powerful, nude torso was indelibly etched on her brain. A man like him was too dangerously appealing for his own good, but he was cutting her no slack with his masculinity, handsomeness or sensuous attire. *Lord, give me strength!* She approached the Rock of Gibraltar.

"Jai, we have to talk," Roderick said an octave lower than his normal tone without a smile anywhere in the vicinity of his face.

"Is this about work?" she coolly asked.

"You know it isn't."

"Then I think we've said it all."

"Well, you thought wrong!" he said firmly. "We're going to straighten out a few things tonight! If you want to hold this conversation here in the lobby, then so be it! But lady, we are going to talk!"

JaiHonnah glimpsed faces turning to look at them. A congressman and his wife were coming into the lobby followed by several reporters who were looking at her and Roderick.

"Lower your voice, Roderick," she said. "You're not on a job site!"

"Then I suggest that we move this discussion to your condo or I'll have a wrecking crew down here in fifteen minutes flat and make it a job site!"

He might just do it, she thought as she stared into those deep, furious pools he called eyes. She had the distinct impression that he would not be dismissed. She relented.

Roderick took up a position in the corner of the elevator diagonally across from JaiHonnah. He wouldn't and couldn't take his eyes off her. She was stunning in her autumn yellow silk-blend coatdress that kissed every sweet curve of her voluptuous body. He had explored every inch of her intoxicating frame. The spot below her right earlobe had sent shivers through her. He had suckled the tasty tips of her full breasts like a newborn babe for hours. The point behind her left knee on the back of her long, firm thighs made her moan with delight and her sweet spot where he drew her sweet nectar made her call out his name in the heat of passion.

However, the box of flowers in her arms gave him reason to pause. Also, where could she have been for hours looking that radiant? She was more beautiful than any woman had a right to be.

The elevator stopped, and they got off. He followed her down the hall watching the mesmerizing sway of her hips, the wisps of hair dangling down her neck around the wide copper choker, the perfectly shaped legs in her brown alligator pumps and the small matching handbag that hung from her shoulder and bounced against her nicely rounded hips. She was irresistible and his body knew it—and showed it.

JaiHonnah's hands were trembling when she reached into her purse to find the electronic door key. She finally found it and tried to insert it in the slot of the door, but she was shaking too badly, and it slipped out of her fingers and fell to the floor. Roderick bent slowly, picked up the key and handed it to her. She still had difficulty inserting it until his hand covered hers and helped her guide the key into the small slot. He was standing so close to her that she could feel his heat and revel in his intoxicating, manly scent. Her knees were feeling as weak as water, and her heart was pounding against her chest cavity like taiko drums. She leaned forward against the door, but it did not open until Roderick turned the knob. She nearly bolted into the wide, marble vestibule and didn't stop until she was in the kitchen. He hadn't spoken a word since they left the lobby, but she knew that he was monitoring every move that she made. She had to be strong. She had to be calm. Most of all, she had to be professional.

"You wanted to talk with me about something?" she asked with her back to him as she half filled a Waterford vase from the kitchen tap.

"Who are the flowers from?"

"You came here to ask me about flowers?" She turned with a factious edge in her voice. "Well, Mr. Baylor, that's none of your business."

"Oh, so now we're back to the social amenities again, are we, *Mrs.* Chapman? Strange, I thought that we had decided to dispense with the social graces long *before* I made love with you! *After* we made love, I would have thought that plain ole honey and baby would suffice! You pick the proper noun, *Mrs.* Chapman!"

She wondered whether he heard her gulp or noticed that she was about to drop the flower vase from her trembling hands. Gingerly, she set the vase down on the centerpost work area and tried to compose herself. She took a deep, calming breath.

"Look, we had a little—I mean, we let things get out of control. Rather, I let things get out of hand. I take complete responsibility for my actions, and I apologize for my behavior, but ...," she said nervously fiddling with the flower box, but not daring to look up into his eyes.

Roderick covered the expanse between them and spun her around trapping her between him and the centerpost kitchen island. He wasn't touching her, but his long, strong arms and hands gripped the countertop on either side of her, blocking any means of escape.

"Look at me." he ordered. "Those damn flowers can wait. Now tell me what I've done to make you act this way. Are you afraid of me? Did I hurt you? Do you hate me for wanting to make love with you? Is this what it's about? Was I too aggressive when I made love to you? Was I insensitive to your needs? Did I not please you in some way? Talk to me, Jai. I don't understand what's going on."

He wasn't to be trifled with, this she knew. She saw his body bobbing and weaving like a cobra trying to find her eyes, which she hid from him.

His body had stiffened and the muscles in his jaw tightened. She couldn't look at him. She rested her eyes on the bulky cables in his sweater. She had to summon the courage to speak. She seized on the only plausible explanation that she could offer.

"It's me!" she shouted. "It's this. This sex thing. It's wrong. It isn't a condition of my contract that I have to sleep with the boss! After all, I am married and you...well, you have a family. If this behavior is what I can expect to be subjected to . . .well, then, uh, well maybe it would be better that I resigned from your company. I've had an offer that I'm considering and..."

Roderick backed away with silent rage and total confusion fixed on his granite-like face. It wasn't just annoyance that she sensed in his demeanor; he was furious, but he wasn't going to intimidate her, she vowed to herself.

"Don't threaten me, Jai. I'm no one you want to fool with. You find sleeping with me so repulsive, so disgusting, so loathsome, then don't give it another thought. I won't make a fool of myself again. Sex is *not* a part of your contract, but you do *have* a contract unless I choose to fire you. You're obligated to provide your good and faithful *professional* talents exclusively to Baylor Construction, its parent corporation, and its subsidiaries for one year. Read the fine print, lady. That means until Labor Day next year. If you try to break that contract, I'll haul you into court so fast I'll leave skid marks. And, oh, by the way, *Mrs.* Chapman . . ." he swept her up into his arms in a New York second and kissed her with such passion and power that her toes curled and a needful whimper grew from her throat. Then he let her go just as quickly. *"Get a divorce!"*

In an instant, Roderick was gone. JaiHonnah jumped when the front door slammed shut, but otherwise stood rooted for some time to the spot where he kissed her. Tiny shivers engulfed her body and fired her imagination. She was in rapt wonder of how that man, with his flagrant sensuality, could so totally fire her desire with a kiss like no man had ever done before. His scent was still hanging on to her senses. She bit nervously at her fleshy bottom lip, trying to regain her composure.

That was a futile effort. Slowly, her trembling legs buckled, and she slid down the cabinet to the floor.

* * *

"Hello, Hawk House."

"Ezra, is that you?" JaiHonnah asked.

"Ms. JaiHawk! Now how are you, little girl?" the old, manservant asked, laughing.

"Not bad, Ezra, but I'm not a little girl anymore," she said lightly.

"You'll always be a little girl to me, Ms. JaiHawk. I can still remember the times you used to jump up on that old black stallion and go flying cross the fields. You went quick as the wind in a prairie dust storm," he said and laughed. "Hair flyin' in the breeze, your face to the sky, arms wide open and you laughing like a loon. Never did take much to you not usin' a saddle like girls 'spose to do. Darndest thing seein' you straddlin' Hawk, and you a girl at that! Couldn't nothin' catch you and old Hawk though. Nothin' but the sunbeams."

JaiHonnah laughed, remembering those days. "Ezra, you don't forget anything," she said and laughed again. "I know it's late, but is my daddy there?"

"Yessum, he round heres some wheres. Can't tell 'bout Big Jake."

"Would you tell him I'm on the telephone, Ezra?"

"Sure thing, Ms. JaiHawk. You be still now and I'll go fetch him."

"Thanks, Ezra. I love you."

"Back at you, lil' dahlin'."

Shortly Jake came to the telephone.

"That you, dahlin'?"

"Yes, Daddy, it's me. I'm calling to thank you for the thirty yellow roses. They're beautiful, but my birthday isn't for another two weeks."

"That ain't all, dahlin'. Got somethin' else comin' at you for your birthday and to show you how proud I am of you for receiving your doctorate degrees. The roses were just to say I miss you."

"Daddy, I don't need anything else. I'm not too happy about this birthday anyway and, as for my degrees, well, it's only pieces of paper. I've still got to prove myself worthy of being called JaiHonnah Reise Hawkins, Doctor of Architecture and Doctor of Civil Engineering. I'd really rather not make a big deal out of either event. That doesn't mean that I deserve a present. The fact that you love me and are proud of being my father are present enough."

"Ain't nothin' but a little ole biddy thing, dahlin'. You'll see. Now when you comin' home so I can show you how proud I am?"

"I have a job, Daddy, a real career. I'm a grown-up person now, remember? I have responsibilities and a life to lead."

The long pause let JaiHonnah know that her father was getting his emotions under control. The fact that he loved and cherished her as he did all of his children was evident.

"Ain't been leadin' too much life, I hear tell. Let me find you a husband so you can come on home where you belong and give me some grandbabies."

"Oh, no you don't, Jake Hawkins," she fussed, amused. "If I ever want a husband again, I can find my own, thank you very much."

"Well, when you gonna go get him? You know my time is gettin' awful short round this earth. 'Fore too long I'm gonna be goin' to meet my maker."

"Daddy, the devil got into you a long time ago." She laughed at his huff. "So don't try to twist me around your little finger about 'going to see your maker'."

Jake's devilish laughter boomed over the telephone. "You're too swift for me, dahlin'."

"Yeah, I'll bet, and just how'd you know what kind of life I'm leading anyway?"

"See what I mean? Thought that one got by ya'."

"Nothing is going to get by me where you're concerned. Now how'd you know?"

"Spent the weekend on that boy's boat, did ya?" He laughed. "Why don't he buy himself a real boat stead of that little bitsy thing?"

"Daddy! It's not a 'little bitsy thing.' It's almost as large as your yacht. Have you still got someone spying on me or something?"

"The eyes of Texas are always upon you, little dahlin'. Now you remember that when you go foolin' around with them little boys up there in D.C. They ain't got no leather in their britches! You're one little lady who's gonna take a heap of tamin'. Takes a real man to stand up next to you," he said and hooted. "You cotton to this boy or what?"

"You're up in my business again," she warned. She didn't know how much Jake learned about Roderick, but she had to be as cagey as her father to keep him from finding out about her feelings for him. "But I'll answer you this time: No, there's nothing going on. Besides, he's a married man with two little girls."

"'Sides that, what's wrong with the boy?"

"He's not a *boy*. He's a wonderful man," she fussed.

"Alright, if he's what you want, I'll buy him for you. How much you think he's gonna cost me?"

"Don't you even try it. He's not a man who can be bought, and I wouldn't want him if he could be bought. Plus you taught me that if I have to ask the price of something I don't need it."

"Oh, so you do want him, huh?"

"Good-bye, Daddy," she huffed, then demurely said. "Thanks again for the flowers, and don't send anything else, including a husband."

Jake gave her another devilish laugh. "Good night, dahlin'."

* * *

It couldn't have happened twice in one night to any other person, Roderick swore, as Office Hochstein invited him to have a seat in his police cruiser. The ride to the precinct still wasn't enough to cool his ire, but sitting in a jail cell with other detainees eyeing his tush did get his mind off the lovely *Mrs.* Chapman. Attorney Bill Chandler, one of Vivian's law partners, and Chuck Montgomery, rescued him before he had to defend his honor against six Mike Tyson-looking gentlemen of questionable sexual orientation who all seemed to have the same or higher voice quality as Tyson and the same penchant for pinching butt. Roderick collected his belongings from the desk sergeant and approached Bill and Chuck.

"Needless to say, JRock, Vivian wasn't pleased to get a call from Officer Hochstein suggesting that she send a 'responsible individual' to get you out of jail and take you home," Bill said with a smirk.

"I only listed her as my attorney. I called Chuck to bail me out," Roderick said.

"Yes, we know, but when Hochstein saw one or two of the gentlemen from the press lurking around, he decided you might need a little more protection for your own good. Hochstein called Vivian and Vivian called me. Seventy miles per hour in a thirty-mile-per-hour zone, three red lights and two stop signs. Well, I think that does it for your driving privileges for a while, my friend. Looks like you'll be hiring a chauffeur. Good to see you contributing handsomely to the D.C. coffers too. They could use it. If I were you, though, I would have simply made a donation to the Police Boys and Girls Club."

"Alright, Bill. I get the point," Roderick said, sighing heavily.

"Well, buddy, give it your best OJ profile. You're about to meet your public," Chuck added solemnly.

"The press?"

"Full court," Bill warned. "Your official comment is, no comment," Bill advised and Roderick agreed.

Chapter 10

And in local news today comes a report that former basketball great turned prominent businessman, J. Roderick Baylor, affectionately known as JRock, was arrested late last night and charged with reckless endangerment and speeding. Shown here leaving the precinct with his attorney, William Chandler, and his good friend and former basketball star, Charles 'Chucky P' Montgomery, Mr. Baylor had no comment. No drugs or alcohol involvement were indicated in the police report. Could JRock find himself pounding hard rock and pulling hard time? Film at 11:00."

JaiHonnah sat fixed to the flat screen in horror as the report continued. God, what had she done to him? she lamented. Not only was she threatening to wreck his family in an illicit relationship, now she had caused him to almost kill himself. She shuddered at the thought. She had to go to him. She had to apologize for making him so angry. *What if something had happened? The girls. My God they might have lost their father!*

JaiHonnah crisscrossed Roderick's living room while waiting for him to come out of his bedroom. She was so nervous she couldn't stand still and so angry that she couldn't sit down. He emerged wearing a silk paisley robe.

"What the hell do you think you're doing, Roderick?" she launched into him.

Roderick held up one hand. "I don't have to hear it from you, too, Mrs. Chapman! I already know that what I've done was stupid and childish. I could have hurt someone racing around the streets like that!"

"Do you understand what you mean to me?" It slipped out, and she had to recover quickly, but she didn't do it fast enough. Roderick arched an eyebrow. "I mean, to the people who care about you, especially Shelly and Shelby? What could anyone say to them if you had ended up in an emergency room or worse, dead, instead of a jail cell? Did you think of that while you were tooling around in your Indy-500 exhibition? And another thing . . ." she ranted on uninterrupted for nearly five minutes while pacing the floor.

Finally, she stopped. Either she ran out of breath or admonitions. Roderick couldn't discern which and really didn't care. He was still angry with himself and her, but even in full temper, she was beautiful in the morning sunlight with her fresh, clear, clean skin; devastating beautiful eyes and sparkling white teeth. He had to turn away from her.

"Didn't take time to dry your hair this morning, Jai, huh?" he asked with a sideways glance.

"Roderick!" She huffed in frustration.

"Look, I've had some time to think about what you said. You're right. I have no right to expect you to sleep with me and I should not have imposed myself on you. It won't happen again. If you want to leave Baylor Construction, I'll release you from your contract. The choice is yours. As for the rest of it, well, I'm a grown man responsible for my behavior. You didn't make me do anything. I did the crime on my own. I deserve whatever punishment I get. I appreciate your concern, Mrs. Chapman, if that's what it is, but save it for someone who deserves it.

"Now, if you'll excuse me, I have to get dressed and your responsibility, Mrs. Chapman, depending on which way the wind is blowing today, is either to go to work or go home." He walked back into his bedroom and slammed the door.

Dismissed? she fumed silently in disbelief. *How dare he dismiss me! He doesn't know who he's fooling with! I'll show him! That man makes me so mad!*

JaiHonnah stormed into her office and slammed the door. She paced furiously until she heard a knock.

"Come in!" she yelled.

Kelley stuck her hand in waving a white handkerchief. Then she stuck her head in. "I surrender," she joked.

JaiHonnah couldn't help the small smile that grew. "Come on in, Kelley. The battle is over," she said, sighing.

"The question is, who's winning the war?"

"Life's a fragile thing, Kelley," JaiHonnah said somberly.

"Yeah, I know. JRock doesn't lose his temper often, and I've never seen him behave this way. He was out of sorts all afternoon yesterday after you two got back, and today—," her voice rose—, "Today he's been a real bear! Everyone's making a wide berth around him, including me. So what's going on between you two?"

"Nothing. Not a damn thing!"

"O-kay," she said, quickly raising both hands. "Looks like open warfare to me, but what do I know? I only work in the war zone. Seems like a lot of pent-up tension to me. Probably needs a little sexual healing," she said, floating out the door.

JaiHonnah pursed her lips and rolled her eyes.

Later in the day, Roderick and JaiHonnah came out of their respective offices at the same time and bumped into each other. Roderick crossed his arms over his chest.

"You're still here I see," he said, expressionless.

JaiHonnah looked away. "Of course I am. What did you expect?"

"I gave you the option of leaving with no strings attached."

"I fulfill my obligations. I'm no quitter."

"So you say," he quipped deep throated as he walked away and down the steps.

JaiHonnah hurried away in the opposite direction along the balcony, but she glimpsed the surprise on the faces of the other employees. She stopped, struck a pose, glaring back at them, and they quickly went about their tasks. She stifled the temptation to scream. Instead, she gnashed her teeth. *The man makes me furious!* Why did she let him get to her so? She had sex with him, that's all. No reason to make a big deal out of that. It wasn't as if they were lovers or anything. They just had an unguarded moment. It would pass, but he vexed her worse than Big Jake did. She shivered purposely. *Men!* Then the memory of that night of passion flooded over her. "Roderick," she whispered, touching her lips and closing her eyes.

Roderick walked through the backyard toward his boat. He hadn't taken the time to clean it after his last trip with JaiHonnah. He went into the galley and started tossing food from the refrigerator in a garbage bag. He cleaned and scrubbed until the galley was sparkling then he started in on the staterooms. He stripped the beds and dusted the furniture before he went to his cabin. When he pulled the sheet from his bed, he caught a whiff of JaiHonnah's perfume. He closed his eyes momentarily inhaling deeply. *Damn! I'm not going to start that again,* he chastised himself as he pulled the covers from the bed. So what if she's the most wonderful creature he'd ever met. It didn't matter that she made him come alive. He pulled the blanket from the floor and JaiHonnah's thongs and lacy white bra flew up at him. "Great! Just great!" he fumed. Her shorts and T-shirt were on the floor along with his. Starring at the lumps of damp clothes on the floor, his hand went to the railing above and gripped it. How they made love, he groaned in frustration. He sat on the bed, his back against the headboard. He pulled his knees up and rested his forehead against them. "JaiHonnah," he breathed.

Roderick was still in a black abyss as he sat on the deck of his yacht. His mind reached back to the days of his childhood, remembering the disenfranchisement he felt living on the other side of that same river. His parents made a good living for the time, but five children would put a strain on anyone's budget. He never felt like they were poor nor did he feel like they had money to burn. He remembered his mother's sorrow-filled face when she said that she couldn't give him money to go to his prom. He wanted to attend and ask the prettiest and most popular girl in the school, Rosalyn Hunter, to be his date. They eyed each other all year, but never really talked. He felt that he was all arms and legs then and not much to look at, but Rosalyn looked. College coaches and scouts were offering him outrageous sums of money and fancy cars, but he knew that the NCAA rules would not allow him to accept. Some of the NBA teams wanted him to forgo college and turn pro. He wanted an education, not just the money. When he told his best friend, Wesley Greenfield, about his dilemma with the prom, Wesley laughed and assured him that he'd be the badest dude in the joint. He hadn't asked Wesley how he was going to go to a prom without threads, scratch and most importantly, a bad ride, but Wesley assured him that he would.

On the strength of Wesley's word, Roderick had asked Rosalyn to be his date. She accepted, much to his surprise, and his seventeen-year-old hormones went into overdrive. On the night of the prom, he thought that he had died and gone to heaven when he appeared at Rosalyn's door clutching a corsage in a clear plastic container. She came down the steps in an organdy gown and floated into her living room. He remembered the smile that she gave him. It had taken his breath away.

The prom was great and all because of his friend Wesley. After the prom they went to breakfast at the International House of Pancakes, a twenty-four-hour restaurant. Later Wesley drove them to the beach near Annapolis, Maryland, and he and Rosalyn laid on the sand on a blanket while Wesley and his date, LaKesha Reynolds, busied themselves in the backseat of the car. Rosalyn had made the first approach to him, surprising him with her boldness. He hadn't given it much thought when she permitted him to have sex with her. For him it was the dawning of a new day. His first real experience with sex.

A few days later he saw her in the hallway at school and wanted to talk with her more, but she turned up her nose at him in such an air of superiority that it had stunned him. He didn't know what he did to deserve that kind of treatment. It hurt him deeply. The first girl that he really had sex with and she had rejected him without an explanation. To this day, he never learned what he had done, but the scar of that rejection had haunted him. JaiHonnah's rejection had brought it all back. It was a painful memory that made JaiHonnah's rejection even more devastating. What had he done to make her change so drastically? he wondered. With Rosalyn he finally just chalked it up to experience. With JaiHonnah it was an experience that he knew he would never forget.

Chapter 11

Vivian and Roderick walked out of the district attorney's office into a bustling hallway. District Attorney Paul Walker shook Roderick's hand and then Vivian's.

"I'm very glad that we could settle this matter amicably, Ms. Jackson, without expending the public's hard-earned tax dollars in a protracted trial. You're quite a worthy adversary in the courtroom."

"As are you, Mr. Walker. Please give my best to Mrs. Walker and tell her that I'll be happy to be the keynote speaker at her book club's luncheon. I'll put her group at the top of the list of my tour once the new book is published."

"I'll certainly do that, Ms. Jackson. She'll be very happy that you'll be able to make time for her. She and her club enjoyed your last two books as did I. They have all been quite thought-provoking and timely." He turned to Roderick. "It's been a distinct pleasure to meet you, Mr. Baylor. I followed your college career and your career in the NBA quite studiously. I'm glad that you've consented to be one of the basketball coaches for the Police Boys and Girls Clubs. Even after your community service tour is over, I hope that you'll continue to be involved."

"Yes, Mr. Walker, I believe that I will."

Roderick and Vivian walked away. "That was close," Roderick said, breathing a sigh of relief as he and Vivian headed toward the elevators. "I thought I would be looking at hard labor the way DA Walker started in on me."

"You would have been, if his wife didn't want me for her book club. She's been after me since my last book was published, but that's life in the big city. *Quid pro quo.*" She punched the down button for the elevator and then turned toward Roderick. "Look, I'm having a little dinner party at my place on Saturday night. You think that you could arrange your schedule to be there instead of in jail, say about eight o'clock sharp?"

"Yeah," Roderick said, snorting, "I owe you one. What's the occasion?"

"Birthday party for a friend."

"You know I'm not real high on social functions, but I'll be there. Uh, may I bring a guest?"

"Should I ask who?"

"If you did, you might not like my answer."

Vivian stilled. "Don't tell me, let me guess," she said, striking a defiant pose and pursing her lips. "One big, seven-foot cowboy from Pennsylvania."

"Uh, that's why you're such a good lawyer. You know what your client is thinking before he even forms the thought." He grinned, looping his arm around her shoulder and gave her a gentle squeeze.

"You must have been talking to the housemates. They've already made the request."

"And what did you opine, counselor?" he asked. When Vivian didn't answer, he asked again. "Well?"

"Seems to be nearly unanimous with one dissenting vote. Bring your man, if you must, but I'd strongly suggest that you bring a woman. Your reputation couldn't stand another blow at this point," she said facetiously as the elevator doors opened and they squeezed into the remaining space.

"Don't worry, Viv. I always let Chuck lead when we dance," he said, grinning.

The other elevator occupants' heads snapped in his direction. Vivian and Roderick eyed each other and could barely contain their laughter.

"Okay, Vivian, I'll be there. What time do you want me?" JaiHonnah asked, sighing.

"At nine, maybe later."

"You sure you don't want any help with this congressional gig?"

"No, it's catered. Just put on your glad rags. Something too sharp to sit in."

"Why all this fuss for a congressman you used to work for?"

"Politics, kid. Now, are you with me or are you with me?"

JaiHonnah laughed. "I said I'd be your co-hostess, didn't I?"

"Fine, and Jai, please try to act like you're enjoying yourself."

"Bye, Viv."

"See you Saturday night."

"Oh, Vivian, uh, did everything turn out okay for Roderick at the district attorney's office? I mean, nothing bad is going to happen to him, is it?"

"Why don't you ask him? He just dropped me off. He should be back in his office shortly."

"Well," she hesitated a beat, "we aren't exactly on speaking terms these days. Not since the night that he was arrested two weeks ago."

"Any particular reason you two aren't talking?"

"He could have killed himself, Vivian. I was so angry I could have spit."

"What did you have to do with his behavior that night?"

"I mean, well," JaiHonnah stumbled, "if you must know, we just had an argument at the condo. When he left, he was a little ticked off at me."

"A little?"

"Well, maybe more than a little. Didn't he tell you this?"

"Nope. Just told me that he went on a foolish rampage. Didn't explain why, and I didn't ask."

"I guess, in a way, it was all my fault."

"I hope that you two can settle your differences soon."

"Why, what's going on?"

"I don't need to tell you that Baylor Construction has some very big development projects coming up, and Roderick's going to need all the help he can get to make it work. For some time, he's been thinking about restructuring his company, maybe taking on some partners or taking the company public to secure an infusion of capital."

"He talked about this briefly in the staff meetings, but I didn't realize that these projects could be pivotal for him."

"Could position him to jump into the big leagues or break him. Everyone in the construction industry, as well as the financial markets, is watching his movements to get the inside scoop on what he's going to do and how. It's a very competitive industry."

"Yes, I know. Daddy used to say that there're a lot of captains of the construction industry holding up the corner stones of some major building sites."

"As far as I know, no one wants to give JRock cement boots for Christmas, but they do want to know what's going to be under his Christmas tree."

JaiHonnah and Vivian spoke for a few more minutes. As JaiHonnah hung up the telephone she heard the familiar happy voices of the twins in the hallway. She rose from her desk and went toward the door expecting them to come barreling in as they usually had a habit of doing. They passed by her door, and she heard Roderick's deep voice distinctly tell the twins not to disturb her because she was working. The twins questioned him, but he offered no explanation that she could hear as he left the building with his girls. It was not clear in her mind why his refusal to let the girls visit with her hurt her so deeply, but it did. She thoroughly enjoyed the little unguided missiles. They were no bother. A pleasant sharing had developed between them, and she missed it. She missed them---all of them. Her eyes misted, and she stifled the desire to cry. She felt a strange yearning unfamiliar to her.

Roderick's manner had not been unfriendly of late, just nondescript. That bothered her too. She missed the easy conversations that they had before that fateful day when they crossed the line and made love on his yacht. Now they were what she had asked for—business associates, employer/employee—nothing more.

Roderick tucked the girls into their child-safety seats in the back of his SUV.

"All safe, ladies?" he asked, smiling at them. They giggled when he gave them both sloppy kisses.

He had chided himself for spending so little time with his daughters, for spending so much time thinking about JaiHonnah and wanting to be with her. He had to get himself back on track. Get back to the point in his life where it was comfortable for him and his girls. No more excuses, he thought. No more trying to find reasons for being in JaiHonnah's presence. His close brush with the law proved to him that he couldn't handle what he was feeling for JaiHonnah, and remain the man that he thought himself to be. A man who didn't need a woman as a permanent fixture in his life. A man who didn't need the touch, embrace or the full-time love of a woman.

Sex was another thing entirely. JaiHonnah had awakened something inside of him that he buried long ago—the need for sexual copulation and gratification. Now his physical needs were aroused and were not to be denied. Knowing that he would have to make time in his life to satisfy his sexual urges, the question was with whom? There were, of course, women in the office, some of whom made sexual overtures to him in the past, which he ignored or directly rejected. He had to admit that there were women outside of his office staff who said that they were attracted to him, but again he deferred to avoid entanglements. These women were looking for more than just an occasional roll in the sack, and that he was not ready for. Washington was full of beautiful, dynamic, and independent women who would not attach a great deal of importance to a purely physical relationship, he thought. At least he believed that to be the case. He hadn't been "out there" in such a long time that he didn't know what was available, but he was going to find out. This time he would make sure that they were "available." Definitely no married women and definitely not JaiHonnah Reise Chapman.

Chapter 12

All the lights were ablaze in the huge, stately, corner house in the wealthy and fashionable Georgetown area of Washington, D.C. The four-level brownstone sat on the edge of Rock Creek Park, a very gracious old property built before the turn of the 18th century and refurbished to accommodate a more modern standard of living. One of Vivian's brothers, Air Force pilot Benjamin Alexander, owned the house and renovated the interior to accommodate his single lifestyle. Later, when he was redeployed to California, he leased the house to Vivian while she attended Georgetown Law Center. Vivian in turn rented five of the six bedrooms to other law school students. She also refurbished the basement into a four-bedroom apartment and rented it to a homeless woman from Peru with her two young children and a Navajo Native American law student.

JaiHonnah got out of the taxicab and stood for a moment before she approached the house. She reflected on the many good memories that she shared with Vivian and her eclectic bunch of house mates during holidays and summer vacations. Vivian and Derrick Jackson, a famous, former professional basketball player come noted pediatrician met during the time that Vivian was in law school. They married the summer after she graduated and passed the bar. Their wedding was held at the National Cathedral and the reception in the backyard of the Georgetown house. It was more like a yard party than a formal event. Derrick was already an established pediatrician and moved Vivian into his condo at the Watergate Complex with the children that they adopted. Less than a year after their marriage, Derrick was dead, and JaiHonnah knew that her friend still grieved his loss. Vivian, rather than stay in Derrick's Watergate condo with too many lost hopes and dreams moved back into the Georgetown house after Derrick's funeral. Now JaiHonnah was living in the condo that Vivian and Derrick had once shared.

She rang the doorbell and a man, clad in a butler's uniform, opened the door.

"Good evening, Madame," he said with a slight nod of his head.

"Good evening," JaiHonnah replied in a similar manner.

She entered and the butler took her wrap.

"Everyone is in the East Salon, miss," he said.

JaiHonnah went to the double doors and opened them.

"Happy birthday!" everyone yelled at her.

JaiHonnah was taken aback, not to mention nearly scared out of her wits when forty or more people yelled, whistled or hooted in unison. Her eyes went directly to Vivian's smug grin. JaiHonnah narrowed her eyes at her college friend and scowled.

"You tricked me!" she fussed, a grin edging her lips.

"Now you didn't think that we were going to let you get by the big one unscathed, did you?" Vivian said and laughed.

"A Happy Meal at McDonald's would have sufficed, Vivian."

Everyone laughed and suddenly office friends, close old school BFFs, like Tina Justice, Cheryl Lawrence, and Kristen Bryant, sorority sisters, acquaintances, and men she had known from other colleges in and around Atlanta whom she had not seen in years surrounded her. They sang an up-tempo version of *"Happy Birthday"* to her, and a blush rose to her face. She spotted Roderick standing back from the crowd next to Savannah Logan, another college acquaintance. She remembered Savannah very well. They were sorority sisters. Savannah won the Miss Spelman Contest in their senior year, while she was third runner-up. Savannah was voted Miss All Everything, too. She heard that Savannah went to medical school after college, but she hadn't kept up with her much, like she hadn't kept up with so many people from her life before marrying Calvin. Seeing Savannah again did bring out her competitive spirit though. In college, they battled each other for so many things that she lost count. Savannah was tall, too, but not as tall as her. She had naturally brown-blond hair and cool, light-brown eyes with a cappuccino-rich complexion. Savannah exuded a lush and provocative demeanor, JaiHonnah recalled, and the long-sleeve, silk sheath in burnt orange flattered her complexion and her body. The passage of time only improved on Savannah's stunning good looks and sculptured form, JaiHonnah noted. She couldn't pull her gaze away from Roderick and Savannah as he smiled at something Savannah said. JaiHonnah found him more irresistible than the first time she met him.

She made her wish, cut the cake, and gave a brief speech about reaching thirty. She had declined to open the mountain of gifts recalling what pranksters some of her old friends were. There was no telling what might pop out of the gaily wrapped packages. When the music began, provided by Roderick's brother, a popular disc jockey on XM Radio and MTV, every man in the room asked her to dance—every man except one: Roderick. He and Savannah seemed to have been engrossed in a conversation all evening. Roderick had barely even looked at her, she thought.

He looked fabulous in his dark blue Adolfo blazer as he rested his arm on the fireplace mantel holding a drink in one hand. His white, band-collar shirt rimmed his muscular neck and perfectly outlined his broad firm chest. Her eyes went to his gray trousers which didn't mask his erection very well, she noticed, as he smiled at Savannah and laughed, too, at whatever she was saying. They were talking so close together that one might suspect them of hatching some conspiracy, JaiHonnah thought. She noticed that Roderick asked the deejay to play *"Feel the Fire"* and then he asked Savannah to dance. Savannah's arms circled Roderick's neck exactly the way that JaiHonnah had that night on his yacht. Roderick's arms rested low on Savannah's waist, and they talked together throughout the record and into the next.

"Care to dance, Sweet Cheeks?" Chuck asked from behind her.

She turned and smiled broadly at him. "I thought you'd never ask."

Chuck swept her into his arms. "You're going to stare a hole through JRock and Savannah, Jai," he whispered against her ear.

"Oh," she said, embarrassed to be caught monitoring Roderick's behavior like a jealous wife. She thought that her glances were more furtive. "It just seems strange to see him flirting. I mean, he's so serious when he's in the office."

"A man's got to do what a man's got to do," Chuck said as they danced. "A woman too, for that matter."

"You know Savannah?"

"Sure. She's on staff at Georgetown Medical. She's been there for about five years. Did her residency there and then went into practice in Derrick's office. After Derrick died Vivian offered Savannah a full partnership in Derrick's medical practice."

"What's her field, Chuck?"

"Obstetrics and gynecology. Very competent woman, but I thought that you two knew each other."

"We were in undergrad together at Spelman. I haven't seen her since we graduated," she said, glimpsing Savannah and Roderick on the dance floor still talking. "Have she and Roderick known each other very long?" she asked Chuck, not sure why.

"Oh yeah," Chuck said knowingly. "They were pretty hot and heavy back in the day. Before Monique, that is. Everyone expected that JRock and Savannah would end up married, but Monique, well, she took one look at JRock and ball game. Savannah, well, she never married."

JaiHonnah noticed that Roderick and Savannah left the dance floor, passing right by her and Chuck as they headed out of the room.

"Steady, old girl. He's a big boy now. He can take care of himself," Chuck said cryptically.

Embarrassed again, JaiHonnah looked in the opposite direction. "It doesn't matter to me what he does," she lied.

"Seems that you're being awfully protective of your boss, Jai," he said with a sideways glance.

She didn't answer him.

JaiHonnah danced with other men at the party and tried to have a good time since she was the guest of honor. The deejay played a line dance at Chuck's request, and her second drink of wine had her a little more loose than she would have been cold sober. She quickly got into step with the other dancers and let the music manipulate her. She was going to have fun no matter with whom Roderick was spending his time.

Roderick had nearly stopped breathing when JaiHonnah walked into the room wearing a hot, little red number, and his erection had sprung to attention to salute her. There was more of her showing than was covered. High fashion European styles accentuated every curve of her exquisite and voluptuous body. Tearing his eyes away from her was, perhaps, the hardest thing he had to do. However, she was *only* Mrs. Chapman, an architect and civil engineer who happened to work for him, nothing more, he kept telling himself. His eyes had darted in her direction many times, but he refused to stare, consoling himself with a lively and provocative conversation with Savannah Logan. Two drinks into the evening, he told himself that he was enjoying himself. When Savannah suggested that he ask his brother to play a few of her old favorites, he forced himself not to look at JaiHonnah enjoying herself with other people at the party, but watching her dancing with other men and with Chuck was too much. He wanted her in his arms, and badly. Savannah's lithe body against his didn't arouse him, but glimpsing JaiHonnah over Savannah's shoulder did, which was why he had suggested that he and Savannah get a little air. He had to clear his thoughts and get the vision of making love to Jai out of his head. Savannah seemed more than willing to take a break from the fun and frivolity in the front salon and move to the library across the entranceway. There he didn't have to feel JaiHonnah's presence or see her beautiful smile when she laughed with others and not him.

"Rod," Savannah cooed, "if you're not busy later, why don't we go back to my place?"

"Uh, Savannah, it's already late. It's nearly two in the morning now."

"How do you like your eggs?" she asked and grinned. "I thought that I would make a big breakfast for us later in the morning—much later."

"Are you suggesting what I think you're suggesting?" he asked, a little chagrinned.

"It's been a long time. I've missed you," she purred against his ear.

"You're an enchanting woman, and I'm intrigued by your suggestion, but..."

"You don't want anything heavy, right?"

"Can you deal with that?"

"About as well as I've dealt with you watching JaiHonnah Chapman all evening," she said, grinning.

"Watching her? I haven't been..." He had to laugh at himself. Was he that obvious? he wondered. "She works for Baylor Construction, that's all. I guess that I've been treating her like a kid sister since she joined the firm," he lied.

"So that's what you call it, huh? Brotherly attention." She smiled. "Well, brother, your kid sister is a grown woman capable of taking care of herself. She's married, I hear. I, on the other hand, am not looking for a brother, and I'm not legally or emotionally tied to anyone—nor do I want to be. I do, however, feel this growing need to mother you in ways that would be considered incestuous."

Roderick grinned knowingly. "Mother me, huh? Well, Savannah, I like my eggs scrambled."

"Then we have a date?"

"Oh, yes, ma'am, we certainly do." He appraised her more closely. "Why don't we say good night to Vivian and go check your breakfast supplies. I think we're going to need a country-sized breakfast much later in the morning."

Roderick escorted Savannah back into the front salon where the remaining guests were dancing like teenagers. The music, loud and raucous, rocked the house with vibrations off the Richter Scale. He immediately spotted JaiHonnah whose rhythmic moves were so sensuous that nearly every man's eyes including his washed over her body and long, shapely legs encased in man-killer stilettos. He didn't move his gaze from her when Savannah excused herself to answer a page and went to use her cell phone in a more quiet part of the house. JaiHonnah was dancing so enthusiastically that her hair loosened from the top of her head and fell on her shoulders and slightly across her face. She put her arms up in a vain effort to recapture her raven locks and then she gave up trying, but that dress held on, defying gravity. His eyes smoldered as she ran her tongue over her lips and her beautiful smile sprang forth. He felt that there must have been some wager on who could dance more sensuously because all of the dancers were gyrating as if the bet was an enormous Lotto-size prize. If so, JaiHonnah would have won easily.

Thirty was nothing but a number to her agile body, he thought. Every sway of her hips, movement of her arms or toss of her head caused his heart to do somersaults in his chest until the music ended and everyone whooped and hollered in glee. Now he knew what the Down and Dirty was. His eyes met JaiHonnah's as the music turned mellow again. He wanted to go to her and take her in his arms, but suddenly Savannah was at his side.

"I've got to go to the hospital. One of my patients has gone into labor, she thinks, but I think it's Bradford Hicks. Here's the key to my place. You remember where it is, don't you?"

"Uh, yes, but don't you think that…"

She kissed him on the lips, a slow, mind-numbing kiss. Then biting his lower lip and soothing it with her tongue she whispered. "I won't be long. Don't start without me."

"Right," he said and smiled, feeling uncomfortable and sorry that he had taken his flirtation to the extreme. He accepted the key to her town house and she left.

When he turned, JaiHonnah had a strange expression on her face. She had obviously seen the kiss that Savannah gave him. Not many people could have missed seeing the key exchange either, he thought. Well, he asked for no-strings-attached sex, and his prayers were about to be answered.

"Great party, Viv," he said, kissing her on the cheek and hugging her.

"You leaving, JRock?"

"Yeah, got something to do," he said.

"So I noticed," she said with a sideways glance and a strange inflection in her voice.

He looked at her quizzically. "Uh, Viv, where's my date?"

"If you mean, Chuck, he's gone. Had to check on a patient or something. At least that's what he told Jai. By the way, I need for you to give her a ride to the condo. It's on your way home," she said with a directed glance.

"Viv, I wasn't going *straight* home," he said.

"Uh, I know, but that doesn't mean that you can't give Jai a lift, now does it?"

"Viv, couldn't someone . . ." he started, but Vivian's you're-dead-meat expression squashed his question. "Is she ready to go?"

Roderick closed the trunk of his Mercedes Benz, took a deep breath, letting it out slowly before he climbed into his car. The engine roared to life, and he pulled out of the parking space.

"It was a nice party, wasn't it?" JaiHonnah asked, looking directly at Roderick's profile.

He didn't look at her, she noticed, nor did he answer her.

"Roderick?"

"Uh, yes, it was a nice party," he said without emotion.

"I really didn't want to celebrate this birthday, but I enjoyed seeing so many of my old friends and acquaintances. I, uh, didn't get a chance to have more than a brief conversation with Savannah Logan. You two seemed to have a lot to talk about."

Roderick gritted his teeth, but didn't answer.

"I understand that she's on staff at Georgetown Medical and a full partner with Derrick's medical practice. Certainly is a small world."

Roderick still didn't answer, and his silence got the better of her.

"Roderick, if you're going to sit there ignoring me, why did you offer to take me home?"

He wanted to tell her that he wasn't ignoring her, but that her perfume was driving him crazy. That sitting so close to her was causing him to have to force himself to breathe. That he wanted to make love with her in the worst possible way. That his erection was enormous and throbbing. That his heart was pounding and his blood was warming.

"Sorry, I have something on my mind," he said casually, hoping that there would be no red lights to keep him in the car that close to her for more than a few minutes longer.

Roderick carried the shopping bags full of birthday gifts into the living room for JaiHonnah and then turned to leave.

"Roderick," she said with her hand on his arm, "wouldn't you like to sit down a moment and...?"

Roderick didn't turn around. "And what?" he asked coolly.

"Couldn't we just talk for a while? I mean, it's my birthday and..."

"I've already given you my best...look, it's late."

"Roderick," she said, moving around to face him, "you're making too much of what happened between us."

He shook his head and snorted. "I don't believe you said that. You drove me insane when you made love with me, then you cut it off like it never happened, and now you tell me that *I'm* making too much of it?" He licked his finger and held it up in the air. "Which way is the wind blowing now, *Mrs.* Chapman?"

"Stop calling me that! You're being cruel!"

"I'd say that's the pot calling the kettle black."

"Stop it, Roderick. You're no bully."

"Good night, *Mrs.* Chapman," he said in disgust.

"Roderick, please don't go yet. I mean, can't you stay just a little while?"

"What do you want from me, Jai? I'm human. Flesh and blood. I still want you, and I'll be damned if I'll let you make a fool out of me twice. Unless you're ready to take me to your bed, I'd suggest that you let me go now. Otherwise I won't be responsible for my actions. I'll have you out of that little red handkerchief you call a dress in a New York second and flat on your back before you can whisper my name..." He caught himself. Her eyes were mesmerizing. Her lips luscious and inviting.

She put a hand to his face and caressed his gritted jaw. "I'm sorry for what..."

He didn't wait for the rest as he sidestepped her and started for the door.

"You're going to her, aren't you? You're going to Savannah's place!" Her staccato voice pinned him to the floor. "I saw the way that you kissed her and the keys that she gave to you."

He turned and looked into her eyes. "What the hell does it matter to you where I'm going?" he asked, slowly approaching her. "You've made it painfully clear that you want nothing to do with me. I've accepted that in my head, but you're playing with fire if you keep this up, Jai. You can't have it both ways. Either you want me in your bed or you don't. If you don't want me in your bed, don't question whose bed I am going to be in. Now what do you want?"

JaiHonnah turned her back to him, hoping to hold back the tears of frustration before he saw them. "Go to her then," she said, summoning what little strength she had left.

"That's what I thought. Happy birthday, *Mrs.* Chapman." he said as he turned on his heels and walked out of the door.

JaiHonnah sat on the sofa cupping her hands over her face. Hot tears ran down between her fingers.

Roderick poured a second hefty drink of scotch and stretched out on the sofa listening to Nina Simone tell him what a sad mood he was in. He certainly didn't need to be reminded. He swallowed the drink in two quick gulps. He couldn't get JaiHonnah out of his head. The way she looked at him tore at his gut. Her eyes were so sad, but he couldn't let that sway him. If he did, he'd never recover. He stood and poured another drink, this time without ice. He vaguely heard Savannah's garage door open. He swallowed the drink in one gulp. He'd get JaiHonnah out of his head one way or the other. He poured another drink. Savannah would make him forget the feel of JaiHonnah's body against his. The excitement he felt when she gave herself to him. The sound of her voice when she called out his name in passion. The touch...

Roderick felt two arms reach around him from behind rubbing his chest suggestively and stroking his manhood through his slacks.

"Hey, good looking, wanna date?" Savannah cooed, nibbling his ear.

He turned in her arms in one fluid motion, pulled her close to him and hungrily sought her mouth. "What took you so long?" he asked against her lips, molding her to his body.

"Well, if I had known that this is the greeting I'd get, I'd have been here a lot sooner," she said before kissing him sensuously.

Savannah turned out the lights and led Roderick up the steps to her bedroom, undressing as they went. By the time they reached her bed, they were bare as newborn babes. Roderick laid her on the bed and Savannah pulled him down on top of her. JaiHonnah's face was the last thing he thought about.

Chapter 13

Mrs. Chapman, I really appreciate this. I don't know where Mr. Baylor is, but he isn't answering his pager or cell phone and I have to leave to be with my husband. He's been taken to the hospital. Kelley is out of town so Shelly and Shelby asked me to call you and…"

"Don't worry about it, Mrs. Betterman. I'd be glad to stay with the girls until Mr. Baylor gets home. I was opening party gifts, but didn't have anything planned for today."

"Thank you, Mrs. Chapman."

"I'll be there as soon as I can."

They hung up. Jai grabbed her keys and purse and put on a leather jacket as she rushed through the halls to the elevator.

The morning air was brisk as she climbed into the taxicab. She was feeling a little rocky and hoped that she was not coming down with a cold or the flu, but considering how much wine she had to drink at her party, the fact that she was coherent at all was a minor miracle. Then after Roderick left her, she and a mimosa keep each other company with their own pity party for the rest of the night.

Mrs. Betterman was beside herself when JaiHonnah arrived. The girls were fine though and seemed thrilled to see her. JaiHonnah bundled the girls into their warm coats, hats and mittens. They took a long walk on The National Mall looking at the beautiful colors of fall foliage that Mother Nature had painted the trees. They visited the National Arboretum and oohed and ahhed over the beautiful flowers. Next they went to the new Native American Museum across from the Arboretum. When they returned home, they had hot cocoa and played together for more than an hour. Roderick still had not come home or called. Finally, she had no choice. JaiHonnah reached for the telephone.

"Dr. Logan," Savannah's obviously sleep-ladened voice answered.

"Savannah, this is Jai Reise. Is Roderick Baylor there?"

"Yes, he is. He's still sleeping, Jai. Can this wait?"

"No, Savannah, it can't. I need to speak with him now."

"Hold on," Savannah said groggily.

JaiHonnah waited and heard Savannah trying to wake him. The thought of him in another woman's bed caused her stomach to churn. She bit down hard to stem the rising nausea. Finally, Roderick came on the line.

"Yes," he answered in a deep, thick voice still not fully awake.

"Roderick, Mrs. Betterman had an emergency. She had to leave. I'm here with Shelby and Shelly..."

"What time is it?" he asked, still groggy.

"Nearly noon!" she said and hung up, slamming the telephone down.

Her heart was pounding. Her blood pressure skyrocketed. Her stomach was about to erupt. She fled to the bathroom. She hadn't had much for breakfast, but what was left came back to haunt her as she held herself over the commode. She rinsed her mouth and washed her face. When she returned to the living room, she noticed the two little cherubs at her feet looking up at her with big, beautiful eyes and quizzical expressions.

"You still mad at my daddy?" Shelly asked innocently, her mouth turned down.

"He's sorry, Jai, he won't do it again," Shelby affirmed, her little bottom lip trembling. "Please don't be mad at him anymore, Jai. He likes you. He hasn't been too happy because you're mad at him."

"Yeah, Jai, my daddy said that you're one of a kind," Shelly added.

In an instant her ire vanished. She dropped to her knees and engulfed the little people in her arms, kissing them wildly. Their sad expressions turned into giggles as they hugged her around her neck.

"Okay, I won't be angry with your daddy anymore," she said, grinning at them, "but if you two don't pick up all those toys in your playroom..." she teased, feigning seriousness, "then we won't hear another Indian princess story after lunch before your naptime."

The girls' eyes widened before they scampered away without another word to pick up their things and put them away. JaiHonnah went to the kitchen and started making lunch, fighting her vision of Roderick making love to Savannah the way that he had made love to her. She closed her eyes for a moment and gritted her teeth against the image and the churning in her belly. She was tired of thinking about it. She could barely sleep the night before thinking about it. Dawn had found her sitting on the breezy terrace wrapped in a blanket watching the sun come up, the half-full mimosa at her feet. God, how she wanted him. She squeezed the thought from her mind. He was another woman's husband and now he had taken a lover—Savannah Logan.

When they were at Spelman together, men had flocked to Savannah in droves. Not many were able to resist her, not that they tried. Now she had taken Roderick. "*Taken?*" she fussed aloud. He had raced out of her condo to be with Savannah. JaiHonnah's heart raced at such a furious pace that it even alarmed her. Why was she so upset at knowing that Roderick was with another woman? She had practically given him *carte blanche* to seek his pleasures with Savannah. There was nothing between herself and Roderick. That was the way that she had wanted it. Wasn't it? That was what she had told him. She blew her nose and wiped the tears from her eyes. She could no longer deny that Roderick meant something to her, something more than a business relationship. He did mean something, damn it! She would have to get him out of her head!

JaiHonnah went into the playroom and then sat with the girls while they worked. Soon the girls finished their chores and they settled onto the sofa for the story that she promised. JaiHonnah hugged them close to her sides, and they listened carefully as she spun another Indian princess tale. JaiHonnah was so caught up in their wide-eyed wonderment and questions and the girls were so engrossed in the story that none of them noticed Roderick standing at the entrance to the playroom listening quietly as they talked. Nearing the end of the story she noticed him. His once very dapper appearance was disheveled, rumpled and wrinkled. They looked into each other's eyes deeply for a brief moment and then she finished the story.

"Tell us another one, Jai," Shelly pleaded.

"Yes, Jai, please," Shelby entreated.

"Not until I get my kisses," Roderick spoke.

Shelly and Shelby screeched with joy and laughter as Roderick knelt to receive his daughters, and they ran into his arms. They smothered him with kisses, and he reciprocated.

"Daddy, Jai said that she's not mad at you anymore," Shelly announced proudly.

"Now can we play with her again, Daddy?"

"Yes, please, Daddy. She thinks that you're special too."

Roderick was without words looking at JaiHonnah's raised eyebrow. "We'll talk about that later..."

"No now, Daddy, pleeezzze," Shelly entreated.

"Now, Daddy," Shelby affirmed. "Tell Jai that you're sorry for making her mad and then you can make up and give her a big kiss like you give us."

Roderick was squirming under the pressure of his daughters' barrage as they continued to prod him to end the spat between them. JaiHonnah seemed to be loving every minute of it. She sat with a wry smile on her lips, arms akimbo, and one leg crossed over the other, her foot waving in the air.

She almost gloated at his obvious discomfort and chagrin. She decided to give him a reprieve. She rose from the sofa and approached him.

"All right, little Indian princesses, it's time to have lunch while your daddy—," she leaned in close to him, sniffed and wrinkled her nose—, "takes a shower and changes his perfume," she said, cutting her eyes at him briefly.

The girls giggled and scampered toward the kitchen. Roderick bent and kissed her lips briefly.

"Thank you," he said barely above a whisper.

She did not answer him, but that kiss rocked her soul. She resented the scent of another woman's perfume on his clothes and the lipstick smudge on his white shirt collar. She wasn't finished with him and she let him know it when she rolled her eyes at him.

"Burn the clothes," she said lowly as she tossed her head in the air and walked out of the room.

Roderick leaned back against the door frame. This was not quite the reception he expected to receive. After she slammed the telephone down in his ear, he bolted from Savannah's bed like a marathon runner at the starting gun. The giant-sized hangover crushing his head felt like two wrecking balls clanging together. He hadn't heard a word that Savannah said as he blindly dressed and rushed still half clothed from her town house to his car. He did remember to drive carefully though, not wanting to repeat his jail experience. He expected to find JaiHonnah ranting and raving at the top of her lungs as Monique would have, but not this quiet, loving scene between her and his daughters. They were plaiting her hair in two long braids, listening to the story and asking questions as they worked. She looked so natural sitting with them. He stood very still so as not to disturb the magic of her tale or the beauty of the Kodak moment.

JaiHonnah tucked Shelly and Shelby in for their afternoon nap. They drifted off to sleep in the middle of another Indian princess story. She drew their blinds and left the dimly lit girls' room. When she entered the kitchen Roderick was stacking the lunch dishes in the dishwasher. She noticed him grab the back of his neck and extend his arms over his head issuing forth an unintelligible groan and a few intelligible expletives. His body fully stretched made goose bumps rise all over her body. Her eyes washed over his tall, statuesque frame in a pair of drawstring sweatpants and a matching muscle shirt. His feet were bare on the heated, stained concrete floors. She had to look away before she began salivating. Gathering the remaining dishes from the table, she carried them to the kitchen counter.

"I'll do that," Roderick said, taking the dishes from her and brushing her hand away. "That was a great lunch. I was starving."

"What? No time for breakfast in bed? I would have at least thought that Savannah would extend her Southern hospitality beyond the sheets."

Roderick narrowed his eyes, put down the dishes and placed his hands on JaiHonnah's arms.

"Nothing happened, Jai. I didn't make love with her."

"Mmm," she murmured. "Where have we heard that before?" She snapped her finger. "Didn't former President Clinton use that line?"

Roderick ignored her facetiousness. "Look, Jai, as far as I know, I passed out before...well, then the next thing I remember was you slamming the telephone down in my ear. After that I didn't have anything on my mind except getting home to you...I mean, to my girls."

Relief washed over her, and she flushed with inner joy. All that torturous night of visualizing him with Savannah was for naught. She had to regroup though. She backed away from him.

"Why are you telling me this? I'm not your wife or your lover. It's none of my business who you sleep with. Isn't that what you told me?"

"I didn't suggest that it mattered to you, but last night and this morning you've seemed particularly focused on my sex life, such as it is."

JaiHonnah's eyes locked into his. "Don't flatter yourself. Your escapades are of no consequence to me," she said, turning away.

"Escapades?" he questioned, snorting. "Yes, I've had sex with other women, but I've only made love to one other woman since Monique, and I'll give you three guesses as to who she was. I don't make a habit of trying to drown my sorrows in a bottle nor do I sleep around. I apologize for inconveniencing you on a Sunday, but I'm not sorry..."

Roderick took her into his arms, raised her face to his and did what he had ached to do since he walked into his home. He drew his breath when JaiHonnah surrendered to him, deepening his kiss and drawing her tightly against his body. He sucked at her bottom lip tasting the fruit. His phallus was engorged and straining for release. He wanted to touch her, taste her sweet nectar, make her his, right there on the kitchen floor.

JaiHonnah groaned from deep in her core. She wanted his hands on her, him on her, in her. She needed him. The tips of her breasts ached for his caress. Her body trembled with needful passion. Her breath quickened at the feel of his penis against her abdomen. She involuntarily tightened her inner muscles straining to maintain control. Then, just as suddenly as he had taken her, he let her go.

"Thanks for taking care of my girls and for the lunch," he said, breaking off the heat.

JaiHonnah hung in mid-air, shook her head to regain her senses, and walked away from him. "Don't mention it." She threw the comment at him over her shoulder as she grabbed her jacket and purse. In moments she was gone.

JaiHonnah had walked at least ten blocks before the chilly late October day reminded her that tears streaked her face. She looked around blindly, not quite realizing where she was. Tourists moved past her, awed by the sights on The Mall between the Capitol Building and the Washington Monument. The dry leaves rustled and swirled around her feet. She found a bench near the back gate of The White House and sat down.

What was wrong with her? she wondered in frustration. Couldn't she be in his presence without wanting to...she shook off the thought. Why couldn't she just stay away from him? Why did he have to be so damn appealing? So handsome? Such a tender lover? Her core still ached for the want of him. She couldn't shake the feeling of wanting to be with him—alone in their rapture. However, it wasn't only about sex. It was more. She dare not utter the word. It was too horrible a thought. Maybe it was just that the old childish competitiveness with Savannah had surfaced, or was she really—jealous? The word stuck in her brain. She wanted to be the one whom he took to bed, but she had her chance and blew it away like the dry, dead leaves beneath her feet. Summer's warmth had ended and winter's chill would soon arrive. He had ignited her passion, her lust for him again. JaiHonnah laughed aloud at herself. Whom was she kidding? Being with him once was not enough.

Chapter 14

Roderick finished preparing the plans for restructuring Baylor Construction Company into Baylor Design and Developers International. He was prepared to take the company public. The timing for entering into the stock market was crucial. He had everything in place. He paused, steepled his hands and sat back in his chair. If only his private life could be solved with the stroke of a pen. If only he could erase the Mrs. from JaiHonnah's name and rewrite...he paused. What would he do? Kissing her had sent him to the outer edges of oblivion. That wasn't nearly enough. Making love with her wasn't enough. He wanted her, not just sexually, but in a total commitment that transcended the physical. There was that word again. The word that waffled through his conscious and unconscious thoughts. He hadn't known her that long, mere months in fact. It couldn't be happening. Not again. Roberta Flack's "*Let It Be Me*" must have been screwing with his head. He turned off the iPod and went to the playroom to be with his daughters.

At the office the Monday after her surprise party, JaiHonnah picked up her telephone.

"Jai, I think that you should come down to reception," Kelley said cryptically.

JaiHonnah rose from her desk, exited her office, and walked down the steps. A crowd had gathered at the windows overlooking the front of the building.

"What's going on?" she asked, approaching Kelley.

"Come with me," Kelley said, taking JaiHonnah's arm and leading her out the front door. The office crowd followed.

"What in the world . . .?" she gasped, her eyes wide in disbelief.

"They were just delivered," Kelley said, looking at the three Maserati Citroens in fire-engine red, eggshell white and midnight blue, all with big yellow ribbons tied around them. "Here's the card that came with them with your name on it," she said, handing it to JaiHonnah.

JaiHonnah opened the card. It read simply, *"Come home soon, dahlin'. I love you."* She didn't have to guess who had sent the cars. The yellow ribbons were an easy clue. "Just a little bitty thing, huh?" she huffed, parroting her father's words.

She turned quickly and slammed into Roderick's chest. She gritted her teeth and stormed. "Please have someone send them all back, Kelley!" She put the card back in Kelley's hand.

"Do *what*?" Kelley asked in disbelief.

"You heard me. Send them back." JaiHonnah raged, re-entering the building and heading back to her office.

Roderick looked at Kelley and shook his head. "What's going on here?" he asked.

"Beats the hell out of me," Kelley said, still stunned.

She read the card and then handed it to Roderick. Anxiety grew in him as he read the card. His head snapped toward JaiHonnah's swiftly retreating form. He started to follow her, but Kelley grabbed his arm. He looked at her hand and then into her warm and gentle eyes. She shook her head slowly, and his haste to follow JaiHonnah waned. His emotions were still peaked though. An emotion infinitely more disturbing than anxiety gripped him as he thought about the note from her husband. Three thousand Maserati wouldn't be enough to make up for what Calvin Chapman had done to JaiHonnah.

"Have someone get that junk off this property," he said calmly to Kelley.

He climbed the steps and saw JaiHonnah talking on the telephone. Her usually serene face was contorted and anguished, he thought. She was very animated as she stalked around her office. He inhaled in resignation of the fact that JaiHonnah had a husband who, regardless of his brutality, apparently still loved his wife and wanted her to come to him. Roderick turned away from her office door and went to his own.

"Daddy, you know that I don't have a license to drive in the US! You send three cars to me and I can't drive any of them! When I'm ready to drive, I can afford to buy a car for myself! Besides, I told you that I didn't want anything for my birthday. You're not going to have your way, Jake Hawkins, and that's final!"

Jake's deep, baritone laugh infuriated her even more. "*Whew*, lil' dahlin', you sure got your petticoat in a pinch," he said. "Told you it was just a little, bitty thing. Now, you go pick one'na them little toys, and I'll get a chauffeur to drive you around in it."

"You're not listening to me, Jake. I don't want a Maserati."

"Well, then, how about one'na them other toy cars, like a Jag or one like that boy drives, that black Benz? I'd rather see you in something like a Rolls or my Silver Shadow, but you youngsters have a mind of your own," he said. "Name it, dahlin', and I'll have it and a chauffeur to your door before you leave that office of yours today."

"I am not going to discuss this with you anymore. Now you send me anything else and I'll...I'll...oooh," she fussed. "I won't come to visit you at all!"

Jake's laughter quelled. "Alright, JaiHawk, calm down. *Whew!* You really know how to hurt your ole man, but go ahead and send the cars back. I can give them away in some charity contest or something," he said with a smirk. "So when you comin' home?"

"Christmas. I'll come home for Christmas, but don't you dare make a fuss like before. If I see anyone other than my family there, I'll turn right around and leave."

"Dahlin', it was only a little ole hundred-piece band. I don't see why you're still bent out of shape about that. That was years ago."

"It was the band *and* two thousand of your closest friends *and* the Texas-styled barbecue that lasted for three whole days and nights!"

Jake roared with laughter. "You c'mon home, dahlin', and I'll tone it down a bit."

"Have I got your word that it will be only the family?"

"But, dahlin'..."

"Your word, Jake," she insisted. She could hear him chewing on his cigar. "Jake," she said in a firm, questioning tone.

"Alright, dahlin', but JaiHawk, I've been lining up these eligible bachelors and checking out their pedigree so you can get busy on giving me my grandson. Can't I have..."

"Absolutely, positively not! Not one person more. Now, do I have your word or not?"

"You sure drive a hard bargain, dahlin'. Must be that Ingine blood in you. Just like your mama."

"I'm half Hawkins, too, remember," she said and laughed.

"But I don't have no stubborn streak in me like that, JaiHawk."

"Yeah, right," she quipped. "Your word, Jake, now. I've got work to do."

"You got my word," he said, relenting.

"Love you, Daddy," she said, smiling triumphantly.

"Love you more, dahlin'," he said, sighing.

"Grandson?" she said, shaking her head and musing to herself. Wasn't likely the way her life was going. After all, the doctors told her that it was very unlikely...she paused at the painful thought. The only way that she might become a mother was through adoption. Well, she sighed inwardly, Vivian loved her adopted children, regardless of who the biological parents were. Jake had better work on her brothers if he wanted a grandson. Not that the idea didn't appeal to her, because it did. Even if the doctors were wrong, she didn't want to make another mistake like Calvin Chapman. Perish the thought that he would father any woman's child.

Maybe artificial insemination, she thought. A lot of women her age, when finding that the odds of ever conceiving were against them and the old biological clock was ticking beyond the eleventh hour, had chosen artificial insemination as an option to fulfilling their maternal needs. Or using a surrogate.

Huh! Stop thinking crazy, Jai, she chastised herself. Then her mind began to wonder what a son of Roderick's would be like. If he had Roderick's eyes, she'd have to beat the women off with a whip before he reached the age of consent. Any young man Roderick fathered would naturally be tall, handsome and muscular. Yep, he'd be trouble alright, she mused. She shook off the thought and went back to work.

* * *

"What's up for your weekend, Jai?" Kelley asked as she bit into her steak and cheese sub.

"Laundry," JaiHonnah deadpanned, and groaned as she chewed on a carrot.

Kelley laughed. "I know the feeling. If there's anything I hate worse than washing dishes, it's washing clothes, but I'm not going to do any of that this weekend and neither are you."

"Oh?" JaiHonnah asked with one raised eyebrow. "And exactly what *am* I going to be doing?"

"We, my dear friend, are going to have a marvelous time shopping."

"Uh, Kelley, if there's anything I hate worse than doing laundry, it's going shopping."

"Yes, that's what Vivian told me, but we three are going anyway. We'll have brunch at the Galleria, then shop until we drop and then go to the opening game of the Washington Metro Men's and Women's Basketball League over at Dunbar High School. Baylor Construction has a team entered in the league. We call it Baylor's Wrecking Crew," she said and laughed. "Chuck Montgomery's team is called The Body Snatchers. Vivian plays on a team of female attorneys and judges called Final Justice."

"And this is supposed to be fun, is it?" JaiHonnah asked with a raised eyebrow.

"Beats the hell outta doing laundry," Kelley said, laughing at JaiHonnah's mutinous expression.

The shopping spree had netted Kelley several great bargains, while Vivian was loaded down with school clothes for her children. JaiHonnah found an interesting oil painting that she thought she might buy, if it were there next year when she returned. The women left the Galleria Mall in the fashionable Chevy Chase area of Maryland and drove across town to the fashionless area surrounding Dunbar High School in Northeast Washington. Vivian parked, pulled her oversized duffle bag out of her Land Cruiser, and slung it over her shoulder. Several other women she knew were also parking very expensive cars in the unprotected school parking lot as they joined up to climb the steps into the high school gymnasium.

"What about your things, Viv?" JaiHonnah asked, looking around at some very unsavory looking characters loitering in the parking lot.

Vivian understood immediately and gave JaiHonnah a slight smile. "Don't worry, Jai. Everything and my car will be here when we get back. This is, for lack of a better term, hallowed ground. Professional and amateur basketball players don't have any problem with theft, vandalism or robbery in this parking lot."

JaiHonnah shook her head skeptically. "Okay, if you say so."

Vivian smiled and joined her other teammates as they entered the gymnasium. The noise level hit them like a runaway locomotive as soon as they opened the heavy metal double doors. To JaiHonnah's surprise the gymnasium was packed to the rafters. There was barely standing room. A game was already underway when they entered.

"Damn," Kelley said. "They must have started early."

"No, we're twenty minutes late," Vivian answered as she stood on the sidelines watching the game. "My team is up next. I've got to go get dressed. I'll see you two later."

Kelley and JaiHonnah weaved their way around the border of the shiny, blond hardwood floor while play momentarily ceased. They squeezed up onto the bleachers at the far side of the arena and found two very cramped seats amid some young men and other ball players watching the game. While JaiHonnah was mildly interested in the play on the floor, Kelley was into the game fully focused until she heard the announcer say, "JRock Baylor in for Stockton" and the crowd erupted in cheers.

JaiHonnah focused on the man sitting on the floor in front of the announcer's table. Roderick stood, striped off his warm-up uniform in one fluid motion, and strode into the game pointing to Stockton who gave him a high and low five as he left the floor and Roderick took his position.

JaiHonnah watched the game intently now and noticed that, although she thought Roderick to be tall and massive, other players were much taller than his six-feet seven inches. Suddenly she feared that he could get hurt out there among the larger men, including Chuck Montgomery's seven-foot stature. As the game progressed, she noticed how Roderick's presence on the court was more of a threat to the opposing team than a risk to his life and limbs. He bobbed and weaved through and around the court with a quickness. Unless a person's eyes were glued on him, he moved so fast that it was hard to tell where he was a split second before. He was a scoring machine and thrilled the audience while they took to their feet chanting, *"Go, JRock! Go, JRock!"*

Later, Roderick was sitting and leaning back against the bleachers intently watching the flow of the game and hadn't notice Kelley and JaiHonnah enter. His daughters, nieces and nephews, Vivian's children and his Boys and Girls Club team were on the next few rungs of the bleachers above and behind him asking him and his teammates tons of questions as they watched the other men playing. Earlier that day he and his brothers, Walter and Francis Baylor, took all of the children to the National Zoo spending several hours before having lunch at Benihana. Roderick had played the first ten minutes of the game, putting the team up by ten points and then sat out to let Eric Stockton, one of his electronics engineers, get some playing time. Roderick was enjoying the camaraderie with his employees, his young team members, and his family on the sidelines, but Chuck's team, The Body Snatchers, was beginning to catch up so the team's coach, another employee on Roderick's sales and marketing staff, sent him back into the game.

Being back in a basketball uniform again and playing with and against top talent in the Washington-Maryland-Virginia area gave Roderick a sense of balance. Basketball was the one sport that traversed his life from childhood to adulthood and had given him not only unbelievable wealth, but also a means through which to dare to make a difference. He invested his multi-year, multimillion-dollar professional earnings well with a fellow sportsman and friend, Nick Collins. Nick was a star football player, who, like Roderick, came up the hard way and left the game at the top of his career because they could and then went into business. Society often labeled jocks like them as having IQs no larger than their shoe sizes. Nick and others had proven that society didn't know jack about intellect and now Roderick lived more comfortably than he thought he had a right to.

His celebrity brought him disappointments too. He met Monique his second year in the NBA when he was drafted fourth by the Miami Heat. Suddenly so many things seemed to fall into place for him. He was offered lucrative contracts just to wear certain sports equipment and clothes, go on nationally sponsored speaking tours to colleges, universities and high schools. He did guest appearances on television news and talk shows, ad campaigns and even cameo appearances on feature films, videos and independent movies. When time allowed, he did color commentary for a national sports show to critique high school and college games. The dollars mounted quickly, and he began to put his plan into action to leave the game and enter the world of business. After his sixth year in the league, an Olympic Gold Medal, record-breaking performances and multimillion-dollar endorsements, he had finally positioned himself to leave professional basketball. He earned two master's degrees—one in business and the other in economics—during the off season and put them to good use. His last year in the NBA he started Baylor Construction and convinced Kelley to leave her top-paying position as a sales and marketing executive with an airline to manage Baylor Construction for him.

Monique lived in Miami all of her life and never traveled. He enjoyed spending what little time he did have with her and was not disappointed when she announced that she was pregnant. Although he was not at all convinced that he loved her, there was no question in his mind that he wanted their baby. He married her and experienced untold joy when the baby turned out to be the two little golden nuggets who cheered for their daddy and warmed his heart.

Dressed in miniature Wrecking Crew cheerleader outfits, Shelby and Shelly were the team's mascots along with some of his employees' children. His girls went with some member of his family to every game with him from the time they were babes in arms. Just knowing that they were close and that he could glimpse them during a game had given him much joy, especially after Monique stopped coming to the games shortly after they were married. He didn't miss her absence since she never developed an interest in what he was doing to earn a living. All she seemed to need was the credit cards and bank account that he established in her name. That truly made her happy. Not him or their daughters.

Vivian's children sent up a cheer when they spotted her walking toward the bleachers dressed to play the game following his. Then when she sat, his brother, Walter, nudged him and pointed to their sister, Kelley and JaiHonnah sitting above Vivian in the tightly packed bleachers. He returned Kelley's wave. JaiHonnah's eyes were fixed on him, he thought, as the team took a time-out before the end of the first half. Just looking at her gave him an emotional boost. She was a basketball neophyte and had admitted that she had never seen him play or even heard of him before she came to Washington to work for him.

JaiHonnah watched as Roderick stood in a huddle with the other team members. His daughters wiped sweat from his brow and gave him bottled water. It was such a precious scene. She noticed that the girls performed that same ritual and then hugged and kissed their father each time he sat down. They were some family unit, she thought, very attentive and loving to each other. Kelley was pointing out her brothers, sister and their respective family members seated in the bleachers behind Roderick. The perfect family portrait, even without Monique's presence, JaiHonnah thought. She had tasted Roderick's forbidden fruit and wondered how any woman could walk away and leave a man like him even for a short time.

Roderick stood walking back into the game after the time out and briefly looked up at the score and the clock overhead. JaiHonnah couldn't figure out why everyone started yelling, *"Jam Rock!"* and stomping the bleachers until they vibrated. She turned to Kelley who was rising to her feet along with everyone else.

JaiHonnah stood, too. "Kelley, what do they mean by 'Jam Rock'?" she asked over the roar of the crowd.

Kelley laughed. "It's JRock's trademark. Less than ten seconds on the clock, the score is tied, and they want to see him do a monster jam."

"How can he do that if everyone knows what he's going to do? Won't the other team know what's coming?"

"Sure they do, but what they don't know is when or how he's going to do it," she said, laughing.

"But he is going to do it, huh?"

Kelley gave JaiHonnah a sideways grin. "Uh-huh, he sure is." Her pride in her brother was evidenced on her face.

As the play unfolded, another player on Roderick's team had the ball passing it back and forth waiting for the seconds to tick off the clock. JaiHonnah's eyes were as wide as silver dollars. She could not believe the agile and quick moves that Roderick had performed. His body was pure poetry in motion, faking out two and three defenders, spinning, reversing, and then leaping, his body as graceful as an Olympic high diver. Then suddenly one of the players lobbed the ball into the air and out of nowhere Roderick caught the ball in mid-air, spun above the rim and jammed it in to the basket just before the buzzer sounded. The packed gymnasium went ballistic.

Kelley turned toward JaiHonnah with a broad smile. "That was for you, Jai. JRock usually doesn't do a Tomahawk Jam. I think he was sending a message."

Chapter 15

Thank you, ladies and gentlemen," JaiHonnah said, smiling warmly at the group of very wealthy financiers and investment bankers surrounding the table where she had just uncovered her vision for a new conference center to be constructed in Fairfax, Virginia. "Your accolades reflect the excitement that Baylor Design and Developers feel for this project." She started the slide presentation on large-screen video monitors and continued her running commentary. "Your excitement is shared by the world-renowned SAIE Exhibition, which has asked Baylor Design to exhibit at its upcoming international exhibition in Bologna next fall. The SAIE recognizes, as do we at Baylor, that the Fairfax Conference and Convention Center will provide a forum for the exchange of ideas while maintaining the charm of the surrounding area. Likened unto the work of the great Brazilian architect, João Batista Villanova Artigas, it remains ecologically and environmentally linked to the future in the style of Robert Asher.

"As you can see on the monitors, out buildings of no more than two stories will capture the old traditions of Virginia as displayed on The Lawn of the University of Virginia in Charlottesville. Thomas Jefferson, when he designed the school, thought of it as a place where ideas were born and nurtured. Not as a place where one sought a degree to attest to individual knowledge. Under Mr. Jefferson's policy, no degrees and diplomas were issued. Out of deference to the founder, it wasn't until after his death that the policy was changed. The new Fairfax Conference Center will hold to the old traditions rather than the new and the procession of academicians will still beat a path to its doors.

"The domed rotunda Arthur Ashe Library will house state-of-the-art electronic information research and retrieval equipment and software.

The Obama Amphitheater will host lectures to crowds that would fill a basketball arena. The main conference center will provide for and accommodate many different groups simultaneously in pods to avoid when necessary, but permit when appropriate, the interaction of diverse groups. Interior general construction, architecture and management services for specialty retailers, restaurants, office interiors and even international banks will be restricted to support, not supplant the purpose of the center, which is to promote innovation in development and encourage interaction between the most advanced technologies and primary market sections worldwide. Countless opportunities will be available for leading professionals to come together privately, exchange information and ideas, and learn new methods to address international issues such as those of the Clinton Global Initiative. This is the vision of Baylor Design and Developers and its leadership, Mr. J. Roderick Baylor," she finished with the slide presentation to rousing applause.

Roderick, sitting at the opposite end of the long conference table, was again awed by JaiHonnah's polish and presence. She held her audience spellbound and that included him. He had heard her presentations to other august bodies in the past months since her arrival, and she excited him anew with her captivating manner on each and every occasion. Nothing seemed to daunt her spirit and ability to handle any situation or crowd. Her award-winning smile never disappeared from morning to night no matter how long or arduous the day. She was a breath of freshness in an otherwise staid business meeting, and her buoyant enthusiasm caused the meetings to sail by as did this one.

"Fine woman, your architect," Rothman Childs, the biggest and most influential investment banker in the metropolitan area, said, nodding toward JaiHonnah.

"You mean, of course, that Baylor Developers has a fine architect and civil engineer who happens to be a woman, don't you, Roth?" Roderick countered.

Rothman's clear blue eyes and white-gray mustache smiled in silent agreement around an unlit Havana cigar. "Rod, my son, you've been playing your hand pretty close to the vest of late. I had to read about this little get together in the *Washington Post* and the *Wall Street Journal* like everyone else. Now, son, that's not how we do business," the crafty, middle-aged man said, guiding Roderick to a more secluded spot in the large conference room. "Why didn't you bring this deal to me first privately? You know we could have struck an agreement without involving these other good old boys. Why, we've done some pretty good business before, haven't we, son?"

"Roth, old man, competition for inexpensive money is tough, you know," Roderick said, wrapping his arm around the man's shoulders in a fatherly fashion. "I'll admit that in the past we've worked on some very interesting projects together. Made a good return on the investments, too, but the cost of that money wasn't as much of an issue as it is in a project the size of the Fairfax Conference and Convention Center.

"Now, unless I miss my guess, I'm going to be getting a call from at least three of your competitors offering far less than market-rate money to build the facility and some pretty hefty tax-deductible gifts as well as a part of their offers, community spirited as we all know they are.

"And then, of course, there's some out-of-town money that's been dogging my heels for some time now. BlackHawk is sniffin' out my trail. But, of course, we don't really need some of that foreign money floating around and about the Virginia countryside, now do we, Roth? I think I can find what I'm looking for much closer to home, say for example, right in this very room. What do you think?"

The older man thoughtfully rubbed his chin, and Roderick knew that the old fox was ready to make an offer. Then the haggling would begin.

"I think that I can see my way clear to find you some five-percent money," he said and grinned.

"Well, Roth, it's always a pleasure to see you. My best to your wife, Betsy, right?" Roderick said, shaking the man's hand, patting him on the back and preparing to walk away.

The old man held a grip on Roderick's hand. "Well, of course, we could make that an adjustable rate, just to see which way the market is running."

"By the way, how's Roth Junior coming with that jump shot of his?" Roderick asked, seeming to have ignored the old man's second offer. "I saw him at a game at Dunbar High School and asked him whether he'd like to help with my Boys and Girls Club team."

"Well, then again, I might be able to find some four percent money and hold your promissory note for twenty maybe twenty-five years."

"You and the family going skiing this season, Roth? I hear that there is some good powder in the Poconos early. You'll have to come with me and Chuck Montgomery the next time we hit the slopes."

"Alright, JRock," he said, frustrated. "What is it gonna take to get me into this deal?"

Roderick folded his arms across his chest and looked Rothman Childs directly in the eyes and gave him his bottom line without blinking.

The old man flushed beet red. "Let go my balls, man!" Roth barked a laugh. He eyed Roderick closely as he chewed hard on the Havana. Roderick never changed his expression or blinked. "You're serious, aren't you?" Roth asked.

"Asked and answered. Any more questions, Roth, old man?" Roderick asked with a twinkle in his eye and a grin on his lips. "Maybe you'll be more seriously interested in some other projects that—."

"I get the first trust?"

"Inked in my lawyer's office first of next week."

"You know my lawyers can cut us a deal tomorrow. You don't need to use that Jackson woman."

"*Cut* being the operative word here, aye, Roth?"

"Now, son, how was I supposed to know that my lawyers had cut in a little extra on that Maxell deal last spring? I don't make a habit of monitoring every little detail of what they do. I just pay them sharks what they ask," he protested with a sly grin.

"Good thing Mrs. Jackson found that *little* discrepancy before I signed the deal. Imagine, that extra two percent could have cost me fourteen million dollars."

Roth cleared his throat roughly. "So where'd you find this architect?"

"She's a very close friend of Mrs. Jackson's."

"I should have guessed!" Roth growled. "Tarnation, it's getting so that a man can't go nowhere anymore or do any business without a woman putting her two cents into it."

Roderick sensed what the man was up to.

"Forget it, Roth. Mrs. Chapman is under an iron-clad contract to Baylor Design and Developers written by Mrs. Jackson."

"Now, son, would I do something like that to you?" the man asked, grinning.

"The Fairfax deal is off if you even try it."

"You'd toss a multi-billion dollar deal on account of a woman?" Roth sputtered.

"Not just any woman, Roth, but Mrs. Chapman specifically, yes. You'd be left holding your golf club with no balls," he said, his eyes fixed on Roth. "Mrs. Chapman is a fine lady, not some ingenue to add to your collection. She has my respect and admiration. Remember that when you speak with me about her. Now, do we have an understanding?"

Roth took a measure of Roderick whose demeanor gave no quarter. He acquiesced without further commentary.

"I'll have my lawyers contact Mrs. Jackson early next week," he said, shaking Roderick's hand. "You sure don't take no tea for the fever. This woman, she mean something to you?"

Roderick deflected the question. "Until next week, Roth," Roderick said, now grinning at the man. The deal was sealed.

Roderick briefly shook hands with the other financiers, cutting off their interest in setting up a deal and gathered his briefcase. With promises to get back to the other financiers with other Baylor Design and Developers projects, Roderick picked up JaiHonnah's laptop and briskly escorted her from the conference room. His ground-eating strides matched his enthusiasm. He was almost giddy as his long legs covered the distance through the wide hallway. JaiHonnah trotted to keep up with him.

"Wait just a minute, Roderick!" JaiHonnah protested, stopping dead still in her vain effort to keep pace with him as he nearly dragged her along. "Where the hell is the fire?"

Roderick dropped everything on the floor, grabbed JaiHonnah up in his arms, and kissed her with heat and passion. Then he let her go as quickly as he had grabbed her. She rocked back on her heels.

"Roderick, what was that about?" she asked and huffed.

"I just closed the biggest deal—the Baylor Plaza Park project just got funded," he said with robust enthusiasm, clenching both fists in the air.

"What? I don't understand. You knew going into that meeting that you'd get what you wanted for the Fairfax Conference and Convention Center. Your only question was how much the money was going to cost you. What does the Fairfax Center have to do with Baylor Plaza Park?" she asked in total confusion.

"How much did I think it was going to cost going in?" he asked.

"You thought maybe four or four and a half percent was the best that you could do."

"How does one percent grab you?"

JaiHonnah's eyes widened and her mouth dropped open in disbelief. She flew into Roderick's arms, rocking him backwards. Her kiss was spontaneous, he knew, but very welcomed indeed. She quickly collected herself and backed away from Roderick.

"Roderick, that's fantastic! I don't know how you did it!"

"Care to continue this discussion over dinner, Jai? I think we have a lot to celebrate, don't you?"

"Dinner, uh, you mean just the two of us?"

He casually looked from side to side and then back at her. "Well, I don't see anyone else around, do you?"

"I don't know, Roderick," she said, studying the utility carpet. "That might not be such a good idea. I mean, we don't seem to be able to control the situation in close quarters."

His thumb and forefinger lifted her chin. "Then you pick the restaurant. Some place spacious and full of people who can protect us from ourselves," he said and grinned.

JaiHonnah rolled her eyes and pursed her lips. "Alright, River House on the Georgetown waterfront."

"Eight o'clock?"

"Seven. Tomorrow is a work day, remember?"

"If I didn't, you'd remind me, I'm sure," he said, then smirked.

Roderick was chatting with some people at the bar in the River House when JaiHonnah arrived. He stood when she was led to him by the maître d'. *Stunning* was the only word for her, he thought, as she approached. He wasn't the only one who noticed. Heads turned and conversations hung in mid-syllable as she walked toward him. Men nodded appreciatively, a few sucking wind. A beautiful woman should always be beheld with such silent reverence, he thought.

"We'll seat you for dinner shortly, Mr. Baylor," the maître d' said.

Roderick nodded his thanks to the man and led JaiHonnah to a bar table for two, but he couldn't take his eyes off her burnt-orange dress and camel-brown suede coat. The deep V cut of the wrap dress immediately captured his imagination when she removed her coat. The epitome of elegance and grace, he thought, and no bra as far as he could see.

"Hurry and pick a topic of conversation. Something that's going to keep you from just sitting here staring at me all evening," JaiHonnah said, noticing his gaze.

Roderick lifted the bar menu in front of his face. JaiHonnah pursed her lips and lowered his hands revealing his face. He had his eyes closed.

"Is it safe to look at you now?" he asked, his eyes still closed.

"I don't see why not. You know what I look like. You see me every day at the office," she said and smiled slightly. "Give a girl a break." She laughed.

Roderick opened his eyes, rested an elbow on the table and his chin on his knuckles.

"*Umph*, you're more than a notion, Mrs. Chapman," he said almost wistfully.

It still bothered JaiHonnah that he called her Mrs. Chapman from time to time, but they had settled into a more comfortable repartee of late, she thought. He would compliment her on her attire, but he often told the women in the office how well they looked. He seemed to treat her no differently than anyone else. It was the times that they found themselves alone together when she would catch him staring at her that recalled the lustful glances he used to give her. If she were true to her emotions, she would admit to herself that having him look at her sent welcomed shivers up her spine. However, she learned that she couldn't trust her own emotions. Especially not where J. Roderick Baylor was concerned. Lately her emotions ran the gamut from almost giddy to deep moods of despair and solace. She was going to find out why though. The mood swings were becoming annoying and too frequent. It was too soon for her to be menopausal. At least she hoped that it was.

"What are you doing for Thanksgiving?" Roderick asked as the waiter brought their drinks.

"I've made airline reservation to go to New Mexico to see my grandmother. She lives on the Navajo Reservation in Shiprock."

"Ah, so that's where all the Indian princess stories originated."

"Well, perhaps, but my mother used to tell me these stories when I was younger, about Shelly and Shelby's ages. They were beautiful stories to a little girl like me. The stories made me very proud of my Navajo heritage. I don't think that I've forgotten any of them."

"Your mother lives on the reservation too?"

"No, she died when I was very young. My mother and father lived outside of San Antonio."

"Your father still living?"

"Oh, yes, very much so," she mused.

"You're fortunate to have at least one of your parents still with you."

"That's what Baylor Plaza Park is all about, isn't it? It's a monument to your parents."

"It's a celebration for what they did, not only for their own five children, but also for so many others in our old neighborhood. They gave so much as did others in their peer group. I want their generosity to be remembered."

"It will be. Baylor Plaza Park is a wonderful and fitting way to show your appreciation to your ancestors. The Navajo nation is big on ancestry," she said, chuckling.

Roderick's heart still skipped a beat when JaiHonnah smiled. No matter when or where she did it, she lifted his spirits. His girls smiled a lot when she was around. His conversations with his daughters did not last long without them including JaiHonnah somewhere in the text or subtext. Actually, he enjoyed talking about her with his daughters. However, what of her family? He had never thought to ask. There was much that he wanted to know about her—beyond her life with Chapman. As he gazed at her, he realized that there was more that he wanted her to know about him too. He hadn't known her long, but maybe he could trust her with his secrets, especially about Monique. She already knew about some of his life, now he wanted her to know about the rest of his life—including his life with and divorce from Monique. Suddenly a thought occurred to him.

"You haven't seen the Baylor Plaza Park job site yet, have you?" he asked.

"No, we've been so busy with so many other projects that I haven't had time. Since your speech at the Black Caucus gala, we've been inundated with requests for proposals. You really know how to stir up your market and get your public talking about you."

"There's only one person I want to stir up," he said, not looking at her.

Somehow she thought that his cryptic remark might refer to Monique, his absentee-wife-turned-actress. After Roderick flew to Los Angeles for a few days with his daughters, it became common knowledge around the office that Monique was slated to have a starring role in an upcoming feature-length film. Monique was in the tabloids quite a bit of late on the arm of one movie magnate or another. Although Kelley had to get rid of a couple of aggressive reporters, Roderick didn't seem to let that kind of thing bother him, JaiHonnah thought. Still waters run deep, she had told herself.

"Do you know who that person is?" he was asking her when she snapped her attention back to him. She was about to answer him when they were interrupted.

"Well, good evening, you two. If I had known that you were here, you could have joined us," Savannah Logan said as she and a couple of doctors wearing hospital scrubs stopped at their table.

"Good evening," they both answered and acknowledged the other people with Savannah. "You're looking well," JaiHonnah said, noticing that Savannah's focus was on Roderick.

"I will be better, won't I, Roderick? We're still on for later, right?"

Roderick uncomfortably cleared his throat. "Uh, yes, I believe so, but if you have a change in plans, I'll understand—."

"Not tonight, handsome. Not an early-term pregnancy in sight. I've even taken myself off emergency call thanks to my friends. It cost me the price of dinner. No interruptions," she said, looking more at JaiHonnah than at Roderick. "It's been real, Jai," she said, grinning.

When Savannah and her friends walked away, JaiHonnah's eyes landed on him like an avalanche—cold and capturing. "So, now we know who it is you want to 'stir up'," JaiHonnah said, leaning forward on the table and lowering her voice to a dangerous level.

Roderick covered his face briefly with one hand and looked directly at JaiHonnah. "You seem to think that I'm the Rock of Gibraltar, but I'm only a man, more like the Walls of Jericho, I need to tumble every once in a while. You can thank yourself for putting the first wrecking ball to that wall. I was content until you came along and destroyed me on sight, literally and figuratively speaking, that is. So don't sit there in judgment of my behavior. You were the co-conspirator who contributed to my demise. Yes, I want to be with a woman. What healthy, heterosexual, red-blooded man doesn't?"

"Just any woman or Dr. Savannah Logan, specifically?"

"Specifically? JaiHonnah Reise Chapman. Generally? JaiHonnah Reise Chapman. Next question?"

JaiHonnah had no further questions. At least he didn't add the "Mrs." this time, she thought. Roderick made himself perfectly clear. It didn't help that twinge of silly jealousy she felt cutting through her gut. She wished that Savannah hadn't let on that she had a date with Roderick for later that night. Now she knew that she would spend another sleepless night thinking about Roderick making love with Savannah. The thought of them together was not just annoying, it was devastating. However, the thought of Roderick with any woman, including his wife, while he was in California had the same effect on her, she realized. When did it happen? When did she become so jealous of any woman who was in his life? Her emotions were going haywire, and it had to stop. She'd call for a doctor's appointment first thing in the morning.

Roderick again failed to keep his vow. He pledged that he would not say or do anything during the evening that would let his feelings for JaiHonnah show or share his secrets with her. Thank his lucky stars that Savannah stopped by the table before he really made a fool of himself, he thought. Changing the subject was a better idea given the circumstances.

"Let's ride out to the Baylor Plaza Park job site after dinner," he suggested.

"Tonight? But it's already seven-thirty, and you have a date remember?" she said stiffly.

"There you go worrying about my sex life again. If you'd stop worrying about it and *do* something about it, we could . . ." he cut his thought. Was he actually getting ready to say that they could get married and end the problem of his wayward wandering? God, where did that thought come from? Had he fallen that far already? *Back up, brother man,* he told himself. *That's what got you into trouble the first time with Monique.* He didn't want a repeat performance of that relationship. Of course, JaiHonnah was legally, as well as morally, outside of his reach. She was still a married woman. That factor became more than an annoyance. One that he was incapable of resolving. They had no future together, a fact that he had to accept.

"We could what?"

"Mr. Baylor, your table is ready now, sir," the maître d' announced.

Being saved by the proverbial bell again was a welcomed diversion, Roderick thought. Maintaining rational thought around JaiHonnah was beginning to be impossible.

* * *

Once they reached the Watergate Complex, Roderick walked with JaiHonnah to her door.

"Why don't you come in for a nightcap, Roderick?"

Roderick flicked his wrist to check the time. "Uh, I don't think that that's wise, Jai. It's been a long day. I'll see you in the office tomorrow. Maybe we can find time to talk a little more about Baylor Plaza Park."

"Why not now? It's not that late. I've got the time now, and I've got some questions to ask you while they're fresh in my mind. I have an idea that I think you'll like."

Roderick looked at his watch again. "Alright, if it will help you focus, we can talk for a few minutes, and then I have to go."

"Yes, I know. Savannah," she said and huffed as she opened the condo door.

"Jai, you and Savannah have some kind of history together or something?" he asked, coming in and closing the door behind him.

"No, why?"

"I don't know, but every time you mention her name you suddenly seem angry. There're some strong vibes there for some reason."

"You're the one who's always mentioning her, not me."

JaiHonnah headed for her bedroom.

"Jai, I don't bring her up, you do, and…where are you going? I thought you wanted to talk."

"I want to get my sketch pad," she called back over her shoulder to him. "Help yourself to a nightcap. I'll have a glass of white wine."

Roderick shrugged out of his top coat, went to the wet bar, and poured two glasses of wine. He picked up one glass and went out onto the terrace overlooking the fully lit John F. Kennedy Center. President

Kennedy's words came back to him. *"Ask not what your country can do for you. Ask what you can do for your country."* Roderick felt that he was finally in a position to take up that challenge. It was his father's dream, too, that spurred him on, challenged him after the 1966 March on Washington. *"Make it better. Make it what it is supposed to be."* He had come a long way in his life, he thought, but not so far that he had forgotten where he came from. Logistically, it was not a very long way from Bad Ass Place to Water Street to the Watergate Complex, a few miles across the Anacostia River, but they were light-years away from one another in terms of economic and social development. More than the river divided Washington, D.C. into two cities; one with the means to control their destiny and the other without. That was going to change. At least it would change in his old neighborhood. Baylor Plaza Park would be the beginning. It would bring new businesses and services to the area as well as new homes, new schools, and more importantly new life. He was on the brink of making that happen with JaiHonnah's help. He had set it into motion with his master plan.

Checking his watch again, he wondered what was taking her so long.

What she was going to do and why she was doing it was no mystery anymore. She didn't care to analyze it to death either, she thought, as she slipped into the black, silk palazzo pants that hung low on her hips and a matching black silk top that barely covered her bare breasts and slipped off one shoulder. Her waistline was exposed down to below her navel. She let her hair fall down her back and finger-combed it. A dab of *Oui* in the right spots and a touch-up with her lip gloss finished the look. He was her boss and a married man. Those were the facts. Now came the reality: She wanted him and needed him. Those were the truths.

Satisfied that she was prepared for her mission, JaiHonnah walked barefoot back into the living room. She saw the glass of wine waiting for her on the bar and noticed Roderick on the terrace. She lowered the lights slightly and slipped an old Roberta Flack CD into the player. She grabbed the wine and her sketch pad, and parked herself on one of the sofas.

Roderick walked back into the living room and instantly became a potted plant, rooted to the spot when he glimpsed JaiHonnah sitting on one end of a sofa, legs folded Indian-style beneath her with the large pad on her lap sketching. Her feet were bare and her long, black, thick hair hung over one bared shoulder as she worked. Her head was bent over her sketchpad as her fingers flew in broad strokes and outlines filling in spaces with the other markers in her hand.

"Uh, Jai, I think I'd better go," he said, placing his empty wineglass on the wet bar.

JaiHonnah looked up, gazing deeply into his eyes momentarily. She looked back at her pad and continued working.

"You've got time," she said, sweeping her hair back behind her left ear, her bare shoulder visible.

Her hair came undone again and she pulled it together twisting a quick loose plait. When she raised her arms, her black, silky top rode up and her fleshy bronze breasts were partly exposed just below the nipples which protruded through the fabric. Finished with her hair, a few more strokes with her pens, she raised the pad toward Roderick who stood transfixed with longing building in his torso. He had to turn his back to her as he grabbed his neck with one hand and the edge of the wet bar with the other to steady himself.

"Roderick, what do you think?" she asked still holding up the pad.

"I think you like driving me crazy," he said, looking blindly at the Kennedy Center. "Do you know, care or even understand what you're doing to me? For God's sake, Jai, please go put on something else. I want you so badly that it hurts. I can't even look at you. If I didn't know better, I'd say that you put on that sultry little number to get my attention. Well, lady, you've got it. Now what?" he asked, rubbing his neck forcefully.

JaiHonnah knew that her attempts at subtlety had failed. Roderick had figured out what she was up to and called her on it. She walked silently toward him and around to face the Rock of Gibraltar. He looked past her, balled his fists and jammed them into his pockets, she noticed. She placed her hands behind her back, stood on her tiptoes and licked at his lips, her unrestrained nipples straining against his chest. She noticed his breathing quicken and his jaw muscles flex, but he wouldn't look at her, touch her or acknowledge her kisses.

"You're the developer," she whispered, against his mouth, "develop something."

Roderick could take no more. She had pushed him beyond his limits. He held her away from him, but finally looked at her. Her beautiful face gave him no refuge from his desire. Flustered with his own yearning and embarrassed by the sheer size of his arousal, he felt a cruel indignation growing in him.

"What, so that you can bring in a wrecking crew in the morning and knock down all of my illusions? Thanks, but no thanks, *Mrs.* Chapman! I've witnessed, firsthand, how devastating a blow you can render. I've stood in the rubble before. I will not put myself in harms way again."

Undaunted and surprised by her own aggressiveness, JaiHonnah moved toward Roderick again with her hands still laced behind her back. Her head lowered, she moved into him, rubbing her hair under his chin and then slowly raising her lips to his throat. She gently kissed and licked at the granite wall.

Roderick held her away, but again and again she approached him.

"Jai, please, I can't stand it and you know that. I don't want just a one-night stand with you. You're not the flavor of the month to me. I won't be able to forgive you if you wave your marriage license or your employment contract in my face and walk away from me again. So if you don't intend that we be there for each other, don't start with me now... Heaven forgive me, I want you so," he groaned unable to hold off any longer. "Jai, don't play with me."

"Come to my bed, Roderick. Make love with me, please. I need you, too, and I'm tired of fighting it. No one's marriage license or contract will stand between us. I don't want to be your lady. I want to be your woman."

"Jai, for Heaven's sake, think about what you're saying. Those words spoken now with you in my arms when you know I can't resist believing you, trusting you again, giving you anything you want, could come back to haunt us both in the cold light of day. I'm still from the wrong side of the river. A pledge like that carries weight there."

"It carries weight on this side of the river too," she whispered against his throat.

Roderick placed his strong hands on her waist, lifted her straight up off the floor, and placed her on the bar to meet his level gaze. He searched deep into her topaz eyes and whispered. "Are you sure?"

Her answer came with a sweet, soft kiss that grew in intensity. She wrapped her arms around his neck and her legs around his waist. She whimpered as she took her pleasure from his mouth. Roderick groaned, carried her slowly to her bedroom without breaking the union until they reached the bed. He released her from her loose-fitting clothes and laid her down.

It was what he had dreamed about, fantasized about, and yes, even prayed over. He began to undress, letting his expensive and well-tailored suit fall in a crumpled heap on the floor. JaiHonnah's eyes appreciatively washed over him as he removed every stitch, and she seductively grinned when he removed his briefs.

"Last chance to back out, Jai," he said, his deep voice, low and thick with passion.

JaiHonnah moved over in the bed making room for him to lay down. He climbed in beside her, reached for her and pulled her on top of him. Her kisses were hot, wet and wildly enticing. He stroked from her back to her butt, reveling in the velvet-like feel of her fresh-scented skin. She straddled him, resting her heated core along his sensitive center. She stoked a fire within him that threatened to consume him in her heat. She moved his arms above his head, giving herself free access to his exposed body. Her long hair draped around them. She took full advantage of her position above him, riding him slowly, but methodically as if she were on a rocking horse. Roderick's deep groans as she teased his raisin-like nipples with her tongue were exciting her and were an indication that he was pleased with her approach. Still a novice at the art of fulfilling the needs of a man, JaiHonnah moved on to explore all the techniques that she had read about in books, improvising as she enjoyed every inch of Roderick's beautiful body.

Roderick was in a place that he had never been before. His emotions whirled out of control, lifting his body like a slow motion Mexican jumping bean as JaiHonnah's hot, elixir-like tongue took charge of him and controlled him skillfully. Not touching her was killing him. When he couldn't take it any longer, he sat up, breathing hard, to suckle at her breasts until he elicited convulsive gasps from her. He laid her on her back and pinned her hands above her head, trailing his hot kisses down her arms to her neck. Her whispered pleasure drew a tortured groan from him. He wanted nothing more at that moment than to please her, but her movement beneath him was drawing him closer to the edge.

Nearly completely lost in her rapture, he took time to protect them both, mounted her and she sheathed him deeper and deeper into her core. They moved together in perfect rhythm. It wasn't long before the first of many orgasms gripped her. Holding on to the edge of his sanity with his fingertips, Roderick brought JaiHonnah back to a heightened state, fighting to hold on to his diminishing control of his own body. When JaiHonnah sunk her tongue into his mouth, he knew that he was lost.

"Roderick!"

"Jai, oh God! Jai!" he answered as his body tightened abruptly and held its stiffness for longer than ever before. It felt like an eternity had passed before his body released him.

However, that was only the beginning of another all-night love feast.

* * *

Roderick rolled to his side searching for JaiHonnah. When he didn't find her warm body, his eyes popped open. JaiHonnah was not next to him. Fearing a repeat of their first experience together, he sat up, looking around the bedroom. "Jai," he called out anxiously. Then he heard the shower running in the bathroom suite. He quickly climbed out of bed and went into the first alcove which held a Jacuzzi then he moved to another alcove that contained the shower room. His heart was thundering in his chest. "Jai," he called to her, "are you alright?"

The double-glass, frameless shower doors opened, and her wet, smiling face beamed up at him. She reached for his hand and pulled him into the shower with her. He groaned as his tense body relaxed with her in his arms.

"You were sleeping so peacefully, I didn't want to wake you. I thought I'd make breakfast for you," she whispered as he held her.

"Breakfast can wait," he said, smiling. "I haven't finished loving you yet."

Roderick and JaiHonnah made love in the shower as the spray beat down on them from three directions. They washed each other's hair and bodies and lathered on fragrant shower oils. Later, they sat at a table in the breakfast room adjacent to the kitchen wrapped in bath sheets, finishing the hearty breakfast that they prepared together. They grinned at each other over the rims of their coffee cups as they tried to suppress the desire to return to their haven between the bed sheets.

"Oh," JaiHonnah said, remembering something important. "I have something to show you."

She rose from the table and left the room soon to return with her sketch pad. She handed it to Roderick. He studied it closely and a smile grew brighter over his countenance.

"Jai, you are a master. This is exactly what I had in mind. How did you know?"

"I didn't really. It's a rendition of an African village and a Navajo kiva combined. There's not that much difference between the two concepts, but they both achieve the sense of community that I think you're looking for. In both cultures, the center of the community was held sacred and made beautiful for all to enjoy. The rest of the village circled the center and grew out in this wagon-wheel effect from there. In this concept, the center will be a fountain and park that everyone can enjoy only by foot. No roads or streets. That will eliminate cars, noise and certain drive-by dangers. The homes will ring the park set off in pods of town homes and villas intermingled with small shops, businesses, schools and medical and other services. No high-rise density that gives the feeling of being trapped in a concrete-and-steel jungle or caged in chain-linked fences. People won't be jammed up on top of one another either. Trees, flowers and shrubs will be the only barriers. All unsightly utility services will be underground. Otherwise it will be spacious and open so that everyone can see the stars at night and not the harshness of halogen lights." She crawled into his lap with her back to his chest. He enveloped her in his arms as they viewed the drawings cheek to cheek. "Roderick, this is going to cost more to build because we won't be trying to squeeze people into every square inch of acreage, but in the final analysis it will be a fairly self-sufficient community attracting more jobs into the development and businesses to buy or lease space. It's like..."

"Small-town America in the big city. Truly an ideal inner city," he said finishing her thought and enjoying the feel of her on his lap. "I'm not looking for a monetary profit from this project, Jai. In fact, I fully expect to lose a bundle, but this needs to be a low-density, not a low budget, village. It's exactly what I wanted. It's a way of reclaiming our heritage and the sense of community and fellowship that I'm after. These are the traditions that are sacrificed by the building trade for a few dollars more on the balance sheet and profit-and-loss statement."

"I have a few ideas on how to save money on the project. I want to use shipping containers to fashion the homes and business.

"That's a unique idea. I've seen a demonstration of how melding together four to six containers can create a sizable home or business.

"That's right and at a minimum cost for each container. Far less than a stick built or prefab building and far more durable than anything on the market today.

"I also want to use geothermal energy to power the homes and a rain barrel system for the water supply and sewer system. If we do rooftop gardens, residents can grow their own fruits and vegetables year round in hydroponics farms."

"These are excellent ideas and they're on the cutting edge of the building and construction industry. If we succeed with this concept and train new employees using the trade funds for a journeyman's school, we could corner the market with new technology construction improvements."

JaiHonnah beamed with excitement as Roderick talked more about the vision for Baylor Plaza Park and her enervative ideas. She was ecstatic and feeling warm and tender thoughts from the man who held her lovingly in his arms. She could imagine herself curled in his lap every morning with little children growing up around them making their lives together complete, but that wasn't going to happen for them. What they had was an affair—not even a love affair but an office romance—doomed to end when his wife returned, and return she would when her movie debut ended. Return to the man that no woman in her right mind could walk away from. Return to the adorable little girls that Monique and Roderick had given life and love to. There was no place for JaiHonnah in that picture, but, for the moment, she and Roderick were sharing a Norman Rockwell rendition of a happy couple having breakfast.

"Jai? What is it, baby?" Roderick asked with great concern showing on his face.

She snapped from her daydream, found a smile, and brought it to the surface. "Nothing. Just doing a little wool-gathering. More coffee?"

"Jai, you felt like you were a million miles away and not too happy. If it's about being with me like this, I don't want you to regret it now, later or ever. You don't have to make any commitments to me that you're not ready for, and I won't take advantage of the position I've put you in by making demands on you or your time."

The words had barely left his lips when he realized that he *did* want to make a commitment to her, a permanent commitment to love, honor and cherish. It wasn't about the sex, which was definitely blissful perfection, but it was about needing to be with her and wanting her to be with him. He couldn't make her marital status go away with a wrecking crew. If he could, he would make it happen. She had to make that decision on her own, and he hoped that she'd come to the same conclusion—soon. He wanted her to be free of Calvin Chapman. Free to come to him and to love him. He wanted her as his wife.

JaiHonnah got up from her perch on Roderick's lap and poured more coffee. Could she trust this man she had only known for a few months with the truth about her disastrous marriage, her family connections? However, she didn't know the answers to those questions. She did remember Monique's threat, but until she felt more comfortable and confident with Roderick, she couldn't risk telling him the truth about her life.

She sat down in the chair across from him and slipped her toes between his thighs as he continued to review her sketches. His eyes twinkled as he tried to pretend that her toes weren't creating havoc with him, but she could feel the hardness growing and see the beads of perspiration on his face, bare shoulders, and chest. His mustache twitched almost imperceptibly and then he landed his intensely smoldering eyes on her. She ignored his gaze pretending to be more interested in the morning newspaper and her coffee. She hazarded a quick glimpse and knew immediately what was about to happen. She almost giggled out loud as she hopped from her seat and sped toward the bedroom with Roderick in hot pursuit. She was not quick enough though as he caught her midway to the living room and lifted her into his arms. They were both laughing hysterically as he carried her back to bed.

"Haven't had enough, huh?" He grinned as he placed her on the bed.

"Not nearly." She grinned devilishly as she released the towel from his waist and her tongue played with the small mole at the side of her mouth. "Breakfast just gave me more energy. I'm ready for lunch."

The sensuousness of that act drove Roderick to distraction. He slowly opened the offending terrycloth towel and gazed on her loveliness until he could stand it no longer. He could look at her forever if that were possible.

"Are you developing something or do I have to start drawing pictures for you?" she asked, her smile sassy and bright.

Roderick's grin grew broader, more deep, and lust-filled.

"Oh it's developed, alright, and you are the perfect picture," he said, lowering himself to her core, his head buried between her thighs. "Dinner is served," he said, groaning.

Roderick and JaiHonnah remained locked together until it was time to go to the office.

Chapter 16

"JRock, you should be feeling pretty pleased with yourself," Vivian said. "This is one hellava good deal."

"I'm very pleased about it. As you know, Rothman Childs is a crafty character so make sure that he doesn't try anything that we haven't anticipated."

"I'll have Accounting go over the details carefully. I think you'll be in a position to sign the deal after the Thanksgiving holiday. Uh, where's Jai?" Vivian asked, observing him closely. "Why didn't you bring her with you today to discuss this deal?"

Roderick recognized that innocent tone in Vivian's voice and her smooth segue into a questions about JaiHonnah. She was on to something. "She's at a conference for architects in Baltimore. She has been very busy lately," he replied, trying to mask the excitement in his eyes. He covered his face briefly then rested his elbows on the comfortable chair armrest and steepled his fingers.

"Uh-huh," Vivian remarked with a flash of a shy smile.

He knew that she had guessed the secret of his heart's and body's delight, but he wasn't going to admit it to her. There were Jai's feelings and reputation to consider. Vivian was Jai's friend and also knew her husband, Calvin. He had to leave the decision of what to tell Vivian about them being lovers up to Jai. Until then, he would protect their secret. He moved on. "I've been relatively surprised, but very pleased, that some of the bigger conglomerates haven't come after the Fairfax Conference Center project and tried to take it away from Baylor Design and Developers. I haven't heard any rumblings from companies like Axel Builders, Sprouse Industries or BlackHawk International. I thought that when I restructured the company, they would come after me with a hostile-takeover attempt."

"You know that those companies take their lead from BlackHawk, but your moves have not gone unnoticed."

"Yes, I do know that, but it's this parade rest that tells me that something's afoot. I come from a long line of old street fighters, so I know that the gangs are out there waiting, but for some reason they haven't armed their weapons."

"Not everyone is gun shy. Porter, Dare and Silver have their pistols loaded."

Roderick's head snapped to attention. "Lionel Porter?"

"The same. It seems that his company has been bouncing around the financial markets trying to find front money to acquire your company. Bouncing is about as far as they have gotten—so far, that is. Everyone is waiting to see whether BlackHawk swoops down on you looking for fresh meat. That's why Porter, Dare and Silver haven't been able to make an affirmative move."

"Then it's still BlackHawk that I need to watch," he said more as a confirmation of his own thoughts than as a question. "I haven't put a lot of time into monitoring BlackHawk's behavior lately, but I think that I ought to. They're a shrewd operation and very diversified. They own a few banks, I understand."

"At least," Vivian said. "You've taken on some high-risk projects before, JRock, and the ones you're aiming for now have you on a high-wire tightrope working without a net."

"That's where I want Baylor Design and Developers to be. I went to a conference last week with the Department of Transportation and Railroad Administration. Since September 11, there is a renewed interest in a national high-speed railroad system. I've been invited to join a fact-finding mission to Japan to study the success of their bullet train. Several Japanese investors have made contact with me about doing a limited partnership to build railroad systems across Africa, South and North America and Austria. That's where the challenges are. I'm going to keep my parachute handy though, but I want you to move forward with the acquisition of Johnson Concrete and Block as well as Harris Masonry as we discussed. I'm also looking at adding a lumber yard."

"These are excellent acquisitions, JRock. I'll contact Johnson's and Harris' corporate attorneys today. They've both been calling to see whether you were going forward with the deals."

"I had to nail down the Fairfax financing before I committed to the acquisitions."

"JRock, about Porter . . ."

"What about him?"

"These moves he's trying to make are very aggressive. Seems to me that it's about something more than business. In fact, it seems personal. I get the distinct impression that there's something between you and Lionel Porter that I don't know about. Do I need to ask the question?"

"I have some things to work out, Viv. Don't ask the question yet."

"You've made a final decision about your ten-year master plan then?"

"Yes, I have, but I'm not ready to discuss it at this point. Something else has my attention at the moment."

Roderick glimpsed a knowing look on Vivian's face. Although curious, patient and calm, her demeanor not otherwise illuminating her thoughts, he wasn't unaware of what she was thinking. With a brief glance at her notes, she asked.

"How are you and Jai getting along?"

Saved by the bell. Vivian's telephone rang with an important conference call. She put the call on hold.

"We'll have to finish this at another time," Vivian said, rising from her desk and locking her arms in his as she walked with him to her office door. "Maybe I should have the family over for dinner, which includes Jai, of course."

Roderick gave her a quick hug and a kiss on her brow. "The girls always enjoy your housekeeper's home-cooked meals, Viv," he teased, not indicating that he caught the reference to the family including Jai.

JaiHonnah was beaming with joy every day in the office and felt as if she were walking on cotton. Her effervescence seemed to surprise no one, though, especially not Kelley, who she believed guessed at the reason for her buoyant disposition. JaiHonnah knew that she was glowing like a neon light, but couldn't find the dial to turn down the brilliance, especially when Shelly and Shelby charged into her office with their daily doses of hugs and kisses. Each evening she would tell them a story after dinner and baths at bedtime and tuck them in with Roderick by her side. Then, she and Roderick would spend time alone in front of the fireplace in each other's arms talking or not talking and listening to relaxing music. No two people could have been happier, she thought.

* * *

The music from the stereo was low and melodic. The lights were off, and only the flames from the fireplace lit the room. JaiHonnah and Rodcrick lay on floor pillows in his living room watching the flames in the grate devouring the logs. Roderick pulled JaiHonnah closer as they lay on their sides spoon fashion. He caressed her breasts and she snuggled into his warmth. A soft moan escaped her as Roderick kissed her ear and her neck. She reached back over her shoulder and stroked the back of his head as he continued to send sparks throughout her body.

"That was a great meal you prepared tonight, Roderick," JaiHonnah said softly as his kisses continued to thrill her, "but if you keep kissing me like this, I'm going to make you my dessert," she teased.

"Promises, promises." He groaned against her ear and moved his leg to cover her thigh. "You've been so busy the last couple of weeks that we haven't had much time to be alone together. However, I have to admit that I talked Wesley into cooking the meal for use. Still, dinner was my way of getting you to come over and keeping you still for a few minutes. I've missed being with you."

"I've missed you too," she said, pressing her butt against his engorged phallus, "but I'm not the only one who's been busy, Mr. Baylor. You've been out of town lately, and when you're at home you're burning the midnight oil, too, you know."

"While I was in Japan I couldn't sleep because I was missing you. You've kept me awake a lot of nights whether I was away or at home. That's why I sneak into your bed every chance I get. I want to take time and do ordinary things with you, Jai, like go to the theatre and have dinner, go to a club and dance, go to the mountains for a long weekend."

"We've both been more than a little preoccupied," she said, sighing. "Between your Boys and Girls Club basketball teams three nights a week, your pro/am basketball games on Sunday and spending time alone with Shelly and Shelby, we haven't had time to catch up with each other."

"I wish that the Baylor Plaza Park project wasn't taking up so many of your nights. You've been meeting with several groups three or four nights a week, I understand."

"It's necessary for me to meet the business, church, school and community leaders to ascertain their needs and desires while I'm still in the design stage of the project. I've also been meeting with a group of young people who are interested in architecture or engineering as a career option. I have been asked to teach a course next semester."

"I've been asked to teach one, too; business and finance."

"Looks like we'll have to pencil each other in for lunch occasionally," she said, turning her head to kiss Roderick's forehead.

Roderick caressed her face and lowered his mouth to hers. He kissed her deeply, savoring her delicious taste and groaning his pleasure. JaiHonnah turned in his arms and put her arms around his neck. He gazed at her, and a lump grew in his throat. She was so beautiful in his eyes. He studied the baby-fine hair that rimmed her face; the dark eyebrows the color of a raven's wing; the soft, smooth, bronze-gold complexion; high cheekbones and luscious mouth. She was perfection. A deep hunger for her grew and smoldered in his eyes. "Lunch could never be enough time, Jai," he said, leaning forward and kissing her tenderly.

JaiHonnah stroked the thick, rich, rough texture of his hair, pulling him deeper into the kiss. He threaded his fingers through her long, naturally straight, silky hair massaging her scalp. His other hand slid inside her panties and palmed her butt. He leaned partially on to her as he kissed her harder, deeper. She lifted her leg between his strong, muscular thighs and began to slowly rub them. His maleness was thick between them. She felt it harden more, causing her need to copulate with him develop more forcefully in her core.

Roderick was completely captivated by the woman who lay beneath him. She was the fire that raced through him and stirred his desire into a blaze. Her lips made him hers and only hers. His mouth covered hers repeatedly, each time causing his need to build. His senses all focused on her as his tongue claimed the treasure of hers. He shuddered as she moved beneath him and between his thighs.

"Jai," he breathed against her throat. He wanted to scream the words, *I love you,* but the fear that she would reject him caused him to hold the words in abeyance. Theirs was such a perfect union, he thought. They never talked about the other's spouse or the fact that they were wrong to be together, each instinctively knowing that to do so would require acknowledgement that what was happening between them couldn't last, that it would only be for a short time until one or the other's spouse showed up, that what was happening between them was both wrong and so right. That there was a commitment that transcended their prior vows, yet reality was just below the surface.

Breath escaped JaiHonnah in her delirium, but her breathing was far from stable. The touch, feel, taste and sight of Roderick usually had that effect on her. Her body was hot for him, her nipples stood on end, pouted, and her soul reached out. *I love this man.* She knew with the certainty that the sun rose in the east. He was her north, south, east and west. He was her center. Nothing she had ever experienced made her feel the way he did. She fought against the image of his wife. He was hers—for the moment—not Monique's. She knew her love for him was wrong and that someday he would leave her, but what they had at that moment was intimate and precious.

He knew that what was happening between them couldn't last. She was another man's wife. A man who didn't deserve to call himself a man, let alone her man. The thought that Calvin Chapman had ever touched her wrenched his gut. She deserved better than Chapman. However, was he any better for her? God, the anxiety he felt, that their lovemaking outside the bonds of her marriage was wrong nearly drove him crazy, but if he and Jai were wrong, he didn't want to be right. She was his, and he'd spite the devil to keep her. He wouldn't ever relinquish what he had with her or extinguish his love for her.

"Roderick," she whispered when her passion and need for him reached a feverish pitch.

"I know, baby. I've got to have you or I'll die," he said, groaning and squeezing her to him.

"The girls," she cautioned. "If either of them wakes up..."

Before she could finish her thought, Roderick was up and lifting her into his arms. He carried her to his bedroom, closing the door behind him. When he let her slide down his body, he knew that was a mistake. The devilish gleam in her dark topaz eyes was electrifying. He turned the lock behind his back as she leaned into him, kissing him tenderly. Then he felt her hand slowly undo his slacks and slip inside his briefs. He let his slacks fall, pooling at his feet. His phallus was bared when she slid her hands inside his briefs and slid them down his thighs. Then her hands went under his bulky sweater until it cleared his head. He stood totally bare before her as she licked and kissed her way across his chest, stomach and abdomen, stroking him as she drove him slowly, but methodically, insane. His knees weakened when she took him into her mouth. Her nails raked his thighs tenderly like feathers. He groaned a loud guttural sound. "God, woman, you're driving me crazy." He could take no more. He lifted her and kissed her with all the passion he still had strength for. He stepped out of his clothes and covered the expanse to his sleigh bed. He removed her sweats and found no bra or panties.

"My God," he growled. "Please give me strength."

A body more exquisite didn't exist, he knew. Being inside her was, he believed, like heaven on earth. She gave new meaning to the term heavenly body. He lowered his head to the center of her passion and drew from her honey like a man possessed. He held her hips, loving her well past several successive orgasms before opening her soft, supple thighs and positioning himself between them.

He found her devilish mouth and tongue waiting to complete his undoing. By degrees he sank into her hot, wet core until no space existed between them. Heat rose from their bodies as they voiced their pleasure. Her clever tongue and warm breath against his ear proved lethal. The low hum that began in his core grew and spread throughout his being as JaiHonnah rocked and rolled beneath him.

Hot, wet sweat from Roderick trickled down between JaiHonnah's breasts and melded with her own. One breast in his mouth and the other between his fingertips her soul nearly leaped from her body. The love feast continued and repeated into the night.

* * *

It was difficult to kiss Roderick good-bye at Reagan National Airport with so many holiday travelers around, but her heart didn't break half as much when he whispered, "I miss you already. Hurry back to me safely and soon, please."

Now sitting on the Southwestern Airlines flight about to land in Farmington, New Mexico, the scent of him still tantalized and clung to her emotions. JaiHonnah had arranged for a car and driver to meet her at the airport. She was driven through the familiar Land of Enchantment toward the Navajo Reservation. The picturesque landscape looked the same as she remembered, as if carved by nature and illuminated by clear, blue skies. On the way she passed golf courses and guest ranches, pueblos and natural wonders, wineries and historic sights. It was all still so magnificent and grand, JaiHonnah thought, recalling summers spent there with her brothers and grandparents. She felt like she was coming home as she asked the driver to stop for bottled water. She stepped out of the car and was surrounded by her people,—*mestizaje*, people from mixed marriages, and *genizaros*, descendants of Spanish settlers whose ancestors were abducted during raids. Her great great-grandfather had ridden with Teddy Roosevelt's Rough Riders and her great grandfather survived the Bataan Death March in World War II. Although she felt equally at home among the Navajo as she did among Americans of African descent, she could trace her mother's ancestry among the Native Americans farther than she could through her father's Louisiana Creole or Cuban ancestry. Knowing not only *who* you were, but also *whose* you were, always of paramount importance to her and her family.

JaiHonnah reached Shiprock late in the afternoon. A towering mountainous peak rose majestically and defiantly before her. She knew when she saw it that she was home. The adobe village was equally spectacular as the bright day gave way to the beginning of a brilliant sunset. When the driver parked the car, she got out and walked only a few yards. Crowds of Navajo people stood silently in a circle surrounding others who were dressed in their brightly colored regalia. JaiHonnah stood silently as well, looking around at the familiar faces awaiting the signal. A blood-curdling scream pierced the calm, and the dance and chant began in an ancient singsong tongue. The singing was lusty, and when the dancing ended the people dispersed quietly. JaiHonnah spoke to her friends of long ago and then waited patiently for the approach of one of the women who had been in the circle. The woman's frame was slight, but steel-like in her constitution, stride and demeanor. Two long thick braids fell to just below her butt. She wore a native band around her head and native clothing. Turquoise stones draped around her neck and hung from her waist and wrists. The two women did not touch.

"*Ya'ha'teeh,* my child. You have been too long away from us," Kiavi Littlefeather spoke in Navajo.

"*Ya'ha'teeh,* Grandmother. It will not be as long between my comings and goings. You are well?" JaiHonnah answered, also in Navajo.

"I will not leave this earth soon. The concern I see in your eyes is not necessary, but I see anguish in your heart not related to my spirit. Come, now that evening prayers have ended, we will take supper together. You will tell me of your journey since you last visited me, and we will discuss the reason for your heart to be so heavy."

They went into the cool adobe hut and talked while Kiavi made dinner over the open flame in the large fireplace. She made tacos heaped with fresh lettuce, tomatoes, refried beans, guacamole, sour cream and fry bread. A rabbit stew with pan dulce simmered in a black pot hung from a wire over the flame.

"You have told me of your journeys throughout Europe, Asia and Africa, JaiHonnah, but you have not told me of this deep sadness within you. I feel your pain, granddaughter. It is deep, but it must come to the surface to be cleansed from your soul. We must speak of this thing now."

Too much wisdom and insight was contained in the slight frame of the woman whose eyes she shared for JaiHonnah to avoid the truth. Kiavi would know it was a lie regardless of how convincingly it was told. Keeping her own counsel would not be permitted in this house. The truth would spill out of its dark dungeon in her soul.

JaiHonnah drew an unsteady breath and told her grandmother of the vicious attack by Calvin months ago. Her grandmother sat patiently on a rug that she had weaved as they faced each other. Kiavi was emotionless as JaiHonnah talked. When she finished, Kiavi said without passion, sentiment or anger, "We will speak with the Shaman."

With that said, they began to serve themselves the meal. JaiHonnah reached for the red chili. Kiavi stopped her and JaiHonnah looked at her quizzically.

"That is not good for the seed that you carry. You are with child, JaiHonnah."

JaiHonnah felt as if her heart had stopped beating. She flushed, searching her grandmother's eyes in total disbelief. The food slipped from her numb fingers onto the rug. She lost all sense of feeling as she shook involuntarily. Blood seemed to rush from her head, and she felt dizzy and nauseous. Her grandmother's caress of her face stopped her gyrations and spinning head.

"You did not suspect?"

JaiHonnah forced herself to breathe. She tried to speak, but could only look in disbelief into her grandmother's eyes. Finally, she found her voice. "I cannot be pregnant, Grandmother." Her voice was but an octave above a whisper. "The doctor said that I had only a slim chance of ever conceiving after I lost my baby."

"The ancestors have chosen to smile upon you. You have suffered much and for much too long. Your pain is not yet ended, but it will end. The Shaman will confirm that I have spoken the truth. You carry a seed here," she said, placing her hand over JaiHonnah's abdomen. "It is a man child, a boy who will be tall like the trees, cunning as the wolf, brave like the bear and strong as the ox. He will have the wisdom of the ancestors to guide him. You will teach him that he is a son of Mexico in Keanu Littlefeather, my husband, and in Amina and Ra Pierro, my parents. A great-grandson of Nimo and Kove, and great-grandson of Matese the Spaniard and Minnel the Apache. That his line goes back to the Mayans, Toltec and Aztecs. He must be taught that he comes from great people through to you. He will need to know these things to be a leader among his people like his ancestors before him."

* * *

The Navajo medicine man entered the room and lit a twist of sage to purify the air. The Shaman, the traditional healer, *hatah'lii* (singer in Navajo), chanted complex and beautiful songs in a flat, nasal monotone, occasionally highlighted by an emphasis. He placed corn pollen in JaiHonnah's mouth and touched her body with a feather. JaiHonnah felt a sense of harmony and well-being when *hatah'lii* left the room

"Grandmother, I live in two realities: I am a Black woman as well as a Navajo woman. It is not that I doubt what you and the Shaman have told me, it is that this seed may be that of my former husband. If it is so, and he has knowledge of this pregnancy, he will have a means to control me. If he has that means, he will seek to use it against my father who he both hates and fears. A man who no longer fears has nothing but hate left. He will attack my father out of hate, and my father will strike back."

"And if this seed is not that of your former husband, which reality can you follow? That of the Navajo or that of the Black?"

"But I am one in the same, Grandmother."

"No, JaiHonnah, the Black woman washes her body of the seed as easily as she washes her clothes. The Navajo woman does not wash her body of the ancestors' gift."

"You were reading my thoughts. It may be better that this seed not grow because of the trouble and despair that its life could bring."

"This seed has life. It is a gift from our ancestors. It must grow because it will erase the trouble and despair that you find in your heart and in your future."

"Future? Grandmother, the other man with whom I have slept is not free. His bonds to his family are strong. He has children, a wonderful set of twin girls. His woman would take his children from him. I cannot bring this matter to him. It is my burden to bear alone if that is what I must do."

"A man separated from his son is only half a man. Once your path is clear, you must tell this man, if he is the father. You would not have given your body to him if you did not love him. A woman who truly loves a man could not hurt him by withholding his son from him. Your soul is still your own. When you can trust him with your soul, share it with a man, you will know the right path to take. You are not alone. Your ancestors will be with you in this. They tell me that what we were, you are now. You carry the seed of the ancestors. What you have been, you are still. Your vision is who you will be."

Kiavi again laid her hands on Jai's abdomen, frowned then smiled slightly, nodding as if in approval. JaiHonnah didn't know what to make of her grandmother's Mona Lisa smile and was too steeped in thought and visions of her own to ask questions.

Chapter 17

Roderick sat before the giant flat-screen in Kelley's large Capitol Hill corner brownstone row house with his brothers and sisters, their families, and his daughters. The Macy's Thanksgiving Day Parade, passing by the camera and commentators dictating everything that was happening, held no interest for him, though as he looked around at his siblings and their happy families.

Restless, he rose from his comfortable seat and went into the kitchen where Kelley was busying herself with preparations for dinner. He sat at the bar that divided the kitchen from the dining room and nibbled at a carrot stick. He rested an elbow on the counter and stretched his long legs out across the other three stools at the bar. He glanced back into the den where he noticed Walter, his oldest brother, put his arm around his wife, Marie, pull her close to him, and absently kiss her on the forehead as they continued to enjoy the parade. Francis, next in line, sat on the floor between his wife Gail's knees as she lovingly stroked his arms and chest. Francis looked up at her eliciting a kiss which she delivered with a warm smile. Karen, his older sister, was busy plaiting one of her daughter's braids as Harold Knight, Karen's husband, stretched out on the floor resting his head on their daughter's lap napping more than watching the parade. The nieces and nephews, including his twins, were sprawled over one another on the floor laughing and talking about the characters in the parade. It was a happy Kodak moment, but he wasn't in the picture. Roderick's thoughts were elsewhere. Wherever JaiHonnah was, he wanted her to be here with him sharing in the day with his family.

Roderick didn't know what emptiness felt like until the Southwestern Airlines flight carrying JaiHonnah pulled away from the gate at Reagan

National Airport. It wasn't until the aircraft rolled out of sight that he noticed the little kids patiently standing before him and asking for his autograph. He wordlessly signed the bits of paper and walked through the airport deep in thought. The chill in the November air caused him to walk briskly to his car. When he opened the door, he noticed an envelope on his seat addressed to him. The carefully penned and colorful calligraphy told him immediately that it was from JaiHonnah. The hand drawing on the card depicted the first Thanksgiving with the Native Americans sharing the bountiful harvest with the settlers. Of course, there were many Black faces depicted, too, also sharing in the feast. The inscription read: *Happy Thanksgiving. I miss you too.* He laughed aloud in the hollow of his vehicle with JaiHonnah's delicate scent still present in the air.

"JRock, if you're going to look that unhappy, you can peel the onions and really have a reason to cry," Kelley joked, snapping him back to reality.

"Not that I'm not willing to help out, but *onions?*" he asked, frowning playfully. "How about the potatoes or the yams?"

"Already done. I need onions for the gravy," she said and smiled knowingly.

Roderick pulled himself from his perch, put a pot of water on to boil and dropped in onions into the water. When the skins loosened, he stripped them off, put the onion in the Cuisinart and pushed chop. Proudly he turned to face Kelley, folded his arms across his chest, leaned his butt against the countertop and crossed his legs at the ankles.

"Next?" he said, grinning.

"That was too easy. Mama always said that you were the best cook in the family," she said, shaking her head.

"I was the youngest. She had more time to work on me," he said, laughing. "The rest of you were out and about getting into mischief."

"That's how you got here, little brother. Daddy and Mama making mischief long after the old biological clock should have stopped ticking," she teased him. "I was expecting to maintain my position as the baby in the family until you came along and changed that."

"You still maintain your position as the baby girl."

"Not so much a baby anymore. I'll be forty-three my next birthday."

"You mean you'll be celebrating the second anniversary of your forty-third birthday, don't you?"

Kelley pursed her lips and rolled her eyes. "Don't remind me." She took a headlong look at him, he noticed.

"What?" he asked and grinned.

"Seems you haven't been balling your fists in your pockets lately," she said with a query laced in her voice.

Roderick only grinned.

"Must have something to do with Pocahontas," his brother Francis Baylor said, breezing into the kitchen and playfully sparing with Roderick.

"Pocahontas?" Karen asked, following him and looking for a can of soda in the tall, clear-glass, beer and wine cooler. "Who's Pocahontas?"

"JaiHonnah," Kelley said, grinning. "I see the girls have been talking to you too."

"Yeah," Francis said, taking the soda from Karen, much to her dismay, and taking a long gulp. "Seems you been spending a little time with an Indian princess, JRock. So what's the story? The adult version, that is."

"When's dinner gonna be ready?" Walter asked, coming into the kitchen.

"Soon enough," Kelley said. "Right now we're trying to solve a mystery."

"Mystery? What mystery?" Walter asked, taking the can of soda from Francis and finishing it in one long gulp.

"Pocahontas," Karen replied. "Seems JRock's been holding out on us."

"Pocahontas? Who's Pocahontas?" Walter asked.

"JaiHonnah," Francis, Karen and Kelley answered in unison.

All eyes landed on Roderick.

"Well, time to make the gravy," Roderick said without further thought to his older siblings' questions.

Roderick knew that he would not get by any one of his sisters or brothers very easily, but getting past all of them collectively took a skill level he hadn't reached yet in his thirty-six years. This time he had to accomplish that feat. Besides, the fact that he and Jai were lovers wasn't just his secret to keep, but hers too. He had not taken the time to sort through his many emotions about JaiHonnah to trust her with his heart and secrets, and he was not prepared to do so with his siblings and all of their children waiting with bated breaths. He would have time later after the college football games had gone into the record books and the remaining turkey, roast beef, and ham became salads or sandwiches to be devoured before the evening passed into history.

Back in his own home, Shelly and Shelby peacefully asleep in their beds, Roderick sat alone before the fireplace watching the flames lick the edges of the logs. He rested easily in the chair, wrapped in his silk robe with his bare feet crossed at the ankles up on an ottoman. He steepled his fingers in a reflective mood, recalling the last time he and JaiHonnah made love on the rug before a roaring fire. The vision was so vivid that it drew a deep, needful groan from his core. Too perfect were the words that entered his thinking. Being with her was too perfect. Making love to and with her was too perfect. Letting himself dream of a too-perfect future with her would be a mistake and consequently his undoing. She was not like Monique in any dimension, but she was capable of rejecting him, of hurting him deeply and entitled to do so given her current marital status. He had no hold on her nor did he have a right to demand anything of her. What JaiHonnah gave to him was a gift, not an obligation, and he recognized that in his head. In his heart, he was beginning to want more—much, much more—but he pledged that he would not make demands on her. He intended to keep that vow. The question was what was he going to do with his need for her emotionally? And could he trust her with a secret that affected not only him, but also his family, his precious daughters? Could he tell her the truth? That Shelly and Shelby might not be his? That he was paying Monique what amounted to a queen's ransom to keep quiet?

Roderick didn't know when it started, but somehow it seemed to be there from the very moment he laid eyes on JaiHonnah. It was a knowledge deep in his soul that they were meant to be together. Something primal, pristine, almost religious swept over him. He got that same sensation when they were together at Chuck's ranch in Prince George's County a few weeks earlier. It was a two-hundred-sixty-six acre spread that Chuck and Vivian found six years earlier quite by accident. The old White Mansion property was then a dilapidated, abandoned farm, but Chuck, after Vivian's marriage to Derrick, buried himself in restoring the old place to its original majesty. Chuck's effort paid off handsomely over the last six years.

Roderick recalled how he and JaiHonnah took Shelly and Shelby, Vivian's children, and his nieces and nephews to pick pumpkins for Halloween, which was the truth, but what he nor JaiHonnah told Vivian was that the pumpkins were on Chuck's ranch. He knew that Vivian would be pissed off once she found out, but it was worth incurring her wrath to see the look on Chuck's face when he and JaiHonnah arrived with Vivian's children. The fact that Chuck loved those little people was evident, and the way that he enveloped them each individually and collectively warmed the heart.

Chuck hired, as permanent ranch and farm hands, more than twenty men from one of the homeless shelters. He pulled his ranch hands away from their daily tasks to walk beside each child as they rode on ponies in the exercise corral, ensuring that none of the children had a chance of injury.

Everyone was surprised, though, when JaiHonnah cut one of Chuck's best thoroughbreds out of a herd, mounted the horse bareback, and raced the steed around a quarter-mile track in record time. Roderick had stood with the children, the farmhands and Chuck at the rail as JaiHonnah whizzed around the track with eyes sparkling, face shining and hair flowing in the wind. There was a determination in her eyes that was unmatched by anything else he witnessed in her. She was single-minded about getting the best from herself and from the thoroughbred—and she did. One of the ranch hands remarked that the horse never ran a faster speed, even in the competitions in which Chuck entered it. Everyone attributed the record-breaking performance speed to JaiHonnah's handling of the steed.

With relative ease and in short order, JaiHonnah made the brown beauty perform a few tricks for her audience. The children's mouths had hung open, and their eyes had popped out of their heads. Shelly and Shelby were walking on clouds when JaiHonnah gathered them in front of her on the horse's bare back as she walked it around the track to cool down. His girls still laughed at him because he was reluctant to climb up on anything so powerful that he could not control, even if JaiHonnah was the driver. JaiHonnah never made him feel badly about his reluctance to ride, but she warned him that, by that time next year, he, too, would be putting that thoroughbred through his paces. He agreed that she could try, but he preferred how she handled him over how she handled the horse.

That night, after they put the girls to bed, she demonstrated just how well she could handle him, but he had no complaints on that score. Nor had she complained when the tables were turned, and he took them both beyond the limits of reality.

Roderick smiled to himself, leaned his head back against the leather chair, mentally stroking off the erection that had grown while he thought about JaiHonnah on that horse. Seeing her soon was uppermost in his mind followed by sleeping with her in his arms. "JaiHonnah," he whispered.

Chapter 18

Roderick stood in the airport impatiently waiting for JaiHonnah's return from New Mexico. It had only been four days since she left. He had practiced being cool, calm and collected, but his patience was failing. He had turned his baseball cap on his head three times finally settling for wearing it in his traditional manner, in reverse. His sunglasses were perched on top of his head over the cap. He had moved them to several different positions as well. His arms were once folded over his chest, then into his pockets and then across his chest again. The waiting was excruciating.

Where is she! he wondered and, then, as if he had said *abra cadabra,* the darkness parted, and the sun rose as JaiHonnah's face came into view at the security checkpoint. Her arrival was tantamount to the birth of a new universe to him. All efforts to remain stoic and put into action what he had practiced diminished when she smiled at him and walked into his open arms. He wrapped her in his leather bomber jacket and pulled her close to him. That was the feeling, the heat, the sensation that his body had craved, had ached for since she left. His body came alive as soon as she touched him. He could not wait for privacy. He lifted her chin and took his pleasure from her treasured mouth. Her whimper intensified his joy, and he deepened his kiss in the treasure beyond her lips.

"Where are the girls?" she asked, her voice husky.

"With Vivian on a shopping trip looking for Christmas presents. They're spending the night and she's taking them to school in the morning."

"How are things in the office?" she asked with a grin.

"What office?" He grinned back.

"Your office, Mr. Baylor. You know, the place that butters my bread?" she teased.

"You want your bread buttered, do you?" he asked with a raised eyebrow and a delicious grin on his lips.

JaiHonnah blushed, he noticed, but something was different. She was radiant, but something he saw in her eyes bothered him, worried him in fact. Her joy at seeing him was real enough, he believed. Her response to his kiss was real, too, but he knew her well enough to know that she was holding something back.

"Let me get you home and you can tell me all about your visit with your grandmother." Roderick felt her tense and saw her brilliant smile slipping slightly. "Everything was alright, wasn't it? With your grandmother, I mean?"

"Yes, she is well. My visit was long overdue, but...well, maybe we can talk about this another time. It was a long trip, and I'm feeling a little weary."

"Then I have just the solution." He grinned guiding her away.

JaiHonnah disrobed and slipped into her short terry-cloth cover up. She loosened her hair and brushed it out as she sat at the vanity in front of the mirror. Roderick was in the Jacuzzi room. She could hear the water running, but he had dared her not to enter, and she had agreed to stay out of his way. She looked at her face in the mirror and wondered if she looked any different. Touching her abdomen with the flat of her hand, a flush colored her cheeks and curved her mouth into a Mona Lisa smile. She knew what she saw in Roderick's eyes when he saw her coming through the airport. His earth-shattering smile had thrilled her. No one had ever greeted her return with such passion and so publicly. The sight of him standing there so straight and tall and so handsome had sent what felt like a punch singing through her system. His kiss was so warm, tantalizing and welcoming that her knees wanted to buckle. His arms were so strong, powerful and protective that she felt safe and loved. Momentarily she had forgotten her pain and her fears. All there was, was him in his splendor, and he was all that she wanted to see.

JaiHonnah looked up in the mirror and saw Roderick standing behind her. He took the brush from her hand and lovingly began to brush her hair. When he finished, he lifted his hand to her and together they strolled into the Jacuzzi room. Scented candles lit the space, bathing it in a warm yellow, flickering glow. Paul Taylor's saxophone played melodiously from the tiny, wall-mounted speakers. Roderick stepped into the bubbling water and gently brought her against his body. He untied her robe and slipped it from her shoulders, kissing her bare skin at the hollow of her neck. He removed the bath sheet from around his waist and sat in the water, bringing her down with him and putting her between his muscular thighs with her back to his front. JaiHonnah leaned back against Roderick as the foaming water enveloped them. He added fragrant bath salts, and the room filed with the intoxicating pleasant aromas. Roderick sponged the warm, scented water over JaiHonnah's body. Then he placed a bowl of freshly cut fruit that was languishing in sparkling cider on the edge of the Jacuzzi. He fed them both the fruit piece by piece until they were full. They closed their eyes, letting themselves drift and feel their senses capture the tastes, smells, sounds and touches that surrounded them. The warm, churning water had a dizzying effect on them. Their caresses added to their excitement. They were drifting away from themselves and clung to each other. The outside world didn't exist in their aquatic cocoon, only the two of them, and they were at peace as one.

As the water began to cool, Roderick lifted JaiHonnah and carried her to the bed, resting her warm, wet body on towels. He turned her onto her stomach, straddled her and began massaging her body slowly and methodically with warmed, scented oils as she moaned with delight. His hands were gentle on her body, feathering his touch in her more sensitive areas. He rolled her over and began the process anew from her toes to her head, stopping to pay proper homage to her sweet spot and her breasts, but no place on her body went unappreciated.

"That was wonderful," JaiHonnah said, lying comfortably naked in Roderick's arms. She smiled as she kissed him gently at his throat.

"There's more where that came from, but I'm going to go now and let you rest."

"Do you have to?" she asked in a whisper, stroking his chest.

"No, I just thought you'd want to rest. I don't have to—."

Her kiss told him that there was nothing more important to her than his being exactly where he was at that moment. Her touch told him that she wanted him, appreciated him and the thought of her need excited him beyond belief. No man had ever felt this much joy, Roderick thought.

"Something else I can do for you, ma'am?" he asked and grinned down at her as she stroked him.

JaiHonnah didn't look into his eyes, he noticed, but he heard something in her voice when she whispered, "Make love with me, please, Roderick. I need you."

He positioned himself between her smooth thighs. "We, at Salon Baylor, aim to please, ma'am," he teased, searching for her eyes, but they were half-closed.

JaiHonnah tried to keep her spirits up and lighthearted, but her inner soul was in torment. She couldn't look Roderick in his eyes or she would collapse into tears. She wanted to trust him, to tell him that she was pregnant with another man's child, but she couldn't bring herself to do so. If she told him he would surely end their affair. Sooner or later the truth would show itself as her body changed and she would lose him, but for a little while longer she would selfishly hold on to the rapture. She wanted joy in her life, and he had been the one to supply it.

"I want the full treatment, sir. That's what I came into your salon for, and I want my money's worth."

"Dollar for dollar, pound for pound?"

"Every cent for every ounce," she quipped.

"You drive a hard bargain, but it's a deal," he said and smiled against her lips as he began the slow, joyous process of joining himself to her, but something was still wrong. Her words were enticing and stimulating, but her eyes had closed him out.

JaiHonnah felt so safe and secure in Roderick's arms. She closed her eyes, let herself drift and felt her senses capture the feel of him, savoring it for the day when they would no longer be lovers. Then he was outside of her reach. She couldn't control her thoughts. Roderick was kissing her feet, her ankles, her legs, her thighs. His hands were gentle as he opened her legs and brought her to a state of euphoria where she had never been before. She felt herself feel for him as she gasped and panted through an orgasm. Finally, when she floated back from her private heaven, she caught his hand and pulled him to her. As soon as he slid into her, another wave of uncontrollable tiny explosions passed within her. Colors, like fireworks, burst in her mind's eye. She was making sounds that she did not recognize, but those explosions were too great for her to focus on anything but holding on tightly to Roderick.

Slowly Roderick moved within her warm, scented body. He whispered in her ear. "Let yourself go, baby. Relax. I'm here with you. No one, but us, Jai. No one in the universe, but you and me."

He was rocking her very core. She wanted to believe that they were the only two people in the universe. She held on tight as she slipped outside herself and felt Roderick's strong arms holding her as the next wave of explosions hit her and took away her ability to control her muscles, her voice, her thoughts. She dug her fingers into his flesh as another wave grew, flooded and took her yet farther away from herself. Her breathing intensified. She panted as the shockwaves hit again and again. Over and over he rolled himself inside her with pleasurable slowness as slow as slow motion, but as powerful as an earthquake.

"Let it all go, JaiHonnah," Roderick whispered. "All of it. We can do this together."

She could not speak. The colors were brilliant. Their bodies stiffened as the perfumed oils mixed with their body heat and sweat, and they slid against each other, intensifying their movements by degrees. JaiHonnah opened her mouth to catch her breath. They voiced their pleasure, flew free and then slowly brought themselves back from wherever their souls had flown.

Roderick's head lay pillowed on her breasts. She cradled him and laid her cheek against the top of his head. Her heart raced out of control.

Roderick lay there holding her as she drifted into sleep with silent tears of sorrow and joy staining her face. She remembered her dream from months ago; from the day she returned to the United States. There was trouble ahead her dream had portended.

Roderick and JaiHonnah slept and woke again through the night, renewing their union, their bodies like addicts in need of another powerful love fix. The next morning when she opened her eyes to the beginning of a new day, Roderick lay beside her, his arms still around her, one hand behind his head, his body fully exposed, one leg bent at the knee. She wanted to touch his smooth, brown skin. She ran her hand lightly over the damp, smooth hairs on his chest and abdomen. Then she felt a twinge in her abdomen. A sensation of excitement that she had not felt in a very long time.

"Good morning," Roderick whispered close to her ear followed by a kiss. "Did you rest well?"

"Yes, very well, thanks to you," she said, snuggling closer to him.

"Now tell me what's bothering you." He kissed her forehead.

JaiHonnah tensed. "Nothing. Nothing's bothering me."

Roderick moved his head to look into her eyes. He lifted her chin. "Jai, something is wrong. I could see it in your eyes when you got home yesterday. I could feel it in your body when we made love. You were wound tighter than a drum. Last night you tossed and turned in your sleep. Tell me that it's none of my business, if you want, but don't lie to me and tell me that nothing is wrong."

JaiHonnah buried her face in his chest. "Could we not talk about it, Roderick? It's nothing really. I'll work it out. I just need a little time."

Roderick's thoughts were troubled. Why was she not being open with him? Was she pushing him away again? Had she had another change in her feelings toward him? Was she feeling guilty for letting another man other than her miserable excuse for a husband, make love to her? Had he hurt her? Been too physical with his needs throughout the night? Maybe she had not gone to see her grandmother after all. Maybe she had been with her husband and was feeling guilty. No thought that crossed his mind gave him any comfort. He gritted his teeth and his muscles tensed. Or maybe whatever was bothering her had nothing at all to do with him.

"Jai, I'm going home. I want to be there when the girls get home from school. I suppose you'll be in the office later," he said, sitting up on the side of the bed. He reached for his watch and ring.

"Roderick," JaiHonnah said, leaning on one elbow and stroking his tense back. "Please, I just have a few things on my mind. I'll talk with you about them when I can, but not now."

Roderick looked over his shoulder at the distress on her face. Turning toward her, he smoothed her brow with his thumb and caressed her face. "I don't think of myself as only your lover, Jai. I consider myself your friend too. I can't help you when you shut me out, when you don't tell me what's going on. I care about you, not just because we have great sex together or because we work so well together, but because I respect you."

She kissed the palm of his hand. "Yes, I know. I feel the same way." She did not offer more.

Roderick dressed, kissed her on the forehead and left. JaiHonnah lay in bed wrapped in guilt, contrition and shame. She could not tell her friend and lover that she was carrying another man's child.

Roderick found JaiHonnah pensive, introspective and self-absorbed in the few weeks that followed her return from the Thanksgiving holiday. They had not had sex since that day. Although they worked steadily together on the Baylor Plaza Park project and others, JaiHonnah seemed otherwise distant, remote, and removed from him, but not from his daughters. With them she remained warm, giving, and affectionate.

* * *

"What's wrong, good buddy?" Chuck Montgomery asked as they finished the third pick-up game of basketball. "You're way off your game this week."

"Sorry, man. Just got a lot on my mind. Just couldn't pull it together."

"Woman trouble, huh?" Chuck asked knowingly.

Roderick gave him a sideways glance.

"C'mon, man, let's go sweat," Chuck said, heading for the sauna.

The two men positioned their nude bodies in the hot, steamy room stretched out on towels talking about their games, the NBA season that was underway and Roderick's boys' basketball squad that played in the Police Boys and Girls Club league. They talked easily together as they relaxed.

"You and Jai, you two got something going?" Chuck asked.

Roderick laughed. "Man, you sure know how to get to the bottom line. Maybe you should give up medicine and come into the business with me full time."

"I sit on your board of directors, and I invest my ill-gotten gains with you, but, for the life of me, I can't get a straight answer out of you with a flat iron. Now, what's the deal? Is she your lady or what?"

"Yes and no."

"Well that's a start. What's the no part?"

"Beats the hell outta me. The last couple of weeks she—well it's been rough."

"I see," Chuck said quietly.

Chuck knew what was going on. More than he was at liberty to discuss with Roderick. JaiHonnah made an appointment to come to his office for a checkup. After he examined her and ran a few tests, he confirmed that she was indeed pregnant. She didn't seem at all surprised by the news, but she was very interested in the approximate date of conception. Since obstetrics and gynecology were not his specialties, he recommended one of the best doctors in that field, Savannah Logan.

"Well, I'm glad you do because I damn sure don't."

"You know, Kenneth Alexander told me something about women a while back that I haven't forgotten."

"Vivian's brother?"

"Yeah, he told me to use the KISS method with them."

"I don't get it. What's the KISS method?"

"Keep It Simple, Stupid."

Roderick laughed. "Probably not bad advice. Especially the stupid part."

"It hasn't worked for me with Vivian, but it may do some good for you in the long run. Like Vivian, Jai is no ordinary woman. If she's looking for space, give it to her."

"Yeah, but, Chuck, you've been in love with Vivian for more than six years that I know of. That's a hellava lotta space."

"You telling me that it's love that you're feeling for Jai?"

"Man, at this point, I don't know what it is."

"Want some advice?"

"Could I avoid it if I said no?"

"No."

"Well, what is it?"

"Don't dive in unless you're prepared to swim, and don't swim until you know how deep the water is."

* * *

JaiHonnah came back into Savannah Logan's office after her examination.

"Have a seat, Jai. I want to go over these reports before we talk," Savannah said.

JaiHonnah sat looking around Savannah's tastefully decorated office. Her impressive degrees hung on one wall. On another was a collage of pictures of babies that she had delivered and the names and birth dates of each. If she decided to keep this baby, she wondered whether Savannah would put her baby's picture in the collage too. She brushed the thought aside. Generally, JaiHonnah was impressed with Savannah's thoroughness and professionalism. She had expected something entirely different from her one-time nemesis. What she found, when she checked with other sources, was that Dr. Savannah Logan was well respected in her field and thought to be highly competent. Her private life seemed not to interfere with her professional one and the reverse was also true.

Savannah jotted notes into her computer and wrote out a prescription. Then she closed the computer file and turned her attention to JaiHonnah.

"There's no question that you conceived in early September. I believe that you should see your bundle of joy in early to mid-June. I'm not going to put you on a diet. Based on your lab results, you seem to be in very good shape. I am concerned about two things. First, your blood pressure seems a little high, but I'll monitor that very closely. Second, your intake of iron. I prefer that my pregnant mothers get their intake of vitamins and minerals from natural, not artificial sources. I suggest that you alter your diet to include more iron-rich foods and calcium. I'll give you a prescription for an iron-therapy medication, but I only want you to take it if your anemia flares up. Otherwise, continue your physical fitness program on a light-to-moderate schedule. I'm going to put you on a regular visitation schedule with one of my nurse practitioners. Now, are there any questions?"

"Savannah, can't you give me a better indication of exactly when I conceived? I mean early September could span as much as two to three weeks."

"That's as close as anyone can get at this point in your pregnancy, Jai. Is there some reason why the exact date is crucial to you? I mean, this is not just idle curiosity on my part."

"There is a reason, but I really don't care to go into it."

"That's fine. I only need to know whether there is some medical involvement that could affect the fetus. I've reviewed your medical history, and I'm aware that this is not your first pregnancy. I spoke with your physician in San Antonio. Frankly, he was very surprised that you were able to conceive again. I want you to know that I don't intend for you to lose this baby, if that's what you're worrying about. I will do everything humanly and medically possible to assure that you carry this baby to term and deliver a healthy child. Your age should not be a problem, but your emotional state could be."

"And if I want to terminate this pregnancy?"

Savannah sat back in her seat, narrowing her eyes before she spoke. "Then you're talking to the wrong doctor. I don't perform abortions unless the mother's life or health is in danger or the fetus would not survive outside the womb. If that's what you're considering, then I can recommend some very fine OB/GYN specialists who do perform the procedure. I caution you, however, that if you are seriously considering abortion as a real alternative, then your time is running out. No reputable physician will perform an abortion in the second trimester. Profession aside, I hope that you will want to carry this fetus to term."

JaiHonnah's eyes met Savannah's. "You haven't asked me about the father."

A wave of Savannah's hand dismissed the comment. "He's not my concern unless there's something in his medical history that can affect the fetus. You and your baby are my primary concern."

Leaning forward on the desk, JaiHonnah penned Savannah with her eyes. "I want this pregnancy kept in the strictest confidence."

Savannah leaned forward and reached for JaiHonnah's hand. "That goes without saying, Jai. We're certainly not silly college coeds anymore. I don't play games with my patients' health."

JaiHonnah took Savannah's hand, squeezing gently. "Thank you, Savannah. I'll let you know whether I need those referrals."

Chapter 19

JaiHonnah finished wrapping the Christmas gifts that she had brought back from the Navajo reservation for Shelly and Shelby. She tucked them away in her office where the girls wouldn't find them, planning to give the gifts to them before she left for the Christmas holiday. She held the Navajo baseball cap in her hand for a moment thinking about Roderick. She would give it to him personally that night, she thought. She decided that she had to share her secret with him. She had to tell him the truth about her marriage to and divorce from Calvin and that she was carrying Calvin's child.

Roderick had been so patient with her over the past weeks since her return from New Mexico. She desperately wanted to be with him, but her mind had been in turmoil. She had finally decided to keep the baby, and she felt that a weight had been lifted from her shoulders. The endless nights of thinking about the potential problems that could occur kept her awake. This turmoil had to end. She knew what she had to do. Kiavi said that once her path was clear, the pain would end. Her pain had to end, and she had to tell Roderick what haunted her. She folded the baseball cap into the box and wrapped it.

That completed, she moved on to the final touches on the Baylor Plaza Park model that she constructed for the presentation and demonstration scheduled before the District of Columbia City Council. She needed a few more photographs for the slide show that she was planning and then she would present it to Roderick. She knew that he was anxious to see the project finally get underway in the early spring. He worked closely with the city planning office to secure the licenses and permits that would be needed before he could start clearing the land for construction of the first phase of the project, the park. The remainder of the project would unfold over a five-year period. Everything was proceeding at pace and few people raised any questions about the need for the project. Those who had were quickly brought over to Roderick's position, she mused. He had a very persuasive style. Just look at how he had swept her off her feet in the space of four short months.

The telephone rang, and JaiHonnah stopped her woolgathering to answer it.

"Jai Chapman," she answer in a light voice.

"Chapman, huh?"

JaiHonnah didn't need to ask who was calling. "Calvin," she said, her voice suddenly tight.

"Have you thought about my deal, JaiHonnah?"

"That's not why I wanted to see you, Calvin. Are you in town yet?"

"Yes, I'll meet you at The Shadow's Restaurant on 19th Street at one o'clock this afternoon, but—."

"I'll see you at 1:00 o'clock." She hung up and inhaled deeply. There was nothing that she wanted to do less than see Calvin Chapman, but it had to be done. If she was going to move on with her life and protect her baby, she had to tell Calvin about their son. She wouldn't let him intimidate her any longer. His constant calls over the past months were nerve-racking, making it difficult to control her blood pressure. She had enough. If he wanted to be a part of his son's life, she would agree, but beyond that, she wanted nothing at all to do with him or his scheme to become head of BlackHawk. She would tell him as much today at lunch.

* * *

"So, you think I can get a villa at this late date?" Roderick asked the corporate head of a very chic, exclusive and fashionable ski resort in Vail, Colorado.

"JRock, for you, no question," Morris Talbot said. "How many guests?"

"Just two."

"Uh-huh, sounds like you've got someone special in mind," Morris said, chuckling.

"Very special," Roderick affirmed.

"Then say no more. I'll have everything arranged. Very discreet. So you'll arrive on Christmas Eve and be with us through New Year's Day?"

"That's correct."

"Fine, JRock. I'm sure that you and the lady will enjoy your stay with us."

"I am, too, Morris. Thanks for making space for us."

Roderick was elated when he hung up the telephone and arranged for the flight on one of Vivian's Adventurer Executive Air jets. He had high hopes that this surprise vacation to Vail for him and JaiHonnah would put their relationship back on track. On track to what though? he wondered. It wasn't just the sex. It never had been. He did hold her in high esteem and admiration. There were no buts about any of that, except what did he want from her and what was he willing to give in return? He had put himself on the line with Monique and had hung himself in the process. He didn't want another woman in his life who didn't or couldn't love him for who he was or one who only wanted him for what he could offer financially. He wanted and needed a partner, a soul mate, someone with whom he could share his dreams and aspirations, his secrets. Someone who understood his desire to make things better. JaiHonnah fit that criteria—completely—but what did she want her life to be?

They both spent endless hours on projects that seemed to drain their energy. They had barely enough time to do more than have a quick lunch together. He was spending his evenings either with the twins, now that they were in school or fulfilling his obligation to coach a basketball team. In the mornings he would drive the girls to school and then pick them up in the afternoon. Of course, they would have so much to tell him about their day before, during and after they did their homework. By the time dinner, evening entertainment, and bath time were over, there was no time for him to spend with JaiHonnah. They would talk on the telephone often so that his girls could repeat the highlights of their day to her, but what he wanted was to hold JaiHonnah in his arms at night and wake with her in the morning. The trip to Vail over the holidays while the twins were with their mother in California would allow him and JaiHonnah the privacy, rest, and relaxation he thought they needed. They would have time to talk about the future. Their future—together.

* * *

When JaiHonnah arrived at The Shadows restaurant Calvin was already there. She took a deep breath before approaching him at the table.

"Well, Mrs. Chapman—," he grinned, eyeing her from head to toe, "you look even better than you did..."

"Let's forgo the social amenities, shall we, Calvin?" she hissed. "I don't want to be here one minute longer than I have to be."

"Hey, Kelley, where's Jai?" Roderick asked as she returned to the office. "I thought you two went to the old neighborhood."

"I dropped her off at that restaurant over on 19th Street, uh, The Shadows. Said she had a business meeting or something."

Roderick thought a moment, trying to remember whether she had mentioned a meeting with anyone. Nothing came to mind, but that didn't matter. He wanted to see her as soon as possible to tell her about the trip he planned for them over the holiday. Well, he thought, he had to pick up a Christmas gift in that neighborhood anyway, so he decided to run that errand first and then meet JaiHonnah at the restaurant.

"Yes, Mr. Baylor, Mrs. Chapman is still here," the maître d' confirmed.

"Don't disturb her meeting, Carl, but ask her to wait for me if she starts to leave before I get there," Roderick said as he drove to the jeweler's to pick up the gift for Jai.

"Very good, sir," the maître d' said.

Roderick made short work of his errand. Privately, he hoped that he and JaiHonnah could steal a couple of hours together after he told her about the trip. The day was sunny for December. Perhaps they could take a walk in Rock Creek Park where they could wile away a few listless hours before he picked up his daughters from school. He parked his car and went into the restaurant. Carl greeted him with a big smile, and Roderick reciprocated, but as Carl motioned to the secluded spot where JaiHonnah sat only a few feet away from two Supreme Court justices, Roderick's smile slipped from his face. His jaw clamped. Something tore at his gut and reached in and then twisted his heart.

Carl started to lead him toward the table where JaiHonnah sat talking to Calvin Chapman. Roderick's rage was immediate and distinct. He held Carl back with a hand on the man's sleeve and a nod of his head back toward the door. Business meeting? What kind of business would JaiHonnah have with a man—her husband? he wondered, trying to reconcile his thoughts and feelings and having no luck. There was only so much that he was willing to stomach.

Roderick noticed Carl's confused expression. "Uh, look, Carl," Roderick said pulling some bills from his pocket and palming them, "we don't have to mention to Mrs. Chapman that I stopped by," he said, shaking Carl's hand.

Carl looked at the gratuity, smiled briefly, then stiffened his stance straightening his tie. "Never saw you, sir," he said and coughed.

Roderick took another look toward the table at JaiHonnah and left the restaurant.

"This is no bargaining chip!" JaiHonnah flashed. "I told you before, if you want in on whatever my father is doing, talk with him yourself!"

"You'll do what I told you to do or I'll . . .," Calvin said lowly, but with a thinly veiled threat.

"You'll what?" JaiHonnah asked with animosity in her tone.

JaiHonnah's head was throbbing, but she couldn't let Calvin see or sense her fear. No fear! she schooled herself, remembering the ordeal that she had just experienced. She had to hold on. To keep Calvin at bay. Too much was at stake for her to back down now. Now she wished that she had not made the mistake of telling him about their child.

"Don't push me, Jai! I've had just about enough of you and your father getting your way! This time you'll both do as *I* say!" he raged, punching his thumb to his chest.

"I will not be intimidated by you, Calvin!"

Calvin leaned deadly close. "Oh, yes you will! That's *my* baby you're carrying! If you and your father don't do what I want, you'll spend the rest of your life in the biggest custody battle this country has ever seen! It will make the O.J. trial look like a Kodak moment. Now get it through your pretty little head, Jai! You have thirty days to get ready! Nothing big. Just a private little ceremony and then we'll sign the deal putting fifty-one percent of BlackHawk International into *my* baby's name with *me* as the executor—uncontested!" he said, gloating and leaning back in his seat. "Now, you run along, little girl, and call your daddy!"

JaiHonnah knew that there was no way of reasoning with Calvin. She flipped her napkin onto the table, rose from her seat and leaned over toward him. "Blow it out your ass!" she hissed through gritted teeth.

Calvin grabbed her arm and held it tightly. "Thirty days, Jai!" he hissed back.

Forcefully she snatched her arm away from him. Gathering her belongings, she turned on her heels and walked swiftly toward the door amid stares from the very notable people in the restaurant. Tears were close to brimming over as she approached Carl.

"Mrs. Chapman," Carl said, concerned for her obvious distress. "Please, may I do anything for you?"

JaiHonnah couldn't answer. She shook her head and tried to catch her breath. Carl helped her with her coat, her body shaking slightly.

"I'll put this on his tab," Carl said firmly, nodding toward Calvin. "Let me get a cab for you."

JaiHonnah agreed with a nod, not trusting her voice.

As soon as JaiHonnah left the restaurant, Calvin pulled his cell phone from his pocket and smiled. He pushed a series of numbers, eased back against the comfortable chair and waited.

"Monique, honey, this is Calvin Chapman. I think I've come up with a way to save your film...and get back at that husband of yours," he said, remembering the beating that he had taken from Roderick. "This is better than I could possibly have imagined." He sipped his drink. "My beautiful wife is pregnant—by your husband.... How do I know?" He laughed. "I know because I had a vasectomy after she got pregnant before. I know Jai very well. She doesn't give her body without a fight, and there is not a mark on her," he said, gloating. "Not yet, at least. Now, this is what I want you to do..."

* * *

Roderick walked into the reception area on the ground floor of his office and started toward the steps. His temper had cooled, but he was still disturbed. Although he recognized that he had no right to ask, he wanted an explanation from JaiHonnah about her meeting with her husband. They would have time to discuss it on their vacation though, he thought as he patted the gift in his breast pocket.

"Mr. Baylor," Mindy, one of the administrative assistants, called to him. "Kelly isn't around so I need your signature on these purchase orders."

Roderick waited for her to approach and signed the documents without looking at

what he was doing. He was still caught in a fog over seeing JaiHonnah with Calvin.

"Oh, and, if you're going up to your office, would you leave these messages on Mrs. Chapman's desk, please? The voice mail program is on the blink."

Wordlessly, Roderick took the folded messages and ascended the stairs. His concern was not on work or the fistful of messages. As he started to put the messages on JaiHonnah's desk, something caught his eye. "Porter?" he said aloud, unfolding the slip of paper and looking more closely at the message.

Mrs. Chapman—Arrangements have been made for your arrival in Atlanta. My partners and I are hopeful that the employment package that we discussed at our last meeting and subsequently offered to you, will be satisfactory. It is also an indication of our sincere desire that you will join our firm very soon. Please call at your earliest convenience to confirm your arrival schedule. Lionel Porter.

Roderick's jaw set tightly, and his rage built. *So that's what this distance is about! She's getting ready to leave!* The hurt and disappointment welded with the feeling of betrayal. He stormed into his office and paced the floor. He was planning to tell her the truth about his divorce from Monique while they were away and ask her to leave her husband. What a fool he had been to start to trust her! Secrets! Damn secrets!

The telephone rang, breaking his concentration.

"What?" he barked.

"Well, I can see that you're in your usual temperament," a sultry voice intoned on the other end of the line.

Roderick raised his eyes to the ceiling and shook his head. "What is it, Monique?"

"I think that it's time to talk about custody of the girls. They're getting older now, and I believe that they need to live with me. Or as an alternative, I think that we should remarry to give them a more stable home environment. Your behavior lately—getting arrested and all—isn't the best influence on their young, impressionable minds. Not to mention your open affair with a married woman."

Roderick's heart had long since hitched with the mention of the words *custody of the girls.* His heart crumbled with the reference to an *open affair with a married woman.* He had to stay calm though. Monique was after something. Her threat was not veiled. It was ominous and even sinister. She knew that threatening to take Shelly and Shelby away from him would paralyze him—and she had nearly succeeded. He took long, deep breaths quietly as she talked, but he had the presence of mind to record his conversation with her as Vivian requested.

* * *

"Jenny, please get Slade Richardson Investigations on the line for me," Vivian said over the intercom to one of her staff members while sitting across her desk from JaiHonnah.

"Yes, ma'am. Right away," Jenny answered.

"Investigator?" JaiHonnah asked with surprise. "Viv, I need legal advice on what, if anything, Calvin can do, not an investigator. I need to know if he can fight me for custody of my baby, even if we're not married," she said with great concern.

"Jai, do you trust me?" Vivian asked, eyeing her closely.

"Yes, of course, I do, but..."

"No buts, Jai. I need to get some answers quickly. Now you take it easy. I don't want you upset anymore than you are already."

"Upset? Viv, Calvin is a *monster*. He said that if I don't remarry him and get my father to sign over half of BlackHawk Industries, he'll..." She choked. "He'll take..." the thought was too much to even utter aloud. The tears overflowed.

Vivian rounded her desk and hugged JaiHonnah close as she shook with emotion.

Vivian waited until JaiHonnah had herself more in control before proceeding. "I know that this is a very personal question, but I have to ask. Are you sure that this is Calvin's baby?"

JaiHonnah raised her eyes to Vivian's. "I'm relatively sure. The timing is about right. Calvin attacked me the first week that I was here. I was only with Roderick once a week later when we didn't use protection. It was the day that we left you at the beach and sailed back to Washington. I wish more than anything that my baby wasn't conceived with Calvin, but all the information seems to indicate that it is his child."

* * *

"Damn!" Roderick bellowed slamming his fist down on his desk after he hung up the telephone. His heart was beating wildly, and his head was throbbing. She wasn't going to get away with it. Not if he could help it. He would go to any extreme to keep custody of his daughters. Marrying Monique again was out of the question.

Someone knocked on his door.

"Yes?" he bellowed.

JaiHonnah's face was contorted in confusion as she entered. "You didn't have to bite my head off," she said a bit annoyed. "I've got good news for you." She noticed that Roderick granite face had not cracked even slightly for a small smile as she had come to expect from him. He did not comment either, she noticed. Abandoning her feeble effort to change his mood, she decided to move on. She wasn't in the best of spirits either, and she felt sick to her stomach. "I've finished the preliminary work on Baylor Plaza Park, complete with model and..."

"I've made arrangements for us to take a vacation, a trip to Vail to do some skiing. I want to leave after the office holiday party," he interrupted, eyeing her reaction closely.

JaiHonnah looked up at Roderick and narrowed her eyes. Where did that come from? she wondered. If it was an invitation, she certainly didn't like the manner in which it was extended. He was almost belligerent, demanding, as if she was only to cower in submission. The hair on the back of her neck began to rise along with the churning in her stomach.

Lifting her chin and narrowing her eyes she said, "I've already made plans for the holidays. You should have asked me before . . ."

"Is that where you've been all day, making plans for your reunion with your husband?"

Something sinister grabbed at JaiHonnah's heart. Temporarily thrown emotionally off balance, she blinked rapidly. How did he know that she had been with Calvin? she wondered. Was he having her monitored like Jake had a tendency to do? Fighting back the urge to retaliate, fractionally she calmed herself. "Earlier this morning I was at the job site. I had to get the remaining pictures for the slide presentation, then a lunch appointment, but I've never had to account to you for my time before. Are you having a problem with my work or the amount of time I put in on doing my job?"

"You're very good at avoiding direct questions, *Mrs.* Chapman. I asked you where the hell you've been today. I'm still waiting for an answer."

JaiHonnah tried to discern what had created this coldness in Roderick. Why he seemed angry and upset, but whatever it was, she was not having any more of it. She resented the tone that he was taking with her. Calvin's bullying was enough for one day. She summoned her courage, stiffening her backbone. "Not to put too fine a point on it," she said with her darken eyes flashing, "it's none of your business!"

"Uh-huh," he growled derisively. "Well, *Mrs.* Chapman, *this* is my business," he said handing Porter's telephone message to her.

JaiHonnah quickly read the message and narrowed her eyes. She nearly froze, and then she looked up into Roderick's coldness. The message could have been interpreted a number of ways, and obviously Roderick had jumped to the wrong conclusion. She had not agreed to go to Atlanta. "I can explain—."

"Don't bother! I think the message is self explanatory."

"Apparently, you've already decided what this is about, so I won't bother to explain it to you!"

"Oh, so you're the innocent in all of this. A victim of circumstances perhaps." His tone lent credence to his skepticism. "You've been preoccupied for weeks. What was it, Jai? Were you just trying to figure out the right time to spring your departure on me? Perhaps after you finished the Baylor Plaza Park presentation? Or just before you left on this sudden vacation, which, I might add, you never mentioned to me before. How were you going to tell me that you were about to betray me with Lionel Porter? Maybe over a candlelight dinner at your place where you could easily let me make a fool of myself again."

Try as she might, JaiHonnah's fury had not dissipated. She was too angry to be coherent. "Whatever you say, *Mr.* Baylor," she said, keeping her voice as quiet as possible, belying the hurt and rage within her as they exchanged long, deep and angry stares. It was not her intention to get into a shouting match with him, especially not today, and certainly not in the office. She turned on her heels to leave.

"I'm not finished with you yet," Roderick said through clinched teeth.

"Is that what you think?" she asked her voice full of sarcasm, "Well, you're wrong!"

"I want the truth from you!"

"In the now famous words of Jack Nicholson, 'you can't handle the truth!'" she retorted.

"Then how about a little honesty from you for a change?"

"At this point, I don't see how it would do any good. You keep asking for the truth. Well I've given you the truth every time I was with you."

"*With me?* Ever since I met you you've shut me out. Pushed me away! Hid behind your employment contract and your marriage license! You want to be with that bastard? Then go to him, *Mrs*. Chapman! I don't give a damn anymore."

The attack cut deep into her core. JaiHonnah's head was spinning and her heart was pounding. It had to end.

"I'm through defending my actions to you or anyone else. You can take this job and shove it. I quit, *Mr*. Baylor."

"No, *Mrs*. Chapman. You're fired."

* * *

If she could just manage to hold back the tears until she was in her condo, she thought as she tried to insert the key card in the skinny slot, but her hands were trembling too much and something was blurring her vision. The tears dripped down her face onto her silk blouse. How long had she been crying? she wondered. Had it started when she got into the taxicab? Maybe that's why the cab driver kept looking at her in his rearview mirror. Or maybe why the desk clerk tried to approach her. Or why people in the elevator took quick, sorrowful glimpses at her. She shook her head, unable to shake off her trembling.

Finally, she was inside the condo. She closed the door and put her back to it. The pain was excruciating. She wrapped her arms around her waist and felt herself sliding to her knees. No sound came out. It was too painful. An ache so deep that it took her breath away.

Sometime later, JaiHonnah awoke with bright lights in her eyes. Muffled sounds were around her, but the light was too bright. She could not see through the glare. Then a voice she recognized was issuing orders. Someone or something was gripping her arm tightly.

"What is going...?"

"Jai, you're in the hospital," Savannah said calmly. "You're going to be fine. I just want to get a new read on your vitals."

"Hospital? How did I...?" she tried to ask.

"Shhh, please, Jai. I'll talk with you in a moment. I have to draw some blood."

"Blood? My baby?" she panicked. "Am I losing my baby?!"

"Jai!" Savannah said firmly. "I want you to focus. I need for you to be calm. You haven't lost your baby. I'm trying to save it, but you have to cooperate with me. Do you understand me?"

JaiHonnah could only nod as she tried to focus on what Savannah was telling her. She hadn't lost her baby. She kept that fact centered in her mind. She closed her eyes, trying to modulate her breathing. The sting of the shunt in the back of her hand brought her back to what had happened. The sharp pain in her stomach. Struggling to the telephone and calling the emergency number for the desk clerk and then nothing. Darkness.

Sometime later the lights clicked off in her face, and she felt the cessation of the hectic orbit around her. She opened her eyes and saw Savannah writing on a chart. She finished and handed it to a nurse then she turned her attention to JaiHonnah.

"You really want me to work for my fee it seems," Savannah said, arms akimbo. "Either that or you're hell bent on ruining my social life."

"What happened to me, Savannah? How did I get here?" JaiHonnah asked.

"Food poisoning, I believe. That combined with a spike in your blood pressure. Apparently you were found unconscious in your condo by the Watergate Security staff. They put in an emergency call and the ambulance brought you here. You're at Georgetown Medical. Chuck was on duty in the emergency room when you were brought in, and he called me—right in the middle of a great dinner with a wonderful man, I might add," she said and smiled. "Chuck's busy right now or he'd be in here with you too. Seems a number of people had an acute attack of food poisoning today. That includes a Supreme Court Justice, a few foreign diplomats, three senators and one very angry head of the Food and Drug Administration. The maître d' at The Shadows restaurant gave us a list of the people who had eaten there today. You were on the list."

"My baby...is my...?"

"Your baby is fine," she said, holding JaiHonnah's hand. "I had to pump your stomach. I'm going to release you from the hospital, but I want you to take some time off and rest. Whatever caused your blood pressure to rise so sharply can't continue, Jai, or you and your baby could be in serious trouble. Do you understand me?"

"Yes," she whispered and nodded. "I understand."

The next day JaiHonnah sat on the sofa in her condo staring blindly at the descending nightfall. She didn't know how long she had been there or even what time it was. She was numb, unable to form a coherent thought. Roderick's angry face was before her, then Calvin's. The horror of it all. The only two men in her life that she had loved, both had taken from her and neither offered anything in return. Sighing deeply, she turned and looked at the cell phone beside her and, with a heavy heart and slow, deliberate thoughts, she speed-dialed a number. "Daddy, I'm coming home."

* * *

Roderick had spent one hellava sleepless night. His neck and back muscles still ached, and his head throbbed. His stomach twisted in knots. Pacing the floor all day had not helped. He sat forward on the edge of an easy chair, elbows on his knees, and knuckles to his forehead. He had been shattered again. He had let himself feel something for a woman, and she had kicked him in his gut. This should not happen to a man twice in a lifetime, he thought. He should have seen it coming though. Just when he was beginning to trust her, JaiHonnah backed away and betrayed him with Lionel Porter of all people. He knew that Porter was trying to marshal his forces to attempt a hostile takeover on Baylor Design and Development when he took the company public. Roderick had divorced Monique because of Porter, now he had to divorce himself of JaiHonnah because of the same man. Was Porter getting inside information from JaiHonnah? Roderick locked one fist in the palm of his hand, resting his chin against it. He wasn't going to be the same fool twice. Love her or not, JaiHonnah Reise Chapman was out of his company and out of his life.

The telephone rang and took his attention away from his brooding. Maybe it was JaiHonnah, he hoped deep in his core. "Yes," he answered.

"JRock, this is Savannah Logan. I've been trying to reach Jai Chapman all day and I thought that you might know where she is."

"I haven't a clue and I don't give a..." He caught himself. "I don't know where she is. Probably with her husband. He's in town."

"Oh," she said, her voice laced with concern and confusion. "Well, this will keep

until after the holidays. If I don't talk with you again before then, I hope you have a good one."

"Yeah, you, too," he said, snorting, then an idea occurred to him. "What are your plans for the holidays?"

"I hadn't decided on anything definite. Why?"

"How does a week in Vail sound to you?"

"Sounds great. Who's going?"

"Just the two of us. You and me."

She paused for the obligatory moment of silence. "Uh, Roderick, if you're joking with me, I don't think that it's very funny. You stood me up before, remember?"

"Pack your skis, Savannah. We'll leave on Friday afternoon." Roderick hung up the telephone and quickly dialed another number. "Roth, your club for lunch tomorrow."

"Sure, Roderick, but you sound..."

"I'll tell you about it then," he said, hanging up.

Roderick went to his computer and called up his ten-year master plan. He began altering it to accelerate some aspects and make them priorities. He was putting his life back on track if it killed him.

Chapter 20

Several days later, JaiHonnah opened the door of the condo, and tears began to stream down her face again. Two powerful arms engulfed her and pulled her into their warm, comforting embrace and held her tightly against a strong, firm chest.

"Daddy, I didn't expect you to come . . ." she said, choking back the tears.

"Shhh," he whispered still holding her tightly. "You're hurting badly. I could hear it in your voice. Of course I was gonna come for you, dahlin'. You've had more than enough tears in your young life to fill the Rio Grand. We're gonna get your things and go home." He lifted her face and smoothed away her tears with his fingers. "Whatever it is, dahlin', I'll fix it. I'll make it right. I promise you that."

"Not this time, Daddy," she whimpered, looking into his eyes. "I got myself into this jam. I'll get myself out."

"Ain't gonna be by yourself, JaiHawk." JaiHonnah heard another familiar voice behind the mountain of a man who held her.

"Ezra?" she asked, hastily wiping her tears and looking behind her father.

"It's me, JaiHawk. Now you come here, little wild thing. These old bones don't move that fast no more." He chuckled and smiled.

JaiHonnah flung her arms around the older man and squeezed him tight. "How did you let Jake talk you into flying, Ezra?" she said through her tears. "You've never flown before."

"Yo' Daddy was over in Japan when he called me and said you'se was in trouble. I told him to come git me on his way to git you. That's the only'est thing that would've got me on one of them contraptions. Man ain't spose to move that fast," he said, smiling. "Unless it's for a pretty little girl."

They hugged while Jake issued orders to two of his constant companions to pack up JaiHonnah's things. The two men set about their task while Jake made a few calls. In no time they were in a limousine headed to Reagan National Airport.

As one of her father's private jets climbed into the dark sky, headed for Hawkinstown, Texas, JaiHonnah looked out of the window at the Anacostia River until it was out of sight.

JaiHonnah curled herself into Ezra's firm embrace and napped as they flew. Roderick's face was in her troubled dreams. She was standing facing him with a widening gulf pulling them apart. His hands stuck down in his pockets, he did not reach for her. A hawk perched on his shoulder. Roderick's eyes looking through her, not seeing her. The hawk. Roderick. She could not move or speak to warn him. Her heart disintegrating before her eyes. Calvin walking away with her baby crying for her in his arms. The hawk. A mist descending around them. The chasm widening. Monique. The hawk. She tried to scream. Something brushed her face, and she opened her eyes.

"You're having a bad dream, JaiHawk," Ezra whispered.

JaiHonnah lifted her head from his shoulder and looked into his eyes. She blinked. "Ezra," she said softly.

"Yes, JaiHawk. Just like when you were a little girl after Skai left us. The bad dreams, the visions, used to wake you in the night. You could see things. Things that were before you came. Things that had not happened yet. Your grammama, she say you have the second sight."

"Or I ate something that I shouldn't have."

"Naw, JaiHawk, you've got your mama's eyes. You can see."

JaiHonnah knew what Ezra was saying, but she dismissed the thought. Her dream had been a nightmare—only something in her illusions—not real. It could not be the future she saw. She saw no future. She only felt the gut-wrenching pain of the present and the disillusionment of the past.

The jet landed on a private runway. When the door to the aircraft opened and the steps extended to the ground, Adam Hawkins' bright smile was the first thing JaiHonnah saw. Their eyes locked as she walked down the steps into his open arms.

"Hey, little wild thing." Adam greeted his sister with a kiss on her forehead.

"Hi, handsome."

"Want to ride?" He nodded over his shoulder and JaiHonnah's eyes widened.

"Hawk!" she exclaimed, moving swiftly to the midnight-black stallion that pranced fitfully, trying to free himself from his holders. JaiHonnah wrapped her arms around the horse's thick neck squeezing him as he settled and nudged her. "You didn't forget me," she cooed to the stallion. "You still love me. I still love you, too, Hawk."

"What about that ride?" Adam asked, stroking the horse's mane.

JaiHonnah shook her head and took Hawk's lead from his handler. "No, let's walk a while," she answered.

Adam took her free hand in his, and they began walking toward the ranch house. The others got into the waiting SUVs, and they sped away into the darkness. The moonlight played hide-and-seek behind the cloudy sky. The night creatures slipped away into the bushes that lined the long, private roadway. Hawk walked peacefully behind her, nudging at her back with his nose.

After a long silence, as she and Adam walked hand in hand, JaiHonnah said, "Daddy said that you were in Africa."

"No small talk, Jai. I want to know what's been going on with you these last four

months. One minute you're in Italy, the next thing I hear is that you've got a job in

Washington. When I saw you in Paris last winter you didn't say anything about coming back to the States after you got your doctorates. You said that you wanted to teach in Spain or Italy, so let's hear it, Jai."

JaiHonnah sighed heavily. "I hadn't planned to come back. I was going to do my post-doctoral work or teach like I told you, but Vivian

Jackson and I went skiing in Visp. You know how determined she can be."

"Yes, you don't have to remind me," he said, not looking at JaiHonnah. She felt his hand tighten on hers.

"Don't change the subject, Jai," he directed as they continued to walk.

JaiHonnah exhaled heavily. She never could get around Adam. He knew her too well. She glanced at his strong, handsome profile and saw his jaw tighten in the moonlight as their matched, steady pace moved them forward. Adam drew her hand to his lips and kissed it. "Alright," he said quietly. "Now keep talking."

"Well, Vivian arranged for an interview with a company owned by a friend and client of hers. She was determined to get me to come back stateside. I came back, got the job, worked for four months, and now I'm home just in time for the holidays."

Adam stopped walking. "If you just wanted to see what it was like to have to work for a living, Jai, you could have taken over the BlackHawk Design Institute. Blair Marantz has been begging you to come work with him for three years. Now, tell me the rest of it, Jai. Not just the surface stuff."

JaiHonnah looked up at him. Tears rimmed her eyes. "I'm pregnant, Adam. I'm pregnant with Calvin's baby, and I'm afraid that I'm in love with another man, a man who doesn't love me or want me. A man who is married with a family."

Adam's handsome face contorted in anguish. "After what he did to you! He dared to touch you again?"

"Adam, please, don't!" she cried, trying to calm him and herself.

"No, Jai. You're not going to convince me that you let Chapman make love to you. I know you better than that! He raped you again, didn't he? He …" Adam's words choked as he buried his sister in his arms, his face in her hair. His body shook with anger. "I'll kill that bastard."

"No, Adam, nothing is going to change the fact that I'm pregnant, and it's his child and mine," she cried, tightly holding her brother.

Adam's voice was still full of anger. "Does Jake know?" he asked through a set jaw.

"No, I haven't told him, but Grandmother knows. I don't know whether Calvin has said anything to Jacob, Jr. I'm not ready to talk about this yet to anyone else. I've got to be calm or I could jeopardize my baby. That's why I came home, Adam. I didn't want to go back to Europe. I need to find some peace in my life. Please, let's keep this between us for now," she pleaded holding him closer. "Please, Adam, let me work this out my way. I love you, big brother, but I'm not a little girl anymore. You have to promise me that you won't do anything."

Adam gritted his teeth, his jaw working the muscles in his handsome face. He looked away from her. "Alright, Jai. I don't want to upset you," he said as he put his arm around her shoulders. They continued their walk toward the house. A few steps later, he said, "What about this man you're in love with?"

Her arm tightened around his waist, but she summoned her courage. "I made a mistake, Adam. I walked into a situation with my eyes open. I knew that he was married, but I couldn't stop myself. I was a fool. A bigger fool than I've ever been."

"Does he know that you're pregnant with Chapman's . . ." he choked.

"No, he doesn't, but it's over anyway. It ended badly a few days ago. It had nothing to do with my pregnancy."

"You say he's married."

"Yes, with a family."

"Not like you to go after another woman's husband, Jai. He must have meant a great deal to you."

"Yes, he did," she answered as the bright, impressive lights of Hawk House lit the night. "But, as I said, that's over now."

"Are you sure?"

"Yes, Adam, I'm sure. We had no place to go with the relationship. It's better this way. If I had stayed with him, we would have only ended up hurting his family. I couldn't do that. I just couldn't . . ." she said as she stopped walking. When Hawk reared up, she settled him by pulling him closer to her. She whispered to him, stroking him gently and removing his lead. "Home, Hawk!" She signaled and the horse raced toward the corral.

The black stallion cleared three fences and mingled with the mares who were hailing his return with nays and whinnies. His majesty was again on his throne. JaiHonnah smiled as Hawk reared up on two legs kicking the air. Then her attention broadened to encompass her childhood home.

Hawk House hadn't changed in the many years that she had been away, JaiHonnah thought with some relief. Actually, the term *house* was a misnomer. The massive and impressive mansion, a replica of antebellum homes that was typical of the ones in the enclaves surrounding New Orleans, Louisiana. The mansion had more than six thousand square feet of living space on one level, and it was three stories high. A veranda circled the mansion on every level with white rounded pillars triumphantly holding up the level above. The manicured lawn, which stretched out for five acres in every direction, was still green and lush. Oak and pine trees surrounded, but did not obscure the house from view. Nothing could because Hawk House was the dominant fixture on the otherwise vast, unadulterated landscape. Corrals, stables and barns sat unobtrusively beyond the house. Cattle grazed lazily on the rolling hillsides. Ten bunkhouses, which boarded over a hundred workers, were obscured from view. Other housing for families was in Hawkins Town, a community a mile away.

A few ranch hands touched the brim of their hats in greeting as she and Adam approached.

JaiHonnah looked up the house's front face and could see a man standing with legs apart and arms akimbo on the top veranda above the immense family crest. Jacob Junior's powerful presence could be felt even under the cover of darkness. The light that illuminated the crest flowed over him. His tall, wiry frame could not hide his magnificent, muscular physique. His hair was a healthy, slick black, the color of hot asphalt and pulled back into a ponytail that naturally curled at the end. His sun-burned, golden-brown complexion added a healthy glow to his appearance, but so did the haute couture designer shorts and polo shirt he wore. The scowl on his face was riveting even at a distance. His hairless countenance drew tight against his square jaw, high cheekbones and narrow nose. He had inherited much of his good looks from their mother's side of the family. Raven-black eyebrows called to mind his African-Creole-Mexican-Navajo heritage, an exalted, brooding mass who stood above it all.

JaiHonnah stared up at her oldest brother without cracking a smile. She knew that her homecoming would be difficult, but she had hoped that he would welcome her back with the least amount of acrimony. His stern stance told her that her return would be anything but harmonious.

Adam pulled her close to him as they ascended the wide, deep, stone stairs to the first veranda. As they entered the house, Jake called Adam into his study, and Ezra took JaiHonnah to her rooms in the south wing of the mansion. As they passed Jacob's wing, they heard the sound of women giggling. JaiHonnah turned to Ezra.

"How many?" she asked.

"Who knows," he said and shrugged. "two, maybe three probably. No tellin' with your brother."

She shook her head. "He's getting to be more like Daddy every day."

"Yo' Daddy's got a heart," Ezra observed. "This one," he said, nodding toward Jacob's hallway. "No heart."

JaiHonnah was not surprised at Ezra's assessment of her brother. Jacob's behavior always stirred the senses with dread. They continued to the wing of the house that she occupied as a child.

* * *

Roth turned three successive shades of red. His contraband, unlit Cuban cigar slipped from his open mouth, and Roderick finally saw the true colors of Roth's eyes as they bulged out of his head.

"Son, you ought not spring something like this on an old man who's only had one drink," he said, slowly regaining his composure as he signaled for a waiter.

The waiter approached.

"Bring me another bourbon—hold the ice. Damn it! Bring me the damn bottle."

"But, Mr. Childs, we can only serve by the glass," the waiter gently protested.

Roth pulled another cigar from his inside pocket and bit off the end, spitting it on the waiter's shoes. The waiter froze under Roth's penetrating glare.

"Make it a bottle from my private stock," he growled menacingly.

The waiter scurried away. Roth lit the cigar, reared back in the high-back, over-stuffed winged chair and drew the smoke, slowly eyeing Roderick before he spoke.

"You're building a war chest, aren't you, son?" Roth asked matter-of-factly.

"I'm planning a few deals. You want in or not?"

Roth's brow furrowed as he chewed his cigar. He glimpsed the woman sitting to Roderick's right.

"Can she be trusted?" Roth asked, nodding toward Kelley.

"She wouldn't be here if she couldn't, and that's not the question. The question is: How far do you trust me?" Roderick asked coolly, locking into Roth's shifty eyes.

"Five billion, you say?" Roth asked thoughtfully and then, using his cigar as a pointer said, "You, son, are going after some big game. I'll have to go to the well on this one."

"Let's cut to the chase, Roth. If you're in, you get five percent. If not, you know what you can do with it. Stock exchange opens every day at nine sharp. Market closed yesterday at four percent," Roderick said, rising from his seat.

"Now, hold on there, son," Roth sputtered. "Let an old man get his mind around this. Mull it over with a—."

"You've got my number, Roth, and my bottom line."

Roth eyed Roderick thoughtfully then rose from his seat and extended his hand.

"You'll hear from Mrs. Jackson," Roderick said, shaking Roth's hand.

* * *

JaiHonnah woke from a deep sleep and stretched. She didn't have to think about where she was. She was at home in her old rooms in her California king-size bed. Remnants of her youth were everywhere she looked. Not quite an adult's room, she thought. An adult wouldn't still have dolls on the shelves or old CDs in the jukebox or high school trophies in the étagères. No, an adult's room would look like the one at the condo in D.C. That's where, for the first time in her life, she had experienced love—or maybe not. Would a man who loved her hurt her so deeply? Would he be so unfeeling and impatient with her? These questions and many more caused her previous night to be a living hell. When she went into the relationship with Roderick, she did so with her eyes wide open. She didn't and couldn't expect anything from him. He was, after all, her boss and a married man. What she did not expect was his coldness, his vehemence, his cruelty and his harshness. He seemed so different from other men, so different from Calvin. She bought into his dreams for rebuilding and making life better. She shared his desire to see their people back on their feet and in charge of their own destiny. She bought into his affection, his warmth, but how could he be that and cruel at the same time? She shook it off. The memory was too painful. She'd have to deal with it at some point, but not now. Now she had to contend with Calvin.

"Yes, come in," she answered to the knock on her door.

Jake entered followed by two servants.

"Time you got up, dahlin'." Jake grinned as he motioned for the servants to set up the breakfast in the glassed-enclosed salon attached to her bedroom suite.

"I'm not very hungry, Daddy," she said and smiled slightly.

"Well, I am. You come along and sit a spell with me," he said, encouraging her to get up by mussing her hair.

JaiHonnah knew what this was about. Jake was ready for her to tell him what was going on. He did not press her the night before the way that Adam had, but Jake was not Adam. Jake had his own method of getting what he wanted. The minute that she told him the truth, she knew that he would have a plan of action formulated and ready for execution—and in this case "execution" was exactly what Jake would do to Calvin Chapman. She wanted to avoid the massacre, if at all possible, but, with Jake, anything was possible. She cautioned herself to be strong, as strong as the man who had amassed a fortune with little more than a sixth-grade education; a cunning unmatched in his peer group and a will of steel.

JaiHonnah sat across from her father sipping orange juice as Jake dug into a hearty meal. She noticed the slight graying around his temples; his firm jaw; his wide-set eyes, which remained deceptively half closed; the broad nose and thick mustache over his full lips; his broad chest and shoulders and large hands. No matter what those hands touched in his nearly fifty years, Midas had been in his fingertips. Folks he knew from his childhood said that her daddy was a man full grown at twelve. He had run away from an orphanage in the Louisiana bayou. Swamp fever had killed his mother and his father. His little sister, Mavis, was his only family, and he had stolen her away from the orphanage the very day that she complained that one of the aides had abused her. No one had come looking for them, but how they made it to San Antonio, Jake never told. And neither did Ezra who had been with her father from the beginning of his rise to power—through the birth of every child and the kidnapping of her only sister the day after her birth. Through the loss of her mother and throughout her childhood, Jake and Ezra had been inseparable. Only twelve years separated their ages, but Ezra was like a father to Jake and often his conscience.

JaiHonnah smiled slightly at her father. He had an imposing size, was strong as an ox, and as healthy as any thirty-year-old man. What surprised her more was how handsome he still was. Not in a pretty way, but in a rugged, rakish kind of way. He still turned women's heads—young and old alike. She wouldn't have been surprised if some young thing was somewhere in the house at that very moment trying to compose herself after Jake's amorous and impassioned lovemaking. Jake was her father, but he was no ordinary man, she mused. She had no illusions where Jake was concerned. He was a loving father, but a fierce businessman who was both admired and hated.

"Ahhh," he moaned in satisfaction leaning back in his seat. "Ezra sure knows how to put on the feed bag. He's gonna be mighty upset that you didn't eat none of his breakfast. You're thin as a rail, dahlin'."

"I won't be for long," she said cryptically looking down at the glass of juice in her hands.

"Look at me, JaiHawk," Jake said with an edge in his voice.

JaiHonnah didn't want to meet his gaze, but she couldn't hold out forever. Jake was going to know the reason for her melancholia or the sun wouldn't dare rise until he did.

"I'm pregnant, Daddy," she said, finally meeting his gaze. "It's Calvin's baby."

The poker face was in place, but the eyes showed a completely different hand.

"I'm alright, Daddy," she whispered reaching across the table to rest her hands on his clenched fists.

Jake took her hands in his, and without breaking his gaze he kissed both of her palms. "I know you will be, dahlin'," he said too quietly for JaiHonnah's comfort. "What does he want?"

"I'll handle it," she said, holding his tensed paws in her hands.

"Sure you will, dahlin'. After all, you're a Hawkins. You'll handle it just fine. Now, what does he want?"

JaiHonnah shuddered slightly from the sharp-edged steel laced in Jake's voice.

"He wants me to remarry him—," she felt the tension filling the room—"and he wants controlling interest in BlackHawk International in the baby's name with him as the executor."

Jake grunted and a menacing grin crossed his lips. "Does he now?"

JaiHonnah could almost see the wheels turning in Jake's head. Those same wheels would roll right over Calvin Chapman and pulverize him the same way that Roderick had done, she thought. Calvin and his father combined hadn't been able to overthrow Jake on their best days. Now she feared that Jake would grind the Chapmans into the dust.

"This is my problem to solve," she said, attempting to quell the torrents of emotion she knew lurked behind his poker face and deceptive grin. "Vivian Jackson is representing me on this. She's put a private investigator to work. I'm not sure what she's looking for, but I trust her. Promise me that you won't interfere. I want your word."

His grin widened, but JaiHonnah's hair stood on the back of her neck in fear, not anger.

"Dahlin', you're carrying my grandbaby inside you," he said an octave above a whisper. "Now, I don't know what them Eastern doctors told you, but two can't survive on what you had for breakfast. I'm gonna have Ezra whip up something for you, and I want you to eat all of it."

"I'm not a little girl, you know," she said, her eyes and voice pleading for understanding. "My doctor said that I'm in fine shape, but what about your promise?"

"Fine for them European woman built like weeds and maybe even for them Eastern women with a lump of two they call tits and ass, but you're a Texan, dahlin'. We grow real women here. Women you can tell their comin' from their goin'," he said, still grinning.

JaiHonnah wasn't fooled. She knew that Jake had already planned what was going to be done.

"Your word, Daddy," she implored.

"We'll talk about it later, dahlin'. Ezra will bring you something shortly," he said with a wink and a grin, patting her hand.

"Jake, I know what . . ." she called after him, but it was too late. He was gone in a flash belying his large frame.

She was too weary to run after him. She realized that she hadn't eaten much since

lunch time a few days ago, and even then she couldn't digest her food with Calvin sitting across the table from her. Food poisoning, she thought. Just looking at Calvin was enough to turn her stomach. The thought caused her empty stomach to churn. It began to erupt, and she fled to the bathroom.

Chapter 21

Vivian wordlessly sat back in her chair eyeing Roderick as he continued pacing her office and wondered what put the mean on his face. Except for the perfunctory exchanges, she and Roderick barely spoke to each other. He e-mailed his plan to her with a message for her to call when she was ready to discuss any of the details that, from a legal standpoint, might prove problematic. She reviewed the plan twice and didn't believe it even after the second reading.

"JRock, this isn't like you," she observed. "This is a vendetta, not a business deal. And as far as Monique is concerned..."

"Are you going to handle it or should I find myself another lawyer, too?" he stiffly interrupted.

"Too? I know that your company is booming right now, but what other jobs are you looking to fill besides mine?"

Roderick kept pacing, slowly crisscrossing his steps. His hands were fisted in his pockets, and he was deep in thought. He had no intention of hiring another law firm to handle his affairs. Vivian didn't deserve that crack, but the unflappable Mrs. Vivian Alexander Jackson had waltzed right by it as if it had never crossed his lips. She did deserve an explanation. "I fired Jai—or maybe she quit. Hell, I don't know," he stated, flinging a hand in the air in frustration, "but the point is, she's out. I'm looking for a new architect. She's your friend, so if you feel a greater loyalty to her than you do to me, then I'll understand."

Ah, now the mist cleared for Vivian. Roderick and Jai must have had one hell of an argument. If Jai was out of Baylor Construction then nothing stood in Jake Hawkins' way. If he wanted to take over Baylor Design and Developers, Roderick had just given Jake the perfect opportunity and, depending on the state of the relationship between Jake's daughter and Roderick, the perfect reason—revenge. Oh, hell,

Vivian groaned silently. Her effort to put a road block in Big Jake Hawkins' way, by having JaiHonnah work with Baylor Design, was being demolished.

"Care to share any of the details that led to Jai's untimely departure?"

"No. Now, can we talk about my plan?"

He couldn't share his feelings with Vivian or anyone at the moment. Since Jai left he'd been in turmoil. His introspection only intensified his anger and confusion. His pain had to end!

"The plan is sound, from a business and legal standpoint. Very bold and aggressive. If any of my other clients had brought this to me, I'd tell them to think about it for a while. Put it away in a drawer for a month or two and then consider it again, but obviously you've thought very carefully about this. A lot of detailed planning went into it, and I don't believe that you'll be dissuaded from doing exactly as described here, but this is truly out of character for you."

"Handle it, Vivian," he said, grabbing his overcoat and slinging it over his shoulder. "Rothman Childs is expecting your call. Be prepared to hear from the others through their attorneys very soon. I'm leaving town today during the holiday office party. I'll be unavailable until after the first of the year. If you need me, you know how to reach me."

"And Monique?"

"I think that you already know the answer to that. I won't tolerate her or any woman jerking me around anymore."

"That's what this is all about, isn't it, JRock? You feel that you've been betrayed, and you're striking out. I don't disagree with your anger and disappointment where Monique is concerned, but I don't believe that Jai should be a casualty in all of this."

He stopped pacing and pinned her with his flashing eyes, his voice deceptively low, but tight. "She had a choice. It was her decision, not mine! All I wanted her to do was to be honest with me and she wouldn't do it! Case closed!"

"JRock, you can be a very stubborn man sometimes. If people don't perform The Law According to Baylor then the sentence is swift and without mercy."

"Something I learned growing up on the other side of the Anacostia River, Vivian. I don't expect you to understand it."

"Oh, I understand it, alright. That's what's driven you to succeed, but don't forget, JRock, the river isn't what divides you from people who care about you. You've done that all by yourself from *this side* of the river."

"And what is it that divides you from Chuck, Vivian?" he tossed out. He regretted the question the moment it rolled off his lips, but, as usual, Vivian's demeanor never changed. He let out a big sigh, tossed his overcoat on a chair, approached Vivian and enveloped her in his arms. "I need this vacation more than I realized," he whispered, holding her.

"Do you want to rethink the decisions that you've made?"

"No. My decisions, all of them, remain unchanged," he said, releasing her and grabbing his coat again. He headed for the door and turned toward her. "Have a good holiday, Viv. I'll see you after the New Year."

"Be kind to yourself, JRock," she said.

Roderick left and Vivian picked up the telephone.

"Jenny, call Richardson Investigations. I have another project for them. Then find JaiHonnah Chapman. Try Hawkinstown, Texas, first. If she's not there, try her grandmother and then her home in Milan, Italy."

Vivian sat back in her chair contemplating what Roderick was about to do. Although his plan was sound, it was fraught with risks. He was leaving himself vulnerable and exposed, but only someone with huge resources and cunning business acumen would be able to take advantage of Roderick's unprotected position. His high-wire act was getting more daring and dangerous. She knew exactly who that person was who could and would seize this opportunity and how interested he had been in moving in and acquiring Baylor Construction until she had put a cog in the wheel—JaiHonnah Hawkins Chapman. She knew that Jake Hawkins wouldn't attempt a hostile takeover bid for Baylor Construction or permit any other company to make a move on Baylor as long as Jai was working for Roderick. Now that Jai was no longer with Baylor Construction, there would be a free-for-all, a feeding frenzy. If Jake found out what his daughter had been through, he'd smell blood in the water, and the old shark would move in swiftly for the kill. Her client's and friend's blood. At this point, however, there might not be anything that she could do to stop the inevitable from happening. She hoped that she was wrong.

Chapter 22

The Christmas party at Baylor Design and Developers should have been a very joyous occasion. The office was brightly decorated, the caterer, a friend from his old neighborhood, Isaac Greenfield, had laid out a veritable feast, and the deejay, his brother, Francis, a popular XM Radio disk jockey and music television host who had shows on MTV was spinning some great tunes. There should have been a great deal of merriment, laughter and spirit considering how successful the past year had been and how bright the future was that lay ahead. There was an absence of all of the above, and Roderick knew the reason.

He distributed the bonus checks, said a few words about the year that had passed and his plans for the future, but there was something missing—there was someone missing. Someone who brightened everyone's day and set his nights afire—JaiHonnah Reise Chapman. What a hell of an impact she made on everyone in such a short period of time. Business acquaintances stopped by the party just to say hello to her and were sorely disappointed when they learned that she was no longer associated with his company. The next question was always "*how could she be reached,*" to which he had no response.

When he couldn't take the constant questions anymore he retreated to the relative peace of his office, picked up the *Wall Street Journal* and read the headline again.

Baylor Developers Boom Into Stock Market with Heavy Volume

Baylor Developers charged onto public market today, generating a huge volume of 42.1 million shares, as the price rose 20% above the initial public offering price of $42 per share. The company raised more than $4 billion when its shares opened on the New York Stock Exchange at $42.87 and two hours later breezed to $72.52. Analysts said strength of overall market contributed *to Baylor's strong performance. Baylor closed at $71.14 down from its high of $73 during the day.*

Baylor only offered 120 million shares at a dollar volume of $3.5 billion, which set U.S. records. Market analysts said frenzied trading activity reflected profit-taking by early buyers and predicted it would settle down in a few days. Based on the stock activity, analysts said that the company probably will be capitalized at about $28 billion. The offering represented only 8% of Baylor's shares. Although J. R. Baylor, reached at his offices, declined to elaborate on the windfall, stock analysts predict that Baylor will hold the rest of the shares, which stock analyst predict could dampen interest in the stock. Turnover was exceptionally heavy, with nearly 3 million shares changing hands each hour through most of the day, following large block sales in opening minutes. Sales were delayed while market specialists set opening price, analysts said.

Flurry of trades reflected hype preceding initial sales underwritten by Morgan Stanley and Goldman, Sachs, which had set low prices several weeks ago. A Standard & Poor's analyst told us that quick profit seeking will move on, leaving mostly institutional traders to deal in shares. Of total offering, 100 million shares are on U.S. markets and 20 million on foreign exchanges, analysts said.

Proceeds will be used to repay about $5 billion in short-term working capital debt and for general corporate purposes, according to Mr. Baylor, whose Baylor Plaza Park inner-city project is being funded in part from his own pocket. Moody earlier assigned Prime-1 short-term rating to Baylor's commercial paper and (P)A2 long-term rating, reflecting depth and breadth of products, dominant market position and Baylor Research's reputation.

BlackHawk International still has 60% of the U.S. development and construction market, but Baylor Developers, with its strong showing, has climbed into the ten largest companies with an estimated $25 billion in annual revenue. Jake Hawkins, head of the powerful BlackHawk Holding and undisputed king of the corporate raiders, stated that he's "delighted to have a new kid on the street—Wall Street, that is. Fresh meat always raises my appetite."

Roderick put down the newspaper and noticed Günter Hewlett heading his way.

"So, Roderick, what does JaiHonnah Chapman's departure mean for the future of Baylor Plaza Park?" Hewlett, head of the D.C. planning board, asked, sipping on Champagne.

Roderick motioned Hewlett to enter and have a seat. "Mrs. Chapman completed the work on the Baylor Plaza Park project, Günter. I'll make the presentation before the city zoning board in mid January."

"Shame she had to leave. She was easy to work with. I liked her ideas and her ideals. Very much like yours, Roderick. You two made a good team."

"I'm closing a deal shortly to bring in a new firm to handle Baylor's architectural and engineering needs. This and any other project won't suffer because of Mrs. Chapman's departure," he said confidently.

"I hope you're right, Roderick. It's not just the project that sold my department on the concept, it was the lady herself."

"No one is irreplaceable…"

"Pardon the interruption, gentlemen. Roderick, the car service is here," Savannah Logan said, standing in the doorway. "It's about time we left for the airport, don't you think?"

"Uh, yes, the holiday traffic was pretty tight," he said, recalling when he dropped Kelley, Shelby, and Shelly at the airport earlier that day for their trip to California to visit with Monique. "We'd better get a move on."

Roderick bid farewell and happy holidays to his employees, friends and business acquaintances and left his office with Savannah. As they rode to the airport, doubts about the wisdom of his decision to invite Savannah to go to Vail in JaiHonnah's place, began to creep into his head. He wouldn't have thought of the trip at all were it not for his desire to be alone with Jai. Now he was off with another woman. No one was irreplaceable, he kept trying to convince himself. No one, not even JaiHonnah.

* * *

"See you still here, JaiHawk," Jacob Junior growled walking into the kitchen wearing only his swimming trunks. He grabbed a mug and poured a cup of black coffee for himself. "You going to be here long?"

"Well, good afternoon to you too, brother," she said with a smile.

Jacob looked over his shoulder at her with one raised eyebrow. "So, how pregnant are you?" he asked.

"You and Calvin still running together or did Jake tell you?"

"Humph, Jake tells me only what he wants me to know," he said and snorted.

"So tell me how you found out."

"Don't ask questions you know I'm not going to answer," he said, grabbing the *New York Times,* scowling at the headlines and tossing the newspaper into the trash bin. Sauntering toward the door, he looked back at her. "You should have had an abortion."

JaiHonnah's head jerked toward her brother, but he left the kitchen and went to the indoor swimming pool. She got up from the table and followed him.

"What did you mean by that crack?" she asked and huffed, then she noticed three young, nude women swimming in the atrium-covered, indoor pool.

Jacob turned and looked in her direction, but didn't answer her. He put his coffee on one of the poolside tables, stripped out of his swimming trunks and dove into the water. The three women mindlessly laughed and giggled as they surrounded him, pawing at his nude, masculine frame. JaiHonnah knew what was about to happen. Hawk House was a man's domain filled with toys of the human variety with which the men played. She turned on her heels and left the pool area in a huff.

As she went back into the kitchen, JaiHonnah and her father made eye contact. She shook her head in disgusted frustration.

"You and your brother at it again, I see," Jake said.

"Still, you mean, don't you, Daddy?" she said, deadpan. "He makes me so angry sometimes. I don't understand it or him."

"Growing pains, I suspect," Jake said laconically. "Healthy competition helps you grow up."

"Competition? Who does Jacob have to compete with? Certainly not me. I'm no threat to him. He's the president of one of your corporate conglomerates, he has all the perks of his executive position and anything and everything he wants he can have with no sweat."

"A man needs to sweat. Needs to feel the pressure. Needs to know that his future is in his hands and that only he can control his destiny. A man has to know his strengths and turn his weaknesses into motivational tools. A man has to be challenged. If he doesn't have to sweat to get what he wants and needs, how can he know what he's made of? He's got to be hungry to appreciate it when he's full. He's got to want it no matter what it takes to get it."

"Jacob can be a bitter pill sometimes, but he works hard," JaiHonnah defended.

"Jacob Junior works smart, but not always hard. You gotta do both, dahlin'. You gotta work hard and smart. Like that boy you were working for."

"Roderick's not a boy. He is as much a man as you are."

"I hear he doesn't mind getting his hands dirty. Goes out to those job sites of his and works shoulder-to-shoulder with his men. All the time thinking how to make it better. I also hear tell that he don't lose no people neither. He pays a good wage and knows good service when he sees it," he said, eyeing his daughter.

She noticed his gaze on her. "What do you want me to say? You're right. He does work hard and smart. Yes, he does run a good operation. Yes, he does know his company from the bottom up and yes, his employees trust and respect him."

"So what's his secret, dahlin'? You seem to know the man."

JaiHonnah gave her father a sideways glance. "If you think I'm going to talk about Roderick Baylor, Daddy, think again. Besides, I don't see what my spat with Jacob has to do with Roderick."

Jake grinned and turned to pour a cup of coffee for himself. "More than a little, perhaps, or nothing at all," he said cryptically.

"Are you keeping something from me?"

Jake grinned. "Nah, dahlin', just thinking, 'tis all."

"Thinking what?"

"Why you quit. You just described a good businessman who keeps his employees. Something you not tellin' me, dahlin'?"

JaiHonnah knew that her father didn't indulge in idle thought. He had built an empire while others slept. She also knew that something was brewing, and she was about to begin her interrogation when a young beauty interrupted.

"Jake, honey," she cooed with a decidedly deep Texas drawl. "I thought you were coming back to bed. I miss you, sugar."

"I'll be there, Lorna Mae. You go on back to the bedroom and see if you can figure out how to work the DVD."

"But, Jake, being with you is better than watching those movies you told me to watch. I've learned a lot being with you."

Jake shook his head. "Yep, a man has to be challenged, alright."

JaiHonnah shook her head and then drank her juice. This woman was clueless, she thought. Jake wasn't into teaching women the ABCs of lovemaking, but if he had resorted to giving this woman X-rated movies to watch, Jake was clearly out of her league. If anything, a woman had to be hip, booted and schooled to hold her father's attention for more than one night. She'd bet real money that this Texas tease would be on the first jet out of Hawkinstown in the morning.

The woman left the kitchen and Jake settled his gaze on JaiHonnah.

"You been lonely too long, JaiHawk."

"Now where did that come from?"

"A woman has choices. Not like when your mama was a girl. You can choose to have a career and a family. Don't have to be one or the other no more."

"I know, Daddy. I'm not alone, and I won't be lonely. I'll have my baby and my family," she said and smiled, rubbing the spot where her baby grew.

Jake silently left the kitchen.

* * *

"Ezra, where is Jake?" JaiHonnah asked as she returned from a long walk.

"Don't rightly know, Miss JaiHawk. Man left early 'fo the sun come up. Said something 'bout a 'dead man walkin.' Didn't say where's he was goin'. Just told me to look out for yous," Ezra said as he put her lunch on the table before her.

JaiHonnah laughed as she picked up an orange slice and bit into it. "Never heard that phrase before," she said as she snuck another piece of fruit.

"Don't have much of a call for it round here."

JaiHonnah narrowed her eyes. "Not much of a call for what, Ezra?"

"Executions, Miss JaiHawk."

JaiHonnah momentarily froze. "Ezra, what do you mean?"

"Calm yo'self, Miss JaiHawk."

"Ezra, who is Jake going to execute?"

"Don't rightly know. Didn't say. Probably some fool who thinks yo' daddy came down with yesterday's rain," he said, laughing. "He ain't long gonna hold that thought though. Yo' daddy, he don't take no tea for the fever."

"Oh no," she anguished, thinking that Jake had gone after Calvin as she rushed to the telephone. "He could get himself into a lot of trouble!" She dialed her father's cell phone, but there was no answer.

All afternoon JaiHonnah tried the line. She knew that her father had the cell phone on him at all times. He had to know that it was her calling him. He could be anywhere in the world by now, even in Switzerland to face down Calvin and his father. Her fears mounted, but there was nothing that she could do until her father came home.

A couple of days later, JaiHonnah sat cross legged in a rocking chair on the wide veranda of her father's ranch and looked out over the landscape that went on forever. The sun danced out from behind swiftly moving clouds and dust devils waltzed on tiptoes across the horizon. In the distance, she could see trails of dust billowing up. The scene reminded her of the first time she saw Roderick coming through the dust cloud at the job site. Had it only been four months ago? So much had happened in such a short time. Christmas had come and gone. In a few days it would be a New Year and then another new life, she thought as she listlessly rubbed her burgeoning abdomen. A new little life was growing inside her, and it would have been a wonderful feeling if it were not for the circumstances of how the baby was conceived. Nevertheless, the baby had nothing to do with that traumatic experience.

Jacob Junior came out of the house swigging on a bottle of beer. He stood at the edge of the veranda observing the scenery. JaiHonnah didn't turn to look at him. Unlike her relationship with Adam, which was close and loving, her relationship with Jacob Junior was often distant and cool. That was particularly true after she divorced Calvin. Jacob and Calvin were college friends before JaiHonnah and Calvin met. Jacob and Calvin ran in the same circles, often jet-setting around the globe seeking the same thrills and adventures, and often sleeping with the same women—movie starlets or heiresses, maids or mistresses, it didn't matter. Both men were devastatingly handsome and had their pick of the female cream of the crop. Even when she and Calvin were married, if Jacob called him from some distant port, Calvin would be on his private jet and gone for weeks at a time. Jacob Junior and Calvin had no commitment to anything except the next thrill. She did not want another confrontation with Jacob. She wished that she had gone with Adam to the outbuilding that held his race cars. Adam was preparing two of his cars for the Grand Prix.

"Interesting woman, Monique Baylor," Jacob mused. "I can't imagine her as a mother and married to that straight-laced, boring Baylor character."

JaiHonnah's head turned toward Jacob. "How do you know Roderick's wife?" she asked with some trepidation.

"I was sleeping with her out in California while you were sleeping with her husband in Washington," he said, grinning. "I must say, she's got a sweet little ass, but more body than brains."

"You slept with her?" JaiHonnah flashed, startled.

Jacob took another swig of his beer. "Yeah. So?" he mused in disdain. "You slept with her husband, didn't you?"

"That was different! I was . . ." the defense choked off. Was she really going to dredge up the fact that she was in love with Roderick Baylor and that's why she had slept with him? No. She couldn't do it. She couldn't tell Jacob that. Especially since she had never told Roderick.

"What was different?" he asked, chuckling. "You thought you had found love and happiness? Well, little sister, see where that got you? You should have been more selective about who you gave yourself to."

"Like Calvin, I suppose?" she quipped.

"That's different. You're a Hawkins woman! Not some cheap whore laying down for the first three-legged animal that crosses your path! Baylor came from nothing and he's going nowhere. At least, with Calvin, you had a name; a name that means something in this country and abroad. His family comes from the highest British nobility. Not some boy who learned how to bounce a ball and now thinks that he's king of the hill."

"We came from nothing," she spat. "I'm not ashamed of that heritage. You think that Calvin gives a flying fig about you, Jacob? That he sees you as his equal just because you could afford the cost of college tuition at an Ivy League school? Well, big brother, you're in for a rude awakening. Calvin is a user, a manipulator. He used you and me to get to Daddy. He wants BlackHawk, and he thinks that, because I'm carrying his child and he knows what family means to Daddy, Jake is going to hand his empire over to him."

JaiHonnah's anger blossomed fully as she stood and walked away to spend time with Adam and his race cars. She couldn't fight Jacob. He thought Calvin was his friend, but from the look on Jacob's face, what she had said to him about Calvin's duplicity was sinking in. Nevertheless, Jacob's words about Roderick had also cut too deep. She had been a fool for falling for the handsome, warm and loving J. Roderick Baylor. She didn't need Jacob's condemnation to prove the point. The tears flowed as soon as she was away from him.

* * *

New Year's Eve in the plush and gaily decorated ballroom sitting at a round table after dinner should have been fun. Before the dancing started, Dorothy Kitt was telling another story and the group sat in rapt attention. Her husband, Gary Kitt, had his arm lazily around her shoulder smiling at her animated gestures. Gary was the butt of the joke and laughed with everyone else. Roderick tried to get into the flow of the group, but no matter how hard he tried, this evening, like the entire week, was an unmitigated disaster.

The week started off well enough and went straight downhill from there.

Strike one came swiftly.

When Roderick and Savannah arrived at the ski resort's main pavilion to register, she ran into people that she knew from her days in Atlanta at Spelman, Clark-Atlanta, Morehouse and Emory Universities. Of course, they planned to meet with her friends later to catch up on old times. As he and Savannah were leaving the pavilion and starting toward their villa, the owner, Morris Talbot, stopped them and said, "Ah, so, Roderick, this is the beautiful woman who you were so anxious to get alone?" Well, what could he say to Morris' smiling face and Savannah's confusion? *No, this is her replacement.* JaiHonnah decided to go with her husband instead of me. Instead, he just smiled and thanked Morris for the outstanding accommodations. Savannah never spoke another word until they were preparing for a romantic evening.

Then came the second strike.

Finally alone before a roaring fire, soft sounds of *Four Play* in the background, Savannah in a stunning red negligee, and him nibbling at her ear, he had committed the cardinal sin. He still didn't realize that he was calling her JaiHonnah as his nature was struggling to rise, but nothing was wrong with Savannah's hearing or thought processes. The argument that ensued landed him in the guest bedroom.

The third strike came the next night.

Roderick handed a small oblong box to Savannah as a peace offering. Not thinking had become a regular routine with him since JaiHonnah left him. The box held a gold charm bracelet. He remembered the inscription the moment the gold heart charm caught the glow of the candlelight, but not fast enough before Savannah read the inscription aloud. *"To JaiHonnah, with Love. JRock."*

Savannah packed and moved out of the villa in ten minutes flat. Morris found accommodations for her in the resort's hotel.

As he sat talking during dinner in a group of eight, Roderick had been the center of attention. Answering an array of questions about his basketball-playing days was not something he wanted to do. Besides, he had forgotten most of the games and the plays that were so vivid in the minds of his dinner companions.

Finally he had been able to turn the conversation away from himself when, all of a sudden, Dorothy asked Savannah, "When was the last time you saw JaiHonnah Chapman?" Savannah had answered without a blink, and a conversation ensued among the group with JaiHonnah as the centerpiece, but his heart stopped at the mention of her name. After that, he buried himself in several bottles of beer.

Later, still sitting at a table with people he met who also knew JaiHonnah and knew that she had worked for him, Savannah was nowhere in sight. She made herself scarce the entire week. She didn't even ski with him. Instead, she was the center of attraction for some other eligible or even some not-so-eligible, virile specimen. Roderick had been left to his own devices in the cozy villa and very much alone.

"Roderick, you've been very quiet this evening," Evelyn Prescott, one of the people at the table commented sitting next to him. "Where's Savannah?"

"I'm sure that she's here somewhere," he said, fingering the condensation on his glass of beer.

"Aren't you two a couple?" Evelyn asked, her gray-green eyes shining.

"We're a couple of friends," he answered, not sure of whether that was even true at the moment.

"She's a very lucky woman." Evelyn smiled, nudging closer to him. "You probably don't remember me, but I heard you speak at the Black Caucus gala last September. You were very impressive."

"There were so many people there that night. I thought the keynote speaker was very well received."

She laughed. "Roderick, you stole his thunder. What else could the audience do but give him polite applause," she said and shrugged.

"Thanks, Evelyn, but that wasn't my intent. My message was an attempt to..."

"Oh, it was clear what your message was," she said, laughing. "It got my vote."

"I'm pleased to hear that someone was listening."

"Everyone was, including Jai Chapman. She was your date that night, as I remember, right?" she asked, sipping her vodka martini. "I didn't get a chance to speak with her, but she looked great sitting on the dais."

The vision of JaiHonnah that night was still so vivid in his mind that it blocked out everything around him. He shook it off, not wanting to talk about Jai or that night.

"She and Savannah, well I see the competition continues," Evelyn blithely dropped the cryptic reference.

"Competition? Between Savannah and JaiHonnah?" he asked, his curiosity getting the better of him.

"Oh, you didn't know? Well, they were always in competition with each other in college. They ran for the same offices in campus clubs, competed scholastically, and the men! Well, we used to call it the Battle of the Sexiest," she said, laughing.

Roderick thought a minute. Was that what he was to JaiHonnah, the object of some youthful competition between her and Savannah? He remembered how JaiHonnah seduced him that night after they ran into Savannah at the restaurant. JaiHonnah was hell bent on keeping him away from Savannah—and it worked. He was so wrapped up in JaiHonnah that he hadn't given Savannah another thought. The reality of that night and next morning with JaiHonnah was emblazoned in his memory. He became semi-erect whenever he thought about her—just as he was then until Evelyn's chatter invaded his thoughts again.

"I'd say that they were about even when they graduated in the upper five percent of our class. Vivian Alexander Jackson beat them both out for high honors though."

Roderick smiled. "I'm not at all surprised. Vivian is my legal counsel."

"Do you know whether she and Jai's father are still playing chess?"

Roderick narrowed his eyes. "Chess?"

Evelyn laughed at his curious expression. "Yes, Jai and Vivian were roommates their senior year. Jai's father taught Vivian how to play chess. Vivian immediately beat him at the game and then they continued playing long distance. I've never seen anything like it. Jai's father would make a move and maybe two months later Vivian would counter it. Last I heard they were still at it."

Roderick hadn't known that about Vivian and Jai's father. Vivian never even mentioned that she played chess, but, of course, he hadn't asked.

"I'll ask her when I talk with her again, Evelyn. Maybe she'll give you a call and bring you up to date."

"I can ask Jai. I hear that she's back home in San Antonio for the holidays. She's not on the social scene though—."

"San Antonio?" he interrupted. "I thought she was from New Mexico. Shiprock, I think."

Evelyn laughed. "Are you sure Jai worked for you?"

"Yes, of that I'm sure," he said, deadpan and then taking another sip of beer. Though he had to admit to himself that he didn't really know much about her. Only enough to know that he loved her.

"Well, you must not have known her very well. Her mother was Navajo, but Jai grew up outside San Antonio. She won the Miss San Antonio Beauty Pageant when she was seventeen or eighteen, the Miss Texas Pageant too. If she hadn't purposefully acted as if she suddenly lost all of her senses, she would have won the Miss America Pageant. She easily could have won that contest, but I think that she had enough."

"Enough? Beauty pageant? I don't understand," Roderick said, becoming more interested than he cared to admit to himself.

"Yes, enough. I've heard Jai give former Texas Congresswoman Barbara Jordon's famous 1976 speech before the Democratic National Convention at least three times, each time flawlessly. Congresswoman Jordon was one of Jai's idols, but I could tell that JaiHonnah missed some lines on purpose. She was tired of the bright lights and photographers and being told how and when to smile. She already won a lot of other beauty contest, too. It was driving her crazy and so was her father. She wanted out of the beauty contest rat race, and she found a way to do it by getting married."

"So you think—."

"I think I've spent too much time talking to you about other women when what I want is to dance with you," she said.

Roderick did not notice that the band started playing. Evelyn was grinning at him like he was bait and she was a shark moving in for the kill. He asked her to dance, as if he had a choice at that point. Once that was over, he began circulating the ballroom and mingling with other people to avoid being trapped in other conversations that somehow always seemed to center around JaiHonnah Chapman and her fabulous life on the continent with her husband. He felt like he was wearing a tag on his forehead that read "Jai's Fool."

Just before midnight, he spotted Savannah and she noticed him, but she was wrapped in the arms of another man. He knew that it was going to be another long, lonely night, but it really didn't matter. He lost his appetite for a woman's warmth and touch. Only one woman could touch him in any way that counted—JaiHonnah Reise Chapman—but she was never going to touch him again. Sorrow mixed with anger still resided in his gut over that fact.

Roderick slipped out of the ballroom into the cold, clear night air and looked up at the night skiers on the slopes and the bright, starry sky. He knew that it would happen. JaiHonnah was on his mind, and the vision of her wreaked havoc with his heart. He folded his arms across his chest and remembered. There was a pain deep in his soul that, try as he had, would not go away. Closing his eyes against the vision held no relief. It was still there. Her essense was still there in his soul. He could feel her in his arms. Smell her scent. Taste her passion. Recall every moment that they were together. See the pain and disappointment in her eyes when he let his jealousy and distrust loose on her without giving her an opportunity to speak. It was seeing her with her husband and seeing the note from Lionel Porter that sent him into a blind, jealous tailspin. As if he was the only one in the relationship who was entitled to be hurt. Memories of Monique's deceit slithered into him, and he turned his malice on Jai. *Well, bro,* he thought, *three strikes and you're out.* He looked to the stars and at the stroke of midnight he whispered, "Happy New Year, JaiHonnah,"

* * *

"Happy New Year, Roderick," JaiHonnah whispered to the stars at the stroke of midnight, her eyes blurring with tears. She walked toward the lighted swimming pool and sat on a lounge chair with her legs pulled up to her chest. Her crimson silk gown waved gently in the breeze and around her ankles. The Texas sky was big, bright, and cloud free.

JaiHonnah sat at a wide, round table at San Antonio Country Club feeling like she'd rather be having a bikini wax than attending a private New Year's Eve party. Though it was after midnight, no one seemed ready to leave. The music was lively and so was the dancing. The open bars were doing a healthy business and the chefs were having the busmen set up the breakfast buffets. In addition to the BlackHawk employees and their spouses, the party was stocked with eligible men by her father like so many trout in one of his spawning farms. How she let Jake talk her into hosting this gala was still a mystery. Although she promised the ranch hands and their spouses that she would attend, she certainly didn't feel gay or happy. The consummate cowboy, Jake cut out a few heffas for himself from the female livestock leaving the rest for Adam and Jacob. She knew that her father would have a few of those women figuratively hogtied and on their backs before the dawn's early light. Jake was still a very virile man who liked his women and his liquor straight. His appetite had not waned in the years that she was in Europe, but he still wasn't the commitment type. He said, many years earlier after her mother died, that there would never be another woman like Skai. He never even came close to a permanent relationship since then.

Jacob Junior was a Jake clone, she thought, as she watched him charming yet another woman, but her heart went out to Adam who, much like her, just wanted someone to love and be loved in return. She knew how it felt to want someone so badly and know that it could never be.

"Ah, dahlin', you look too pretty to be spending your time nursing that soda water," Kevin Harris said, leaning in too close to her. "I think you ought to let this old cowboy lasso you for a little do-si-do around the dance floor."

"Thanks, Kevin, but I'd rather not. It's late and I'm a little tired."

"It's the shank of the evening. Can't be that bad a dancer, dahlin'. You trusted me at your cotillion," he said, smiling. "Now come along and let's re-create that memory."

Kevin took JaiHonnah's hand, and she relented. They danced slowly and the music made her think of Roderick. She loved to dance close to Roderick, his arms holding her just right. She fit in his embrace. She could almost smell Roderick's intoxicating manliness. She closed her eyes and swayed to the music, remembering every detail of Roderick's body. She remembered how much she enjoyed his tenderness and the seductive touches that awakened something in her that she longed for, but had never known before him. He unleashed passion in her for the feel of his bare body against hers, the exploration of paradise that they made together locked in each other's arms, the heat that they generated writhing uncontrollably against each other, the whispers of his passion in her ear that caused her to shudder in ecstasy as he spoiled her for any other man. They had moved in perfect rhythm and symmetry together, why were they so out of step now?

"You're a million miles away, Jai," Kevin whispered in her ear as they danced.

His voice startled her and snapped her back from her erotic remembrances. "Not quite a million, Kevin," she answered, wanting not to remember Roderick, but feeling powerless to stop herself.

"You know, Jai, I thought, way back there when you graduated from that private high school, that we could have had something serious between us. I know that my parents would welcome you into our family. I sure wish we hadn't grown apart, but now that you're back home, I'd like to come a courtin'," he said, smiling against her cheek.

"That's sweet, Kevin, but—."

"Now don't turn me away again so easily, Jai. I know things aren't real right with you and Calvin Chapman, but I never believed that he deserved to be with a woman like you. The man should have been on his knees every day thanking The Almighty that you chose him over all the men you had to choose from—me included. Now, unless you tell me no, then I'm not gonna let this opportunity pass—."

JaiHonnah stopped dancing and looked up at him. She brushed his cheek with her

hand. She wanted to say that when you've had your best lover, everyone else pales by comparison. She had the best—J. Roderick Baylor.

"Kevin, we will always be friends, but we'll never be lovers. You're a wonderful man, so it's not you that I'm saying no to, but I'm—."

"Obviously in love with your husband," he said, finishing what he thought she was about to say.

"I don't think that I'm in . . .well, it doesn't matter," she said, sighing. "Let's just say that it's not the right time and leave it at that."

Why was she in such torment? she wondered. She didn't want to lock herself away again, but she couldn't stand the pain any longer. Fool that she was, she wanted to be with Roderick and only Roderick. Only time would extract him from her head and heart, but time was passing too slowly.

JaiHonnah stood on the patio of the country club and wrapped her arms around her waist. It was quiet, except for the music playing inside. The stars were clearly visible, and she looked up at them as she heard the beginning of Auld Lang Sang. *"Shall old acquaintance be forgot and never brought to mind,"* she thought as the music played. In this case, yes. There were no options where that was concerned. She had to put Roderick Baylor in the past. It was over.

A while later, Jai felt her fur wrap being slipped around her shoulders, and she quickly wiped her tears. "Ezra, I've been such a fool," she said quietly. "I'm so ashamed."

"No, dahlin', you just learnin' how to be a woman. Something yo' daddy and me couldn't teach ya, though we tried. But we failed. Yo' daddy, he thought he was doin' the right thing letting you marry so young to that Chapman boy, but he been sorely tried for dat mistake. He ain't fixin' to make dat mistake again."

"Neither am I, Ezra. Neither am I," she declared solemnly.

"Sounds to me like you done fixed yo' mine on a plan, JaiHawk," Ezra noted, drawing on his pipe as he stood beside her in the moonlit night.

"I have, yes. Something that I should have done long ago."

"You ain't gonna do nothin' foolish, now is you, JaiHawk?"

"I'm through doing foolish things," she said with steel laced in her voice.

The older man's eyes were shining as he pulled on his pipe. He knew that she was ready to handle her business, but he felt her pain and sorrow nonetheless.

* * *

The day was warm despite the late January date. The winter had not been hard although it was not yet over. JaiHonnah was in San Antonio for a few days to meet with potential clients who were interested in hiring her to design office buildings and shops to be built on the famous River Walk in the downtown area. She walked along the trendy River Walk cobblestone paths, making a few notes about the existing architecture and the unique façade that added to the popular attraction. The San Antonio River ran through the village-like district bordered on both sides with sidewalk cafes, haute courant boutiques, book stores, card shops and other businesses. Music filtered out of restaurants, coffee houses, and clubs. Breezes caught in the cypress trees, swaying them slightly. Aromas tantalized from sidewalk vendors and dinner boats. Brightly colored river taxis cruised by, and a kaleidoscope of sensations immersed JaiHonnah in the richness of the Tex-Mex cultures. Chic nouvelle with an attitude. That was the San Antonio she loved and missed. The promise of outrageous night life in hideaway clubs would inspire the night, she thought. She rubbed her burgeoning belly. *Wish you were here,* she thought silently.

JaiHonnah padded her way toward an interesting little bistro and took a seat outside by the railing overlooking the river. She stared blankly at the water rushing by her and thought about the Anacostia River so many miles away. The gurgling and rippling melody of the water caught her memory up in its gentleness, and she looked away from her notes for a moment to remember. The river moved on forever toward the sea to be devoured by the Gulf of Mexico. She likened her life to the rushing water, bending and twisting around obstacles to make its way to oblivion.

"Jai?" a voice said, trying to get her attention. "Earth to JaiHonnah," she said again touching JaiHonnah's shoulder.

The thoughts began to clear and permitted JaiHonnah to realize that someone was speaking to her. She turned mechanically toward the voice, devoid of expression. Then she saw Evelyn Prescott smiling quizzically at her. Her mouth curled in a lazy smile. "Evelyn, I'm sorry. I didn't see you there."

"Or hear me either, girlfriend," Evelyn said, smiling back and moving to press her cheek against JaiHonnah's. "Now that's what I call total focus," she said, taking a seat at the little bistro table across from JaiHonnah and placing several shopping bags in an empty chair.

JaiHonnah smiled. "I was working on an idea, but that can wait. How are you? I haven't seen you in years."

"Well enough," Evelyn said. "I heard from some of our old crowd that you were back in the States. I saw you at the Black Caucus gala, but there were so many people there that I didn't get a chance to talk with you before you left that night. Then I bumped into Rich Thompson. He told me that Vivian Alexander Jackson gave a big party for your last birthday. He said a lot of the old crowd was there."

"I had a job in D. C. until just before Christmas," JaiHonnah said as she felt a pang of remorse and didn't want to dwell on the painful memory. "So what have you been doing?" she asked and smiled broadly.

"Headhunting," Evelyn said and laughed.

"What?" JaiHonnah asked, with confusion on her smiling face.

"I own a placement company now. I have clients who are looking for talented people or people who have specialized skills to offer. I match corporate needs with individuals who can fulfill those needs and *voila,* I get paid," she said, animated.

"Oh, I see. That's great, Evelyn."

"Well, it's a living and it's getting better. I was just up at Vail during the holidays looking for more contacts, doing some networking, and I ran into some of the old crowd from Atlanta. You know Carrie, Sonia, Paulette, Savannah and Gwendolyn. It was like old home week. I heard that Constantina Justice is somewhere in California. KC is in Chicago, you know, and so is Cheryl. The only ones missing were you and Vivian."

"Sounds like it was fun. How is everyone?"

"Married and happy, except for a few, like Savannah and me," she said, "but maybe Savannah won't be in that category for long."

"Savannah? What, is she getting married?" JaiHonnah asked, surprised.

"Well, you know Savannah. She doesn't go after something half assed. She was with this guy, Roderick, uh, Roderick Baylor. Real tall, good looking and built! You know, that basketball star?"

JaiHonnah stopped breathing.

"You know him, don't you, Jai?"

"Uh, yes, I do, I mean, I did, uh, yes. I worked for him," she stumbled over her words.

"That's what he said. He didn't seem to know that you were from Texas though. He thought that you were from New Mexico."

"We weren't that close," she lied. "I mean, he was my boss, but he has a family."

"Oh, I didn't know that. I saw you two together at the Black Caucus gala . . .Jai? What is it, Jai?" Evelyn's worried expression growing deeper when JaiHonnah rose from her seat. "Jai, you're pregnant!"

"Uh, yes, uh, I have to run, Evelyn. It was good to see you...uh." JaiHonnah bolted from the table, leaving Evelyn with her mouth agape. The thought of Savannah and Roderick together—on a romantic getaway, the one that he had planned for her—was too painful for her to bear. She picked up her pace and walked swiftly to a cab stand. Her heart thumped, then settled down to its normal rhythm as she sat in the taxicab headed for the airport. All she wanted to do was go home to Hawkinstown.

$$\mathcal{C}hapter\ 23$$

The holiday trip to Vail was a pitiful memory, a month later. Roderick was sitting in his office working on bids for other projects that were on his agenda. Suddenly, he heard a commotion outside his office door that grew louder and more boisterous as it got nearer. He heard shouts and then the door to his office flew open shattering the glass which crumbled onto the carpet.

"*You bastard!*" Lionel Porter's voice boomed. "*You mother-fucking bastard!*" He stalked into the office, his light-complexioned face blood red, twisted in anger and spitting the words with venom through his bared teeth and tensed lips.

"You'll pay for this, Baylor!" Lionel thundered as he backed away. "You'll be sorry you ever . . ." Roderick raised menacing eyes to Lionel silencing him before Lionel turned and fled the Rock of Gibraltar.

A few days later, Roderick sat next to Vivian who sat next to Kelley in one of Vivian's law office conference rooms. They were poised across the table from Lionel Porter and his battery of lawyers who had been holding a filibuster for nearly an hour. Roderick had not spoken, but listened patiently with his hands steepled before him resting against his lips. Now it was time for their response, and Roderick took the lead.

"Lionel, you're out. A new board chairperson will be named soon. In the interim, Kelley Baylor takes over as president and CEO of the company next month," Roderick said calmly, as if bored with the rhetoric, utterances and discourse.

"That's it? Just like that I'm out of a company that I built from the ground up? *No! Hell no!*"

"You have no choice, Lionel. Baylor Design and Developers holds controlling interest in Porter, Dare and Silver Architecture and Engineering. With controlling interest, Baylor Design and Developers is entitled to restructure the company, name a new president, chairman of the board, and board of directors. I've done that. Your partners, Dare and Silver, have asked to buy in to the new subsidiary corporate structure, Baylor Architecture and Engineering, and I'm considering their proposals. As far as you're concerned, you can stick a fork in it. It's done. It's over and you're out."

"I'll take this to the SEC. I'll take you to court. I'll see you in hell before I...."

Roderick held up one hand, silencing Lionel, and then leaned forward.

"Bail out in that golden parachute you've got, Lionel, before I clip the strings, slap you with an injunction, and have the federal district attorney bring you up on criminal charges for misappropriation of corporate funds, tax evasion, and stock manipulation." Lionel's swollen demeanor puffed more as Roderick continued. "And, another thing. I want you to submit to a DNA test," Roderick added.

Vivian's hands went to her laptop keys Roderick noticed, but she said nothing.

"This isn't business." Lionel raged. "This is personal. This is about me and Monique. Sure I slept with her, but so did everybody else. I wasn't the only one. You want her? She's yours. I don't want her, never did, but you can't have my company."

"Monique? You think that this is about Monique?" Roderick railed. "You are a foolish man, Lionel. There are none so blind as those who will not see. A very foolish man. And I thought I was the fool. I don't want Monique."

"You want her all right. She's your wife, isn't she? She's all the time telling me that you can't resist her; that you'd do anything to keep her."

"And you believed that? You're more of a fool than I thought."

"Then, if it's not about Monique, what the hell do you want? What will it take to get my company back?"

"Hell freezing over. I want you out of my business, Lionel, and, by the way, take Chapman with you when you go."

"*Chapman?* Who the hell is...." he thought a moment. "JaiHonnah Chapman? Is that who you're talking about?"

"Don't try to play me for a chump, Lionel. She works for you."

"Man, what have you been sniffin'? Jai Chapman doesn't work for me or my company. Last I heard she was working for you."

The revelation rocked Roderick. Vivian interceded.

"I'm sure that your attorneys will advise you, Mr. Porter, that Mr. Baylor has every legal right to assume control of the company as outlined in the new corporate structure. All transactions have been made known to the Securities and Exchange Commission. Nothing in what he or Baylor Design and Developers have done is in any way actionable under state or federal law. There won't be any litigation, Mr. Porter. All current contracts will remain in force. No new business will be conducted without Ms. Kelley Baylor's approval, but I strongly suggest that you cease and desist from any attempt to withdraw funds from any corporate account. As of yesterday, all accounts have been audited and closed. New accounts were opened under the new corporate structure this morning.

"As for your prior unauthorized and questionable use of corporate funds, the information has been turned over to the proper authorities. Rather than issue threats against someone who just saved the company from going into receivership, I'd strongly suggest that you spend your time preparing your defense against charges that will likely be brought against you by the federal government.

"Now," Vivian stood and extended her hand. "Since there is no other business to discuss, I bid you and your legal team a good day."

Dejectedly, Porter's attorneys shook her hand, stuffed their papers back into their briefcases and urged the now despondent Lionel Porter to depart without further comment.

Leaving no question that he had been summarily dismissed, Porter rose from the conference table and gave Roderick a backward glance.

Roderick's head never turned toward Lionel when he said, "I want those DNA tests done today!"

Lionel's mouth moved silently, but it was clear to all that there was no use in further discussion. His plan to take over Baylor Development had failed. He left the room a beaten man.

Vivian fixed her stare on Roderick's profile. He sat with his body hunched forward staring straight ahead with narrowed brow.

"Audio and video off," she ordered to the air and then waited while the recording system shut down. "Was he right, JRock? Did you do this as a vendetta not about Monique, but about Jai?"

Roderick turned only his head toward her, his hands still steepled and his brow still furrowed. "No, it wasn't," he answered coolly. "This was about Lionel Porter trying to raid Baylor Developers so that he could gut my company to shore up his own failing business. He mismanaged his company, and he was after mine to cover his losses on contracts to design and build arenas and other projects for the Olympics. He thought that I was vulnerable when I purchased the lumber yard and then the brick, block and concrete company and that I'd let him walk all over me. He started coming after me years ago after he and Monique . . ." he cut off his thought. Then he looked away from her. "This had nothing to do with Jai. You should know me better than that, Vivian. If Lionel Porter had come to me and asked for my help, I would have given it. Personally, I don't like the man, not just because he slept with Monique and then had the temerity to rub my nose in it, but because he's a thief. He's still a frat brother though. For that reason, and only for that reason, I would have helped him get back on his feet."

"Then explain to me why you wanted Porter to take JaiHonnah with him when he left the company."

"I need people working for the new company who I can depend on to be loyal. Not someone who'll turn and run when the going gets tough. Jai Chapman has demonstrated an inability to stick with it. She, apparently, interviewed with Porter and was going to leave my company to join his. She wasn't even going to give me a chance to match or better his offer. It's going to be hard enough fulfilling the contractual obligations that Porter wrote without having to wonder when one of my primary architects and engineers is going to up and take a walk."

Kelley rose from her seat clearly frustrated and finally spoke. "She's not Monique, JRock. She was not going to Porter, Dare and Silver. She told me that Lionel offered her a very lucrative contract, but she told him that she wouldn't accept his offer because she was morally and contractually obligated to Baylor Developers. She was going to stay with Baylor Developers, that is, until you gave her a reason not to stay." Then to Vivian, Kelley said, "Vivian, I'll call you later when I've had an opportunity to look over the Atlanta operation more closely. JRock, I'll see you back at the office."

Roderick just stared at her, confused. After she left, Vivian sat alone with Roderick.

"I sense that you were surprised by what you heard here today," she said, modulating her voice. "What are your feelings toward Jai now?"

Roderick impatiently rose from his seat, jammed his fists into his pockets, and walked around the conference room toward the sliding glass doors that led to a balcony. He looked out into the cold, late February day, which offered no solace. Icicles clung to the railing and matched his mood.

"Nothing has changed," he said, not looking at Vivian.

"That means that you're still in love with her," Vivian said, gathering her papers.

Roderick turned with a jerk and looked at Vivian. "That means that she's still out of the company and out of my life. She remains Mrs. JaiHonnah Reise Chapman, former employee, period!"

* * *

JaiHonnah strolled around her father's huge library reviewing again the documents in her hand. When the double doors opened, she laid them on her father's solid oak desk and looked up.

"Mr. Calvin Chapman III," Ezra announced, not giving any clue as to his real feelings about the man who followed him into the library.

"Thank you, Ezra," JaiHonnah said calmly.

Calvin's pompous frame strolled into and then around the room, possessively eyeing every detail of the posh enclave. He clasped his hands together and rubbed them as if the friction was an aphrodisiac. A grin curled around his lips as a languid finger trailed the length of one of the overstuffed, dark-red leather sofas. Moving on to a matching high-back leather chair near the desk where JaiHonnah rested one hip on the edge of the pool-table sized, solid oak desk, he leaned his arms against the top of the chair and eyed her slowly and lasciviously from head to toe. A gleam grew in his eyes and a possessive grin on his lips.

"Pregnancy agrees with you, Jai," he said, his voice low and full of lust. "You're more beautiful than the day you walked out on stage at the pageant. Took me a while, but I finally got that old buzzard to agree that you would marry me." He looked around the room casually. "It was right here in this very room. I liked the look of it, but after we're married, I want to make a few changes. Modernize the place a bit. Nothing too drastic, you know." He settled his gaze on JaiHonnah again. "After this baby is born, I want you to have a tubal ligation. There won't need to be any more babies. I want you as lush and trim as you were when you were competing. I remember it like it was yesterday."

JaiHonnah folded her arms. "We're not here to reminisce, Calvin."

"Yes, you're right," he said with a broader grin, eyeing her. "Let's get the show on the road. I've got a hard-on for you. I want to get to the honeymoon. This wedding ceremony shouldn't take long, and then we can be alone together again just like before." He glimpsed his watch. "Where's the preacher and the old buzzard, anyway?"

"Sign these documents, Calvin," she said, holding a pen out toward him.

Calvin straightened from his rested position against the back of the chair. He took her hand with the pen in it and raised it to his lips.

"I wouldn't do that, if I were you," JaiHonnah spoke through a locked jaw, "until you've read the agreement," she added.

Calvin's grin broadened. "Right," he said. "You're not legally my wife yet. I wouldn't want you to be able to claim that I sexually harassed you. We'll get to the good parts later." He took the pen from her hand and fixed his attention on the documents on the desk. His grin slowly slipped from his face and then his face contorted in anger. "*What the hell? What is this?*"

JaiHonnah stood and faced him. "It's an agreement that I, and thirty other women, will not press criminal charges of rape, assault and battery, and a whole panoply of other offenses, against you. We will only do this in exchange for your agreement to: (a) acknowledge your crimes against each of us, (b) pay restitution of one hundred thousand dollars to each woman, except me, of course, and (c) enter a sex-offenders clinic of my choice and not leave until the doctors can assure me that you're sufficiently cured so as to never be a threat to another woman again.

"The agreement goes on to assure that you relinquish all claims on my baby or any eventual inheritance that my baby might receive and that you give fully and freely all custody rights to my baby to me without future action, should I meet with some early or unexpected demise. Should that happen, my attorney becomes the exclusive legal guardian over my son, my estate, and you surrender all rights of recourse.

"You will, of course, be permitted to see our child at my discretion and only under supervised visits, but if you come anywhere near me or my child without my expressed permission, all bets are off. Now, sign the damn document and get the hell out of my face."

Calvin's jaw tightened convulsively and the color bloomed in his face. "The hell you say. I'm not signing a damn thing. You get your father in here right now. I won't put up with your shit."

"My father has nothing to do with this. If you don't agree to the terms and conditions of this agreement, you'd better start putting your affairs in order because you'll be spending damn near the rest of your life in prison in eight different states and on three continents."

The reality was not having a sobering effect on Calvin, Jai noticed. He looked wildly into her eyes as his rage grew. His hand raised and suddenly Ezra cocked the rifle, freezing Calvin in mid swing. JaiHonnah never faltered or took her stare from Calvin's raging eyes.

"I ain't got nothin' to lose, boy!" Ezra raged, holding the rifle steady with a bead on Calvin.

"Ezra, that won't be necessary! Please, put the gun down!" JaiHonnah said, stepping between him and Calvin.

"He ain't gonna hurt you no more, JaiHawk. Lem'me kill him and I'll go to my grave a happy man."

"Then who will help me raise my son, Ezra? I need you with me. Just like always," she said calmly. "This is not the way of my people."

JaiHonnah's words were strong and firm. After a humming moment, Ezra lowered the rifle. JaiHonnah turned, picked up the pen again and held it up to Calvin. "Sign it!" she ordered.

Calvin snatched the pen from her hand and scribbled his signature on the documents. He stared at her impenetrable form, turned and stalked from the room. JaiHonnah picked up the documents and checked that all were properly signed. Then she turned to Ezra.

"Please witness his signature, have these documents copied and sent by express mail to my lawyer in Washington, Ezra. She's expecting them, and,—" she kissed his cheek,—"thank you for standing by me."

"You done good, JaiHawk. Yo' daddy would be proud ifin' he knew what you done here today..."

The sound of a thumbnail on a wind match caught their attention. They saw the fire catch, and turned toward the mountain filling the doorway. Jake brought the match to his cigar and drew the smoke easily, letting it drift out of his mouth unaided by breath. His glance was wicked as the grin curled his full lips. He held the match momentarily then extinguished it with a finger and thumb. He winked at JaiHonnah and nodded slowly.

"Said you was gonna make me some spoonbread, dahlin'. Sure would like a mess of yo' fried okra and green tomatoes. Picked some fresh ones out in the hot house. Left them in the kitchen for you to wash up for me, Ezra."

"Sure thing, Mr. Jake," Ezra said with a wink. "Gonna get right to it soon as I get these old bones to movin'."

"How's 'bout a game of racquetball about 3:00 o'clock, Ezra? Like always," he added. "Our girl is tired of whippin' on us."

When Ezra left the room, Jake fixed his gaze on JaiHonnah. Hands on hips she gave him a sideways glance.

"Thought you were out of town, Jake."

"Just went for a little ride up to the cabin. Good fishin' up there this time of the year." He drew the smoke lazily.

"Who was the bait?" she asked, sizing him up.

"Don't go for no jail bait, dahlin'. The lady in question was over the age of consent."

"Maybe my being here is cramping your style, Jake."

"I ain't a greedy man. I gits my share," he said and grinned. "Now 'bout that lunch, I got me some trout in the bucket waitin' for you to fry 'em up."

JaiHonnah shook her head slowly and smiled at her father.

"Broiled or baked, Jake?"

"Just carve 'em up the way you did Chapman, JaiHawk. I like the taste of it raw too," he said and winked.

"Put out that cigar, Jake. It's bad for the baby. If I'm going to hang around here, you go smoke outside," she said and smiled.

"Done," Jake said.

Chapter 24

The cherry blossoms were in full bloom around the Tidal Basin. People were out in droves enjoying the spring air and warm sunshine. Roderick, Shelly and Shelby swept the winter debris from the deck of the boat and started scrubbing the chrome. His daughters' little hands worked steadily for hours, Roderick noticed, and he smiled at their accomplishment. They were as happy as they could possibly be, he thought as he took a moment to watch them working. He couldn't help the joy that grew across his face watching the two little women. They were bossing him around like he was the child, and he loved it. Nothing was more special than the relationship between father and daughter, he thought.

"*Dad-dy.*" Shelly frowned, hands on hips. "You're not working," she scolded.

"Yes, ma'am," he said, grinning. "Thought we'd take a little break. Just for a few minutes. You young ladies have been working me all morning."

"Okay," Shelby said and gave an exaggerated huff. "You sit down and I'll get a soda for you. You can't have any beer today 'cause you had two yesterday."

Roderick laughed. "Yes, ma'am, Ms. Shelby."

"That's Shelby Sunbeam to you, Daddy," she corrected.

Roderick's smile slipped slightly. After all these months his daughters hadn't forgotten JaiHonnah for one minute. How could they? They had Kelley track Jai down in Texas and his mounting telephone bill bore evidence to the fact that they talked with her nearly every day. He had even overheard some of the conversations they had with her each night before he tucked them into bed or in the afternoon when they returned from school. They couldn't put their books down fast enough before they would speed dial her telephone number and tell her all about their day at school while he or his housekeeper, Mrs. Betterman, made a snack for them. Each conversation that his daughters had with JaiHonnah ended with "We love you, Jai. Please come home soon." He wondered what her answer was to that, but the girls never told him, and he wouldn't ask.

Shelby handed a bottle of orange soda to him and one to her sister. They all sat down at a table on the deck of the yacht.

"Daddy, Shelby and I have decided that we want to call *The Mighty Magic Heat The Navajo Princess* from now on."

"Oh?" he said, surprised by her directness. "You've talked about this, have you?"

"Yes, Daddy, we have. The corporation voted and we agreed. Now when you agree it will make it unna - no... I can't say that word, Shelby, you say it."

"I can't say it either, Shelly. You know what we mean, don't you, Daddy?" Shelby asked innocently.

"Unanimous. Yes, I know what you mean, sweetheart."

"Well, Daddy, will you do it?" Shelly asked. "Can we call the boat *The Navajo Princess*? Maybe then Jai will come back to us, and we can all be happy again."

The comment tugged hard at his heart. His stomach did a slow dive. He caressed Shelly's small face, smoothing her wiry, golden brown, flowing locks from her furrowed brow.

"I thought we were happy, sweetheart. We're the corporation, remember? Me, you and Shelby."

"But it's not the same without Jai, Daddy," Shelby whined. "You used to be real happy when Jai was here. You used to kiss her on the lips and smile all the time."

"Yeah, Daddy, and then you'd make those funny sounds when you and Jai thought we were asleep."

"And then you and Jai would be makin' those funny sounds again, but we couldn't tell what you and Jai were saying. Sounded like some kinda foreign language or something," Shelly said and giggled.

Roderick covered his mouth to hide his amusement at his twins' animated behavior. He had smiled a lot then, he remembered as the girls continued to talk. How could he not smile when Jai was anywhere in the vicinity? She put a smile on his heart like no other person, place or thing other than his daughters. Even now, when he missed JaiHonnah so desperately, he couldn't stand it at times. He could no longer smile when he remembered her touch, her kiss, her scent, her feel against him—his joy and hers in their union of ecstasy. It was unbridled passion that he felt for her, he tried to tell himself, but in his heart he knew that Vivian was right. He was in love with the Navajo princess—deeply and unavoidably in love with JaiHonnah Reise Chapman.

"Can we, Daddy, pleeezzze," Shelly entreated.

"Yes, baby, we can do that," he said soberly, gathering his girls in his arms and kissing them both.

His daughters returned his affection, squeezing him around the neck and wildly kissing his face. He laughed heartily and held them closer. He wanted JaiHonnah to be with them too.

* * *

The film clip was just about over. Roderick silently sat watching the details in each frame. Vivian jotted notes on her laptop. Roderick's eyes shifted toward Monique and her attorneys, some of whom sat in rapt fascination and others who covered their faces at the sights and sounds on the film strip. This was not going to be pretty, he thought, but it had to happen. Monique's most recent demand, for two million dollars more a year or she would start custody proceedings to take the girls and discuss their divorce on every national talk show, had been the last straw. He didn't know what Vivian was up to, but the film starring Monique Baylor in the title role of *Luscious Lips* was a good clue. He would have laughed out loud at Monique's lack of acting talent, if his girls' future didn't hang in the balance. The film ended, and Vivian took the lead.

"Well, I presume that we are all on the same page here. The former Mrs. Baylor signed an agreement that the funds contributed by Baylor

Pictures would be used to produce a family-oriented film, which would garner a general audience rating by the Motion Picture Association of America. As we have demonstrated, the film, *Luscious Lips,* would barely garner a triple-X rating by the MPAA. The only hint of a family is the opening shot of Mr. Baylor's and Ms. Baylor's daughters playing on the front lawn of the Baylor's Beverly Hills estate. Beyond that I believe that the film appeals to prurient interest, since subsequent to the opening frame, Ms. Baylor appears in no less than twenty scenes copulating various sizes of male genitalia.

"There doesn't appear to be any socially redeeming value, since the dialogue consists of a series of tonal grunts and groans from your client, except when she winks at the end of the film, licks her lips and coos the title of the movie.

"Finally, the film appears to be patently offensive, at a minimum, because of Ms. Baylor's inability to act and, at the other extreme, her poor selection of location, sound, video quality and directorial prowess."

Vivian pulled her wire-rim glasses down her nose with one finger and peered over the top of the glasses across the table to Monique and opposing legal counsel. "In other words, Ms. Baylor and esteemed counsel, the flick is legally obscene by contemporary standards. Now, please don't misunderstand Mr. Baylor's position here. He does not object to Ms. Baylor's desire to be gainfully employed in whatever career she so chooses. In fact, he applauds her efforts. Mr. Baylor's generosity in financing Baylor Pictures is well documented and was geared toward that position. Notwithstanding his full support for her career aspirations, he has patiently contributed again and again to Ms. Baylor's endeavors. However, it is our contention that Ms. Baylor has failed to act in good faith. Moreover, she has used their children in this film in violation of child labor laws. I must hasten to add that she did so in contravention of the custodial parent's expressed request that their daughters' time be spent with Ms. Baylor in a mother/daughter bonding period to give the girls a sense of well being. That has not been the case. Ms. Baylor, on each occasion when the girls were in her care, left them with a nanny spending less than one hour a day with them over a two-week period. We have affidavits signed by the nanny and their aunt, Ms. Kelley Baylor, attesting to that fact as recently as last year when she accompanied the minor girls to California during the holidays.

"In further evidence of Ms. Monique Baylor's malfeasance as a parent, I direct your attention to this most recent act. Ms. Baylor claims that she has sole right of guardianship over Shelly and Shelby Baylor, because, according to her, Mr. Baylor is not the biological father of the minor children. She further claims that Lionel Porter is, in fact, the father of the offspring. Yet, even if that were true, which we are prepared to demonstrate that it is not, Ms. Monique Baylor is willing to permit the girls to remain with Mr. Baylor, if he would increase his already generous alimony payments by two million dollars a year."

Vivian removed her eyeglasses, folded them on the conference table before her and then leaned back in the high-back leather chair.

"My esteemed colleagues," she continued, "with all due respect, Mr. Baylor respectfully declines your client's offer, and with the same level of due deference to Ms. Baylor, my client withdraws *all* alimony and/ or other support save one hundred, fifty thousand dollars a year. Mr. Baylor will continue to maintain the Baylor Beverly Hills estate until their daughters, who we have DNA evidence to prove are biologically his, reach the age of twenty-one at which time the title to the estate will transfer to Shelly and Shelby Baylor. Ms. Baylor's agreement with the terms and conditions of the contract made between her and Mr. Baylor in September of last year, goes into effect immediately. Mr. Baylor is fully prepared to submit the film for judicial scrutiny and will do so by filing with the D.C. Circuit Court of Appeals this very afternoon, documents to have the film declared legally obscene and thus in violation of federal statute. Mr. Baylor will do so to exculpate himself from any criminal charges that the Department of Justice may want to bring. Are there any questions?"

Monique and her attorneys sat motionless, mouths agape. Clearly, Roderick observed, they were in a stupor. Finally, Monique found her voice.

"One hundred, fifty thousand? I pay my gardener fifty thousand."

"Sounds like your gardener is due for a reduction in his standard of living," Vivian quipped.

"You can't do this to me!" Monique railed. "Lionel will not stand for it! And neither will Calvin Chapman! I know what you're after! You can't fool me, Roderick Baylor! You want Calvin's wife! You want that half-breed Indian bitch! Well, you can't have her! She's seven months pregnant with Calvin's baby! He's not going to give her up no matter what you want!"

"Pregnant?" Roderick whispered, the wind knocked out of him.

Nothing else in the room moved for him while Monique's tirade continued. He was lost in a fog. His eyes saw nothing. His ears heard nothing. His body felt nothing. His brain only repeated over and over *JaiHonnah is pregnant*. He didn't notice when the room cleared. Only Vivian's gentle voice penetrated the dense orbit he found himself in.

"JRock," Vivian said softly, her hand on his shoulder.

He found his voice. "Vivian, I know and understand your position on not divulging any information about your clients, and I respect that position, but I have to know...please tell me the truth," his voice labored and low. "Is JaiHonnah pregnant?" His eyes searched hers. She did not have to answer. He saw it in her face. He laced his fingers together against his lips. "That's why she was distracted. That's why she asked me to be patient with her, isn't it, Vivian? She's carrying that bastard's baby, and I treated her like . . ." the words were like a dagger plunged deep in his heart. "I treated her like a..."

"JRock, I've talked with Jai many times. She's doing well. She's looking forward to the birth of her child. She's not angry with you for what happened between you before she left. She only has the highest respect for you and wishes you and the girls all the best. She hopes that you don't object to her staying in touch with Shelly and Shelby and that maybe you'll let them visit with her someday. In the meantime, now that she has time on her hands, she's working on some ideas that she thinks might be good additions to the Baylor Plaza Park project. She'll send them to me when she's finished. She doesn't expect payment for her work..."

Roderick abruptly rose from his chair. He walked to the window and covered his face with one hand. "God. What a fool I've been. That maniac raped her and abused her and I've done the same thing to her. After all of that, she's still thinking about how to make my dream of Baylor Plaza Park come true. God!" He rubbed his brow, but it did not soothe the wrenching in his gut. He breathed deeply, trying desperately to quell the emotions surging through him. He was nearly numb.

"JRock," Vivian said, a hand on his arm. "It's alright. She's fine."

"It's not alright, Vivian. It will never be alright for her as long as Calvin Chapman is with her. God knows the two of us have caused her enough pain and suffering to last her a lifetime. I wanted her to trust me, but I didn't give her my trust in exchange. I saw in her another Monique. A woman who only knew how to hurt and manipulate. How many fools does it take to make a man? My girls knew that she was special immediately and without question. They respect her, trust her, and, above all, they love her, and so do I."

Chapter 25

JaiHonnah finished her sketches and picked up the stack, moving toward the window in her studio. She clipped the sketches to stays hanging from the ceiling and then stepped back to look at them. Baylor Plaza Park would have an indoor and outdoor sports arena including an Olympic-size pool to be built adjacent to the Greenfield Community Center building. She didn't know why she hadn't thought of it before. Now, after reading an article in *The Wall Street Journal* about Baylor Developer's innovative plans for the renovation of the Olympic stadiums, it all fell into place. There would also be an equestrian center and the community hydroponics' farm concept that she had suggested where flowers could be grown along with edible crops for training young adults and for sale to the public in an open-air, fresh food market.

She crossed her arms over her breasts and smiled at the additions. They would fit well into the original plan and she hoped that Roderick would agree to include them. She recognized that the additions would strain the project's budget, but she was willing to contribute to the other donations that had been collected to match the funds and services being contributed by Roderick personally.

The sun creased the horizon, and JaiHonnah looked through the atrium wall of glass toward the east and the rising sun. She had not been able to sleep long the night before. Her little constant companion had been very active and in want of her attention. Her constant arguments with Jacob, when he was not out making BlackHawk richer, also troubled her. He had, what appeared to be, an obsessive hatred for Roderick personally and Baylor Design and Developer's success particularly.

The night before she sat in her rocking chair rubbing her stomach for more than an hour. Two trips to the bathroom later, she figured that the baby must have been playing racquetball using her bladder as the ball. Finally, she got up and walked through the quiet house toward her studio on the east wing. Hearing voices coming from the kitchen, she crept toward the door and peeked in fully expecting to find Jake and some young thing, raiding the refrigerator. Much to her surprise she found Ezra and her grandmother, Kiavi, locked in a passionate kiss. The ageless couple touching each other tenderly. Backing away quietly, she smiled to herself. She never would have guessed that, when her grandmother came to be with her at her request, Kiavi and Ezra would find each other. She couldn't think of two people who deserved to be together more and share their boundless love with each other. The thought made her almost giddy.

"Can't sleep again, huh, dahlin'?" Jake asked, smiling at her from the doorway.

JaiHonnah turned and smiled broadly at her father. He was dressed in a silk robe and boxers. His fists dug deep into the pockets. An image of Roderick flashed in her mind. She had to blink to remember that, although the two men had the same build and imposing demeanor, Roderick was as far from her as the sun was from the next galaxy. It was her daddy's gentle voice that had spoken to her.

"This little JayHawker has been up all night." She smiled, rubbing her motion-filled abdomen.

Jake approached her and put his arm around her shoulder. "May I?" he asked.

JaiHonnah took her father's free hand in hers and placed it on her abdomen. A brilliant smile bowed Jake's mustache, and his eyes lit to almost watery.

"Kid's a Hawkins, alright," he said enthusiastically, kissing JaiHonnah's temple and guiding her to a rocking chair. "You shouldn't be on your feet too long, dahlin'. Doc's kinda worried about you. He's not happy that you haven't been in to see him."

"I'm fine, Daddy. I just haven't had the time to go in for more tests. I don't know why old Doc Jameson wants to run this sonogram anyway, but he says that there's nothing to worry about. Just something

Savannah wanted him to do. Why, I don't know, but she's been following my treatment since I've been home."

"Fine doctor that Savannah Logan turned out to be," Jake said. "Now if I can just get rid of that lawyer of yours."

JaiHonnah laughed. "So Vivian's taking you to the mat again, huh?"

"Tarnation! That woman don't know when to quit vexin' me!" he growled with a smirk, but without the heat. "Shoulda never let you go east to that Spelman College. Maybe then my life would be my own."

"Uh-huh, you've got that court case coming up in Chicago soon. The one where Vivian is representing the Sierra Club."

"Them conservationists are gonna ruin my business, and that Vivian Jackson is leadin' the pack of them. Seems that woman's been put on this earth just to get in my way. Can't make a move without her sunny face poppin' up. That Southern Belle ain't no lady neva! She got more brass balls than a brammer bull!"

"You two still playing that same chess game, I see," JaiHonnah said, looking at her father sideways.

Jake grinned. "I got her on the run though. Thought she had me back a while ago, but I caught onto her game real quick. I moved my pawn to her rook. Twenty more moves, and she buys the steak dinner anywhere in the world I want," he gloated.

"How long did it take you to make that last move, Daddy?"

Jake cleared his throat coarsely. "Uh, when you gotta go see old Doc Jameson?"

"Dad-dy," JaiHonnah implored with a lopsided grin.

Jake rolled his eyes away. "Five months. Since you came back to the States," he said, frustrated.

JaiHonnah shook with loud laughter. Jake noticed.

"Nice to see that pretty face you wearing again, JaiHawk," he said tenderly, caressing her face.

"I'm feeling better, Daddy. Much, much better. The clinic called yesterday to say that Calvin's treatment is going very well, but that he has a long way to go. I hope that when this son of ours is born, he and Calvin can develop a real father/son relationship."

"The man should be pushin' up daises, not sittin' in some cushy rest home! Ezra should have followed his first instinct and dropped the bastard where he stood!"

"What would that have done to my son? He would have grown up not knowing who his father was. No matter how bad we think Calvin is, he's still this baby's father. That fact can't be changed."

"You're right, dahlin', but sometimes I wish Jacob Junior never brought Calvin Chapman to your beauty pageant and that he'd never laid eyes on you. Ezra says that if Calvin Chapman comes anywhere near you again, he's a dead man walking."

JaiHonnah laughed. "Ezra might have his hands too full with Grandmother. I happened on them this morning in the kitchen."

"Oh, that," Jake said and snorted. "Been goin' on for years. Long, long years. Kiavi is a stubborn ole woman. Can't forget her wedding vows to yo' granddaddy who's been dead since Jesus was born. Told that old man to go find him another woman to warm his bed, but he swears by Kiavi Littlefeather. Goes up to the reservation ever now and again hoping she'll change her mind and come live here with him. Man's crazy to let one woman tie him up in knots like that."

"You did it," she said, grinning. "You gonna tell me that Skai was just a woman who warmed your bed, Daddy?"

"Draw it mild, JaiHawk. Skai Hawkins was yo' mama and the only woman ever loved me."

"And the only woman you ever loved. Mama's been gone a long time, Daddy, and you haven't settled down with anyone since she died. So don't tell me that Ezra is the only one-woman man in this house."

"We're Hawkins, JaiHawk. We love deep and long. You know what I'm talkin' 'bout. You been pining over that boy up there in D.C. I sees your eyes when you talk to them children of his. You miss 'em, don't ya, dahlin'? You miss 'em somethin' awful."

JaiHonnah looked away from her father. "They're all well and happy, Daddy, but yes, I do miss them."

* * *

"JRock, wake up!" Kelley was calling and shaking him out of another dream about JaiHonnah. "Telephone's for you."

Roderick buried the heels of his hands deep in his eyes. "Who is it, Kelley?" he asked, rolling over and burying his head under some pillows.

"It's someone from Vivian Jackson's office. Says she's missing."

Roderick sat straight up and snatched the phone.

"This is Baylor! What's this about Vivian being missing?!"

"Can't find her anywhere, JRock," Bill Chandler answered. "She came back from a trip to Chicago yesterday. She won her case for the Sierra Club. She came into the office and then she met with Professor Feyhey, one of our former professors from Georgetown Law. They had lunch at his club and he told her that her name has been submitted to Congress by the President for a judgeship on the D. C. Circuit Court of Appeals. After that, Feyhey doesn't know where she went or with whom."

"Bill, have you called the police yet?"

"No, if Vivian just needs some time alone to think about whether she wants this judgeship, she'd have my ass if I called the police."

"I'll have your ass if you don't!"

"That's a pleasant thought, JRock, but I don't have time to act on it right now. I'm worried because it was Derrick Junior's birthday yesterday. Vivian wouldn't miss his fifth birthday for anything in this world. I just called to see whether you knew where she might be."

"I haven't talked with her in weeks, but she might have gone to Pennsylvania to visit Derrick's grave. I know Chuck goes up there every year too."

"I didn't think about that. I'll call Chuck's family and Derrick's in Pennsylvania and have them go to the grave site."

"Keep me posted, Bill. In the meantime, I'm calling this cop I know on the police force."

"Alright, it's your ass if Vivian gets pissed off."

"I'll take the weight gladly," he said as he hung up.

Roderick quickly called Officer Chadwick Hochstein, whom he had gotten to know very well over the past months. Hochstein was concerned and said that Vivian had lots of friends in the police department and court system who wouldn't sit easy until she was found. He said that he would put an APB out on her with a "report to headquarters only" notice. Then, ignoring the fact that it was predawn, Roderick began to call everyone who knew Vivian. Once they knew the reason for his call, no one complained about the early hour. That task completed, all Roderick could do was wait and worry.

Later after breakfast he dressed the girls and went to Vivian's house in Georgetown. No one was there. He assumed that Bill had taken the children out and waited for nearly two hours for them to return. When they didn't come back, he locked the house and went back to his place. Later in the morning he left the girls with Kelley and drove to Chuck's ranch. He had not called Chuck fearing that Chuck would not be able to cope if anything had happened to Vivian. He knocked on the door and, when it opened, there stood Vivian, barefoot, wearing one of Chuck's plaid shirts. Roderick swooped her up in his arms and then put her down just as quickly.

"You have some explaining to do, counselor!" he scolded.

Vivian smiled sleepily around a yawn. "Uh, good morning, JRock. What brings you out so early in the morning?"

Roderick was fit to be tied. "Don't give me that innocent look! Where have you been for the last twenty-four hours?"

"Well, for the last few hours she's been seducing me," Chuck said, appearing with a towel wrapped around his waist and kissing Vivian on the neck."

Roderick shook his head slowly at the pair. "Seduced you, did she?" Roderick asked his ire dissipating.

"Yeah, over and over," Chuck said, laughing. "Come on in, man."

Roderick followed Chuck and Vivian into the massive country kitchen and had a seat at one of the trestle tables.

"Coffee?" Vivian asked.

"And answers," Roderick said.

Vivian poured three cups of coffee before she sat down. "I finally realized that loving Chuck wasn't a betrayal of Derrick or his memory.

It's as simple as that. Derrick's death tore me to shreds, but I wasn't the only one who loved him and missed him. Chuck knew and loved Derrick longer than I did, and I was making him pay for that. I was wrong and I've said so."

"And she asked me to marry her, too," Chuck said, smiling broadly.

Vivian pursed her lips and rolled her eyes. "Now for that lie, Dr. Charles Patrick Montgomery, you can make breakfast before the children get up. We have a lot to discuss with them. I'm going to take a shower and get dressed." She kissed him quickly and started to move away. Chuck engulfed her in his arms and kissed her with passion.

Vivian winked at Chuck and smiled. "Later, baby."

Chuck was glowing, his clear, porcelain complexion and early morning beard not hiding his excitement. Nor was his bath towel. Roderick shook his head bemused at Chuck's glee as he set about making breakfast.

"So she seduced you, huh?"

"Man, I was a goner the day I first laid eyes on Vivian Lynn Alexander. Sort of like a bolt of lightning, or an explosion of TNT, or like . . ."

"The earth moving under your feet," Roderick said, finishing Chuck's thought.

"Exactly. You know the feeling?"

"All too well, my friend. All too well. So, what are you two going to do with this newfound love of yours?"

"I'm going to let her make an honest man out of me. I was ready to call the Justice of the Peace and hold the wedding today, but Vivian says she wants to give me time to think about it. Is she lunar or what? I wait eight years to be with Vivian and hold her in my arms and tell her how much I love her, and she wants me to *think* about it? Man, time for thinking was over when I kissed her for the first time last night." he said, laughing. "Now all I want is for her to say 'I do' and, believe me, my friend, I will!"

"Yes, it must be great," Roderick said, somewhat melancholy.

Chuck noticed. "Well, man, whenever Vivian chooses to make my life complete, I'm going to need a good man standing beside me. Think you can handle that?"

Roderick extended his hand to Chuck. "Any time, brother. Any time."

Chapter 26

"Breathe, JaiHawk!" Jake ordered. "C'mon, dahlin', you can do this! I've got faith in you! You're a Hawkins! Remember that! Now breathe!"

"You breathe, Daddy! I'm too busy right now having a baby! Or didn't you notice that little fact?"

"Out of here, Jake Hawkins," Kiavi Littlefeather ordered. "This is woman's work."

"But I can't leave my little girl! She needs her daddy."

Kiavi fixed her glare on Jake, and he left the birthing room in the hospital.

"Couldn't we do this tomorrow or next week, Grandmother?" JaiHonnah asked, panting between labor pains.

"Now is your time. It will not be easier tomorrow. The Shaman has sent this," she said producing a piece of bark.

"Grandmother, I'm afraid. The baby is so late. Doc Jameson wanted to run some tests, but I kept putting it off. What if something is wrong, and I ignored it?"

Kiavi put the bark back between JaiHonnah's teeth and smoothed her worried brow. "It is through the wisdom of the ancestors to say when they will send another to this land. You must trust the ancestors to guide this birth."

Another pain grabbed JaiHonnah, and she bit down hard on the bark. She kept her eyes fixed on Kiavi through the gut-wrenching pain. She screamed again and again for what seemed to her to be an eternity. She nearly lost consciousness. At the end, the bark broke in her teeth. Suddenly she felt a jolt and the baby's head spurted out, but the pain did not decrease. Again she screamed as her grandmother held her, another baby rustled himself from her body and slid into the surprised doctor's waiting hands. The nurses quickly attended to the twin boys while the doctor pressed on her abdomen.

JaiHonnah didn't understand why she was crying, but the tears rolled down her cheeks and on to her grandmother's warm hands. The nurse placed the wrapped babies in JaiHonnah's arms. As she looked at her sons' facial features and complexion, her eyes widened in bewilderment and disbelief. "*Oh. My. God.*"

Later, Jake and Ezra stuck out their chests as they looked through the glass in the hospital nursery at the twin boys. Jake had extra guards stationed near the nursery. He was taking no chance that his grandsons would be abducted as his daughter had been more than thirty years earlier.

"Them's Hawkins alright," Jake chortled proudly. "Look just like me."

Ezra cocked his head from one side and then to the other looking at the twin boys.

"Them's JaiHawk's boys alright, but ain't none of that Chapman boy in 'em," he observed.

Jake yanked the long, unlit cigar from his mouth and his smile along with it. He peered at the two bundles more closely. His massive brows furrowed as he met Ezra's gaze.

"*Tarnation!*" he uttered in disbelief.

* * *

JaiHonnah hung up the telephone and smiled at her bundles of joy.

"Well, my little men. Looks like your restaurant is going to be in Aunt Vivian's wedding," she said and smiled at her gurgling and cooing boys. "It also looks like I'm going to have to introduce you to the bottle."

Someone knocked at the door and then called out.

"You decent, dahlin'?"

"Usually," JaiHonnah joked. "Come on in, Daddy."

Jake bounded into the nursery, making a beeline for the twin boys. He gingerly gathered them up in his arms.

"Well, men, it's time for yo' granddaddy to take over," he said and laughed.

"Careful, Daddy, they just had lunch," she said as she watched her father juggling the boys in his arms.

"We gots us an understanding, them and me. This is time for the men to be together. Now you run along, lil' dahlin', and draw something pretty."

JaiHonnah's fists punched her hips. "Oh no you don't, Jake. It's time for them to take a nap. You're not going to sit there holding them all afternoon. Now you can spend a few minutes with them, but then you're outta here. Go raid some corporation or something."

"Ain't got much of a taste for raidin' these days, dahlin'. Me and my boys been keeping company these last couple of months right regular."

"Yeah, I've noticed. You sit up half the night looking at them."

"I don't want them to want for nothin'," he said soberly.

JaiHonnah rubbed her father's back soothingly. "They won't, Daddy. I can take care of them. As soon as I get back from South Carolina, I'll open my own business. The freelance work that I've been doing is paying off well enough for me to hire a staff. The boys are going to be fine."

"My boys are gonna have the best, JaiHawk. The best that money can buy."

"Daddy, what my boys need is your love, not your money."

"They gonna have both, I swear that oath. They'll never have to ask a man how much."

"They better ask or I'll know the reason why not," she scolded mildly.

Jake grinned. "See, boys, yo' mama ain't learned yet what we men know. Everything's got a price, but it don't matter none what that price is when you want something real bad." He kissed the boys and laid them in their cribs. Then he turned to JaiHonnah. "Gotta go outta town for a day or two, Jai. You watch over these boys real careful,"

JaiHonnah smiled. "Must have gotten those taste buds back in gear. I pity the company you're getting ready to raid. The owner won't know what happened to it till it's over, will he, Daddy?"

"You better bet it, dahlin', 'cause it's a sure winner."

* * *

Without even so much as a knock, Big Jake Hawkins strode into Roderick Baylor's office wearing his Stetson and a scowl. Roderick was standing at a flat screen illustrating a point to twenty staff members when the huge man entered. Roderick narrowed his eyes.

"You Baylor?" Big Jake barked.

"Who's asking?" Roderick barked back.

"You know who I am, boy. Now let's clear this here room so we can dicker. Dismissed!"

Mouths agape, everyone looked back at Roderick.

"You certainly are," Roderick fired back. "And don't let the door knob hurt you on the way out!"

The two mountains glared at each other from across the room. The silence was deafening.

"I mean to speak to you, boy. I don't rightly care whether everyone hears it or not."

Roderick strode toward the man and got dead in his face.

"I got your *boy*, mister!" Roderick sidestepped him and crossed the hall to another conference room with Jake following.

Inside the conference room, Roderick stiffened his stance—head up, shoulders back, with his fists in his pockets. "Speak whatever it is you came to say. I've got business to do," he said, scowling.

"You've got balls. I'll give you that, boy," Jake said and grinned menacingly.

"I'm waiting, *old man*, but my patience is running low. What is it that you want?"

"I already got what I want. Now I aim to keep it. You been sniffin' around some of my companies for a couple of years. Buying up stock a little at a time. You're gettin' real close to my last nerve. I've had my eyes on you. It's been interesting, boy." Jake looked around the room casually. "You've built a nice little operation, and I wanna thank you for making it prosperous for me, but I'm a little tired of swattin' at flies." Jake took an envelope from inside his top-coat pocket and slapped it down on the conference table. "Now I *own* you, boy! You got sixty days to pay up or you're out on your ass,—lock, stock and no barrel!"

Roderick picked up the envelop and opened it. Inside was the five-billion-dollar promissory note that he had signed with Rothman Childs. "BlackHawk," Roderick muttered with disgust as he read the deal that Jake had made with Rothman. Then Roderick grinned. "You got taken, old man," Roderick said with a certain amount of amusement. "The old swindler, Rothman Childs, took you to the cleaners. Well, if you want to take a bath, I'll hose you down too. You'll have your five billion in less than sixty days." Roderick's face hardened. "Now, if you have nothing else to say, I have a business to run—*my* business."

Roderick started toward the door.

"I ain't finished with you yet, *boy!*"

Roderick turned and flashed a broad smile. "Yes you are, *old man*. Lessons are over for the day. Better luck next time."

"I want you out of my daughter's life—for good!" Jake struck a wind match with his thumb nail and held up the five-billion-dollar note. "You swear to stay away from her, and I'll forget about this here petty cash. That's the deal."

"Your daughter? Somebody let you birth a daughter? I pity the woman whoever the hell she is, but I haven't got a clue who you're talking about." He blew out the match. "Go home, old man. They're probably looking for you at the rest home. I don't want your daughter, but you'll have your money as promised."

Roderick turned again to leave.

"JaiHonnah Reise won't be needing your sympathy, thank you very much."

Roderick froze and spun around. "JaiHonnah? You're JaiHonnah's father?"

"Tarnation, boy, who the hell did you think I was?"

"Some old blow hard, rest home escapee, and my opinion remains the same."

"We can stand here trading insults all day, but I've got your business under my thumb. I'm waiting for your word, boy! You agree to stay away from my JaiHawk, and I'll burn this here note."

Roderick didn't tarry. He got up in Jake's face. "Call the note, old man!" he growled. "Sixty days or less."

"Does this mean you won't stay away from my Jai?"

"I didn't stutter, now did I, old man?"

He didn't blink, shift his eyes, flinch or cower, Jake observed as he eyed Roderick's stiffened demeanor. Despite himself, he liked the boy. It proved to him that J. Roderick Baylor deserved the respect that everyone he contacted about him offered willingly.

"I'll double the offer. Stay away from Jai Reise, and you'll be ten billion to the good."

"Not for one hundred billion! Y'all have a nice day now, ya hear?" Roderick mimicked the southern drawl.

As he opened the door to leave, Roderick's daughters tumbled in.

"Look, Daddy!" they yelled. "Look what we made in camp today!"

Roderick stooped to receive their kisses and hugs. He lifted them both in his arms.

"Who's the nice man in the big hat, Daddy?" Shelby asked, pointing to Big Jake.

"Nice? Looks can be deceiving, honey. He's not someone you need to know. Now run along upstairs and . . ."

"Why, howdy, lil' ladies. My name is Jake Reise Hawkins, but you can call me Big Jake. All my ladies do. You must be Shelly and Shelby. JaiHonnah talks about you all the time."

"JaiHonnah!" the girls squealed in unison.

"You know JaiHonnah?" Shelby asked excitedly.

"Is she here, Daddy?" Shelly squealed. "Is she, Daddy?"

"No, dahlin', she's not here," Big Jake smiled at the girls as he took them from Roderick's arms. "She's back home in Texas, but she tells me you two are doing real good in riding school. Says you're both smart as a whip and good little Indian princesses too."

"We're doing very well in school, Mr. Big Jake, but when is JaiHonnah coming home to be with us?"

"Don't rightly know, dahlin'. I'll tell her you asked after her though. She'll be real happy to hear it."

"Let's go call her now, Shelly!"

"Yes, let's go!"

The girls scampered down and to the door. "Bye, Mr. Big Jake," the girls said and waved.

"Bye, little dahlins'," he said and waved back.

So this was the Jake Hawkins who had set the business world off its axis. And he was Jai's father. Thoughts whirled into Roderick's mind. Jai had mentioned her father and so had Evelyn, but neither had mentioned his name. *Vivian.* It came to him that Vivian had always known who Jai's father was. She had played chess long distance with him...and bested him in a recent court battle. More things began to fall into place as Roderick watched the older man with his daughters. He hated to admit it, but he liked the old buzzard. The girls seemed to like him, too, and they were good judges of character, but he wasn't going to let Jake Reise Hawkins off the hook no matter whose father he was.

Jake straightened his stance, head up, shoulders back and eyeball to eyeball with Roderick. "Nice girls," Jake growled. "Sorry they got a fool for a daddy."

"JaiHonnah has my sympathy, too," Roderick growled back.

"Sixty days, Baylor."

"Done, Hawkins."

* * *

After his meeting ended, Roderick called Rothman Childs for an explanation. In his gut he felt that something was amiss, but couldn't quite put his finger on it. Promissory notes were bought and sold by banks and other financial institutions every day. That wasn't unusual. What tripped his interest was why Hawkins was offering to burn the note and give him five billion too. That was a hell of an incentive to stay away from Jai. There was more to this than a straight business deal, and Roderick was determined to find out what it was that the great Jake Hawkins was up to.

"Why didn't you call me, if you were going to sell my promissory note, Roth?"

"Son, we're talking 'bout Jake the JayHawker here. That man eats raw bankers for breakfast. Don't no man this side of sanity say no to the JayHawker. He swoops down on you and picks you clean before you can bleed. Now, son, when the man himself showed up in my office and said he wanted your promissory note, what could I say? I got to live in the same world with that man."

"He's not the one you need to worry about, Roth," Roderick threatened. "By the way, his daughter is JaiHonnah Reise Chapman."

"Holy…!" Rothman sputtered. "Son, I only asked her out to dinner a few times. I never laid a hand on her. I swear!"

"My best to Mrs. Childs, Roth," Roderick said as he hung up.

Then Roderick went to see Vivian.

"So, Big Jake visited you personally, huh?" Vivian said and laughed. "Must be after something big for him to put in an appearance."

"Yeah, like my ass. He put the fear of God into Rothman Childs and bought my promissory note. Gave me sixty days to come up with the five billion or he'll call the loan due."

"Uh-huh, what else did he want besides your ass on his trophy wall and five billion?"

Roderick looked away from Vivian, dug his fists in his pockets and hung his head slightly. "He wants me to stay away from Jai. Offered me ten billion to leave her alone."

"And after you told him where to shove his deal, what did he say?"

"You must have been listening."

"No, but I'd loved to have been a fly on the wall during that little exchange. You two are cut from the same cloth, my friend."

Roderick's head snapped around toward Vivian. "If you want to insult me, Vivian, say something derogatory about my mother or father, but don't put me in the same category with that egotistical, narcissistic, self-centered . . ."

"Proud, stubborn, overbearing... enough?" she asked.

"Enough," Roderick agreed reluctantly.

"Can you raise the scratch?"

"Yeah, no sweat. Chuck and some of the boys in the NBA and NFL want in on this deal."

"So what are you concerned about?"

"Jai. How she's going to take it when I level her father."

Vivian laughed. "Jai's a big girl, JRock. She's crazy about Big Jake, but she's had to take Jake down a peg or two herself from time to time. She'll handle it just fine."

"I hope you're right. She and my girls are very close, and I don't want to do anything to interfere with their relationship. They talk to her at least twice a day every day. Sometimes more."

"And what about your relationship with her?"

Roderick cut his eyes at Vivian. "After what I did to her, I'm just thankful that she didn't have me shot at sunrise."

Vivian laughed.

"Uh, Viv, is she alright? I mean, Chapman hasn't hurt her again or anything, has he?"

"I can safely say, without violating attorney-client privileged information, that Jai is handling Calvin Chapman just fine."

"And their baby?"

"Uh, JRock, your girls aren't the only ones who know how to use a telephone. You want to know how she is, I suggest you get on the telephone and call her."

"Right, and get my head handed to me. Uh-uh, no thanks."

* * *

Jake experienced the Wrath of JaiHonnah as soon as he set foot back in Hawkinstown. JaiHonnah went up one side of him and down the other.

"But, Jai, it was business, not personal," Jake pleaded.

"I don't give a flying fig what you call it, Jake Hawkins! You knew when you left here last week that you were going to see Roderick, and you didn't say a word to me because you knew I'd hit the roof."

"You're done that a few times already, dahlin'," he said and grinned sheepishly. "Look, I made the boy a good offer for his businesses. He's thinkin' it over."

"Thinking it over? If I know J. Roderick Baylor, he told you where you could stick your offer without benefit of Vaseline!"

"Draw it mild, dahlin'. The man's stubborn as a ginny mule. Thinks he's ready to play in the big leagues. Well, we'll see about that little thing."

"Jake Hawkins," she fussed, wagging her finger in his face, "if you've been messin' in my business again, hell won't be far enough for you to hide from me. And by the way, where have you been for the last five days? Why didn't you answer when I called you?"

A broad, uncontrollable grin creased Jake's handsome face. "Had a little business in Atlanta. Nice city. Thinkin' 'bout flying back there in a couple of days."

"Uh-huh, what's her name, Jake?" JaiHonnah asked dryly hands on hips.

"Who says this is about a woman?"

"If you've spent five days in Atlanta, it's about a woman, and a hellava woman at that."

"You got that right," Jake said and grinned, thinking about Kelley Baylor. "A hellava woman."

JaiHonnah shook her head and exhaled in frustration. Her father was in too good a mood for her comfort. Whatever he was up to, she'd have to be on her toes. She hit upon a plan.

"Jake, I'm going to leave the boys here while I go to Vivian's and Chuck's wedding. Will you stay here with them while I'm gone? I'll only be away a few days, and I don't want them to miss me too much."

"Yeah, dahlin'. I won't move a muscle. You know that."

JaiHonnah cocked an eyebrow at him.

Chapter 27

Roderick tested the engines on the *Navajo Princess* as he prepared for the journey with Chuck, the other groomsmen, most of whom were Chuck's brothers, and the rest of his entourage to South Carolina. They were sailing the yacht to Myrtle Beach and then driving to Goodwill, Summer County, where Vivian's relatives lived. The wedding would be on her family's farm. Chuck's large family motored down in mobile homes and other recreational vehicles so that they could camp out for the week's worth of pre-wedding activity leading up to the wedding on Labor Day. Roderick had met many of Vivian's family members, who numbered in the hundreds, but between the two families, the Alexanders and the Montgomerys, the number of wedding guests would resemble a small army.

"Ahoy, *The Navajo Princess*," Chuck yelled from the dock, trailed by the groomsmen.

Roderick smiled. "Ahoy, yourself. Come on aboard, gentlemen, we've got to get Chuck to the church on time."

"Not to worry, my man. This is one wedding you'd have to kill me to keep me away from. Let's head 'em up and move 'em out!" he said, laughing.

Chuck, Roderick and the other groomsmen had a great time on what was a great booze cruise and deep-sea fishing along the way. They talked for hours about so many things that they hoped their futures held. Chuck was looking forward to having lots of children with Vivian. Even though she would be sworn in and robed as a sitting judge on the federal appellate bench, she was only thirty-one years old and looking forward to having babies with Chuck. Adopting more children was also not out of the question either. Chuck's ranch could hold a football team-sized family with room to spare. He brought along a little five-year-old boy who had been brutalized and abused by his biological parents. Chuck and Vivian put the wheels in motion to adopt the child who had many health challenges ahead of him.

"So where are you two going on your honeymoon?" Roderick asked.

"Ain't tellin'," Chuck said and laughed. "Vivian and I are going to leave all forms of communication at home. The children are going to stay with her family until we get back. I want this lady all to myself for at least ten days."

"Sounds like some serious baby-making time," Roderick said, laughing.

"Speaking of babies, you talk with Jai lately?"

Roderick eyed Chuck suspiciously. "Shelly and Shelby talk with her all the time, but what's this about Jai and babies?"

"You know that she was pregnant?"

"Yes, I know. Vivian said that she's doing fine."

"She's going to be at the wedding. She's Vivian's matron of honor."

"Yes, Vivian told me. She wanted to give me a chance to back out of the wedding if I couldn't take the heat," Roderick said and laughed.

"So you can handle this alright?"

"Only test is to do it."

"Famous last words," Chuck quipped.

* * *

JaiHonnah saw Roderick's sleek, muscular frame before the chauffeur opened the car door for her. She thought that she would be well prepared to see him again, but she was wrong. He still sent a warm gust up her spine with his earth-shattering smile. A proud African warrior would have cowered in Roderick's presence. He was standing, feet apart, arms across his chest and wearing his trademark baseball cap turned backward on his head. She noted that it was the cap that she had planned to give to him as a Christmas present before she left Washington. On the brim it read *Navajo Warrior*. She told Kelley where she stashed the Christmas presents and asked her to give them to Roderick, his twins and the Baylor Construction office staff. That seemed like such a long time ago, but actually she had known Roderick almost one year to the day exactly. That was when her life drastically changed from a female afraid of living life to a woman who now lusted for what life had to offer—even another woman's husband.

Why did she have to be even more beautiful than the last time he had seen her? he silently asked himself. That hourglass figure was even more defined. Her sun-kissed, supple-looking bronze complexion was exquisite against her raven-black hair worn down and straight back in a loose plait. A walking, talking vision, he thought, as he watched her emerge from her limousine in front of Vivian's parents' home in Goodwill, South Carolina. He didn't have to question why his girls raced toward her as she got out of the limo. She took his breath away with the Academy-Award winning smile she gave Shelly and Shelby as she scooped them up in her arms and swung them around and around. He couldn't take his eyes off her. He didn't even want to try.

He wanted another man's wife, baby and all. His thoughts ran the gamut from paying Chapman to leave her to breaking Chapman's neck with his bare hands. The thought of any man touching her with anything other than love in his intent tore at Roderick's gut. The thought of any other man with her was even more devastating. Even after all these months away from her, what he felt for her couldn't be duplicated or substituted. He learned that lesson well with his trip to Vail with Savannah. He had not thought of another woman since then. JaiHonnah was the only constant in his conscious thoughts. His love for her was so deep it had no bottom, so great that it had no beginning and no end, and so high that he hadn't been able to get over it or her. It was a hopeless situation, but he loved her still, even more.

Shelly and Shelby smothered her with kisses, and she reveled in their warmth. Although they talked constantly since she left Washington, she missed them so much that she squeezed them for a long time. They were little chatter boxes as they nearly dragged her to their father, but they fell silent and disappeared to join Vivian's children when they finally had JaiHonnah face-to-face with Roderick.

"Like the hat," she said and stuck her hands in her pockets to keep from reaching out to touch him, to take him in her arms and to ravish his mouth the way she wanted to do.

Roderick couldn't help the smile that grew on his face. "So do I. It's my favorite. Thanks, Jai. It's good to see you again." Roderick's deep, melodious voice thrilled her as he extended his hand.

"You too, Roderick," she said, accepting his hand. For a lifetime they silently looked at each other. His thumb was stroking the skin on the back of her hand as she called forth her voice from wherever it had hidden. "I understand that things are going very well at Baylor Design and Developers. You're getting rave reviews from the business press and news media."

"I pay them well to say nice things about my company," he joked, but he didn't feel happy. Not without her in his arms. "It's the cost of doing business."

She withdrew her hand from his and dug them in the pockets of her slacks again. "Speaking of which, I, uh, understand that you've met my father." She looked at the ground and dug the toe of her boot into the gravel. "I was very upset with Jake when your girls told me that he came to see you." She forced herself to look up into his eyes and took a deep breath before she continued. "I want you to know that I had nothing at all to do with Jake's visit. He said that he offered to buy your company."

Roderick chuckled. "He said that, did he?" Then he sobered. "Why didn't you tell me that Jake Hawkins is your father?"

JaiHonnah shrugged absently and looked away from Roderick. "I want to be judged on my own merits, not by some yardstick used to measure my family name."

"BlackHawk has been one of my chief competitors for years, though I never met your father until he came to my office."

"I wasn't trying to deceive you, Roderick. I would never divulge Baylor Company information to anyone, not even my father. Jake can be very cunning. He intimidates most people who meet him." JaiHonnah then turned back to face him. "In Jake's defense, I can tell you that he would never use me to get to you. He is a proud, principled man, and I love him fiercely. Nevertheless, I'll do everything that I can to keep him from interfering with Baylor Design and Developers. I sit on his board and I will block any attempt he might make to raid your company."

"Your father doesn't intimidate me, Jai, and I don't believe that you're an industrial spy for him." Roderick looked down at the patch of ground between them. "I've been trying to find the words to apologize to you for the way that I've treated you; the accusations that you were being disloyal and dishonest. I found out that you weren't planning to leave when I acquired Lionel Porter's company. I still didn't understand why you had been so remote until sometime later when I learned that you were pregnant with Chapman's baby. It must have been very difficult for you to handle. I certainly wasn't patient with you. I had my own family problems to deal with." He looked back up into her eyes. "You didn't deserve what I put you through, the demands I made on you. I was wrong and I'm sorry. I hope that you'll be able to forgive me."

JaiHonnah smiled agreeably. "It's already forgotten." Then she brightened. "How are Kelley and the crew and Marilyn and...Baylor Plaza Park?"

He chuckled at her excitement. "Everyone is well. Wesley Greenfield came on as project manager. Kelley is in Atlanta now managing our operation there. By the way, I've incorporated your new suggestions. They were brilliant. A mini training facility for future Olympians is a great idea. I'm also thinking of funding a new school system based on the one here in Summer County. Vivian and I have asked Rosalyn to head it up."

"I'm pleased that you liked my suggestions and where you're going with the project. I hope that you'll allow me to stay minimally involved."

Roderick and JaiHonnah continued to talk about people at Baylor Design and Development and those involved in other projects, but neither chose to raise the burning issue between them—their deep and abiding love for each other. Each giving due deference to the other's marital status. Roderick couldn't help but wonder whether JaiHonnah missed him as much as he missed her. Whether her pain was as deep as his. No, he thought. She couldn't. It wasn't humanly possible for anyone to endure that much pain and treat their meeting so casually after so many months of being apart.

JaiHonnah was taken aback anew by the sensuousness of the mountain that moved beside her as they walked around the Alexanders' farm. Roderick had the power to make her sweat on a bone-chilling day. She could look at his finely chiseled face forever, she thought. She remembered every inch of his body that she had explored. The strong, muscular frame that rippled under her touch, smooth texture of his skin, the feel of his mouth on her and the thrill of his fully engorged nature pumping and pulsating inside her. Something palpable raced through her, and she could no longer ignore the throbbing of her core. Her heart pumped rapidly against her chest. He was magnificent, and the pain of the secret she kept from him tore at her. She saw him in her boys' eyes even now when they were so young. There was no question that the boys were Baylor stock. She had only been the conduit for them.

Naturally, they wandered into one of the barns where horses moved around in their stalls. JaiHonnah walked to each stall enticing a few of the horses to come to her, feeding them apples, and rubbing each between the eyes and down the long bridge of its face to its nose. She spoke to each horse in soft Navajo tones, and the horses seemed to respond to her coaxing calmly. At the back of the long row, Roderick spotted a ladder that led to the hay-filled loft. He climbed up and helped JaiHonnah up after him. They sat side by side quietly for a while. Roderick laid back in the sweet-smelling hay, his fingers laced behind his head and his long legs crossed at the ankles. JaiHonnah sat Indian style twirling strands of hay between her fingers.

"Relax, Jai. I'm not going to bite you," Roderick said, looking at her back and sensing the tension in her frame.

She didn't turn to look at him. His blatant masculinity was all too apparent, too potent. "I still feel like I owe you an explanation...about Porter."

"Don't give it or him another thought. He isn't worth it," he said.

"I should have told you myself that I met with him, but, at the time, I was confused about a lot of things, and I didn't think that it was such a big deal."

"It wasn't, but that had nothing to do with you. It was more about me venting my frustration over a relationship between Monique and Lionel. They had an affair, and, at the time, I thought that..."

She looked at him over her shoulder. "Roderick, you don't have to tell me this. I don't need to know about what goes on between you and Monique," she interrupted nervously. She didn't want to exacerbate the situation between Roderick and his wife by telling him that her brother claimed to have slept with Monique. Or that the investigator Vivian hired had pictures of Monique and Calvin *flagrante delicto*.

"You're right. That's over with now and best forgotten." He rubbed her back gently. Studying the barn and its structure, he said, "I like this farm. I've been thinking of buying one where the girls can ride once they are a little older."

JaiHonnah worried her bottom lip as his hand on her back singed her senses. She wondered whether she should tell Roderick that her brother, Jacob Junior, claimed to have had intimate relations with Monique too. And, to her certain knowledge, since Calvin had Monique, then so had Jacob. She quickly dismissed the thought. She didn't want to be the one to insert herself into Monique's and Roderick's marriage. Even if it might cause them to break up. No, she loved Roderick too much to do that to him. She wanted Roderick in the worst possible way, but she wouldn't use what she had been told by her brother or the photographs she had of Calvin and Monique to re-insert herself into Roderick's life. Yet, the fresh sexual tension was driving her insane as it was.

When she didn't comment, he worried that something was wrong. "Are things good with you, Jai? I mean, really good?" he asked, the deep timbre of his voice enthralling her.

"Yes," she said weakly. "My family keeps me busy, and I have my work. I'm doing some freelance designs for an architectural firm, Tyson and Covington. The firm has several properties on the San Antonio River Walk. It's an interesting project. I've got others in the works too."

"When do I get my share?" he asked quizzically. "Tyson and Covington is a very prestigious firm and they pay their contractors handsomely, I hear."

JaiHonnah looked over her shoulder at him. She immediately knew that was a mistake. His prone body brought clearly to her mind their lovemaking. The sight of him was overwhelming.

"Your share? Your share of what, may I ask?" A cryptic smile rounded her lips.

"A share of your moonlighting for other companies. Remember, you're under contract to Baylor Construction," he said teasingly.

She gave him a sideways look. "Oh, no, Mr. Baylor, you fired me, remember? I'm a free agent."

"But that you were," he said, his voice heavy with something that JaiHonnah recognized as longing. Then his tone changed. "Well, I seem to remember the circumstances differently. As I recall, you told me that you quit," he said, laughing, "*before* I fired you. So my firing you didn't count."

"Ah, but you forget, Mr. Baylor," she said, teasing him in return. "My contract was only for one year. A trial run, you called it. My time in your servitude ends this very weekend, if I recall correctly."

"It appears that I'm going to have to have my legal counsel look into this matter in order to get my share."

"Since your legal counsel and my legal counsel are one in the same, I do believe that there is a serious conflict of interest."

"Hmmm, you may have a point, especially since our legal counsel will be gracing the federal bench soon. I guess we'll have to settle this another way then," he said, sitting up and pulling JaiHonnah across his lap.

Her yelps as he tickled her made him roar with laughter.

"You're a beast," she sneered between bouts of laughter and tossing hay at him.

"Oh, now you're really going to get it," he said menacingly as he captured her and tickled her until she begged for him to stop.

"Okay, okay, I'll give you anything you want," she said, laughing breathlessly, anything to get him to stop tickling her.

Roderick stopped and released his hold on her slightly; just enough so that JaiHonnah thought that she could scamper out of his grip. She was wrong. The innocent expression on her face had not fooled Roderick, and he tackled her, pinning her with his body in the hay.

"Uh-huh!" he said. "And you thought that you could get away, did you?" He laughed as he lay atop her.

Her surprised, innocent expression melted into a broad smile until she found herself in a compromising position with her hands locked together above her head where Roderick could tickle her with his free hand unencumbered. Then the knowing grin crossed Roderick's face, and JaiHonnah sensed the devilishness in his eyes.

"Oh no! Oh no!" she screeched, trying to worm her way out from under him, but it was too late. He tickled her until tears were welling in her eyes from laughter. Her body undulating, twisting and gyrating beneath him.

Roderick was enjoying the merriment and playfulness that was passing between them in the hay. It was reminiscent of the fun they used to share as lovers. He laughed at her efforts to free herself until the movement of her body beneath him recalled different times and places. Another kind of playfulness. His heart thumped against his ribcage, heated his pulsating blood then he knew it—he had to have her. His eyes smoldered and the playfulness left him by degrees as he looked down into JaiHonnah's beautiful face. Her laughter quelled slowly as she gazed up at him. They stared into each other's eyes. Roderick lowered his head by degrees until his mouth touched down lightly on hers. JaiHonnah did not recoil from him or turn away. He licked at her lips, feathering his touch until she opened to him and joined their tongues in a slow, mesmerizing dance amid mounting moans. Roderick released her hands and her arms went around his neck, pulling his head deeper into the kiss. Without the hot air to breathe, they would have both fainted with the thick passion between them. The urgency was great as Roderick opened and unzipped JaiHonnah's slacks, rolling her just enough to slide them down her hips. She was violently aroused and heaved her body against his hand between her warm thighs.

"Roderick . . ." she breathed, her need for him growing along with her fear. If he touched her she would be lost.

"Shhh, baby, can you tell me that you don't want me to touch you?" he whispered as his hands met the dampness of her lacy shield. "Tell me that you don't want to touch me."

"No . . ." she breathed, closing her eyes to the lie. "I can't want you ever again."

"Be honest with me, Jai. I want you. I *need* you," he breathed the words with urgency. "I can't wait or be patient or act like you're not here with me. You can't lie to me any longer. Your body is telling me something other than your words."

"I can't think when you're this close to me," she said, turning her face away. "When you touch me, I come undone."

Roderick moved off her. "Look at me, Jai!" he commanded.

JaiHonnah feared that looking into his eyes would make her lose her resolve, and she was right. She turned her head toward him slowly and opened her eyes.

"How far away do you want me?" His desire rose effortlessly with the hot, wet signal that she was ready for him. He stood before her.

"That's not fair, Roderick," she whimpered. She could see his phallus straining for release against his cut-off jeans. She wanted him. She wanted him buried inside of her. Her core ached for the reunion that would make her a whole woman again. The union that invaded both her sleep and her day dreams.

"I'm not touching you. I'm not crowding you, but know what you do to me. You know how much I want you. Tell me that you don't want me as much as I want you. Tell me that you don't want me buried deep inside you, loving you."

JaiHonnah stood slowly, her hands moving up his body. They had nearly the same conversation on his yacht a year earlier, the night when his seed had fertilized her womb and created two precious lives. Then and now she didn't care whose husband he was. She wanted him. She wanted him for herself. Vaguely she thought about how lovers betrayed their spouses. She had been betrayed and never wanted to inflict that type of pain on another woman, but all sense of responsibility for her actions left her. She pulled Roderick's T-shirt out of his jeans, raising it until it cleared his head. Then she unzipped his jeans as he moaned, lathed her neck with his tongue, annoyed by the shirt and bra she wore. She captured her heart's desire, moaning at the thrill and feel of him pulsating against her hand. He pulled down his jeans along with his briefs in one fluid motion until they were no longer a barrier to his urgent need for JaiHonnah.

"Take off your clothes," he growled, his voice thick and low. "I've got to feel you, taste you."

Dutifully, needfully, she stripped. Roderick captured a breast in his mouth and brought her slowly down into the hay. The sensation of having this hot, sweet woman again began to drive him to take her hard and fast. JaiHonnah's soft hands on his shaft guiding him to her core flung his control into oblivion. With a quickness he spread her thighs and thrust himself into her.

JaiHonnah's body bowed up to meet him thrust for thrust. She thought she would surely go insane from all the sweet sensations that Roderick's moist muscular body created. The suctioning of her breast took her breath away. His fingers teasing her core caused her heart to pound erratically. His strong, sure advance into her body forced unintelligible sounds from her throat. The muscles and sinews of his butt under her grip, moving his shaft back and forth inside her rocked her world. The first orgasm hit her with the intensity of a white-hot branding iron, searing her flesh into a fiery sheathing. Igniting her. She collapsed her inner muscles around him like a vice clamp.

Roderick rolled over and brought her on top without breaking the union. Sweat poured from his flesh, molding the sweet hay to his back. JaiHonnah freed her mind and her body followed settling into a wicked gyration, exercising his muscle in her inner grip. He sucked in wind through his clenched teeth, barely holding off his release deep inside her fiery caldron. He groaned deeply as their bodies moved back and forth against each other in excruciatingly perfect rhythm. The pressure building in his groin was enormous. The sight of her moving above him, with hay clinging to her loose, raven locks, and her flat belly dancing provocatively was nearly more than he could bear. Her low moans, whispering his name, caused him to accelerate his pace.

The second climax was more traumatic than the first. JaiHonnah shuddered, her chest heaving in short, breathless pants. A cry rushed forth to the rafters above. Roderick sat up and pulled her shivering body to him, burying his face between her breasts, his perspiration mixing with hers. He feathered his kisses up to her neck, bracing himself against the urgent need to release his nature. JaiHonnah, her body barely recovering from her last eruption, felt the growing need within her. She wanted him more than ever before and needed him again and again.

Roderick lowered her onto her back again and raised her knees to his shoulders.

"Look at me, Jai," he whispered. "I need to see your eyes. I have to know whether I've pleased you."

JaiHonnah opened her eyes slowly. Tears of joy rimmed her eyes, and a faint smile curled her lips.

The energy left to restrain the release of his nature was rapidly dwindling when JaiHonnah smiled at him. His eyes locked into hers as he began the slow and steady process of bringing her to another cataclysmic eruption.

This time she would not be alone. Roderick's mellifluent voice called to her to join him as his tumescence spoke to her womanhood. Shuddering with unlocked desire, JaiHonnah gave to him all that had been locked inside her since the moment she saw him—everything except the truth. For the first time since she'd stepped out of the limousine, she knew that she couldn't tell him about the boys. Visions of having to live outside of his life haunted and hurt her. She could love him and make love to him, but that wouldn't change the facts. He was a married man. She couldn't make Monique go away in the heat of passion. She could only temporarily fill the caverns of her body with another woman's man. She wanted and needed more. Much more. She wanted all of him, not just stolen moments between visits by his wife. She had to love him and then leave him for the last time.

Roderick's back arched as his nature dictated. JaiHonnah's nails tightened around his nipples as she called his name in blissful utterances until her breath nearly ceased to flow from her lungs. Roderick's cannon roared, and they reached the peak together.

"JaiHonnah," he whispered as he captured her mouth in a deep, wet, sensuous kiss. He pulled her close while they drifted in a euphoric haze and then slept.

JaiHonnah took a long, last look at Roderick's beautiful nude body as she wiped tears from her eyes. Silently, while he slept, she left the barn and climbed back into the limousine. It sped away.

Roderick woke to find JaiHonnah gone. She had run away from him again. Back to her husband, no doubt, he angrily thought as he sat in the hay resting his arms and his head on his knees. The thought of her with her husband drained and infuriated him.

* * *

The day that Chuck and Vivian recited their wedding vows to each other, Roderick and JaiHonnah stood paralyzed and galvanized by the meaning of marriage. Neither wanted to tread on old ground, but the heat of passion between them was visible, even to them. As they danced at the reception, Roderick couldn't keep his attention on anything except the woman in his arms. JaiHonnah's emotions were so strong that she feared she would crumble in his embrace.

"What now, Jai?" he asked as she looked at him with her beautiful eyes. "Help me connect the dots. Are you going to be my woman the way you once told me that you wanted to be? Are you coming back to me or are you going to try again to forget what has happened between us? What we are together? Can you see us together the way that I do every waking moment and every sleepless night?"

"I'm not wearing some kind of cloaking device, Roderick," she flashed. "I can't hide what I feel for you. Some images are too jarring, and you know that I can't resist you. You proved that in the hayloft. I can read the top line of the eye chart too. I see what we are together. I knew what I was letting myself in for when we were together that very first time, but I've got to practice self-preservation. Marriage is still a sacred institution to me. It always has been and that hasn't changed although I've come too close to being sacrilegious. My hypocrisy does know some boundaries. There are too many lives at stake, your family and mine. Coming back to Washington wouldn't solve anything for either of us. We'd be together when we could, but we couldn't be together."

"Leave the bastard!"

"That's not the issue, Roderick, and you know it."

"Jai, we can work anything out if we want to. I want you and your baby near me."

"No, Roderick. It's best left as it is."

"Then you're leaving me again?"

"I'm going home, Roderick. There's no way that I can come back to Washington. Not now."

"This is too important to run away from, Jai."

"Run away? I'm not running away."

"Call it what you want to, but, the bottom line is, you have to face the net loss that your decision will mean." Roderick stared at the woman he loved. It was killing him that she wouldn't love him in return. "Now who's being cruel, Jai?"

JaiHonnah refused to let her pain and yearning for Roderick color her expression. She was unable to answer him. She turned on her heels and walked away. So many things had happened in the short time since she'd met Roderick. She would carry the memory of him for the rest of her life. After the bride and groom departed, JaiHonnah immediately left for Hawkinstown, Texas.

*   *   *

Roderick boarded his yacht and made his way back to Washington with his girls, locked in turmoil so great, he barely spoke a word to the family and friends who accompanied him through the long journey. That last night on the boat, when he dug down into a drawer for fresh towels after the girls showered, he found the proverbial straw that broke the camel's back: the clothes that JaiHonnah had left in his cabin the first time they made love, nearly a year ago to the day. He had washed the lacy underwear with care and placed them in the drawer intending to return them to her at his first opportunity. Now he wasn't willing for opportunity to come knocking. He had to make something happen or he'd go out of his mind.

Chapter 28

JaiHonnah tore across the seemingly endless expanse of the BlackHawk Ranch, galloping at a breakneck speed on the bareback of KnightHawk, her black stallion sired by Hawk. He was more nimble than his father and loved to run. She raced him full out with tears streaming down her face cooled by the wind as she rode. Nothing that she did could ease the pain.

She held her sons for hours after her return from South Carolina. That was all that she would ever have of the man that she loved so deeply—his sons. She wanted desperately to tell him that he was the father of twin boys, Rodney and Reise, but she feared his reaction and that of his wife. JaiHonnah clearly remembered Monique's threat to take his daughters from him if Roderick was unfaithful to her. Though, in her mind, Monique Baylor was no better than an alley cat, JaiHonnah couldn't face the pain that she knew Roderick would experience if she were the reason that he lost Shelly and Shelby. How or when she would tell Roderick about his boys was left in her hands, but Vivian and Chuck both knew her secret and begged her to tell him. She failed to do so. So now she rode the vast plains blinded by her tears and heartache.

* * *

"How do I get to Hawkinstown?" Roderick asked a porter as he picked up his luggage at the San Antonio Airport. "I couldn't find it on a map."

"Son, you must not be from round here," the porter said and chuckled.

"If I were, I wouldn't be asking for directions, now would I?" Roderick quipped.

"Hold your horses, son. How soon you need to be there?"

"This millennium would be good."

The porter smiled. "Well, son, if you got a couple of days to kill, drive west of town. Once you past the San Antonio county limits you're in Hawkins County, but you have to just keep driving for a spell. There ain't but one road, straight as an arrow too. You won't miss the place. Now if you want to get to the ranch house today, old Jake Hawkins owns BlackHawk Air. Keeps a few jets down yonder the concourse there. Now, how you fixin' ta go?"

Roderick didn't answer as he and his girls headed for the BlackHawk Air terminal. The airline attendants responded as if this was an everyday occurrence: Someone walks up asking to be flown to the Hawkins' ranch and, without a second thought, the aircraft is loaded and ready to go. *That's juice,* Roderick thought. It was a shame that he was prepared to level Jake Reise Hawkins to man size. Somehow he knew that old Jake wouldn't be down for long and certainly not out for the count.

The aircraft flew low and wide over the miles and miles of green farm land, oil wells, Texas Longhorn cattle herds, horses and pristine timberlands. The fictionalized Ewing family could never have dreamed of a home so large and diverse, Roderick thought, as he looked at the unfolding horizon.

"Look, Daddy!" Shelly squealed, peering out of one of the aircraft's windows.

Below them appeared to be a stampede of wild horses. One rider was out ahead of the pack, raven-black hair flying in the wind on a raven-black steed.

"It must be a Navajo!" Shelby squealed. "JaiHonnah says that the Navajo ride like the wind, Daddy."

"Well, baby, JaiHonnah was right. Whoever that rider is, is poetry in motion," he said and smiled at his daughter's glee.

JaiHonnah saw the shadow of the aircraft on the ground as it passed over her headed toward the private landing strip near Hawk House. She was leading a group of wild horses to one of the corrals. She didn't have time to look up or wonder who was on the aircraft. Probably some of her father's friends or some lady friend that he was importing for the evening, she surmised. While her father entertained his guests, she'd make herself scarce. She was in no mood to be around people. Roderick was imprinted on her brain and in her heart.

"Well hello, lil' dahlins'." Jake Hawkins grinned broadly as Shelly and Shelby flew at him, hugging and kissing him.

He delighted in their openness and warmth, but Jake watched Roderick peel himself out of the SUV and stride up to him big and bold as brass.

"Nice little place you got here, Hawkins. Now, where's Jai?"

"Son, we don't cotton to no tenderfoot invading the territory uninvited. Now the girls can stay, but..."

"Don't give me grief, old man. I'm 'bout two seconds off you for putting me through hoops over a little piece of change. Now, I asked you a question, and I expect an answer. I'll take this place apart piece by piece if I have to, but..."

Suddenly the ground began to tremble under their feet. All eyes turned toward a ridge where a huge dust cloud rose up into the sky. The rumbling grew louder, the ground trembled like an earthquake, and a lone rider sprinted ahead of a herd of wild horses. The rider bent low over the horse's head when it took flight and cleared the coral fence. Ranch hands began to herd the wild horses. The dust cloud blew toward them and engulfed them. As the dust began to clear, Roderick saw a very familiar sight. JaiHonnah, covered in dust and dirt atop a magnificent, powerful, prancing black stallion. Her hair was loose whipped wildly by the wind. She was majestic, an African queen, an Indian princess in one magnificent form, he thought.

JaiHonnah couldn't believe her eyes as she sat astride KnightHawk's mighty, prancing flesh. Shelly and Shelby were jumping up and down, giggling and squealing and calling her name. She barely stopped the KnightHawk's forward motion before she slid from its saddle-less back in one fluid motion and raced over the coral fence to meet the girls. They laughed and giggled together as if they had not seen each other in years, when in fact, it had been less than two weeks.

Her eyes then caught a sight that had only been a distant thought in her mind. Jake and Roderick standing side by side looking like twin mountains. She never thought of it before, how much they resembled each other in so many ways. Like two strong, mighty African warriors. She approached them cautiously, confusion worrying her face and her bottom lip.

"You know what I'm here after," Roderick spoke, his voice raw with emotion.

"You can't have them now. They're too young. They need me," she said defiantly.

Confusion drew Roderick's eyebrows together.

"Uh, JaiHawk, dahlin', I think the man—," Jake tried to interrupt.

"I can speak for myself, old man," he said, not taking his eyes from JaiHonnah's. "Oh, by the way," he said, pulling an envelope from inside his jacket pocket and slapping it against Jake's broad, hard chest, "here's your five billion—with interest. I also picked up enough stock in BlackHawk International to seat myself on your board of directors. My bride-to-be and I will be opening a new company, JR Baylor, Limited, a closely-held, privately-owned partnership between JaiHonnah Reise and John Roderick Baylor and family. Now run along, old man, and raid some other company while I figure out how to get my woman to marry me."

Jake chewed on his cigar and grinned. He'd be *damned* if he didn't like the way the boy did business. He had his investigator, Henry Tillery, posing as a sales manager for his plumbing supply and equipment company, dating Kelley Baylor, and watching J. Roderick Baylor for nearly two years. Tillery, the poor sod actually fell hard for Kelley Baylor, but, of course, Jake had designs on Kelley himself, so he abruptly transferred Tiller to shadow Adam.

Jake knew that Vivian Alexander Jackson wouldn't back a man who wasn't worthy of respect or didn't have honor, but he must have done something to peak her interest because she countered his move by inducing Jai to come back to the states and plopping her right down in the middle. That Alexander woman was no lady. He had her boxed in though. He had whispered her name into the right ears and got her nominated to take a judgeship at the circuit court level. Not that she didn't deserve it, because she certainly did. She was a hellava attorney and he loved her like a daughter. Still, she was too dangerous to leave as a free agent available to take on clients and cases at her discretion. Silently, he grinned. Yeah, he had her where he wanted her—married to a man he admired and she loved. And she had tipped him off about Roderick Baylor, a man who could and would one day take Jake's place at the helm of BlackHawk Holding with JaiHonnah at his side.

He'd purposefully let those stocks loose so that Roderick would find them. Made him work hard for them too, but John Roderick Baylor knew how to bargain for what he wanted. So did Jake. He would have done even more to secure his daughter's happiness, but he saw the look in his daughter's eyes and in Roderick's. His help wasn't needed anymore. Now with his plans working out nicely, he would have time to romance the very intriguing Kelley Baylor. As soon as he had his daughter married to Roderick, he was planning to take up residence in Atlanta. He already bought the house next door to Kelley's.

Yes, everything was falling into place.

"You want to marry my daughter, huh?"

"I do, yes. I'll overlook the fact that you're her father because I love her with everything that I am," Roderick said, still looking into JaiHonnah's eyes.

"Humph," Jake snorted. "Then do it the old-fashion way, boy," he said, leading the little girls into the house.

Roderick's brows bunched. "What's that, old man?" Roderick called after Jake.

"Ask her," Jake said and laughed, his booming voice trailing off as he entered the ranch house.

Roderick again landed his gaze on JaiHonnah. "Is it possible that it's that easy?" he asked with confusion painted on his face. "All I have to do is ask you to marry me?"

"Not until you get a divorce, it isn't," she snapped with hands on hips.

"A divorce? You want me to get a divorce, do you? Well, I'm sorry. I can't do that," he said, grinning.

"And why not?" she flashed. "I'm in love with you, John Roderick Baylor. I love you more than you will ever know or understand. So why can't you get a divorce?"

Roderick swept her up in his arms and kissed her as never before. He let her go only enough to look into her eyes.

"Because I'm not married," he said, smiling. "Now tell me again how much you love me."

"Not married? Don't lie to me, Roderick. You're married to Monique."

"Not for a very long time. She and I divorced the year the twins were born. I'm in love with you, JaiHonnah Reise. I have loved you since the very first time I saw you. Now I want you to tell me again how much you love me."

"Uh, better still, I'll show you."

"I like the sound of that. And if you didn't know it, I intend to be your husband."

"God, I hope so. This unwed mother business is getting radical."

Roderick stopped and looked at her quizzically. "Unwed mother?" he asked. "You mean that you and Chapman aren't married?"

"Nope, we're not. We were divorced the same year that you were."

They stood looking at each other and then said in unison. *"Vivian!"*

JaiHonnah led Roderick into a front parlor where Jake sat grinning at them both. Roderick looked away from JaiHonnah momentarily to see each of his girls holding a baby in her arms. His stunned expression was priceless. He slowly approached his girls and looked at the identical babies they held. He looked into JaiHonnah's tear-filled eyes, she nodded yes to his unspoken question.

"I want you to meet Rodney and Reise Baylor," she was saying. The introduction was unnecessary because he immediately knew that they were his sons. His laughter was mixed with tears as he took them in his arms, holding them gently and kissing them reverently as he cried. His joy was overwhelming, and JaiHonnah's tears overflowed. Jake and Ezra even dabbed at their eyes and the twins were beside themselves that they had baby brothers.

* * *

Later, after the children were in bed, Roderick and JaiHonnah were alone in her bedroom suite. Joy spread through her like wildfire, and the excitement she felt when she first saw him more than a year ago flooded over her. She had viewed Roderick then as just a handsome face and beautiful body. Now he was so much more, and it heightened her love for him. No matter what happened to them, she realized that this was the natural result, and she no longer feared her emotions. The ancestors bestowed many blessings on her.

Roderick caressed JaiHonnah's beautiful face. "God, I've missed you."

JaiHonnah shivered pleasantly at his touch, gazing into his eyes with newfound wonderment. She melted against his bare chest, and her man closed in around her.

Roderick felt new and alive for the first time since JaiHonnah left him. His heart was bursting with joy so great that it defied description. He tilted her chin to meet his gaze. Her soft topaz eyes caused his heart to thunder in his chest.

"I tried to stay away from you, Roderick," she said softly. "I love you so much that I was afraid of my own feelings and emotions. I would have been your woman whether you were married or not. I didn't care anymore. I just wanted to be with you, but there were the children to think about, yours and ours."

"I was ready to call Chapman out on some historic battle to the finish. Only one man would be left standing, and I was determined that man would be me. I couldn't stand the thought of you being with anyone but me. Adultery? Baby, I was ready to commit justifiable homicide for your love. I came here to ask you to leave Chapman and to marry me. And you have given me the greatest gifts: your love and our sons. You don't know how happy you have made me. When I look at you and at them, I realize that no man could be so blessed," he said, his voice thickening with emotion.

JaiHonnah rose to her tiptoes in his arms, her mouth on his, softly licking at his lips. A warm groan grew from his throat. She increased the pressure against his lips, and he enveloped her mouth with his. He possessed her tongue as all thought of anything or anyone but her ceased.

Their tongues danced away months of separation, trepidation and fears accompanied by the unintelligible sounds that filled the space around them. They were joined together, the heat of their need for each other engulfing them.

Roderick's magic began to overwhelm JaiHonnah as her body molded itself into her familiar places against him. Her hands traversed his body, visiting every muscle that she had recalled and held sacred in her dreams.

"God, I love you so," Roderick breathed against her ear and down her neck to her shoulder. His nature rose and stood at full attention to her touch.

"Don't ever leave me, please, Roderick. I couldn't stand to lose you again," she said haltingly as she nearly fainted from the near-orgasmic sensations that he created in her.

She needed him with such vehemence as she molded his flesh in her hand, her senses unleashed, raw and throbbing, his scent intoxicating and teasing her sanity.

Roderick groaned the sweet torment that her supple body played against him as her tongue whipped him into a near frenzy. Her soft hand on his shaft coaxed a deeper, more guttural groan from his core. He knew that if he died at that moment, no man's passing would have been more sweet.

"JaiHonnah, JaiHonnah," he murmured as if saying a fervent prayer for salvation, drawing her soft, satin-like body as close as two magnets could get.

His hands, on a long overdue mission, spanned her buttocks, feeling the soft, full fleshiness. His mouth found her taut nipples and suckled their sweet nectar.

"Tell me it's true, that I'm not dreaming, that you're mine," he murmured, his voice thick with passion.

JaiHonnah's breath left her. She could hardly think, let alone speak as he drove her to near madness. She whimpered her response, "Yes, yes, yes, I'm yours forever." Her body trembled from her love for him as his lips burned a trail across her abdomen where his seeds had rested and blossomed. Her pulse beat at her throat as he reached her core and suckled there as he had her breasts.

The air was teeming with sexual tension when Roderick lifted JaiHonnah and carried her to the bed. His eyes, his hands, his mouth bathed her in love from head to toe. JaiHonnah's heart danced with the sight of him before her; every muscle of his exquisite frame promising of the excitement to come. So much delight in the feel of his skin, the touch of his hands, and the elixir of his lips. He came to her with purpose in his eyes and etched in his muscle. She opened to him without thought or hesitation and took him home. Roderick gazed on his woman who had borne him sons and knew that this day would bring new life to her core. He felt the serum that would fertilize her building and straining for release. It also would not rush him to the ultimate explosion. He gained some semblance of conscious thought as he lowered his taunt muscle into place.

JaiHonnah whimpered her excitement at receiving her prize—her man. Her inner muscle clamped around her gift and rendered the elixir of life from his nature. The rhythm of his stroke signaled her body that it was time to release the essence of new life on its journey to reality. No words could describe the sensation she felt with clear certainty that Roderick had called upon the ancestors to send them more life to love.

"Oh, Roderick, my love, my life," she cried in sheer ecstasy.

"I know, Jai, I know," he groaned. "I'll always be here for you. We will always be together."

The sweet, tortured release to climax was reached in perfect harmony. Another unguarded moment had passed.

AUTHOR BIO

Ann Jeffries is a native of Washington, D. C. She is an only child who enjoyed the benefits of a private school education at Allen in Asheville, NC, and a public education at the University of Maryland. She began writing fiction for her own amusement. An Unguarded Moment is the 4th manuscript in the Family Reunion: The Wisdom of the Ancestors series.

Ann is the recipient of many awards for leadership and public service. A speaker at colleges and universities and conferences and conventions, she has extensively traveled the North American continent, Asia and Europe. Among other things, she is an entrepreneur, an avid viewer of public television and a voracious reader of fiction.

Ms. Jeffries' pride and joy are her family, particularly her Fabulous Four grands. She lives in Maryland and South Carolina.